UNWRITTEN: ORIGINS

-SELENE-

By Adger R. Matthews II

Soul Forged Studios LLC

UNWRITTEN: ORIGINS - SELENE

Published by **Soul Forged Studios LLC**
Website: www.soulforgedstudio.com
Email: adger@soulforgedstudio.com
ISBN: 979-8-9932504-2-7

ACKNOWLEDGMENTS
Cover design: Soul Forged Studios LLC

CONTENT WARNING

This book is intended for mature audiences (18+) and contains explicit content including but not limited to: graphic violence, strong language, adult themes, death, trauma, and morally complex situations. Reader discretion is advised.

Printed in the United States of America

SOUL FORGED STUDIOS
Forging Stories. Shaping Worlds.

For the ghosts we carry,
for the scars that shaped us,
and for the fire we never meant to survive

Table of Contents

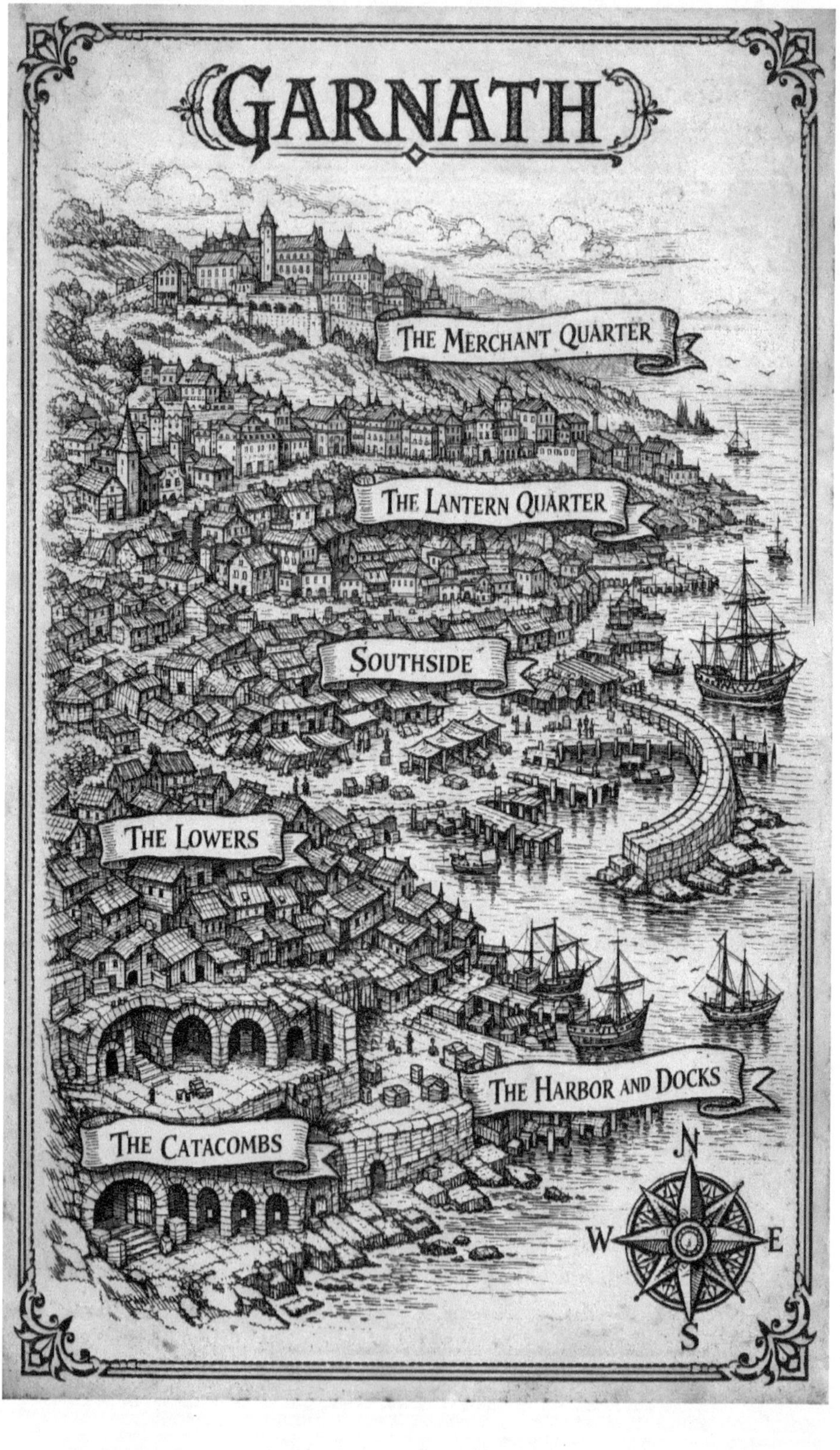

GARNATH

THE MERCHANT QUARTER

THE LANTERN QUARTER

SOUTHSIDE

THE LOWERS

THE HARBOR AND DOCKS

THE CATACOMBS

N

W

E

S

PROLOGUE: The Making of a Survivor

Rain slicked the alley stones.

Selene pressed her spine against the wall, tracking the man's approach through the downpour. He moved like water finding cracks in masonry. Patient. Inevitable. Already where he needed to be before she registered him coming.

Daven. She'd heard the name three days ago from a dock rat who owed her a favor. Headhunter. The kind who didn't send runners to do his work. The kind who came himself when the contract mattered.

His coat shed rain in sheets. His hands stayed loose at his sides. No weapon drawn. He didn't need one yet.

She'd felt him for three days now. Eyes in every reflective surface. The pressure of being watched by someone who knew what watching meant. Not the desperate grab of street thugs or the clumsy pursuit of Watchers running down a lead. This was different. This was a man who had already decided how this ended and was simply walking toward the conclusion.

"You should have stayed hidden." His voice carried no heat. Just observation. Like pointing out that rain was wet or that alleys smelled like piss.

Selene shifted her weight, fingers finding the hilt at her hip. The leather was slick. Cold. "Wasn't planning on being found."

"Then you planned poorly."

He moved.

Fast. Faster than the size of him suggested he could. His hand caught her wrist before the blade cleared the sheath, thumb pressing into the soft meat between tendons. The spot that shut a hand down. Her fingers went slack. The knife clattered against wet stone.

She drove her knee up. He pivoted, took the impact on his thigh instead of his groin, and his other hand came around in a tight arc. Not a punch. A strike. Clinical. The heel of his palm connected behind her ear where skull met spine.

The world tilted.

Stone rushed up. Her palms hit first, scraped raw against the wet cobbles. Rain soaked through her coat in seconds, cold seeping through wool and linen to find skin. Everything cold except the heat spreading from where he'd connected. Her vision stuttered. Doubled. Came back wrong.

He crouched beside her. Not gloating. Just watching her consciousness come apart at the seams.

"Not wise," he said, "taking jobs you don't understand."

"Who have you told?" His voice was distant now. Or maybe she was distant. Fading. "Who else knows what you saw?"

Knows what? she tried to ask. Her mouth wouldn't work. Her tongue was thick and wrong.

"We'll find out," he said. "We always do."

The alley blurred. Rain became smoke. Stone became wood. The copper taste of blood in her mouth became something else. Something older. Something she'd buried so deep she'd almost convinced herself it wasn't there.

Flour.

Lavender.

The smell cut through everything. Through rain and pain and seventeen years of walls built brick by brick. Through all the layers between then and now.

Flour and lavender and her own breathing, too loud in a space too small.

Don't come out. No matter what you hear.

Darkness took her down.

***

The stew was thick with carrots and potatoes and chunks of mutton Mama said cost too much. Selene ate fast, scooping the broth with a heel of bread while Papa talked about a ship that had come in from the northern kingdoms.

"Big as a house," he said, gesturing with his spoon. A drop of broth landed on the table. Mama gave him a look. He grinned and wiped it with his sleeve, which made Mama's look sharpen, which made his grin widen. "Sails like clouds, little star. White as fresh snow. You should have seen the men unloading her. Muscles like oxen. Took six of them to move one crate."

He reached over and tapped the small wooden star hanging at her neck. Mama had carved it for her last birthday. Five points, smooth from her fingers always finding it.

"What was in the crates?"

"Couldn't say." Papa winked. "Some things aren't meant for dock workers to know."

"But you know everything about the docks."

"I know everything worth knowing." He tapped his temple. "The difference between worth knowing and not worth knowing is whether it gets you in trouble."

Mama set a second helping in Selene's bowl without asking. The meat was warm and soft, falling apart on her tongue. Tomorrow there would be more stew. Mama always made enough for three days. The day after that, Papa would bring home fish from the morning boats, and Mama would fry it with onions until the whole house smelled like salt and heat.

That was how things worked. Mama cooked. Papa told stories. Selene ate too fast and asked too many questions, and both of them laughed at her like she was the best thing that had ever happened to them.

"Tell me about the dragons again."

"Not tonight, little star. Eat your dinner."

"Please?"

Papa glanced at Mama. Some conversation passed between them that Selene couldn't read. Adult language, spoken in looks instead of words.

"After dinner," Mama said. "If you finish your vegetables."

Selene shoveled carrots into her mouth. They were soft and sweet, cooked until they melted. She'd eat a hundred carrots for a dragon story. A thousand.

Papa's spoon clattered against the bowl's rim.

Metal on ceramic. Loud in the sudden silence. His head jerked up mid-sentence, body going still in a way she'd never seen. His eyes went to the door. Then the window. Then to Mama.

Something passed between them. Something wordless that made Mama's hand freeze, the wooden serving spoon hovering over the pot. Her face changed. Softness draining out. Something harder underneath.

Papa's expression shifted. Gentle father to something else. Something that looked like the men who worked the rougher docks, the ones Mama told her to stay away from.

"Hide." Sharp. Wrong. Nothing like the voice that told dragon stories. "Both of you. Now."

Mama didn't ask questions. Didn't hesitate. Just grabbed Selene's arm and yanked her from the chair so fast her knee cracked against the table edge. Pain bloomed hot and immediate, but Mama was already moving, bare feet silent on the floor, pulling Selene toward the cupboard in the corner.

The cupboard was storage. Flour sacks stacked against the back wall. Jars on the upper shelf. Onions hanging from hooks, papery skins rustling as Mama yanked the doors open. The smell hit her: dust and grain and Mama's lavender sachets tucked between the sacks to keep moths away.

Mama's hands found Selene's shoulders. Pushed. Shoved. Selene stumbled into the cramped space, her spine hitting the wooden slats at the back. Her knees crushed against her chest. The position hurt, but Mama kept pushing, adjusting, making sure she was deep enough. Hidden enough.

"Stay quiet." Mama's voice was high and tight. Her hands shook. Selene had never seen Mama's hands shake. "Don't come out. No matter what you hear."

"Mama, what's . . ."

"Promise me." Mama's fingers dug in. Not gentle anymore. Desperate. "Promise me, Selene."

Mama never used her full name unless it was serious.

Selene's throat closed. She didn't understand, but she understood enough. Mama was afraid. Mama was never afraid.

"I promise."

"Good girl." Mama's hand found the wooden star at Selene's chest, pressed it flat against her sternum. "Strong and smart and survive. That's what Araveth women do. Don't let go of this."

The cupboard doors closed.

Darkness swallowed everything.

Selene's heart was beating too fast. So fast it hurt. She could feel it in her throat, in her temples, behind her eyes. The flour dust tickled her nose, and she pressed her hand over her mouth and nose, terrified she'd sneeze, terrified she'd cough, terrified any sound would bring whatever Papa had heard straight to her.

Through the thin crack between the doors, she could see a sliver of the kitchen. Her bowl on the table, stew going cold. Papa's chair pushed back. The door to the front room standing open.

Footsteps. Mama running. Toward the bedroom maybe. Or toward Papa. Selene wanted to call out. Wanted to scream, Mama come back, hide with me, don't leave me alone in the dark.

She bit her lip until she tasted copper.

Not enough time.

The front door exploded inward.

Not opened. Exploded. Wood splintering. Hinges tearing free with a shriek of metal. The door slammed against the wall so hard Selene felt the impact through the cupboard floor, through her bones, through the teeth she was clenching so hard her jaw ached.

Her whole body started shaking. Not trembling. Shaking. Violent, uncontrollable. Her teeth chattered, and she clamped her jaw tighter, pressed her hands harder over her mouth, curled smaller and smaller like if she could just be small enough, she'd disappear.

Boots. Heavy. Fast. Multiple sets hammering across the front room.

Mama's gasp. Cut short by impact. The wet thud of body hitting wall. Plaster cracking. Something small falling and shattering.

Mama.

Selene's hands dropped from her mouth. She reached for the cupboard door. Mama was hurt. Mama needed help. She had to . . .

Don't come out. No matter what you hear.

Her fingers stopped an inch from the wood. Shaking. Everything shaking.

I promise.

She'd promised.

She pressed deeper into the corner. The wooden slats bit into her shoulder blades through her dress. Her knees ached from how tightly she held them. The star dug into her palm where she gripped it, five points biting into soft flesh.

Through the crack, she could see her bowl. The stew congealing. Steam rising thinner now. Already it looked like something from a different life. Something that belonged to a girl who didn't exist anymore.

Shadows moved in the front room.

"Please." Mama's voice. Frightened. Wrong. This wasn't Mama's voice. Mama sang while she cooked. Mama laughed at Papa's terrible jokes. Mama was never scared. "Please, we don't . . ."

"Shut up." A man's voice. Flat. Empty of anything human. Like speaking was work he resented. "Get him."

Papa fighting. Furniture breaking. Wood cracking.

Selene's mind built pictures for every sound. Papa swinging. Papa missing. Papa's face when the first blow landed, the way his eyes would go wide, the way his mouth would open. She couldn't see it, but she saw it anyway, saw it clearer than if she'd been standing in the room.

His grunt of pain. More impacts. Fist on flesh. Flesh on floor.

Papa's face hitting the floor. Blood on his teeth. Blood on the wood.

She was shaking so hard now the flour sacks rustled against her. She grabbed her own arms and squeezed, trying to hold herself still, trying to hold herself together.

Then dragging. The scrape of boots, of something heavy being hauled across the room.

Papa trying to speak through whatever they'd done to his mouth. Words turned to wet sounds. Thick. Gurgling.

His jaw. They broke his jaw. That's why he can't talk. They broke Papa's jaw.

Hot liquid spread between her legs. Warmth soaking through her dress, pooling on the cupboard floor beneath her. The smell of it mixed with flour and lavender.

She'd wet herself.

The shame hit almost as hard as the fear. She was seven. She hadn't wet herself since she was four. But she couldn't stop shaking, couldn't stop the fear from taking everything, couldn't stop her body from betraying her in the dark.

"Sit. Both of you."

Bodies being forced down. Chairs scraping. Mama whimpering. Mama never whimpered.

"Now." The flat voice. Calm. Conversational. Like nothing was wrong. Like this was just business. "You were at the docks today."

Papa's breathing was wet. Bubbling. "I work the docks."

"You saw what we were burning. The excavation recovery. The crates from Southside."

A pause. Papa trying to breathe through whatever was broken in his face. "I mind my own business."

"Your daughter was with you."

Selene's lungs stopped.

They knew.

They knew she'd been there. She went to the docks all the time. Papa took her when he couldn't leave her home alone. She'd watched men unloading crates today, bored like always. Watched them burning papers in metal barrels, smoke rising black and thick against the gray sky.

She hadn't thought anything of it. People burned things at the docks all the time.

This was her fault.

"Where is she?" The flat voice.

This is my fault. They're here because of me.

"My daughter is my business." Papa's voice changed. Harder. Colder. Even through the broken sounds, she could hear it. The voice of a man who knew he was going to die and had decided how. "Not yours."

Papa, no. Tell them. Tell them where I am. Don't . . .

"WHERE IS SHE?"

"You have a problem with me, I'm right here."

PAPA, NO.

The impact made her whole body jerk. A wet crack. Bone breaking. She knew what bone breaking sounded like now. She'd never forget.

Papa's grunt turning into a sound that wasn't a word anymore. Another impact. And another. The distinct rhythm of men doing work they'd done before.

Selene shoved her fist into her mouth and bit down. Bit until she tasted blood. The pain was the only thing keeping her from screaming.

Don't come out. Don't come out. Don't come out.

Mama's voice in her head. The promise she'd made. No matter what you hear.

She heard everything.

Her mind made pictures for everything.

Papa's face. Papa's hands trying to block. Papa's body curling on the floor while boots found his ribs, his back, his head.

Stop. Stop. Please stop. Please.

She was crying. Silent crying, tears streaming down her face, mixing with the snot running from her nose. She couldn't breathe right. Couldn't think right. Could only sit in her own piss in the dark and listen to her father die.

Papa stopped making sounds.

The silence was worse.

Then Mama screaming. High and sharp and animal, the sound a person makes when something essential breaks, when the thing they love most in the world stops moving and they understand what that means.

"Shut her up."

A short, hard sound. Meat and bone. Mama's scream cut off.

Another sound. Softer. Wetter. Like a bag of grain dropping from a cart.

Mama hitting the floor.

Then nothing.

Selene couldn't breathe. Her chest was locked. Her throat was locked. Everything was locked. She sat in the dark with her fist in her mouth and her eyes streaming and her whole body shaking and she couldn't breathe, couldn't move, couldn't do anything except exist in this moment that wouldn't end.

Mama. Papa.

Mama. Papa.

Mama.

Boots moving. Coming closer. Into the kitchen.

Selene's body went rigid. Every muscle locked.

A man stepped into view through the crack. Big. Weathered face. Nose broken and healed crooked. Scars along his jaw in pale lines. Eyes the color of dirty ice, sweeping the room methodically. Professionally. Looking for something small and hiding.

He crossed to the table. Looked at Selene's bowl. The cold stew. The bread heel she'd left behind.

His eyes went to the cupboard.

He walked toward it.

Selene couldn't feel her own heartbeat anymore. Couldn't feel anything. Just cold and shaking and the taste of blood in her mouth and the smell of piss and flour and lavender.

Stay small. Stay quiet.

The man's hand reached for the cupboard door.

Pulled it open.

Light flooded in. Blinding after the darkness. Selene pressed back as far as she could go, wedged between flour sacks and the wall, making herself nothing, making herself invisible, making herself disappear.

The man looked right at her.

His pale eyes found hers. Held them. She saw something move behind his expression. Recognition. Understanding. The calculation of a man deciding something.

He'd found her.

She was going to die now. Like Mama. Like Papa.

"Anything?" Another voice from the front room.

The man stared at her. Seven years old. Pressed into a corner. Covered in piss and tears and snot. Trembling like a caught rabbit.

His jaw shifted. Once. Like he was chewing something that tasted bad.

"Nothing here," he said. Loud enough for the others to hear. "Just storage."

He closed the cupboard door.

Darkness again. His footsteps moved away. Back toward the front room. Back toward whatever waited there.

Selene didn't breathe. Didn't move. Didn't understand.

He'd seen her. He'd lied.

She should feel relief. She should feel grateful. She felt nothing except the shaking that wouldn't stop.

"Burn it." Someone else. Bored. "Make sure."

Oil splashing. The sharp smell spreading through the house, cutting through flour and lavender and piss and everything else. The sound of liquid hitting wood, hitting fabric, hitting things that would catch.

Flint striking. Once. Twice. Metal scraping stone.

Then the whoosh of fire catching. The heat bloom reaching even through the cupboard door. Orange light flickering through the crack, dancing shadows where there had been none.

More oil. More fire. They were thorough.

Boots moving toward what remained of the front door. Leaving. The sounds growing distant. Then gone.

Just the fire now. Crackling. Growing. Eating the house.

Selene stayed in the cupboard. Mama said don't come out. Mama said no matter what. She'd promised. She'd promised, and she'd already broken everything else tonight, she wouldn't break this, she wouldn't . . .

The smoke came first. Thin wisps curling under the cupboard door, gray against the darkness. Then thicker. Lower. Filling the small space like water filling a cup.

Selene coughed. Tried not to. Coughed again. Her eyes burned. Her throat burned. Each breath was harder than the last, like trying to drink the air through wet cloth.

The heat grew. The cupboard walls were warm against her back. Getting warmer. The flour sacks were hot through her dress.

Stay quiet. Stay small. Don't come out.

But Mama also said survive.

Strong and smart and survive. That's what Araveth women do.

Which one, Mama? Which one did you mean?

The smoke was thick enough now that she couldn't see the crack of light. Couldn't see her hands. Just smoke and heat and the sound of fire eating everything Papa had built.

Her chest hurt. Each breath was harder. Like trying to breathe underwater. Like drowning in air.

Stay or go. Obey or survive.

She'd promised.

But dead people couldn't keep promises.

Selene's hand found the cupboard door. The wood was hot against her palm. Not burning yet. But soon.

She pushed.

The door swung open and smoke poured out, poured in, everything was smoke and heat and orange light. The kitchen was on fire. Walls, table, chairs. Papa's fallen chair was burning. Her bowl was still on the table, stew blackening in the heat.

She couldn't see Mama. Couldn't see Papa. Just fire and smoke and the shape of what used to be home.

Selene crawled out of the cupboard. Stayed low like Papa taught her once when a warehouse caught fire near the docks. Smoke rises. Stay low. Breathe shallow. The wooden star swung free of her dress, cord pulling at her neck. She shoved it back against her chest and kept moving.

The floor was hot through her dress, through the wet fabric that had already started to dry in the heat. The air was thick and wrong. She moved toward where the door should be, where outside should be, where not-burning should be.

Behind her, something collapsed. Wood and plaster. The ceiling maybe. The sound of structure failing.

She kept crawling.

Found the doorframe by touch. The wood was hot but not burning yet. Found the step down. Found cobblestones under her hands, wet and cold.

Night air hit her lungs. She gasped. Coughed. Gasped again. Crawled until she hit the opposite wall of the alley, then pressed her back against it and just breathed.

Her lungs felt like they'd been scraped raw. Her eyes streamed tears that cut tracks through the soot on her cheeks. Her ribs ached. Her palms stung where she'd scraped them on stone. Her dress was damp with piss and sweat and now rain-wet cobblestone.

But she was out. She was breathing. She was alive.

She'd broken her promise.

Mama said don't come out. She came out.

But Mama also said survive. And she survived.

Which one was right, Mama?

Mama?

Smoke poured out of the house behind her. Flames licked through the windows, orange and hungry. The roof was burning now, sending sparks into the night sky. Everything Mama and Papa had built was burning.

When her eyes cleared enough to see, Selene looked back at the doorway.

The smoke had thinned there. Just enough. Just barely.

She saw them.

Papa was on the floor of the front room. Face down. But wrong. The shape of his head was wrong. Flattened in places it shouldn't be. A dark pool spread around him, black and shining in the firelight. His hand stretched toward Mama, like he'd been trying to reach her even while they beat him, even while he died.

Mama was by the wall. Crumpled. Her neck bent sideways, chin almost touching her shoulder, at an angle that necks didn't bend. Her eyes were open. Glassy. Staring at nothing. At everything. At Selene.

Mama.

The word tore out of her before she could stop it. Raw. Broken.

"MAMA!"

She was on her feet without deciding to stand. Running toward the doorway without deciding to run. Mama was in there. Mama was hurt. Mama needed . . .

Heat hit her like a wall. The fire roared, greedy, and the doorframe cracked and shifted and she stumbled back, arms up, face burning.

She couldn't get to them.

She couldn't get to them.

"MAMA! PAPA!"

The fire didn't answer. Just kept burning. Just kept eating.

She screamed until her throat tore. Screamed their names over and over. Screamed at the fire, at the night, at the city, at the men who'd done this, at herself for hiding, at herself for surviving.

She pounded her fists against the alley wall until her knuckles split and bled.

She kicked and thrashed and fought nothing, fought air, fought the whole world that had taken everything from her in the space of minutes.

Her parents were dead.

Her parents were dead, and she'd hidden in a cupboard and listened to it happen.

Her parents were dead, and the last thing Mama ever did was shove her in a cupboard and tell her to survive.

Her parents were dead, and she couldn't even hold them, couldn't even touch them, couldn't even tell them she was sorry, she was sorry, she was so sorry . . .

The grief hit like a physical blow. She doubled over. Fell to her knees on the wet cobblestones. The feelings were too big for her chest, too big for her body, crushing her from the inside out.

She curled on the ground and sobbed. Ugly, animal sounds. Snot and tears and spit. Her whole body convulsing with it, her mother's name and her father's name tangled together in her throat until they stopped being words.

The fire reached them while she cried. She saw it through blurred eyes. Saw flames crawl across the floor to Papa first. Saw his clothes catch. His hair. Saw the fire take him.

She screamed again. Tried to stand. Fell. Tried again.

The flames found Mama. The dress Mama had sewn herself. The hair Mama braided every morning. The hands that had held Selene's face and said, *Promise me.*

Selene watched her mother burn.

Something broke.

Not her heart. Her heart was already broken. Something else. Something deeper.

The feelings that had been crushing her started to drain away. Like water through a cracked cup. Like blood from a wound. Pouring out of her onto the cobblestones with her tears and her snot and her spit.

She should feel this. She should feel all of this. This was the worst thing that had ever happened, would ever happen, and she should feel every second of it.

But the feelings were leaving. Draining out. Running away.

And she let them go.

Because it was too much. Because she couldn't hold it. Because her mind was seven years old and too small to contain this much grief, this much horror, this much loss all at once.

So she let it go.

The screaming stopped.

The tears slowed.

The shaking quieted.

She sat on the wet cobblestones and watched her parents burn and felt the last of the feelings drain away until there was nothing left. Empty. Quiet. Just her and the fire and the smoke and a city that didn't care.

The fire burned hotter. The roof collapsed, sections falling inward with sounds like thunder. Sparks rose into the night. Selene watched it all.

She should feel something. She knew she should feel something.

She didn't.

No one came. No one called her name. Behind her, carts still rolled on the main street. Voices still haggled over copper coins. Garnath kept breathing, kept moving, kept being loud and alive while her parents burned twenty feet from a public road.

Nobody noticed.

Nobody cared.

Selene stood. Her legs worked. Her body worked. Everything worked except the part that was supposed to feel things.

She walked deeper into the alley. Away from the fire. Away from what used to be home.

She found a gap between two buildings where the walls almost touched. Old construction. Poor repairs. A space barely wide enough for a child to squeeze through. She pressed into it. Made herself small against the cold stone.

Different small than cupboard small.

Alone small.

Strong. Smart. Survive.

Mama's words. Mama's voice. But Mama was ash now. Papa was ash. The house, the stew, the dragon stories, tomorrow. All of it ash. Even the feelings that should have been tearing her apart.

She was what was left.

The wooden star pressed hard against her ribs where she'd shoved it. She pulled it out. Held it in her palm. Five points. Mama had carved it. Mama was dead.

She should feel something about that.

She didn't.

Selene closed her fingers around the star. Pulled her knees to her chest. Made herself as small as possible in the gap between buildings. The stone was cold against her spine. The night air bit through her thin dress. The smell of piss and smoke clung to her skin.

She didn't cry. The tears were gone. She didn't shake. The shaking was gone. There was only the cold stone at her back and the smell of smoke in her hair and the emptiness where everything else used to be.

She closed her eyes and let the cold have her.

***

In the days after, Selene learned hunger.

Not the kind where Mama told you to wait until dinner. Real hunger. The kind that made your stomach twist and cramp. The kind that turned the smell of baking bread into physical pain. The kind that made you understand why people did desperate things.

The first week she ate from garbage. Whatever she could find in the piles behind taverns and bakeries. Stale bread. Rotting vegetables. Things she would have refused a week ago. Things that made her sick at first, body rejecting what her mind accepted.

She got used to it.

The second week, she learned stealing.

Baker's stall in the market square. Loaves cooling on wooden racks. People everywhere, buying and selling and arguing over copper coins. Easy to slip through the crowd. Easy to be small and invisible.

She grabbed a roll. Still warm. Turned to run.

The baker's hand caught her wrist. Big hand. Strong. Calloused. Squeezed until bones ground together.

"Thief." Not angry. Tired. Like this happened every day. Like she was just another problem in a city full of problems.

He dragged her into the alley behind his stall. Threw her against the wall. Her head bounced off stone. White light. Then pain.

"Steal from me again," he said, "and I break both your hands."

He didn't break them this time. Just hit her. Fists on ribs, on stomach, once across the face. Measured beating. Enough to teach. Not quite enough to kill.

When he was done, he left her in the alley.

Selene stayed there until she could breathe without gasping. Until the pain faded enough to think. Until she could stand.

No roll. Still hungry. Ribs screaming. Face swelling.

But lesson learned.

She stole again the next day. Different stall. Different approach. Watched longer first. Found the gaps in the vendor's attention. The moments when his eyes went to customers instead of product.

The roll was in her pocket, and she was three streets away before anyone noticed.

She ate it in a doorway. Slowly. Making it last.

Strong. Smart. Survive.

She was learning.

***

Rain on the alley stones. Present day. Consciousness clawing back from wherever it had gone.

Selene opened her eyes.

The sky was gray overhead. Dawn maybe. Or dusk. The rain had stopped, but everything was wet. Her coat was soaked through. Her cheek pressed against cold cobblestones. Her head throbbed where Daven had hit her.

She was alone.

No Daven. No boot on her neck. No blade at her throat. Just empty alley and wet stone and the sounds of Garnath waking up around her.

He'd left her alive.

Selene pushed herself up. Her arms shook. Her vision swam. She made it to sitting and stayed there, back against the wall, breathing through the nausea.

He'd knocked her out and left her in an alley like garbage. Taken nothing. Done nothing.

Why?

She checked her belt. Knife gone. The one he'd knocked from her hand. But the second blade was still in her boot. The coins in her hidden pocket were still there. The message she'd been carrying was still tucked against her ribs.

He'd taken nothing.

He'd let her live.

Just like the man in the cupboard. Seventeen years apart, two men looking at her and deciding she wasn't worth killing. Not yet.

Not mercy. Men like Daven didn't do mercy. This was something else. A message. *I can reach you whenever I want.* Or worse: *You're not worth killing yet. You're not the job. You're just the path to the job.*

Her hand went to her chest without thinking. Found the shape of the star under her shirt. Still there. Still five points pressing against her skin after seventeen years.

Her fingers were shaking.

Selene stared at her hand. At the tremor she couldn't stop. She hadn't shaken like this since . . . since the cupboard. Since the flour and the lavender and the sounds she couldn't unhear.

She pressed her palm flat against the cobblestones. Pressed until the cold bit into her skin. Until the shaking slowed. Until she could breathe without tasting smoke that wasn't there.

Seventeen years between then and now. Seventeen years since she'd felt the grief drain out of her on a rain-wet alley floor. Seventeen years of the emptiness that had moved in to fill the space.

One smell had almost cracked it open.

Almost.

They were never stone. Just old wounds. And old wounds rip open fast.

She stood. Slowly. Using the wall for support.

Mirael would be worried. Selene had been gone all night. Maybe longer. Mirael would be pacing their room above Viena's, checking the window, writing in that journal she thought Selene didn't know about.

Selene started walking.

The city swallowed her the way it always did. The street took her weight without noticing. Garnath moved around her and did not look back.

CHAPTER 1: Survival Lessons

PART ONE: THE STREET YEARS

The first winter after the fire, Selene learned that cold could kill you just as dead as a blade.

She was seven. Small for her age. Thin in a way that made her ribs show through her shirt when the fabric got wet. She'd found a spot behind a tannery where the vats leaked heat through the walls, and she pressed her back against the stone until her skin burned because burning was better than freezing.

The smell was terrible. Rotting hides and chemicals that made her eyes water. But the rats stayed away from the stench, and so did most of the people, and Selene had already learned that people were worse than rats.

She stole her first loaf of bread three days after the fire. Her hands shook so badly she almost dropped it. The baker saw her, shouted, chased her two blocks before his wind gave out. She ate the bread in an alley, stuffing it into her mouth so fast she nearly choked, and then she threw it all up because her stomach had forgotten what food felt like.

The second time, she didn't run. She walked. Calm. Steady. Like the bread belonged to her, like she'd paid for it, like she was someone's daughter on an errand.

No one chased her.

That was the first lesson: people see what they expect to see. If you look like you belong, they assume you do.

***

By eight, she knew the shape of Garnath's belly.

The Lowers, where the streets ran with piss and the buildings leaned against each other like drunks. The Middens, where the tanners and dyers worked and the air tasted like copper and rot. The Warrens, where the Guild kept their ledgers and their secrets and their enforcers. The Merchant Quarter, where the coin flowed and the Watchers patrolled in pairs.

She learned which rooftops connected, which alleys dead-ended, which doors were left unlocked after dark. She learned the schedules of the night soil carts and the patrol routes of the Watchers. She learned that the fishmongers threw out their unsellable catch at dawn, and if you got there early enough, you could eat something that had only been dead a day.

She learned that other children disappeared.

Mira was the first one she noticed. A girl about her age, maybe a little older, who worked the same stretch of the Merchant Quarter. Quick hands, quicker feet. They never spoke, but they knew each other the way strays know each other. By sight. By smell. By the way they moved through the same hunting grounds without fighting over scraps.

Then one morning Mira wasn't there.

Selene waited three days before she stopped looking. Four more before she stopped thinking about it.

Dex was the second. A boy with clever fingers who'd taught her the basics of picking pockets. He'd shown her the feint, the bump, the lift. He'd laughed when she fumbled and laughed harder when she got it right.

They found him in an alley off Coppersmith Row with his hands broken. Both of them. Every finger snapped backward at the knuckle.

He was still alive. Still breathing. His eyes found hers, and there was nothing in them but animal terror.

She ran.

She didn't go back.

She didn't ask who did it or why. She already knew the answer: someone with power, someone with reach, someone who wanted to make a point. The specifics didn't matter. The lesson did.

Don't be noticed. Don't be remembered. Don't give anyone a reason to make an example of you.

***

The first man she killed was an accident.

She was nine. Thin and fast and desperate. He caught her lifting his purse in the Middens, near the tanner's district where she still slept some nights when the weather turned.

He didn't shout for the Watchers. Didn't call for help. Just smiled with yellow teeth and grabbed her wrist and dragged her into the alley.

"Little rat," he said. "Little thieving rat. You know what happens to rats?"

She knew. She'd seen it happen to other girls. Heard it happen through thin walls. The sounds that came after the grabbing, the dragging, the trapping.

Her hand found the knife she'd stolen two months ago from a drunk who'd passed out near the docks. It was dull and the handle was cracked and she'd never used it for anything but cutting rope.

She used it now.

The blade went in under his ribs, angled up the way she'd seen butchers angle their knives when they opened pig carcasses. She didn't think about it. Didn't plan it. Just felt the grab of flesh and the wet give of something softer underneath and the way his grip on her wrist went slack all at once.

He made a sound. Not a scream. More like a cough, surprised and wet.

His body hit the alley floor. His blood spread out beneath him, black in the moonlight, steaming in the cold air.

Selene stood over him and felt nothing.

That was wrong. She knew it was wrong. She should feel something. Fear. Horror. Guilt. Triumph. Something.

But there was just the cold, and the smell of copper and shit, and the practical understanding that she needed to leave before someone found her standing over a corpse with a bloody knife.

She wiped the blade on his coat. Took his purse. Walked away.

She didn't throw up. Didn't cry. Didn't shake.

The Hollow had been growing inside her since the cupboard, since the fire, since she'd watched her parents burn and kept breathing anyway. The man in the alley just made it bigger.

She slept that night behind the tannery, and her dreams were empty, and when she woke she felt exactly the same as she had the day before.

PART TWO: THE SHADOW

She met him three weeks after the man in the alley.

The Merchant Quarter was busy that morning. Market day. Bodies pressed together, voices shouting prices, the smell of spiced meat and fresh bread and too many people in too small a space. Perfect hunting conditions.

She picked her target: a man near the cloth merchant's stall, well-dressed but not wealthy, the kind of middling trader who carried enough coin to matter but not enough to hire protection. He was haggling over the price of linen, distracted, his coat hanging open just enough to show the purse at his belt.

Easy.

She bumped a woman carrying a basket of eggs. Apologized in a high, childish voice. Used the distraction to slide past the trader, her fingers already reaching for the purse strings.

Her hand got exactly one inch into his coat before something clamped around her wrist like iron.

She tried to pull away. Couldn't. Tried to twist. Couldn't. The grip wasn't painful, but it was absolute. Like being caught in a trap that had decided not to bite. Yet.

"If you're going to rob me, little shadow," a voice said, "at least try to be good at it."

She looked up.

The man was older than she'd thought. Twenty-two, maybe. Hard to tell with the stubble and the weathered skin. His clothes were well-made but worn, the kind of quality that spoke of better days behind him. His eyes were grey like slate. Like knife blades left out in the rain.

He was smiling, but it wasn't a kind smile. It was the smile of someone who'd caught something amusing and was deciding whether to let it go.

"I am good at it," Selene said. Because she was. Because no one had caught her in six months. Because this felt like failure, and failure made her angry.

"You're adequate." He released her wrist. Didn't grab for her, didn't call for the Watchers. Just let her go and watched her with those slate eyes. "Your approach was right. Your timing was acceptable. But you telegraph with your shoulders. You lean before you reach. Anyone paying attention would see you coming." He paused, let that sink in. "Watch the shoulders, little shadow. They'll betray you every time."

Selene rubbed her wrist. Stared at him. She should run. Every instinct said run. But something held her there, something she couldn't name, something that felt like the moment before a coin landed and you didn't know yet if you'd won or lost.

"Who are you?" she asked.

"No one important." He turned back to the cloth merchant, resumed his haggling like she wasn't there. "Go practice on easier marks. Come back when you've fixed that shoulder."

She should have left. Should have vanished into the crowd and found a different quarter to work and forgotten this man with his grey eyes and his iron grip.

Instead, she said: "Show me."

He paused. Looked at her over his shoulder. Something flickered in his expression. Surprise, maybe. Or recognition. Or just the calculation of a man deciding if a stray was worth feeding.

"Why would I do that?"

"Because you caught me." She held his gaze, refusing to look away. "That means you're better. And I want to be better."

Silence. The crowd flowed around them, oblivious. The cloth merchant was staring, confused, waiting for his customer to finish his business.

Then the man laughed.

A short, sharp sound of genuine amusement that cracked his weathered face into something almost human.

"You've got bite," he said. "That's good. Most your age have had it beaten out of them by now."

She didn't answer. Didn't need to. The fact that she was still standing here, still watching him, still *hungry*—that was answer enough.

"No," he said, more to himself than to her. "You're something else."

He tossed a coin to the cloth merchant, waved off the linen, and walked away from the stall. Didn't look back. Didn't check if she was following.

She followed anyway.

***

His name was Rook.

At least, that's what he told her to call him. She didn't know if it was real, and she didn't ask. In Garnath, names were currency. You didn't give them away for free.

He had a room above a butcher's shop in the Lowers, one room with a bed and a chair and a window that looked out over an alley full of rats. The walls were thin and the floor was warped and the whole place smelled of blood and rendered fat, but it had a door that locked and a roof that didn't leak and that made it better than anywhere Selene had slept in two years.

He didn't let her stay. Not at first. He'd teach her, he said, but she had to earn her own shelter. Charity bred weakness, and weakness bred corpses.

"You've survived this long on instinct," he said that first night, sitting in the chair by the window while Selene stood awkwardly near the door, unsure where she was allowed to exist. "Instinct will get you killed. What you need is discipline."

“I have discipline.”

“You have stubbornness. They’re not the same thing.” He pulled a knife from his belt, held it up in the lamplight. Not threatening. Just showing her. The blade was dark, almost black, shorter than most knives she’d seen. Built for quick thrusts rather than slashing, balanced so perfectly it seemed to float in his grip. When he turned it, it caught the light in a way that made it look alive. “Discipline is doing the right thing even when your gut tells you otherwise. Stubbornness is doing the same thing over and over because you’re too proud to learn.”

“What’s the right thing?”

“Depends on the situation.” He flipped the knife, caught it by the blade, offered her the handle. “For now? The right thing is learning to hold a knife without looking like you’re about to drop it.”

She took the knife. It was heavier than she expected. Better balanced. The kind of weapon that cost real money, not the kind you stole off drunks by the docks.

“Your grip is wrong,” he said.

“My grip works fine.”

“Your grip works for stabbing men in alleys who aren’t expecting it. It won’t work for someone who knows what they’re doing.” He stood, crossed the small room, positioned himself behind her. “May I?”

She tensed. Every muscle in her body screaming danger, stranger, trap.

But his voice was calm. Patient. And he’d asked permission. No one in Garnath asked permission for anything.

“Yes,” she said. Her voice came out smaller than she meant it to.

His hands closed over hers. Not grabbing. Just guiding. Repositioning her fingers on the hilt, adjusting the angle of her wrist, shifting the blade until it sat differently in her palm.

“Thumb here. Index here. Relax your grip. You’re not strangling it; you’re holding it.”

His skin was warm against her knuckles. Rough with callouses. She could smell him this close: leather, woodsmoke, something sharp like metal. Her breath stuttered and she didn't know why.

Stupid. That was stupid. It was just a hand.

But when he stepped back, some traitorous part of her wanted him to put it back.

"There," he said. The warmth vanished. The cold rushed back in. "Now it's an extension of your arm, not a rock you're waving around."

She swung the blade experimentally. It felt different. Lighter somehow, despite being the same weight.

"Better," he said. And the word settled in her chest like something warm she hadn't known she was missing.

***

He called her Shadow.

"Because that's what you are," he said when she asked. "You move like one. Think like one. You know how to disappear when people look too hard."

It was the nicest thing anyone had said to her in two years.

She didn't tell him that. Didn't tell him anything, really. He didn't ask about her past, and she didn't offer it. That was the deal. That was how it worked.

He taught her three mornings a week for the next four months.

How to move without sound. How to read a room before entering it. How to watch exits, count bodies, track threats. How to fall without breaking bones. How to throw a blade and actually hit something.

And most importantly: how to fight someone who knew how to fight back.

"You're fast," he said during one of their sessions, circling her in the cramped room while she tried to track him without moving her head. "Speed's an advantage. But it's not enough. A fast corpse is still a corpse."

"Then what is enough?"

"Awareness. Anticipation. Reading what someone's going to do before they do it." He feinted left. She didn't fall for it. His eyebrow rose a fraction. "Better. You're learning."

She was learning. She could feel it. The world was starting to make a different kind of sense, like she'd been looking at a painting upside down her whole life and someone had finally turned it right-side up.

And she was starting to feel things she didn't have names for.

***

It happened in the third month.

They were working on close-quarters defense, the kind of fighting that happened in alleys and stairwells and other places too tight to swing properly. He'd shown her a wrist-lock, a way to control someone's knife hand without giving them an angle to cut you.

"Watch the shoulders," he said as she practiced. The same correction he always gave. "You're still telegraphing."

"Again," he said.

She went through the motion. Her hand closed around his wrist, twisted, pulled. She was supposed to step in, drive her elbow into his solar plexus, create space.

She fumbled the step. Her foot caught on a warped floorboard. She stumbled forward.

He caught her.

One hand on her shoulder, steadying her. One hand still trapped in her grip. His face inches from hers, closer than they'd ever been.

She looked up. He looked down.

Something passed between them. Something she couldn't name. His eyes weren't cold anymore. They were just grey. Just human. And for one stupid, impossible second, she thought he might . . .

He stepped back. Released her. Turned away.

"Your footwork needs practice," he said. His voice was flat. Professional. Like nothing had happened. "Again."

She went through the motion. Her hands were shaking. She didn't know why.

That night, lying in her spot behind the tannery, she pressed her fingers to her shoulder where his hand had been. The warmth was long gone, but she could still feel the shape of it. The ghost of contact.

She hated how much she wanted it back.

***

The fourth month, he started smiling at her jokes.

It wasn't much. Just a crack in the stone, a flicker at the corner of his mouth when she said something sharp. But it was more than anyone else gave her. More than she'd gotten since before the fire, since before her world turned to ash and her parents turned to smoke.

"You're a smartass," he said one morning, after she'd made a crack about the rats in his walls being better fed than she was.

"I'm honest. There's a difference."

"No there isn't. Honest people know when to keep their mouths shut. Smartasses don't."

"And which one are you?"

He paused. Looked at her with those slate eyes. And then his mouth curved, just barely, just enough to make something warm unfurl in her chest.

"Both," he said. "That's why I'm still alive."

She filed that away. Stored it somewhere deep. The way his face changed when he wasn't being careful. The way his voice softened when he wasn't trying.

She knew better than to want things. Wanting was dangerous. Wanting got you hurt.

But somewhere, in the part of her the Hollow hadn't quite reached, she wanted him to smile at her again. Wanted him to look at her like she was worth something. Wanted this, whatever this was, to last.

It didn't.

PART THREE: THE LESSON

She woke up on the day everything changed and she didn't know it was different.

The sky was grey. The air smelled like rain. She did her morning rounds, checked her caches, stole a breakfast of stale bread and overripe fruit from the market square. Normal. Ordinary. A day like any other.

She went to the butcher's shop at the usual time. Climbed the stairs to his room. Knocked the pattern he'd taught her: two, pause, three.

No answer.

She knocked again. Waited. Tried the door.

Unlocked.

The room was empty.

The bed was made. The chair was pushed in. The lamp was cold. Even the knife, the dark blade he'd let her practice with, was gone.

The room smelled wrong. Too clean. Too still. The leather-and-woodsmoke scent that had always clung to the walls was fading, replaced by something flat and dead. Even the dust looked confused, settling on surfaces it had never been allowed to touch before.

No note. No message. No explanation.

She stood in the center of the room and breathed it in like she was trying to swallow the ghost whole. It didn't help. The smell faded with every breath she took, like she was killing it by wanting it too much.

She stood in the doorway for a long time, waiting for him to appear. Waiting for the joke to reveal itself, for him to step out of some shadow and call her gullible, call her slow, call her Shadow and mean it the way he always did.

The room felt colder than the cupboard had ever been. Colder than the night her parents burned. At least that cold had made sense.

He didn't come.

She searched the neighborhood. Asked questions she knew better than to ask. Bribed the butcher's wife with copper she couldn't spare. No one had seen anything. No one knew anything. He'd been there, and then he wasn't, and that was all.

She went back three more times. Three days in a row. Stood in that empty room and breathed air that no longer smelled like leather and woodsmoke and metal.

She checked the butcher's stairs again on the fourth morning. And the fifth. By the sixth day she hated herself for it. Hope was a stupid thing to feel, but her feet kept going anyway.

The seventh day, someone else had moved in.

She didn't go back after that.

***

For the first week, she told herself he was coming back.

People left all the time in Garnath. They went on jobs, took scores, disappeared into the Warrens on business that wasn't her concern. That's what this was. Business. He'd be back when he was done. He wouldn't just leave without saying something.

The second week, the hope started to curdle. Turned to something harder. Something that sat in her stomach like a stone.

He wasn't coming back. She knew that now. Knew it the way you knew the sun would rise and the guards would patrol and the rats would eat whatever you left unprotected.

He was gone.

Not dead, probably. She'd have heard if someone like him had died. Word traveled fast in Garnath, especially word about violence. No, he was alive somewhere. Just . . . somewhere else. Somewhere that didn't include a nine-year-old stray with too much bite and not enough sense.

She'd been so stupid. So fucking stupid. Thinking this was different. Thinking he was different. Thinking that because he'd taught her things, because he'd smiled at her jokes, because his hand had been warm on her shoulder that one time, because he'd called her Shadow like it meant something.

It didn't mean anything. It never meant anything.

She should have known that. She did know that. She'd learned it in the cupboard, in the fire, in every moment since. People left. People always left. The ones who hit you and the ones who helped you, the ones who hurt you and the ones who taught you, they all left in the end.

The only difference was the shape of the wound they carved on the way out.

***

She was nine years old and she had already learned the only lesson that mattered.

If someone can leave you, they will.

She filed Rook away in the same place she kept her parents. The same place she kept Mira and Dex and everyone else who'd vanished from her life without warning. A locked room inside the Hollow, where things went to stop hurting.

It didn't work.

Some nights, in the dark behind the tannery, she caught herself reaching for her shoulder. Pressing her fingers to the spot where his hand had been. Trying to remember the weight of it, the warmth of it.

She hated that the only warm memory she had left of him was that hand on her shoulder. Hated it. Hated him for giving it to her. Hated herself for wanting it back.

She couldn't remember anymore. The ghost was fading. Soon there would be nothing left of him but techniques and scars and a name that probably wasn't real.

Shadow.

He'd named her Shadow. And then he'd walked into one.

She caught herself listening for his laugh once. That short, sharp sound that cracked his weathered face into something almost human. She listened for it in the market crowds, in the tavern spill, in every alley where footsteps echoed wrong.

She stopped listening after that. Some habits deserved to die.

She practiced the moves he'd taught her. Perfected the grip, the stance, the wrist-lock that had made her stumble. She became what he'd told her she could be: fast and quiet and lethal. A shadow in truth, not just in name.

Two weeks after he disappeared, a man tried to grab her from behind in the Warrens. She felt the shift of air, the telegraph he'd taught her to read, and she was already moving before his hands closed on empty space. She broke his wrist with the lock Rook had drilled into her muscles. Left him screaming in the alley.

She lived because of him. That was the worst part.

She kept his lessons. She buried everything else.

And when the hurt tried to surface, she made a joke. Something dark. Something sharp. Something that cracked the tension and deflected the attention and kept anyone from seeing the wound underneath.

Just like he'd taught her.

The sarcasm was armor. The humor was a blade. And the thing that had cracked open in her chest when his hand touched her shoulder, the wanting, the warmth, the stupid dangerous hope?

She locked it in the room with everything else. Threw away the key. Pretended it had never existed.

Whatever softness had lived in her chest those four months didn't survive the empty doorway. She left it there with the fading smell of leather and the dust that had nowhere to settle anymore.

She was nine years old, and she was alone again, and she was exactly what Garnath needed her to be.

A survivor.

A shadow.

A girl who told herself she'd never let anyone close enough to leave her again.

CHAPTER 2: The Stray

Garnath always smelled worse after rain.

The water didn't wash anything away. It just woke the rot up. Fish guts and sewage and old smoke rose from the stones as the sun dragged itself over the rooftops, turning the streets into a throat you had to walk through.

Selene moved with the morning crowd, head down, eyes up. Hands in her pockets, fingers resting against the knife she kept there. She took in everything without looking like she was taking in anything at all.

Rule one: stay small. Rule two: see first.

Dock workers shouldered past in thick coats, boots thudding, voices rough with sleep and last night's drink. Stall owners shouted about fresh bread and cheap fruit that was never as fresh or as cheap as they claimed. Street kids wove through it all, hunting dropped coins and loose purses.

She knew most of them. Who'd cut your throat for half a crust. Who'd trade you to a gang for the promise of protection. Who'd pretend to be your friend until you closed your eyes.

Today, someone new broke the pattern.

She saw the girl at the mouth of the alley behind the tanner's. Thin in the wrong way for Garnath. Not gutter-hard, just newly emptied out. Her clothes had been good once. The fabric was quality, the cut wrong for this part of the city. The hem was dirty, knees stained from too much time on stone, but someone had paid real coin for that dress before the streets got to it.

Light hair, matted now, but she could tell it had been brushed daily, braided probably. Back when someone cared whether it tangled. The girl held herself wrong for Southside too. Spine straight. Chin tucked. Like she was trying to remember how to be smaller and didn't quite know how.

Three boys had cornered her. Local rats. Selene knew their faces, their bad teeth, their worse tempers. The tall one was Crel.

Ran with the Southside pack, thought he was climbing ranks. The other two were nobodies, the kind who followed whoever seemed strongest that week.

They were laughing the way boys laughed when they thought they'd found something weaker than them.

The girl had her back to the wall, arms folded tight across her stomach, like she was holding herself together. Her eyes were wrong too. Brown, clear, wide open. Not empty enough yet.

Selene watched for a moment from the edge of the crowd. Counted exits. Counted bodies. Counted how many steps it would take to get there if she chose to be stupid today.

She didn't owe the girl anything. Strays came through all the time. Some lasted a week. Some didn't. The city ate them and never noticed.

One of the boys reached for the girl's dress.

Selene turned into the alley before she decided to move.

The tanner's stink hit her first. Chemicals and old leather and something that had been animals once. It burned the back of her throat. The boys turned at the sound of her footsteps, like dogs who'd heard a cart.

Crel's face changed when he saw her.

Just for a second. A flicker behind his eyes, the kind that said he knew exactly who had just walked into his alley. She'd seen that flicker before. On other faces. In other alleys. The moment when someone's gut told them they'd made a mistake their mouth hadn't caught up to yet.

But his friends were watching. The girl was watching. And Crel had spent too long building a reputation to let a ten-year-old girl make him flinch in front of witnesses.

So he did what boys like him always did. He puffed up instead of backing down.

"Well, well." He spread his arms wide, showing his empty hands like that meant something. "The little knife. Thought you stayed north of the tanneries."

"Thought you had better instincts," Selene said.

One of the nobodies shifted his weight. Nervous. He'd heard stories, maybe. Or seen her work. His hand kept drifting toward his belt, toward whatever dull blade he kept there.

"We got here first," Crel said. "Find your own."

Selene let them see the knife as she stepped closer. Not raised. Just there. Loose in her hand, the way it was when she meant it.

"She's not yours to claim."

Crel's jaw tightened. He was doing the math now. Three of them, one of her. He was older, bigger, had reach and weight. His friends would back him. Probably. The numbers said he should win.

But the numbers didn't know about the boy she'd opened up behind the fishmonger's last winter. The one who'd thought size meant safe. He'd lived, but he'd never held a knife right again. Word got around. Word always got around.

"You're ten years old," Crel said. Like he was trying to convince himself.

"And you're still talking."

The nobodies exchanged looks. The nervous one took a step back. Not running, not yet, but making sure he had room to run if he needed to.

Crel saw it. Saw his support crumbling. His face went ugly with the kind of anger that came from fear wearing a mask.

"You think you're something special?" He stepped forward, closing the distance, trying to make his height matter. "You think because you cut up some drunk last year, the rest of us are supposed to bow down? You're just another gutter rat, same as us. Same as her." He jerked his chin toward Mirael. "Only difference is you got lucky. Luck runs out."

"You're right," Selene said. "It does."

She moved.

Not toward Crel. Toward the nervous one. The one who'd already decided he didn't want this fight. She closed the gap before he could react, knife flicking out in a short arc that opened his forearm from wrist to elbow. Shallow. Bloody. The kind of cut that looked worse than it was but bled like a slaughtered pig.

He screamed. Stumbled back. Blood splattered the stones, bright red against grey.

The third boy ran. Didn't even look back. Just bolted for the street like the alley had caught fire.

Crel stood frozen. Two seconds ago he'd had numbers. Now he had a bleeding friend and an empty space where his backup used to be.

Selene turned to face him. The knife dripped. She didn't wipe it.

"Your move," she said.

Crel's hands had curled into fists. His whole body was rigid, caught between fight and flight, pride and survival. She watched the war play out across his face. Watched him realize that winning wasn't the same as walking away whole. Watched him calculate what she might take from him if he pushed.

"This isn't over," he said.

"It never is."

He grabbed his bleeding friend by the collar and hauled him toward the street. The nervous one was still whimpering, still dripping, leaving a trail of red behind him like a wounded animal.

At the alley mouth, Crel looked back. His eyes found Selene's and held them.

"You'll slip," he said. "Someday. Everyone does."

"Maybe," Selene said. "But not to you. Not ever." He disappeared into the crowd. The blood trail faded into boot prints and cart tracks, swallowed by the city that didn't care whose it was.

The alley felt bigger without them. Quieter. Just the rain drip from the eaves and the distant shout of the market and the copper smell of fresh blood mixing with the tanner's stink.

Selene turned.

The girl hadn't moved. Still flat against the wall, fists clenched in the fabric at her sides. Her eyes flicked from Selene's face to the knife and back again.

"Thank you," she said.

The voice caught her off guard. Calm. A little hoarse, like she hadn't used it much recently, but steady enough.

She heard good schooling in it. The right cadence. The clean city vowels you only heard in houses with doors that locked.

Selene wiped the knife on her trouser leg and slid it away.

"Don't thank me," she said. "Find a better alley."

The girl blinked. "I didn't pick the alley. It was just . . . there."

Selene snorted. "That's how they get you. 'Just there' turns into dead fast."

She turned to go. This was already more involvement than she could afford.

"Wait."

The word was soft, but it pulled at her feet.

Selene looked back.

The girl pushed herself off the wall. Up close, the differences were sharper. Her face still had softness under the grime, the kind that came from regular meals not too long ago. Freckles crossed the bridge of her nose under a layer of street dirt. There was a bruise starting along her jaw, yellow and purple, half-hidden by her hair.

"You live here?" the girl asked.

"Here as in Garnath?" Selene said. "Or here as in this alley, because if you think this is a home, I really misjudged you."

The corner of the girl's mouth twitched. It might have been trying to be a smile.

"Here as in . . . out here." She gestured toward the street. "Without a house. Without . . . people."

Selene shrugged. "Four walls and a door don't mean you have people. They just mean you have more things someone can burn."

The girl flinched at that. Subtle, but there. Selene filed it away.

"Why are you asking?" Selene said.

The girl hesitated. Her fingers found the hem of her ruined dress and twisted, working the fabric between them.

"Because I don't," she said. "Not anymore."

There it was. The drop.

"How long?" Selene asked.

"Two weeks." The answer came too fast to be a lie. "Maybe three. I lost count a little."

Two, three weeks. That explained the clothes, the posture. Too new to know the rules. Long enough for the city to start stripping the polish off.

"You eat?" Selene said.

"Sometimes."

"Bad answer."

The girl's hands tightened in the fabric. She looked down at her feet.

"I had a crust yesterday," she said. "Someone dropped it near the market. And there was a man who threw me the end of a sausage if I helped him carry boxes. So yes. I ate."

Not lying. Not boasting either. Just stating fact because that was all she had.

"What's your name?" Selene asked.

The girl opened her mouth. Closed it again.

Silence stretched. The sounds of the street rolled past the alley mouth, distant and uncaring. Selene watched the struggle in her face.

"You have one, don't you?" Selene said. "Name?"

"Yes," the girl whispered. "I just . . . it doesn't feel like it belongs to me right now."

Selene understood that more than she liked.

"Fine," she said. "You can be 'hey you' for now."

The girl's eyes flicked up. There was something almost like amusement in them.

"Hey you," Selene said, keeping her voice flat. "If you stand here long enough, something else will try to eat you. Boys. Men.

Hunger. Doesn't matter. The city doesn't care what gets you as long as you go quiet. You want to live, you need rules."

"Rules," the girl repeated. "You have rules?"

"Three," Selene said. "I used to have more. The others broke."

She stepped closer so the girl could see her properly. See the star at her throat if she looked, the one thing Garnath hadn't managed to take. See the way her stance never really relaxed.

"Rule one," Selene said. "Never look lost. Even when you are."

The girl listened like she was memorizing.

"Rule two. Never be the hungriest person in the room. Hungry people do stupid things."

A faint flush crept up the girl's neck. She wrapped her arms around herself like she could hide the hollow there.

"And rule three," Selene said. "Never trust anyone who offers you something for free."

The girl frowned. "But you just . . ."

"I didn't offer you anything," Selene cut in. "I scared some rats off. That was for me. They annoyed me."

It was a lie. They annoyed her, yes. But she could have walked past. She had walked past a hundred scenes like that before.

The girl looked at her for a long moment. Her eyes had that weighing quality Selene had seen in older people. People who'd lost things they couldn't name.

"You didn't have to help," she said.

Selene shrugged.

"You want a roof tonight?" she asked. "Four walls, dry corner, nobody who'll rob you in your sleep if you keep your hands where they can see them?"

The girl's breath hitched. That tiny, sharp sound people made when hope slipped past their guard.

"Yes," she said. Too fast. Too naked. She swallowed. "Yes. Please."

"Then walk," Selene said. "Close. Watch my back."

"What about your name?" the girl asked as Selene started toward the street.

Selene glanced over her shoulder.

"Today?" she said. "You can call me Selene."

The girl repeated it under her breath like a prayer.

"Selene," she said. "I'm Mirael."

There it was. The real name after all.

Selene nodded once.

"Stay close, Mirael," she said. "This city bites."

They stepped out of the alley and into the river of people.

Selene didn't take the direct route. There was no direct route, not if you wanted to live. She cut left through the fish market, weaving between stalls where the vendors shouted prices and the smell of salt and scales hung thick enough to taste. Mirael scrambled to keep up, her shorter legs working double time.

At the corner where the fish market met the cloth district, Selene stopped. Pretended to examine a bolt of cheap linen. Her eyes found the reflection in the brass pot hanging from the next stall over.

No one following. Not yet.

Mirael stopped beside her, breathing hard. She didn't ask why they'd stopped. Just watched. Learning.

Good. That was good.

Selene moved again. Through the cloth district, past the money changers with their scales and their armed guards, into the tangle of side streets that led toward the eastern docks. She doubled back once, cutting through a courtyard she knew had three exits. Checked their trail in a puddle's reflection. In the polish of a door handle. In the eyes of an old woman sitting on her step who tracked movement the way cats tracked mice.

Mirael watched all of it. Selene could feel her attention, the way she filed each turn, each check, each small survival trick. The girl learned fast. Faster than most.

The streets narrowed as they moved east. The buildings here were older, leaning into each other like drunks holding each other up. The smell changed too. Less fish, more tar and rope and the particular salt-rot of the working docks.

Past the docks, into the warehouse district. Half the buildings here were abandoned, too damaged or too disputed to be worth claiming. The kind of place where people disappeared and no one asked questions.

Home.

Selene stopped at a building that looked like all the others. Three stories of weathered wood and broken windows and a door that hung crooked on its hinges. She didn't go to the door.

Instead, she ducked into the alley beside it. Counted bricks from the corner. Pushed one that looked like all the others, and a section of wall swung inward on hinges so quiet they barely whispered.

Mirael's eyes went wide.

"Don't tell anyone about this," Selene said. "Ever."

"I won't."

"I mean it. You tell someone, they find this place, I find you. And I won't be helping you that time."

Mirael swallowed. Nodded.

Selene believed her. Something in the way she held the information, like it was precious. Like she understood that trust was the only currency that couldn't be stolen.

They slipped inside. Selene pulled the wall closed behind them.

The space had been a storage room once, back when the warehouse stored things worth storing. Now it was a narrow corridor that led to a ladder, and the ladder led up to a room on the second floor that Selene had spent three years making into something like a home.

She climbed first. Listened at the top. Pushed open the trapdoor and scanned the room before pulling herself through.

Everything was where she'd left it.

The blankets in the corner, folded the way she folded them, with the corner tucked just so. The trip-wire at the window, still intact, still connected to the tin cans that would rattle if anyone tried to come in that way. The loose board by the far wall, covering the hole where she kept the things that mattered.

Three exits. The trapdoor they'd come through. The window, if she cut the trip-wire first. And the hole in the ceiling that led to the roof, hidden behind a beam.

Mirael climbed up behind her. She stood in the middle of the room, turning slowly, taking it all in with those too-wide eyes.

"This is yours?" she whispered.

"For now." Selene moved to the loose board. Pried it up. Inside: a knife that was better than the one she carried, wrapped in oilcloth. A handful of coins, copper mostly, one silver. A chunk of dried meat that was three days old but still good. Half a loaf of bread, harder than she'd like but not moldy yet.

She pulled out the bread and the meat. Broke both in half.

Mirael stared at the food in Selene's outstretched hand like it might be a trick.

"Rule two," Selene said. "Never be the hungriest person in the room."

"But you said not to trust anyone who offers something for free."

"I'm not offering. I'm telling you to eat. Difference."

Mirael took the food. Her hands were shaking. She bit into the bread and her eyes closed, and for a moment she looked like she might cry.

Selene looked away. Gave her the privacy of not being watched while she remembered what it felt like to not be starving.

She ate her own share standing by the window, looking out through the crack in the boards at the city below. The sun was getting low. Orange light stretched across the rooftops, making even Garnath look almost beautiful.

Almost.

"The blankets are there," Selene said without turning around. "Take the one on the left. The other one's mine."

"Where do I . . ." Mirael trailed off.

"Wherever you want. Just not by the window and not by the trapdoor. I need clear lines to both."

She heard Mirael move. Heard the blanket shift. Heard her settle into the corner farthest from both exits, her back against the wall.

Smart. She was learning.

Selene waited until the light faded and the city went dark. Then she moved to her own corner, her own blanket, her own piece of floor that she'd slept on for three years.

Ten feet away, Mirael lay curled under the other blanket, her eyes still open, watching Selene like she was afraid this might all disappear if she stopped looking.

"Go to sleep," Selene said.

"Okay."

She didn't close her eyes.

Selene turned away. Let her watch if she needed to. Eventually, exhaustion would win out over the fear. It always did.

***

That night, in the back corner of the warehouse on the east side, Mirael lay awake long after Selene's breathing went slow.

The roof didn't leak. The corner stayed dry, just like Selene had said. The blanket was moth-eaten but warm enough, and for the first time in weeks, her stomach wasn't empty.

Mirael watched the rise and fall of Selene's chest in the dark and listened to the rain on the roof and thought:

I would have died in that alley if she hadn't walked past at the right moment.

She didn't know why Selene had stopped. Didn't understand what made her turn into that alley instead of walking by like everyone else. The rules said don't trust anyone who offers something for free, but Selene had offered a roof and asked for nothing.

Maybe that was different. Maybe offering wasn't the same as giving. Maybe Selene had her own rules that bent when she wanted them to.

Or maybe she was just tired of being alone too.

Mirael pulled the blanket tighter around her shoulders and closed her eyes.

Tomorrow she would learn the rules. Tomorrow she would figure out how to stop looking lost. Tomorrow she would become whatever this city needed her to be to survive.

But tonight, for the first time in three weeks, she wasn't alone.

That was enough. It had to be enough.

Ten feet away, Selene slept with one hand on her knife and the wooden star pressed against her chest.

Mirael watched the slow rise and fall of her breathing and let her eyes close.

If Selene walked tomorrow, she would walk too.

CHAPTER 3: The Promise

The warehouse burned on a Tuesday.

Not their warehouse. The one three streets over, where the Kellman brothers ran their fence operation. Someone had finally gotten tired of their rates, or their mouths, or both. The fire started before dawn and burned until there was nothing left but black bones and ash.

Selene and Mirael watched from their rooftop, wrapped in the same blanket because the night was cold and warmth was warmth. The flames painted the sky orange and red, and the smoke rolled across the district like fog, carrying the smell of everything the Kellmans had spent years accumulating.

"Could have been us," Mirael said.

"Wasn't."

"Could have been."

Selene didn't argue. It was true. Any night could be the night someone decided their corner of the warehouse district was worth taking. Any morning could be the morning they woke up to smoke and screaming.

That was just life. That was just Garnath.

They climbed back down through the roof hatch as the sun came up. The warehouse felt different in the grey morning light. Smaller. More fragile. The hidden entrance, the three exits, the trip-wire at the window. All of it suddenly seemed like not enough.

Mirael started a fire in the small pit they'd dug in the center of the room. The smoke rose through the hole in the ceiling, same as always. The warmth spread slowly, pushing back the cold that had crept in overnight.

Selene sat by the window, sharpening her knife. The whetstone made a sound like whispered secrets. Scrape. Scrape. Scrape. Rhythm she could lose herself in when thinking felt too heavy.

"Two years," Mirael said.

Selene looked up. “What?”

“Two years ago today. You found me in that alley.”

The smoke was still thick outside. Drifting past their rooftop, curling through the gaps in the walls. It smelled like the Kellmans’ life burning. Like wood and cloth and years of accumulated things turning to nothing.

It smelled like her mother’s kitchen the morning everything ended.

Mirael hadn’t meant to think about it. But the fire dragged the memory out of her chest where she’d buried it for two years.

Her mother’s voice first. Sharp. Cold.

Liar. Dirty little liar.

Then the slap.

Not a warning. Not a tap. Her mother’s full hand across her face, hard enough to snap her head sideways, hard enough to send her stumbling into the wall. The sound of it louder than the words that followed.

How dare you say that about him. How dare you try to ruin this family.

Mirael’s cheek burned. Even now, two years later, sitting in a warehouse on the other side of the city, she could feel it. The ghost of her mother’s palm printed on her skin. The sting that never quite faded. Some nights she woke with her hand pressed to her face, checking for the heat that wasn’t there anymore but somehow still was.

Then the door. Then the shove. Then the street, still dark, still cold, her nightdress too thin for the autumn air. Her cheek throbbing in time with her heartbeat.

She’d waited on the step until dawn. Because mothers came back. Mothers always came back. Even angry mothers. Even mothers who hit. They came back and they apologized and they let you inside and everything went back to how it was supposed to be.

Except that day.

When the sun rose and the door stayed closed and no one came, Mirael learned the only rule that mattered:

If someone can leave you, they will.

She'd carried that rule through three weeks of alleys and hunger and boys with bad teeth who looked at her like she was meat. She'd carried it into the alley behind the tanner's, where she'd been too tired to run and too broken to care if they hurt her.

And then Selene had walked in. Ten years old with a knife and eyes like winter. And she hadn't left.

Not that day. Not any day since.

Two years of not leaving. Two years of coming back. Two years of "we" instead of "I" and shared blankets and someone who said her name like it belonged to a person instead of a problem.

The smoke curled past, thick and grey, and Mirael felt the old terror clawing up her throat.

If someone can leave you, they will.

But Selene hadn't. Not yet.

Mirael looked at her across the fire. Watched the blade move against the whetstone. Watched the girl who'd saved her life without meaning to, without even knowing she'd done it.

And she understood exactly why she needed the promise today.

"You remember the date?" Selene asked, not looking up from the knife.

"I remember everything about that day." Mirael kept her voice steady. Kept the memory locked behind her teeth where it couldn't escape and ruin everything. "The smell of the tanner's. The sound your knife made when you cut that boy's arm. The way you looked at me like I was a problem you hadn't decided to solve yet."

Selene set down the whetstone. "You were a problem."

"I know." Mirael smiled. It was the smile that had become familiar over two years. Soft. Devoted. The kind of smile that made Selene uncomfortable in ways she couldn't name. "But you solved me anyway."

"I gave you rules. You followed them. That's not solving. That's partnership."

"Is that what this is?" Mirael finally looked at her. The firelight caught her eyes, made them glow amber. "Partnership?"

"What else would it be?"

Mirael didn't answer. She turned back to the fire, and for a long moment there was only the crackle of burning wood and the distant sounds of the city waking up outside.

Then she said: "I want to say something. And I need you to let me finish before you decide it's stupid."

Selene's hand found the knife again. Not for threat. Just for something to hold. "Okay."

"We've been doing this for two years. Living together. Working together. Watching each other's backs. And I know you think it's just practical. Just survival. Just two street rats who figured out that two is better than one." Mirael pulled her knees up to her chest, wrapped her arms around them. Made herself small. "But it's more than that. To me. It's more than that."

"Mirael . . ."

"Let me finish."

Selene closed her mouth. Waited.

"I don't have anyone else," Mirael said. "I had a family once. A house. A name that meant something. And then I didn't. And then I was going to die in an alley and you walked in and you didn't have to help me but you did." Her voice cracked slightly. She swallowed it down. "You're all I have. The only person in this whole city who knows my name and says it like it matters. The only person who's stayed."

The words felt heavy. Too heavy. Like she was handing Selene something fragile and expecting her to know what to do with it.

"I'm not going anywhere," Selene said. Because that was true. That was the practical answer. "We're partners. That means something."

"Does it?" Mirael's eyes found hers again. Desperate. Searching. "Because I need it to mean something. I need to know that this isn't just . . . convenient. That you won't wake up one morning and decide I'm more trouble than I'm worth. That you won't just . . . leave."

"Leave and go where? The palace? I hear they're hiring."

"Selene."

"I'm not going to leave. Where would I even go? We have a good thing here. Roof doesn't leak. Mostly. The rats are manageable. You do that thing where you count the coin three times, which is annoying, but I've learned to live with it."

Mirael's jaw tightened. "I'm being serious."

"I know you are." Selene set down the knife. Rubbed her face with both hands. "Look. I don't know what you want me to say. We're partners. We watch each other's backs. We split the take. We don't die. That's the deal. That's been the deal for two years. Why does it suddenly need to be more than that?"

"Because I need to hear you say it."

"Say what? That I'm not going to wander off? That I'm not secretly planning to sell you to a gang and retire to the countryside? What?"

"That we matter." Mirael's voice dropped. Almost a whisper. "That this matters. That I'm not just . . . convenient."

Selene stared at her. Eleven years old. Firelight on her face. Looking at Selene like the next words out of her mouth would determine whether she lived or died.

"You want me to promise," Selene said flatly.

"Yes."

"Like a blood oath? Should we cut our palms and press them together? Maybe find a priest? I think there's one down by the fishmarket who'll marry anyone for three coppers. We could make it official. Get matching scars. Pick out curtains."

"Stop it."

"I'm just trying to understand what you're asking for. Because it sounds like you want me to swear some kind of eternal vow, and I don't know if you've noticed, but eternal vows don't mean much in Garnath. People promise things all the time. Then they die, or they leave, or they find something better. Words don't change that."

"Your words do." Mirael's hands were shaking now. "To me. Your words mean something. So when I ask you to promise, I'm not asking for a blood oath or a priest or matching scars. I'm asking you to say it. Out loud. So I can hold onto it when things get bad. So I have something to believe in that isn't just . . . hope."

Selene went quiet.

The fire crackled. The city murmured beyond the walls. Rain started again, soft against the roof, filling the silence between them.

"We only have each other now," Mirael said. Voice barely audible. "That's true, isn't it? We only have each other."

And there it was. The thing Mirael had been circling around. The words she needed to hear.

Selene could say no. Could explain that promises were just words, and words meant nothing when the fire came. Could tell her that depending on one person was a weakness, a crack in your armor that the world would exploit.

But Mirael's eyes were wet now. Not crying. Just . . . full. Like everything she'd been holding for two years was right there at the surface, waiting to spill over.

And Selene couldn't be the one to break her. Couldn't be another person who left. Another door that closed. Another fire that took everything.

Not tonight. Maybe not ever.

"Okay," Selene said quietly. "You want the words? Fine. We only have each other now. That's true. That's been true since the alley. That'll keep being true until one of us is dead or gone, and I'm not planning on either."

Mirael's breath caught.

"We're partners," Selene continued. "That means we survive together. Protect each other. Don't abandon each other. We don't sell each other out. We don't leave each other behind. We don't wake up one morning and decide the other person is inconvenient." She held Mirael's gaze. "That's the deal. That's always been the deal. I didn't think I needed to say it out loud, but if you need to hear it, fine. I'm saying it."

"Promise." The word came out broken. Desperate. "Promise me."

"I promise."

Mirael made a sound. Small. Wounded. Like something had cracked open inside her, and the pressure was finally releasing.

"There," Selene said, trying to pull back to something lighter. "Happy? Should I write it down? Sign it in blood? We could get it notarized. I'm sure there's a clerk somewhere who'd do it for a few coppers. Make it all official. Frame it. Hang it on the wall next to our matching curtains."

Mirael laughed. Or sobbed. Something in between that came out wet and shaky. "You're such an ass."

"You knew that when you followed me home."

"I did." Mirael wiped her eyes with the back of her hand. "I really did."

The tension in the room shifted. Settled. Like something had been decided that couldn't be undecided.

Mirael reached out. Touched Selene's hand. Just fingers brushing fingers. Three seconds of contact before she pulled back.

It felt like more than it was.

Selene let it happen. Didn't pull away. Didn't name what she saw in Mirael's eyes. Just accepted the touch as gratitude. As bond acknowledged.

Not as something else. Not as devotion looking for permission. Not as love being given a word it could hide behind.

"We only have each other now," Mirael said again. Soft. Reverent. Like she was praying.

"Yeah," Selene agreed. Practical. Grounded. Like she was confirming a supply run.

Same words.

Different religions.

Mirael went back to tending the fire. Selene went back to sharpening her knife. The morning continued. The warehouse sounds continued. Normal partnership sounds.

Everything was fine.

Everything was exactly what it needed to be.

***

The knock came three hours later.

Not at the hidden entrance. At the window. Three taps, pause, two more. A code Selene had learned six months ago from a woman who dealt in secrets and opportunities and things that fell off carts in the night.

Mirael tensed. Her hand found the knife she kept in her boot.

"It's fine," Selene said, but her voice had an edge to it. Irritation, not fear. "She always picks the worst times."

She crossed to the window, checked through the crack in the boards, then undid the trip wire and pushed the shutters open.

The woman who climbed through moved like she owned the place. Maybe nineteen or twenty. Tall. Dark hair pinned up in a way that looked careless but probably wasn't. She smelled faintly of jasmine and something sharper underneath, like secrets kept too long in closed rooms. Her clothes were good but not flashy. The kind of clothes that said money without screaming it.

"Relax," she said to Selene, brushing dust off her sleeve. "If I were here to kill you, you'd already be quiet."

"Viena." Selene's voice was flat. Guarded.

Viena's eyes swept the warehouse with an expression that managed to be both approving and pitying. Then her gaze found Mirael, still crouched by the fire with her hand on her knife, and something in her face softened.

"Oh," she said. Gentle. Almost warm. "So this is your shadow."

Mirael didn't know what to say. No one had looked at her like that since before. Like she was a person worth noticing. Like she mattered.

"She's not my shadow," Selene said. "She's my partner."

“Even better.” Viena smiled, and it wasn’t the practiced smile of someone selling something. It was real. Or close enough to real that Mirael couldn’t tell the difference. “You brought her in. That means she’s yours. And yours are mine.”

“She’s not yours.”

“Not yet.” Viena’s smile didn’t waver. “But give it time. Everyone needs someone who knows things. Sooner or later, that someone is me.”

She crossed the room like the warehouse belonged to her, stopping a few feet from the fire. Up close, Mirael could see the details. The small scar at the corner of her left eye. The callouses on her fingers that didn’t match her soft clothes. The way she held herself like someone who’d learned to be underestimated and turned it into a weapon.

“I’m Viena,” she said to Mirael. Not waiting for Selene to introduce them. “I run a house in the Copper District. Among other things.”

“A house?” Mirael asked.

“A brothel,” Selene said flatly. “She runs a brothel.”

“I run an establishment,” Viena corrected, unbothered. “Where people come to forget their troubles and share their secrets. The forgetting costs coin. The secrets cost more.” She tilted her head, studying Mirael with those knowing eyes. “You have good bones. Good posture. Someone taught you how to sit like you belonged somewhere better than this.”

Mirael felt her face flush. “I . . . my mother. Before.”

“Before.” Viena nodded like that single word explained everything. Because it probably did. “The befores always leave marks. Some visible. Some not.” Her voice dropped, softer now. Almost kind. “You’re safe here. With her. She doesn’t keep things she doesn’t value.”

Selene made a sound of irritation. “Are you done recruiting?”

“I haven’t even started.” Viena turned back to her, that curved smile returning. “Speaking of which. The offer for steadier work is still open. I could use someone with your skills.”

"In your house?"

"Out front." Viena's smile widened. "You'd be surprised what men pay for a girl who looks like she might kill them."

Selene snorted. "Pass. I don't have the temperament for smiling at customers."

"Who said anything about smiling? Half my girls don't smile. The mysterious ones make twice as much."

"Still no."

"Because you'd have to be nice to people?"

"Because I'd have to be in a room with them." Selene crossed her arms. "I don't do well in rooms I can't leave. And I don't do well with people who think they've bought something."

"Fair." Viena didn't seem offended. If anything, she seemed pleased by the answer. "Can't say I didn't try." She reached into her coat and pulled out two things: a small leather pouch, which she tossed to Selene, and a folded piece of paper, which she set on the crate by the fire.

Selene caught the pouch without looking. Weighed it. "This the Merchant Quarter payment?"

"Delayed. My contact had complications. But it's all there." Viena nodded toward the paper. "That's something else. A name. An address. A shipment that's going to be lighter than it should be three nights from now."

Selene's eyes narrowed. "Why are you giving me this?"

"Because you'll use it well. And because someday you'll have something I need, and you'll remember that I gave before I asked." Viena shrugged, elegant even in the gesture. "That's how it works. That's how everything works."

"I don't like owing people."

"Then don't think of it as a debt. Think of it as an investment." Viena glanced at Mirael again. "In both of you."

She moved toward the window, then stopped. Turned back. Her eyes found Mirael's and held them.

"Take care of her," Viena said. And all the practiced warmth fell away, leaving something real underneath. Something almost like concern. “She’s sharper than she knows. Sharper than she should be, at her age. That kind of sharp cuts both ways. She’ll need someone to remind her that bleeding isn’t the same as winning.”

Mirael opened her mouth to respond, but Viena was already climbing out the window, disappearing into the grey morning light like she’d never been there at all.

Selene reset the trip wire. Closed the shutters. Her jaw was tight.

Mirael watched her for a moment, then looked at the folded paper on the crate. “Are you going to read it?”

Selene snatched it up before Mirael could touch it. Unfolded it. Read. Her expression flickered through something complicated before settling back into neutral.

“Well?” Mirael asked. “Is it helpful?”

Selene hesitated. Which was an answer.

“Viena’s version of being helpful,” she finally said. “Which means it’s probably accurate, definitely dangerous, and comes with strings she hasn’t mentioned yet.”

“But you’ll use it.”

Selene folded the paper again. Tucked it into her belt. “We’ll use it. She gave it to both of us.”

Something warm bloomed in Mirael’s chest. We. Us. Both of us.

“She’s . . . not what I expected,” Mirael said carefully. “For someone who runs a brothel.”

“She’s exactly what you’d expect if you knew what to look for.” Selene picked up the coin pouch, finally opened it, started counting. “Viena collects people the way other people collect coin. She finds the broken ones, the useful ones, the ones nobody else sees. And she gives them just enough to survive. Just enough to need her.”

“That sounds . . .”

“Dangerous?”

“I was going to say kind.”

Selene looked up. Met Mirael's eyes. Something flickered there, too fast to name.

"It's both," she said quietly. "That's what makes her good at it."

Mirael didn't say anything. She watched Selene's hands move through the coins, watched the firelight play across her face, and thought about a woman who smelled like jasmine and secrets. Who looked at her like she was worth seeing. Who said yours are mine like it was a promise and a warning wrapped in one.

Selene had other people. Other connections. Other loyalties.

But for the first time, that didn't feel like a threat.

It felt like a door opening.

***

Later that night, after Selene's breathing had gone slow and steady ten feet away, Mirael pulled out the journal.

She'd stolen it three months ago from a merchant's cart. Good paper. Leather binding. The kind of thing she would have owned a dozen of back when she was someone else.

She'd never written in it. Never known what to say. But tonight, the words were there. Burning in her chest like the fire that had eaten the Kellmans' warehouse. Needing to get out before they consumed her.

She opened to the first page. Smoothed her hand across the blank paper. Found the stub of charcoal she kept wrapped in cloth.

By the dying firelight, her shadow huge against the warehouse wall, she wrote the first line:

She promised.

The rest came pouring out. Everything she couldn't say. Everything she'd been holding since the alley, since the warehouse, since the first night Selene had given her a blanket and a corner and a set of rules to live by. Two years of watching and wanting and pretending it was enough.

She wrote until her hand cramped. Until the fire was nothing but embers. Until the words stopped burning and settled into something she could carry.

Then she closed the journal. Wrapped it carefully in oilcloth. Hid it beneath the loose floorboard, next to Selene's cache but separate from it.

Her own secret. Her own space. The only place where she could be honest about what this was.

She lay down. Ten feet from Selene. Close enough to hear her breathing. Far enough to maintain the distance Selene needed.

The warehouse was quiet. The city beyond was never quiet, but it had faded to a murmur, the late-night sounds of Garnath grinding on.

Inside their corner, their claimed space, their almost-home, they were safe. Warm. Alive.

Together.

Mirael watched Selene sleep. Watched the wooden star rise and fall against her chest with each breath.

There were so many things Selene never talked about. So many walls she'd built that Mirael couldn't climb.

But tonight, she'd said the words. We only have each other now. And she'd meant them. In her way. In the only way she knew how to mean them.

Mirael closed her eyes.

Ten feet away, the gap between what Selene had promised and what Mirael had heard stretched wide in the darkness.

CHAPTER 4: The Veiled Lantern

Twelve years changed a lot of things.

The warehouse was gone. Burned three winters after the Promise, same as the Kellmans', same as half the district when the dry season fires swept through. They'd lost everything except each other and the clothes on their backs, and they'd rebuilt from nothing. Again.

They'd done it so many times now that the loss barely registered anymore.

The Veiled Lantern sat in the Lantern Quarter, three streets back from the harbor where the money was old and the secrets were older. Red paper lanterns hung from the eaves, casting soft light across cobblestones worn smooth by centuries of feet. The building itself was narrow, four stories of dark wood and leaded glass, the kind of place that looked expensive because it was.

Selene pushed through the front door, and the smell hit her first. Jasmine and sandalwood, layered over something sweeter underneath. Incense burning in brass holders. Wine warming by the fire. The particular musk of bodies pressed close in rooms where pleasure was currency.

The common room was half full. Merchants in silk. Minor nobles pretending to be merchants. A few faces Selene recognized from jobs she'd rather forget. Nobody looked up when she entered. That was the point of places like this. You came to the Veiled Lantern to be unseen.

Mirael was already at their usual table, tucked into the corner where two walls met and the angles gave clear sightlines to every door. Her hair was braided back tonight, practical, and she wore the dark-green coat that made her violet eyes look almost black in dim light.

She'd grown into something beautiful over the years. The kind of beautiful that made men stupid and women jealous. She hated it. Said it made her visible when she needed to disappear. Said it drew the wrong kind of attention.

Selene thought she was probably right. But she also thought Mirael didn't see herself clearly. Never had.

"You're late," Mirael said.

"The Harker job ran long." Selene dropped into the chair across from her, back to the wall, facing the room. Old habits. "Their courier took the scenic route through the Lowers. I had to improvise."

"Did you get it?"

Selene pulled a leather tube from inside her coat and set it on the table between them. Mirael's eyes tracked it, then tracked the room, checking for watchers. Finding none.

"Sealed documents," Selene said. "Shipping manifests for the next three months. Every cargo coming through the eastern docks."

"That's worth . . ."

"More than they paid us. I know." Selene flagged down one of the servers, a young man with dark curls and a practiced smile. "Wine. The Valdrian red. Two cups."

He nodded and disappeared toward the bar.

Mirael was still looking at the leather tube. "We could sell this twice. Three times, maybe. Different buyers who don't talk to each other."

"We could. But we won't."

"Because?"

"Because that's how you end up floating in the harbor with your throat cut." Selene leaned back, watching the room. "One sale. Clean. Then we burn our trail and move on to the next job."

"There might not be a next job."

The words hung between them. Selene didn't respond.

The server returned with wine. Poured. Left.

Mirael lifted her cup but didn't drink. "The Hendricks route is closed. Maren's people won't touch us anymore. I tried to set up a meet with the Castellan buyer last week, and his man told me to find another line of work."

"He say why?"

"He didn't have to." Mirael's jaw tightened. "Word is out. Someone's been telling traders we're bad luck. That working with us brings attention nobody wants."

"The Guild."

"Probably. Maybe. I don't know." Mirael finally drank. Set the cup down harder than necessary. "What I know is that three months ago we had six steady routes and a waiting list. Now we have this job and whatever Viena throws our way, and even Viena's been careful lately."

Selene sipped her wine. Let the silence stretch.

They'd been independent for twelve years. No gang affiliation. No Guild membership. No protection except what they could provide themselves. It had worked because they were good, and careful, and smart enough to stay small. Small enough that the big players didn't notice. Small enough that crushing them wasn't worth the effort.

But somewhere along the way, small had become visible. Jobs had gotten bigger. Reputation had spread. And now the machinery of Garnath's underworld was starting to pay attention.

"She's upstairs," Mirael said. "Viena. She sent word she wanted to see us."

"Both of us?"

"Both of us."

Selene drained her cup. Set it down. "Then let's not keep her waiting."

***

Viena's office was on the fourth floor, past the private rooms where her workers plied their trade. The sounds followed them up the stairs. Soft laughter. Rhythmic creaking. Someone moaning in a way that might have been pleasure or performance. Selene had been in those rooms enough times to know that the line between the two was thinner than most people thought.

The office door was polished dark wood with brass fittings that probably cost more than everything Selene owned. She knocked twice. Waited.

"Come."

Viena was at her desk, writing something by candlelight. The room smelled like her: jasmine and secrets and something underneath that was harder to name. Power, maybe. Or patience. The two were hard to tell apart in Garnath.

She looked up when they entered. Smiled that curved smile that never quite reached her eyes.

"My favorite strays," she said. "Sit. Drink. You look like you've been running."

"Walking, mostly." Selene took one of the chairs facing the desk. Mirael took the other. "Your message said urgent."

"Did it? I thought it said important. There's a difference." Viena set down her pen. Folded her hands on the desk. The rings on her fingers caught the candlelight. "Urgent means now. Important means soon. I try to be precise with my words."

"And yet here we are now."

"Here you are. Which tells me you understood the subtext." Viena tilted her head. "You completed the Harker job?"

"An hour ago."

"Good. Payment's already in your account at the moneylender. Minus my percentage, of course."

"Of course."

Viena studied them both. Her eyes lingered on Mirael, softened slightly, then moved back to Selene. "You've heard the rumors."

It wasn't a question.

"We've noticed our options narrowing," Selene said. "Mirael thinks someone's been talking."

"Someone has." Viena rose. Moved to the window. The city stretched out below, a maze of rooftops and lantern light and shadows that swallowed everything. "The Guild's been making inquiries. Asking about you. Your methods. Your contacts. Your vulnerabilities."

Selene's hand found the knife at her belt. Habit. "Why?"

"Because you've become inconvenient." Viena turned back to face them. "You're too good, Selene. Too visible. You've been taking jobs that used to go to Guild contractors. Undercutting their prices. Making them look slow and sloppy by comparison. And you've done it all without paying tribute, without asking permission, without kissing any of the rings that are supposed to be kissed."

"We're independent. That's not against any law."

"There is no law. There's only power and the people who have it." Viena's voice dropped. "The Guild is having conversations about you. The kind of conversations that end with bodies in alleys and businesses burning down."

Mirael's hand found Selene's under the table. Squeezed.

Selene didn't squeeze back.

"What kind of conversations?"

"The kind where someone suggests you might be more useful inside their organization than outside it. And someone else suggests you might be more useful dead." Viena moved to a cabinet. Poured three glasses of something amber. Handed two to them. "They haven't decided yet. But they will. Soon."

"And you're telling us this because?"

"Because yours are mine." Viena said it simply. Like it was obvious. "And because I'd rather not lose two of my best freelancers to Guild stupidity. You're useful to me. I protect useful things."

Selene turned the glass in her hands. Didn't drink. "What do you suggest?"

"Keep your head down. Take smaller jobs. Stop making waves." Viena smiled, but there was no warmth in it. "Or don't. Take bigger jobs. Make more waves. Force them to either recruit you or move against you. Either way, you'll have clarity."

"That's not helpful."

"It's honest. That's better." Viena sat back down. Picked up her pen. "There's a job. The Guild's been running something out of the Warrens. Their headquarters in the old catacombs. I have a buyer who wants to know what."

"You want us to infiltrate Guild headquarters."

"I want you to get close enough to find out what they're planning. Shipments, contracts, whatever's making them bold enough to start squeezing independents." Viena's eyes glittered. "High risk. High reward. The kind of job that either gives you leverage or ends your career."

"The catacombs are a maze. Even the parts they've mapped."

"Which is why most people stay in the parts they know." Viena leaned back. "But you're not most people. And right now, information about what the Guild is planning might be worth more than any job they could offer you."

Selene looked at Mirael. Mirael looked back.

Twelve years of reading each other's faces. Twelve years of knowing when to push and when to fold.

Mirael gave the slightest nod.

"We'll think about it," Selene said.

"Don't think too long. The offer won't wait forever." Viena was already writing again. Dismissal clear. "And Selene? There are people you can steal from and people you cannot. Make sure you know the difference before you choose your next job."

Selene stood. Mirael stood.

At the door, Selene paused. "This job. The buyer who wants the intel. Who is it?"

Viena didn't look up from her writing. "Does it matter?"

"It always matters."

"Then find out yourself. That's what I pay you for."

They left.

***

The hallway outside Viena's office was quiet. Thick carpets absorbed their footsteps. Brass sconces threw soft light across wallpaper that probably cost more than most people made in a year.

"Well," Mirael said. "That was terrifying."

"That was information." Selene started down the stairs. "She's scared. Or close to it. Viena doesn't give warnings unless she thinks the threat is real."

"Which means the Guild is actually moving against us."

"Which means we need to figure out our next move before they make theirs."

They reached the second-floor landing. The sounds were louder here. A woman laughing. A man's voice, low and urgent. The creak of bedframes and the particular rhythm of bodies moving together.

Selene stopped walking.

Mirael stopped too. Waited.

"Go back to the table," Selene said. "Order food. I'll meet you in an hour."

Something flickered across Mirael's face. Recognition. Understanding. The kind of hurt she'd learned to hide behind careful blankness.

"Selene . . ."

"An hour. Maybe less."

Mirael didn't argue. She never argued about this. She just nodded, once, and continued down the stairs without looking back.

Selene watched her go. Watched the straight line of her spine and the careful way she held her shoulders and the slight tremor in her hands that most people wouldn't notice.

She noticed.

She always noticed.

She went looking for Lira anyway.

***

Lira was in her usual room on the second floor. Third door on the right. A brass plaque on the door showed a crescent moon, her symbol, the sign that told clients what kind of company to expect.

Selene knocked.

"It's open."

The room was small but well-kept. A bed with clean sheets. A washstand in the corner. Candles burning low, filling the space with soft light and softer shadows. Lira was sitting by the window, wearing a silk robe that hung open to show the body underneath.

She was beautiful in the way all of Viena's workers were beautiful. Dark hair. Dark eyes. Curves that caught candlelight like they were designed for it. A mouth that knew how to smile and when.

"Selene." The name came out like a greeting and an invitation wrapped together. "It's been a while."

"Three weeks."

"Longer, I thought." Lira rose. Moved closer. The robe slipped off one shoulder. "You've been busy."

"I'm always busy."

"And yet here you are." Lira's hands found Selene's belt. Started working the buckle. "Viena keep you late?"

"Business."

"Always business with you." The belt came loose. Lira's fingers moved to the buttons of Selene's shirt. "Most people come here to forget business."

"I'm not most people."

"No." Lira smiled. Pushed the shirt off Selene's shoulders. Let her hands trace the scars that mapped Selene's torso like a history lesson. The thin white line across her ribs. The puckered mark on her shoulder. The older ones, faded to silver, that she'd stopped explaining years ago. "You're not."

Selene caught Lira's wrists. Stopped her hands. "I'm not here for slow."

Lira's smile didn't waver. It never did. That was what made her good at this.

"Then tell me what you're here for."

Selene told her.

With her mouth. With her hands. With the weight of her body pressing Lira back toward the bed.

Rough. Efficient. The kind of touch that took without asking and gave nothing back.

Lira knew. She always knew. She let Selene push her down onto the sheets, let Selene's hands find the familiar geography of her body, let Selene take what she needed without asking questions about why.

The silk robe fell away.

Lira's body was a study in contrasts. Small breasts that fit perfectly in Selene's palms, nipples already hardening in the cool air. A flat stomach that dipped and tensed under Selene's fingers, the muscles there twitching when she traced the line from ribcage to hip. And that ass, tight and round, the curve of it something Selene's hands remembered even when her mind tried to forget.

Selene's mouth found the hollow of Lira's throat. Tasted salt. Felt the pulse hammering beneath thin skin. Her hands moved lower, mapping the familiar terrain, the soft give of inner thighs, the heat radiating from the center of her.

Lira's breath caught. Her back arched off the bed, pressing those small breasts against Selene's chest.

Selene's fingers found the slick heat between Lira's thighs. Pressed inside. Felt the muscles clench around her, heard the sharp gasp that could have been real or rehearsed.

Selene didn't care which. The answer changed nothing.

Function. Release. The only way she knew to quiet the thing inside her that never stopped screaming.

She worked Lira with practiced efficiency. Two fingers curling inside, thumb circling the swollen nub above. She knew exactly where to press, how hard, how fast. Knew the rhythm that would build toward release. Lira's thighs trembled against her hand. Her hips rolled, chasing the friction, and those small breasts rose and fell with quickening breath.

When Lira came, it was with a sound caught somewhere between gasp and moan. Her inner walls clenched tight around Selene's fingers, pulsing, and her whole body went taut as a bowstring before collapsing back against the sheets.

Selene withdrew her hand. Wiped the slickness on the bedsheet.

Lira's hands reached for her then, and Selene let them. Let those clever fingers work the laces of her trousers, push the fabric down her hips. Let Lira's mouth find the flat plane of her stomach, trace lower, breath hot against the sensitive skin of her inner thigh.

When Lira's tongue found her, Selene's eyes closed. Her fingers twisted in dark hair. Sensation built in slow waves, pressure mounting, the hollow ache that lived in her chest temporarily drowned by something simpler. Cruder. The wet heat of Lira's mouth. The suction. The practiced rhythm that knew exactly how to make her body respond even when her mind was somewhere else entirely.

The climax hit like a fist. Her thighs clenched around Lira's head, her spine arched, and for one blinding moment there was nothing but white noise and release.

Then nothing.

Selene rolled off. Lay on her back. Stared at the ceiling while her breathing slowed.

The candles flickered. Somewhere down the hall, someone was laughing.

"You're getting worse," Lira said quietly. She'd turned on her side, watching Selene with those dark eyes that saw too much. "The way you are after. The emptiness."

Selene didn't answer.

"It used to help. When you first started coming to me. You'd leave looking lighter. Now you leave looking exactly the same." Lira's hand found Selene's shoulder. Gentle. Almost tender. "Whatever you're trying to fill, this isn't working anymore."

"It's not about filling anything." Selene sat up. Reached for her clothes. "It's about shutting something up for a while."

"Is there a difference?"

"There's always a difference."

She dressed quickly. Efficiently. The way she did everything.

At the door, she paused. Pulled coins from her belt pouch. Set them on the table by the bed. More than the usual rate.

"For your time," she said.

Lira didn't touch the coins. Just watched her with that quiet understanding that made Selene want to hit something.

"She's still downstairs, isn't she? Your partner."

"Yes."

"And she knows you're up here."

"Yes."

"That must be hard for her."

Selene's jaw tightened. "She manages."

"Everyone manages until they don't." Lira pulled the silk robe back around her shoulders. "Take care of yourself, Selene. Whatever's eating you, it's getting hungry."

Selene left without answering.

***

Mirael wasn't at the table.

Selene scanned the common room and found her at the bar, leaning against the polished wood with a wine cup in her hand. She was talking to one of Viena's male workers. Tall. Broad shoulders. The kind of jaw that probably made other women stupid.

Mirael laughed at something he said. Tilted her head in that way she did when she wanted someone to look at her neck. Her hand found his forearm, fingers resting there just a moment too long.

Selene walked over.

The man saw her first. Something flickered in his eyes, recognition or warning, and he straightened slightly. Mirael turned, and for just a heartbeat her expression was open. Searching. Looking for something in Selene's face.

She didn't find it.

"Ready?" Selene asked.

Mirael's hand slipped off the man's arm. The searching look shuttered into careful blankness. "I ordered food. It's at the table."

"Good. I'm hungry."

Selene walked to their usual corner without looking back. Didn't check if Mirael was following. Didn't acknowledge the man at all.

Behind her, she heard Mirael say something soft to him. An apology, maybe. Or a goodbye. It didn't matter.

Mirael slid into the chair across from her a moment later. There was food on the table. Bread and cheese and sliced meat. Two cups of wine, one mostly empty now.

Selene reached for the bread. Started eating.

"You were quick," Mirael said. Her voice was level. Too level.

"Wasn't in the mood for conversation."

"You never are."

Selene looked up. Met Mirael's eyes. Saw the hurt there, bright and sharp, the hurt that Mirael had tried to bury under flirtation and wine and a pretty man's attention.

She saw it. She always saw it.

She looked back down at her food.

"Eat something," Mirael said quietly. "You look like you haven't slept in days."

"I haven't."

"Then eat. Sleep later." Mirael's voice shifted into something more controlled. More careful. The voice she used when she was holding herself together by force of will. "We need to talk about Viena's offer. The Guild job."

Selene ate. Drank. Let the silence stretch.

Twelve years, and they'd never talked about this. Never talked about the rooms upstairs or the workers Selene visited or the ways Mirael tried to make her feel something, anything, in return. It sat between them like a third person at the table, present and painful and utterly unacknowledged.

"Infiltrating the Warrens is suicide," Selene finally said. "That's Guild headquarters. Watchers everywhere. We get caught down there, we don't come back up."

"We've done dangerous before."

"This isn't dangerous. This is stupid." Selene tore off a piece of bread. Chewed. "But Viena's right about one thing. If we knew what they were planning, we'd have leverage. Something to trade. Something to use."

Mirael picked at her bread. Didn't eat. "And if we don't take it? If we keep our heads down like Viena suggested?"

"Then we wait for the Guild to make up their mind. Recruitment or elimination. Those are our options."

"Neither sounds great."

"Neither is." Selene drained her wine. "But at least if we're moving, we're not sitting still. Sitting still gets you killed."

Mirael nodded slowly. "So we take the job."

"We think about it. Sleep on it. Decide in the morning when we're not half-drunk and exhausted."

"Since when do you sleep on anything?"

"Since someone I trust told me to eat something and sleep later." Selene stood. Held out her hand. "Come on. Upstairs."

Mirael looked at the offered hand. Something complicated moved behind her eyes. Want and hurt and hope and resignation, all tangled together.

She took the hand.

They left the common room together, climbing the back stairs that led to the upper floors. Past the rooms where Viena's workers plied their trade. Past the sounds that filtered through thin walls. Up to the fourth floor, where Viena kept a few rooms for people who weren't customers. People who were useful in other ways.

Their room was at the end of the hall. Small. Cold. Two narrow beds pushed against opposite walls. But it was theirs, and it was safe, and in Garnath that counted for something.

Selene dropped Mirael's hand as soon as they were through the door. Put the familiar distance between them.

Ten feet. Same as always.

Below them, through the floorboards, someone was laughing. Soft and warm and far away.

Mirael didn't look down.

She never did.

CHAPTER 5: The Watcher's Interest

The Paladin outpost on Bridgewater Street smelled like ink and old stone and the slow rot of an institution that had stopped believing in itself.

The building had been a courthouse once, back when Garnath still pretended justice was more than a transaction. Now the scales carved above the doorway were worn smooth by decades of rain, and the holding cells in the basement stored furniture instead of prisoners. Easier that way. Fewer questions about who got held and who got released and whose coin made the difference.

Weston turned another page. The report was three months old, written in the cramped hand of a clerk who'd been more interested in finishing than accuracy. Suspected contractor activity, Merchant Quarter. Two bodies recovered. No witnesses. Professional work.

He set it aside. Picked up the next one.

Outside his window, Bridgewater Street was waking up. He could hear the fishmongers' carts rolling toward the harbor, wheels grinding against cobblestones that hadn't been repaired in years. A woman was arguing with a vendor about the price of salt. Somewhere further off, a hammer rang against metal, steady as a heartbeat. The smiths on Ironmonger's Row starting their day.

The sounds of Garnath. The sounds of a city that kept moving no matter how much blood soaked into its stones.

The stack on his desk had grown over the past year. Twenty-seven incidents that shared the same handwriting, even if the penmanship changed. Clean entries. Clean exits. Targets who had earned their deaths through the usual channels: betrayal, debt, information sold to the wrong buyer. The kind of work that kept Garnath's underworld in balance, one corpse at a time.

He should have passed the file to enforcement months ago. That was procedure. Accumulate evidence, build a case, hand it off to the men with swords and warrants. Let them do the hunting.

Instead, the file stayed on his desk. Growing thicker. Growing stranger.

The morning light came through the narrow window behind him, falling across papers that told a story he couldn't quite read. From where he sat, he could see a slice of the street below: a boy sweeping the steps of a tailor's shop, a drunk sleeping it off against a lamp post, two women in servants' clothes walking quickly with their heads down. The ordinary machinery of a city that had learned to step over its own corpses.

Weston rubbed his eyes with the heel of his hand. His tea had gone cold an hour ago. He drank it anyway, grimacing at the bitter dregs. Maren would have laughed at him for that. She'd always said he'd drink dishwater if someone put it in front of him while he was reading.

Four years since the fever took her. He still made two cups every morning.

Eighteen years of service, and he still couldn't shake the feeling that the obvious answer was usually the wrong one.

"Commander?"

He looked up. Brennan stood in the doorway, young face carefully neutral. Third year in the order. Still believed in the work, which made him either admirable or doomed. Weston hadn't decided which.

"What is it?"

"The Harker matter. Magistrate Vollen wants to know if we're pursuing."

"Harker was a fence who got caught between two gangs. The magistrate knows that."

"He says there's pressure from the Merchant Council. They want someone held accountable."

"Someone. Not the right someone. Just someone."

Brennan's neutrality flickered. He'd heard this tone before. "Sir, I can tell him you're still reviewing the evidence."

"Tell him the evidence points to gang retaliation, and there's nothing for us to pursue. If he wants a scapegoat, he can find one himself."

The younger man hesitated. "The Guild's been sending representatives. To the magistrate's office. They're offering cooperation on several open cases."

Weston's hand stopped on the file in front of him. "Cooperation."

"That's what they're calling it."

"And what are they asking in return?"

"Consideration. On certain matters of mutual interest." Brennan's voice was flat. Reciting. "Political sensitivities, they said."

The words hung in the air like smoke.

Weston looked at the stack of files on his desk. Twenty-seven incidents. Clean work. Professional work. The kind of work that made the Guild look slow and the order look useless.

"Thank you, Brennan. That will be all."

The young man left. His footsteps faded down the corridor.

Weston turned back to the reports. Picked up the one he'd been avoiding.

Dockside. Six weeks ago. A warehouse that had been running smuggled goods for three different operations. Someone had walked in, killed four men, taken a single ledger, and walked out. The whole job had taken less than ten minutes. The guards never raised an alarm.

The bodies told the story. Quick kills. Efficient angles. No torture, no messages carved into flesh, no theatrical flourishes. Just four men who'd been alive and then weren't.

And at the bottom of the report, a note from the examining physician: No evidence of civilian casualties. Structure cleared before action commenced.

Weston read that line twice.

He pulled another file. The Kellerman job, four months back. Three dead, all confirmed enforcers for a protection racket that had been squeezing Southside merchants. The racket had collapsed within a week. No one had stepped in to fill the vacuum.

Another note, different physician: Premises contained evidence of recent habitation, likely homeless individuals. All absent at time of incident. Appears deliberate.

He kept reading. File after file. The pattern held.

Then he stopped.

The Thornway warehouse. Seven weeks ago. A messy situation involving a smuggling operation that had branched into selling children to the brothels along the harborfront. Four dead, all confirmed participants. The examining physician's note was longer than usual, more detailed. What caught Weston's eye was a single line buried in the middle:

Recovery team found one survivor. Male, approximately 14 years. Bound in rear storage, unharmed. Subject reported that masked individual instructed him to "close his eyes and count to five hundred." When he finished counting, the building was empty and quiet.

Weston set the paper down. Stared at it.

A contractor who told a child to count. Who made sure the boy didn't see what was about to happen. Who cleared the building and left one living witness.

That wasn't restraint. That was a code.

He picked up his cold tea. Drank the last of it without tasting. Then he pulled a blank sheet of paper toward him like he was committing a small treason.

Whoever this was, they didn't kill bystanders. They cleared buildings before they worked. They targeted people who had earned targets on their backs, and they did the job without splash damage.

That wasn't how contractors operated. Not the Guild ones, anyway. Guild work was about reputation. About making examples. About leaving enough mess that people remembered to be afraid.

This was something else. Someone who killed because it was necessary, not because it was profitable. Someone who drew lines and didn't cross them.

Weston closed the file. Stared at the stack.

He should hand it over. Let enforcement do their job. Let the Guild have their cooperation and their political sensitivities and whatever else they were buying with Magistrate Vollen's conscience.

Instead, he opened his desk drawer. Pulled out a blank sheet of paper. Started writing.

If he was going to understand this, he needed to do it himself. Before the Guild's cooperation turned into something else. Before the political sensitivities became standing orders.

Before whoever this was became just another body in an alley.

***

Garnath at night was a different animal than Garnath by day.

The same streets that bustled with merchants and servants and children chasing hoops became corridors of shadow and silence after the lamps were lit. The Merchant Quarter kept its streets bright, oil lamps on every corner, private guards walking regular patrols past shops that sold silk and silver and secrets. But south of the Bridgeway, the city darkened by degrees until the only light came from tavern windows and the occasional torch guttering in a wall bracket that no one had bothered to replace.

Selene moved through the Narrows without sound. The district smelled like rotting vegetables and tannery runoff and the particular sourness of too many bodies packed into too little space. Wooden buildings leaned against each other like drunks holding each other upright. Laundry lines crisscrossed overhead, clothes hanging limp in the still air. Somewhere nearby, a baby was crying. Somewhere further, a man and woman were arguing about money. The eternal sounds of poverty grinding against itself.

Mirael followed ten feet behind, a shadow among shadows. They'd taken the long route, through the Narrows and around the back of the slaughterhouse district where the smell of old blood masked the smell of everything else. The warehouse district lay ahead, a jumble of stone buildings and wooden loading docks that served the merchant ships in the harbor.

They climbed.

The rooftops were another city entirely. Up here, Garnath spread out like a map drawn in lamplight and darkness. To the north, the Merchant Quarter glowed against the night sky, warm light spilling from tavern windows and the great houses on the hill. The Silver Hand garrison was a dark mass beyond that, its towers barely visible against the stars. To the east, the harbor was a forest of masts and rigging, ships at anchor waiting for morning and the tide. To the south and west, the city faded into darkness, district after district of cramped housing and narrow streets where the lamps had been sold for scrap years ago.

From up here, you could see the shape of it. The way the wealthy districts clustered around the harbor and the trade routes while the poor districts spread like a stain toward the outer walls. The way the streets didn't quite connect, as if the city had grown in pieces that were never meant to fit together. The way the fog rolled in from the water, creeping through the alleys, turning the lower streets into a gray soup that swallowed sound and light.

Garnath. Three hundred years of rot, and the city kept finding room to grow.

The warehouse roof was slick with yesterday's rain.

Selene moved along the peak, weight balanced, eyes on the courtyard below. Three guards at the main entrance. Two more walking the perimeter. Standard rotation, standard spacing, standard blind spots that whoever ran security should have noticed and hadn't.

Mirael was twenty feet behind her, tracking a different angle. They hadn't spoken in an hour. They didn't need to.

The air up here tasted like salt and coal smoke. The harbor was close enough that she could hear the water slapping against the pilings, the creak of rope and wood as the ships shifted in their berths. A bell rang somewhere out on the water. A night-watch signal, or a warning, or just a drunk sailor who'd found something to hit.

The target was a lockbox in the counting house on the north side of the compound. Inside: records of payments made to Watcher captains over the past six months. Names, dates, amounts. The kind of information that could end careers or start wars, depending on who held it.

The buyer was paying enough that the job was worth the risk. Barely.

Selene counted the guard rotation again. Watched the pattern. Found the gap.

She signaled Mirael with two fingers. Moving in ninety seconds.

Mirael's response came back. Three fingers, then a closed fist. Adjustment. Something off on her side.

Selene shifted position. Found the problem.

A sixth guard. Standing in shadow by the counting house door. He hadn't been there ten minutes ago. Someone had added coverage, which meant someone was nervous, which meant the lockbox was more valuable than their buyer had let on.

Standard procedure said abort. Reassess. Come back another night when the variables were known.

Selene watched the new guard. Young. Fidgeting. Kept touching the sword at his hip like he wasn't sure it belonged there.

Not a guard. A clerk, maybe. Or a junior accountant who'd drawn the short straw. Someone's nephew doing a favor.

She looked back at Mirael. Held up a single finger, then pointed at the new man.

Mirael's response was immediate. She shifted left, disappearing behind a chimney stack, moving to a position that would put her between the counting house and the main building.

Sixty seconds.

Selene descended the roof on the blind side, using handholds she'd mapped on the approach. The wall was old brick, mortar crumbling in places, gaps where a careful foot could find purchase. She moved without sound, body pressed close to the stone, gravity her enemy and her tool.

Forty seconds.

She reached the ground. Pressed herself into shadow beside a stack of empty crates. The patrol was passing on her left, footsteps steady, voices low. Complaining about the cold. About the hours. About wives who didn't understand.

They passed. She moved.

Thirty seconds.

The counting house door was fifteen feet away. The nervous guard was shifting his weight, looking at everything and seeing nothing. His sword was still sheathed. Good. Drawing steel made noise.

Selene covered the ground in three breaths. Her hand found his mouth before he could turn, her knee found the back of his, and he folded without a sound. She eased him to the ground. Checked his breathing. Still alive, just unconscious. He'd have a headache tomorrow and a story he'd probably never tell.

She didn't kill amateurs. That was noise.

The door was locked. Three heartbeats with the picks and it wasn't.

Inside, the counting house smelled like paper and candle wax. Shelves of ledgers lined the walls. A desk in the corner, ink pots and quills arranged with the precision of someone who believed organization was a form of prayer.

The lockbox was behind a loose stone in the floor. Selene had paid good coin for that information, and it was accurate. The stone came up. The box came out. The lock was better than the door, but not by much.

Inside: papers. Folded, sealed, exactly what she'd been sent to retrieve.

She tucked them inside her coat. Replaced the box. Replaced the stone. Left the room exactly as she'd found it, minus the contents that mattered.

When she slipped back outside, the unconscious guard was still breathing. The patrol had completed another circuit. The main entrance guards were still complaining about their wives.

Mirael materialized from shadow as Selene reached the perimeter wall. No words. Just a nod. Clear.

They went over the wall together. Dropped into the alley beyond. Walked into the maze of Southside streets like they'd never been anywhere else.

Three blocks later, Mirael spoke.

"The extra man."

"Noticed."

"Someone's nervous about those records."

"Someone should be."

They kept walking. The city swallowed them the way it always did. Two more shadows in a city of shadows.

Ten feet of distance between them, same as always.

The sky was shifting by the time they reached the edges of the Merchant Quarter. Not dawn yet, but the deep black of true night had softened to something closer to charcoal. The hour when the last drunks were stumbling home and the first bakers were firing their ovens. Garnath's brief pause between one kind of hunger and another.

They moved through the transitional streets where Southside bled into more respectable territory. The buildings here were taller, better maintained. Fewer broken windows. Fewer rats bold enough to cross your path in the open. The smell shifted too: less rot, more woodsmoke and the faint sweetness of rendered fat from the soap makers on the next block.

A woman was setting out buckets in front of a laundry, her breath fogging in the cold air. A boy pushed a cart of yesterday's bread toward the poor market, wheels squeaking with every rotation. Somewhere nearby, someone was singing, voice rough and tuneless, the kind of song you sang to keep yourself awake through a long night's work.

The city was stirring. Waking up to do it all again.

Candlemaker's Row was three streets north of the Bridgeway, tucked between a street of cobblers and a street of tailors who catered to merchants who couldn't afford the Merchant Quarter but wanted to pretend. The name was old, from back when the street had actually been full of candlemakers. Now only two remained, their shops huddled together at the far end like survivors of a siege, but the smell lingered. Decades of melted tallow and beeswax had soaked into the cobblestones until the whole street carried a faint sweetness that never quite went away, even in the rain.

The buildings here were narrow and tall, three and four stories of old brick and older timber, leaning toward each other across the street until the upper floors nearly touched. Good for shade in summer. Good for trapping sound. Good for ambush.

Selene noticed the architecture the way she noticed everything. The doorways set back from the street. The windows that could hide a crossbow. The alley mouths that offered escape routes or killing grounds depending on which side you were standing on.

She noticed the boy with the matches two blocks before Candlemaker's Row. Fourteen, maybe fifteen. Dirty face, quick eyes. Standing at a corner with a tray of matches he wasn't actually trying to sell, watching the street with the kind of attention that had nothing to do with commerce.

He saw them. His hand moved, a gesture that looked like scratching his neck but wasn't.

Selene kept walking. Mirael adjusted her pace slightly, falling back another half-step.

***

The Watchers found them at the corner of Candlemaker's Row.

Three of them, stepping out of a doorway like they'd been waiting. Which they had.

Selene kept walking anyway. Running invited chase. Standing still invited violence. Walking said you knew exactly what was happening and didn't consider it a problem.

The one in front was older. Scarred hands. Eyes that had stopped being impressed by anything years ago. He positioned himself where the street narrowed, blocking the direct path without making it obvious.

"Late night," he said.

"Early morning, technically." Selene stopped. Mirael stopped beside her, half a step back and to the left. The angle that gave her options. "Something you need?"

"Conversation."

"I'm not feeling chatty."

"That's fine. I'll talk. You'll listen." He smiled. It didn't reach his eyes. "The Guild's been watching you. Both of you. For a while now."

"I'm flattered."

"You shouldn't be." He tilted his head slightly, studying her. "You're good. Better than most. Clean work. Professional. The kind of reputation that gets noticed."

"That sounds like a compliment. From the Guild, I assume it isn't."

"It's an observation. The compliment is that we're talking instead of something else." His hands stayed visible. Relaxed. Nothing about his posture suggested imminent violence, which made him more dangerous than if he'd come in swinging. "The Guild doesn't like competition. You know that. Everyone knows that. But competition can become cooperation, with the right arrangement."

"You're offering me a job."

"I'm offering you a conversation about your future. Which is more than most people get." He glanced at Mirael. "Both of you. The Guild has room for talent. Good pay. Protection. The kind of stability that's hard to find when you're independent."

"And if we prefer independence?"

"Then you've made a choice." His voice didn't change. "And choices have consequences. The routes that are open today might close tomorrow. The buyers who return your messages might stop returning them. The city has a way of getting smaller when you're on the wrong side of certain conversations."

Selene let the silence stretch. Let him think she was considering.

"We'll think about it," she said.

"Don't think too long. The offer isn't patient." He stepped aside, clearing the path. His men moved with him. "And a word of advice, from someone who's been around long enough to know: there are people in this city you can steal from, and people you can't. Lines you can cross, and lines that cross back."

"I'll keep that in mind."

"Do." He started to turn away, then paused. Something flickered across his face. Not quite concern. Not quite warning. Something older. "You don't want Serith noticing you. Trust me on that."

The name dropped into the air like a stone into still water.

Selene's expression didn't change. Her body didn't react. But she filed the name away in the place where she kept things that mattered, and she saw Mirael notice her filing it.

"I'll keep that in mind too," she said.

The Watcher nodded once. Then he and his men walked away, disappearing into the predawn gray like they'd never been there.

Selene waited until their footsteps faded. Then she started walking again.

"Serith," Mirael said quietly.

"Heard it."

"You know the name?"

"No." Selene kept walking. "But I will."

Mirael's step faltered. Half a beat. Barely noticeable unless you were watching for it, and Selene was always watching. When Mirael spoke again, her voice was too even. Too controlled.

"You filed that away. The way you do when something matters."

"I file everything away."

"Not like that."

Selene didn't answer. Didn't look at her.

They walked in silence after that. The city was starting to wake up around them, first light touching the rooftops, vendors beginning their morning routines. Somewhere nearby, a cart wheel shrieked against cobblestone. A bell tolled from the temple district, marking the hour.

Mirael's fingers brushed her sleeve. Once. Then pulled back.

Ten feet of distance between them. Same as always.

***

The room was small and dark and smelled like candle smoke.

Daven stood by the window, though there was nothing to see. Heavy curtains blocked what little light might have crept through. The only illumination came from a single candle on the desk, casting shadows that seemed deeper than they should be.

The man behind the desk didn't look up from the papers he was reading. His pen moved occasionally, making notes in margins. The scratch of nib on parchment was the only sound.

Daven waited. He was good at waiting.

"You're certain," the man said finally. His voice was quiet. Cultured. The kind of voice that never needed to be raised.

"I've been watching her for two weeks. It's her."

"After seventeen years."

"She was seven when the house burned. She's twenty-four now. Contractor. Works with a partner, a blonde woman, minor noble blood from somewhere east. They've built a reputation in Southside. Clean work. Professional." Daven's jaw tightened slightly. "She uses twin daggers. Fights like someone taught her young and she never stopped practicing."

Silence. The candle flame bent as the curtains shifted.

"The dock worker's daughter," the man said. "Still alive."

"She should have been dead seventeen years ago. Someone was sloppy."

"Someone was thorough. The house burned. The parents burned. The child was confirmed deceased." A pause. "Apparently, the confirmation was premature."

"She's not a child now. She's connected throughout Southside. Partner watches her back." Daven shifted his weight. "This isn't a loose thread anymore. This is a problem."

"Yes." The man pulled a fresh sheet of paper toward him. Began writing. "It is."

"What are your orders?"

"Find out what she remembers. What she knows. Whether the fire left anything in her head worth worrying about." The pen scratched steadily. "Then close the file. Permanently."

"The partner?"

"Collateral. Acceptable."

Daven nodded. This was the work. Clean. Simple. The kind of job he'd done a hundred times before.

"And if she's told others? If she's been talking?"

"Then the file gets larger." The man finished writing. Set down the pen. Looked up for the first time.

His eyes were pale in the candlelight. Patient. The eyes of someone who had learned long ago that problems were just tasks that hadn't been completed yet.

"Seventeen years is too long to leave a thread hanging," he said. "Don't make it eighteen."

Daven took the paper. Folded it. Tucked it into his coat.

"I won't."

He left without another word.

The man sat alone in the dark room, the single candle casting his shadow long against the wall. He stayed that way for a long time, thinking.

Then he reached for another file. Opened it. Began to read.

The machinery of consequence continued to turn.

CHAPTER 6: The Firefly

The market on Tallow Street wasn't much of a market.

Three vendors with carts, selling bruised vegetables and day-old bread to people who couldn't afford better. A woman with a basket of eggs she guarded like gold. A boy hawking candle stubs salvaged from the temples, wax scraped together and remelted into lumpy shapes that burned uneven and smelled like old prayers.

Selene moved through it without stopping. They were cutting through Southside on their way back from a morning meeting with a buyer who'd tried to renegotiate terms after the job was already done. The conversation had been short. The buyer had reconsidered.

Mirael walked ten feet behind, as always. The streets here were narrow enough that they had to go single file in places, ducking under laundry lines and stepping over gutters that ran with something that wasn't entirely water.

This was Mother Gessa's territory. Or close to it. The old woman ran a cellar three blocks east where the street children could get soup and a safe corner to sleep, as long as they followed her rules. No stealing from each other. No fighting. No bringing trouble through her door. Selene had never been inside, but she knew the place existed the way she knew all the safe corners and dangerous ones in Southside. Information was currency. You collected it whether you needed it or not.

The morning was gray and cold, the kind of damp that seeped through wool and settled into bone. A few drops of rain spattered the cobblestones, not enough to drive people indoors, just enough to make everyone miserable. The vendors hunched under oilcloth tarps. The customers hurried through their purchases and disappeared into the warren of streets.

Selene was thinking about the buyer. About the way his voice had cracked when she'd explained, calmly, what would happen if he tried to short them again. About whether he'd actually learned or whether she'd need to have another conversation in a few weeks.

She wasn't thinking about the doorway on her left.

But her feet stopped anyway.

The girl was pressed into the shadow where a tenement wall met a collapsed awning, making herself as small as possible. Black hair, tangled and unwashed, falling across a face that was more bone than flesh. Eyes too large for her head, the way children's eyes got when they stopped eating regularly. She couldn't have been more than six or seven, dressed in a coat three sizes too big that had probably been pulled from a trash heap.

She was watching the bread vendor.

Not begging. Not moving. Just watching, with the kind of stillness that came from learning that stillness was safer than asking.

As Selene watched, a man carrying a bundle of firewood walked past the doorway. He didn't slow down. Didn't look. His shoulder caught the edge of the girl's oversized coat and he kept walking like he'd brushed against a post or a pile of garbage. Something in his way. Nothing worth noticing.

The girl didn't flinch. Didn't make a sound. Just pressed herself deeper into the shadow and kept watching the bread.

A woman came out of the tenement behind her, bucket in hand, and shooed her away from the doorway with a sharp gesture and sharper words. "Get out. Go on. Find somewhere else to die."

The girl moved. Quick, silent, no protest. She found another doorway three buildings down, another shadow, another corner where she could disappear. The woman dumped her bucket into the gutter and went back inside without a second glance.

Garnath. The city that ate its children and called it natural order.

Selene had seen this a thousand times. Ten thousand. Street kids were part of the landscape, like rats and garbage and the smell of the tanneries. You stopped seeing them after a while. Stopped noticing the ones who got thinner and thinner until they stopped being there at all. Stopped wondering where they went when winter came and the cold killed the ones who couldn't find shelter.

The vendors knew. The shopkeepers knew. The guards who walked these streets knew. Everyone knew, and everyone looked the other way, because looking meant seeing and seeing meant feeling and feeling was a luxury that Southside couldn't afford.

The girl had found her new doorway. She was pressed into the shadow again, still as stone, eyes fixed on the bread vendor. Calculating distance. Calculating risk. Calculating whether she was fast enough to grab something and run before anyone could catch her.

Selene knew that calculation. She'd made it a thousand times. Sometimes you were fast enough. Sometimes you weren't. Sometimes you got a beating that left you pissing blood for a week. Sometimes you got worse.

The girl's eyes were blue. Pale blue, like winter sky, like water under ice. Like the eyes that looked back at Selene from mirrors she tried not to use.

Something shifted in her chest. A crack in a wall she'd spent seventeen years building.

The bread vendor saw the girl looking. His face twisted into something ugly, and he picked up a rock from beside his cart. Not throwing it. Just holding it. A promise.

"Try it," he said. "Go on. I'll break your fingers."

The girl's eyes dropped. She pressed deeper into the shadow. Made herself smaller. Disappeared into the gray.

The vendor went back to his bread. The market kept moving. No one had noticed. No one cared.

Selene knew that feeling too. The smallness. The invisibility. The way the world made you understand, over and over, that you were nothing. That you didn't matter. That if you died in an alley tonight, they'd step over your body in the morning and complain about the smell.

"Selene?"

Mirael's voice, behind her. Careful. She'd noticed the stop.

Selene didn't answer. She walked to the bread vendor's cart, bought a small loaf without haggling, and kept walking. Past the girl.

Past the doorway. She stopped at a broken crate near the mouth of an alley, set the bread on it like she was adjusting her boot, and continued on.

She didn't look back.

But she listened.

Footsteps. Small. Quick. The rustle of fabric. Then nothing.

***

They walked for two blocks before Mirael spoke again.

"Who was that?"

"Who was who?"

"The child you just fed."

"I didn't feed anyone. I set down some bread because my hands were full."

"Your hands weren't full."

"They felt full."

Mirael made a sound that might have been a laugh if it had any humor in it. "That's the best you can do?"

"I'm tired. Give me a minute; I'll come up with something better."

They turned onto a wider street. The rain was picking up now, fat drops that splattered against cobblestones and ran in rivers toward the gutters. A cart rolled past, wheels spraying dirty water. Selene sidestepped it without breaking stride.

"You stopped," Mirael said. "In the middle of the market. You stopped and stared at a child for thirty seconds."

"I was thinking."

"About what?"

"Whether the bread vendor's prices were fair. They weren't. I overpaid."

"You never overpay."

"First time for everything."

Mirael moved up beside her, close enough that their shoulders almost touched. Her violet eyes were fixed on Selene's profile, reading her the way she always did. Looking for the cracks. Looking for the tells.

"You're deflecting," she said.

"I'm walking. There's a difference."

"You're deflecting while walking. You can do both. You're talented that way."

Selene almost smiled. Almost. "Flattery won't get you answers."

"What will?"

"Nothing. There's nothing to answer. I saw a hungry kid, I had bread, I left it where she could find it. That's not a mystery. That's barely an event."

"You bought the bread specifically to leave it for her."

"I bought the bread because I was hungry."

"You're not hungry. You ate this morning."

"I'm always hungry. It's a condition."

Mirael was quiet for a moment. They passed a tavern that was already serving despite the early hour, the smell of cheap ale and cheaper food spilling out into the street. A drunk was slumped against the wall outside, muttering to himself about debts and women and the general unfairness of existence.

"She looked like you," Mirael said.

Selene's step faltered. Half a beat. She recovered, kept walking, but the damage was done.

"I don't know what you're talking about."

"Yes you do." Mirael's voice was patient. Relentless. The voice she used when she'd found a thread and intended to pull it until something unraveled. "Black hair. Blue eyes. The same bone structure. The same way of holding herself, like she was trying to take up as little space as possible."

"Lots of kids have black hair and blue eyes."

"Not like that. Not like you."

"You're seeing things that aren't there."

"I'm seeing things you don't want me to see. There's a difference."

The rain fell harder. They were both getting soaked now, coats darkening with water, hair plastered to their faces. Neither of them moved for cover.

"It doesn't matter," Selene said.

"You felt something."

"I didn't feel anything."

"I saw your face. When you looked at her. When you watched the vendor threaten her with that rock." Mirael's voice dropped, softer now. "Something in you moved, Selene. I've known you for twelve years. I know what it looks like when something moves."

Selene stopped. Turned. Mirael was standing three feet away, rain running down her cheeks like tears, violet eyes fixed on Selene with an intensity that bordered on painful.

"What do you want me to say?" Selene asked. Her voice came out harder than she meant it to. "That I saw a starving kid and it reminded me of something? Fine. It reminded me of something. That's all."

"That's not all."

"It's all I'm going to give you."

"Because you don't trust me with more?"

The question hung in the air between them. Selene felt it land like a blade, felt the edge of it against something she didn't want to examine.

"Because there isn't more," she said. "Because a kid who looks like me isn't me. Because feeling sorry for someone doesn't change anything. Because the bread I gave her will last one meal and tomorrow she'll be hungry again and I won't be there and that's how it works. That's how it's always worked."

"And yet you stopped."

"And yet I stopped. Congratulations. You found a crack. Write it in your journal."

Mirael flinched. It was small, barely visible, but Selene saw it. Felt the meanness of what she'd said settle into the space between them.

She didn't apologize. Apologizing meant admitting she'd been cruel, and admitting she'd been cruel meant admitting she was protecting something, and admitting she was protecting something meant letting Mirael see it.

They stood there, in the rain, the street empty around them. Somewhere nearby, a shutter banged in the wind. A dog barked twice and went quiet.

Mirael's expression didn't change. But something behind her eyes shifted. Closed. Like a door being shut very carefully so it wouldn't make a sound.

"Alright," she said. "Let's go."

She started walking. Selene watched her for a moment, then followed.

Ten feet of distance between them. Same as always.

***

The room above the tanner's shop was cold when they got back.

Selene stripped off her wet coat and hung it near the window where it would drip onto the floorboards instead of the bedding. Mirael did the same, moving around the small space with the efficiency of long practice. They'd lived in this room for three months. Before that, a room above a butcher's. Before that, a warehouse loft near the harbor. You learned not to accumulate things that couldn't fit in a bag.

The rain hammered against the window. The light through the glass was gray and flat, making the room feel smaller than it was. The smell of the tannery below seeped through the floorboards, chemical and sharp, the kind of smell you stopped noticing after a few days but never quite forgot.

Mirael sat on the edge of the bed and started working the tangles out of her wet hair with her fingers. Her movements were precise, controlled. The way they always were when she was thinking about something she didn't want to say.

Selene stood by the window, looking out at nothing. The rooftops of Southside stretched away into the gray, broken by chimneys and clotheslines and the occasional church spire. Somewhere out there, in one of those thousands of doorways, a girl with black hair and blue eyes was probably eating bread and wondering if it was a trap.

"You're thinking about her."

Mirael's voice, quiet, from across the room.

"I'm thinking about a lot of things."

"But mostly her."

Selene didn't answer. She watched a crow land on a nearby roof, shake water from its feathers, and take off again.

"You can talk to me," Mirael said. "You know that."

"I do talk to you. I'm talking to you right now."

"You're deflecting. Again."

"It's a talent. I practice."

Mirael was quiet for a moment. Selene heard her stand, heard her footsteps cross the small room. Felt her stop a few feet away, close but not touching. Never touching. They hadn't touched in years, not really. An accidental brush of fingers. A hand on a shoulder during a job. The kind of contact that meant nothing, that you could pretend meant nothing.

"What happened to you?" Mirael asked. Her voice was barely above a whisper. "When you were her age. What happened?"

Selene's jaw tightened. "You know what happened."

"I know pieces. I know there was a fire. I know your parents died. I know you lived on the streets until you were ten." A pause. "I don't know what it felt like. I don't know who you were before."

"I wasn't anyone before. I was seven."

"Seven-year-olds are someone."

Selene finally turned. Mirael was watching her with that expression again. The one that was too careful, too controlled. The one that hid everything behind a mask of patience. But underneath the mask, in the depths of those violet eyes, something was waiting. Had been waiting for twelve years.

"I used to be like that," Selene said. She wasn't sure why she said it. The words just came, pulled out of her by the weight of

Mirael's attention. "After. The first year. I looked exactly like that. I was that thin. I had that look in my eyes. That . . . calculation. Every minute of every day, just trying to figure out how to survive until the next minute."

"What happened?"

"I survived. That's what happened. I stole and I hid and I ate garbage when there was nothing else and I learned that people will step over you like you're a dead dog and not even slow down." She shrugged, a sharp motion that didn't match the weight in her chest. "That's the story. That's the whole story. Nothing happened. I just didn't die."

"Something happened." Mirael's voice was gentle. Insistent. "Something that made you stop today. Something that made you look at that girl and see something besides another street kid."

Selene was quiet for a long moment. The rain kept falling. The tanner's shop below them was silent, the old man who ran it probably huddled by his fire, waiting out the weather. The whole city felt muffled, wrapped in gray, like the world was holding its breath.

"Someone gave me soup," she said finally. "Once. When I was eight or nine. I don't know why. I never asked. She was just a woman with a pot of soup and she gave me a bowl and watched me eat it."

"Who was she?"

"I don't know. I never saw her again. I didn't even look at her face. I was too busy eating." Selene's mouth twisted into something that wasn't quite a smile. "I burned my tongue. The soup was hot and I was so hungry that I just kept eating anyway. I remember that. I remember the exact way it hurt, and I remember not caring, because at least I was full. At least for one hour, I was full."

Mirael was quiet. Waiting.

"She didn't ask for anything," Selene continued. "Didn't want anything. Didn't even tell me her name. She just gave me soup and let me eat and then I ran, because that's what you do when you're a street kid. You take what you can get and you run before someone changes their mind."

"So you bought the girl bread."

"I left bread where a hungry kid could find it. That's not the same thing."

"Isn't it?"

Selene looked away. Out the window. At the rain, the gray sky, the rooftops of Southside bleeding into the mist.

"I don't know what it is," she said. "I don't know why I stopped. I don't know why I bought the bread. I don't know why I care whether some kid I've never met eats today or doesn't." Her voice was rough now, the edges of something sharp underneath. "I shouldn't care. I trained myself not to care. I built something inside me that doesn't feel things like that, and it's worked for seventeen years, and now . . ."

She stopped. Didn't finish.

Mirael was silent for a long time. When she spoke, her voice was barely above a whisper, and there was something in it that Selene didn't want to name. Something that sounded like grief.

"Twelve years," Mirael said. "We've been together for twelve years. I've watched you take knives for me. I've watched you walk into rooms you knew might kill you. I've watched you bleed and fight and survive things that should have broken anyone."

Selene turned. Mirael was standing in the gray light from the window, wet hair clinging to her face, violet eyes bright with something that might have been tears or might have been rain.

"And in twelve years," Mirael continued, "I have never seen you look at anything the way you looked at that child. I have never seen anything crack you. Not like that. Not for a second." She paused. "Not for me."

The words hung in the air between them. Heavy. Sharp.

Selene opened her mouth to say something. A joke. A deflection. Something to fill the space and push the moment away.

Nothing came.

"I'm going to change," Mirael said. Her voice was level now. Controlled. The mask back in place. "We should eat something. I'll go down to the tavern on the corner once the rain stops."

"I can go."

"No. You stay. Rest." A pause. "You look tired."

She moved away. Selene heard her open the small trunk where they kept their spare clothes, heard the rustle of fabric, heard all the ordinary sounds of their ordinary life together.

She kept looking out the window.

The girl was probably somewhere dry by now. Mother Gessa's cellar, maybe, if she knew about it. Or some other corner, some other doorway, some other shadow where a child could disappear until the world forgot to look.

Selene hoped she'd eaten the bread. All of it. In one sitting. The way Selene had eaten that soup seventeen years ago, burning her mouth, not caring, just filling the hole inside her until it stopped screaming for a while.

She hoped the girl hadn't tried to ration it. Hadn't hidden half for later. Hadn't done all the things that street kids learned to do because tomorrow was never certain.

She hoped, just this once, someone had been hungry and then full.

That was all. Just that one small thing.

The rain kept falling. The gray afternoon stretched toward a grayer evening.

And somewhere in Selene's chest, behind the wall she'd built, something shifted. Not warmth. Not mercy. Just a crack she couldn't quite close. An irritation at her own numbness. A refusal to look away that she didn't understand and couldn't name.

Her throat was tight. Her hands wanted to curl into fists.

She hated that she cared. She didn't stop herself anyway.

CHAPTER 7: Mother Gessa's Cellar

She told herself it was a shortcut.

Three days after the bread, three days after the girl with the blue eyes, and Selene found herself walking through Southside alone. Mirael was meeting with a buyer across the city, negotiating terms for a job that would keep them fed through the winter. Normal work. Normal evening.

Selene had said she was going to check on a contact near the harbor. She wasn't.

The streets near Tallow Market were quieter after dark. The vendors had packed their carts and gone home, leaving behind the smell of rotting vegetables and the particular silence that came when poor people stopped pretending to have business and retreated to whatever shelter they could find. A few lamps burned in windows. A dog barked somewhere in the distance. The city settled into its nighttime skin, meaner and more honest than its daytime face.

Mother Gessa's cellar was down a narrow alley off Candlemaker's Row, beneath a building that had been a tannery once and was now just a shell where the desperate found corners to sleep. The entrance was a set of stone steps leading down to a wooden door that had been painted blue a long time ago, the color now faded to something closer to gray.

Selene had never been inside. She'd known about the place for years, the way she knew about all the safe corners and dangerous ones in Southside. Information was currency. But knowing about a place and going to it were different things.

She didn't go to it now, either.

Instead, she found a shadow across the alley, a recessed doorway where she could see the cellar entrance without being seen. She pressed her back against the cold stone and watched.

Children were arriving.

They came in ones and twos, slipping out of the darkness like small ghosts. Thin faces. Worn clothes. The particular walk of kids who had learned to move without being noticed. Some of them Selene recognized from the streets. Others were new, or new to her. Southside churned through its children like a mill grinding grain.

They went down the steps. The blue-gray door opened for each of them, spilling warm light into the alley for a moment before closing again. The smell of soup drifted up, faint but unmistakable. Real soup. Vegetables and salt and something that might have been meat.

Selene's stomach tightened. Not from hunger. From memory.

She had been one of these children once. Not here, not at Mother Gessa's, but somewhere like it. A cellar. A back room. A place where someone had decided that feeding hungry kids was worth the trouble, even when no one was paying them to do it.

She couldn't remember the woman's face anymore. Couldn't remember her name, if she'd ever known it. Just the soup. The warmth of it. The way it had felt to be full for the first time in days.

The last child disappeared down the steps. The door closed. The alley went quiet.

Selene should have left. There was no reason to stay. No job here. No contact. Nothing she needed.

She stayed anyway.

***

The cellar had a window.

Not much of one. A narrow rectangle of thick glass set into the stone foundation, barely a foot wide, crusted with years of grime. But it let light out, and if you crouched in the right spot in the alley above, you could see through it into the room below.

Selene found that spot.

The cellar was larger than she'd expected. Stone walls, stone floor, a fireplace at one end with a real fire burning in it. Candles on rough wooden tables. Blankets piled in corners. The kind of place that had been made comfortable through years of small efforts, each one adding something until the whole became more than the sum of its parts.

A pot of soup hung over the fire. Real soup. Selene could see vegetables floating in it, could smell the broth even through the window. Someone had paid for that. Someone had carried those vegetables through Southside streets, had chopped them and cooked them and ladled them into bowls for children who had nothing to offer in return.

Mother Gessa sat on a stool by the fire.

She was older than Selene had imagined. Sixty, maybe seventy, with a face that had been weathered by decades of Southside living. Gray hair pulled back in a practical knot. Hands that were rough and capable, the hands of someone who had spent a lifetime doing work that no one thanked her for. She wore a plain dress, patched in places, clean despite everything. There were dark circles under her eyes, the kind that came from too many late nights and too little rest, but her back was straight and her voice was steady.

She was counting the children with her eyes. Selene watched her do it, watched the way her gaze moved from face to face, cataloging. Not just counting. Checking. Looking for new bruises, new thinness, new signs of the damage Garnath did to its smallest residents.

Seven children tonight.

A boy with a fresh cut on his cheek sat closest to the fire, holding his soup bowl like someone might snatch it away. Next to him, a girl with red hair and a face full of freckles was trying to sit still and failing, her legs bouncing with restless energy. Two children who might have been siblings huddled together under a shared blanket, the older one's arm wrapped protectively around the younger. A boy with dark hair and scared eyes sat apart from the others, watching everything, trusting nothing.

And there, at the edge of the group, not quite part of it but not quite separate either, sat the girl with the blue eyes.

Mother Gessa's voice drifted up through the window, muffled but audible. "Kira, child, slow down. No one's taking it from you."

Kira. So that was her name.

Selene didn't know anything else about her except what she'd seen in those two brief encounters. The stillness. The hunger. The way she calculated every moment like survival was arithmetic and she was always doing the math.

The girl was eating soup from a wooden bowl. Slowly now. Deliberately. Her grip white-knuckled on the spoon. Selene knew that control. Knew what it cost. The girl wasn't savoring the food. She was proving she could be trusted not to make a mess of the gift. Her black hair was still tangled, her clothes still too big, but she looked . . . less desperate than she had three days ago. Less like she was waiting to die. Her eyes kept darting to Mother Gessa, then away, then back. Watching. Wanting to trust but not quite able to.

Something shifted in Selene's chest. That same crack from before, widening slightly.

Mother Gessa reached for a cloth and wiped soup from the chin of the youngest child, the one tucked under the blanket with her sibling. The gesture was automatic, practiced, the kind of small tenderness that came from years of caring for children who had no one else. She didn't make a fuss about it. Just wiped and moved on.

How long had she been doing this? How many children had passed through this cellar, eaten her soup, listened to her stories? How many had she fed and sheltered knowing most of them would disappear back into Garnath's hungry streets?

Mother Gessa set her cloth aside and settled back on her stool, her tone shifting into something older, more practiced. The voice of a storyteller.

"Tonight's story is an old one," she said. "Older than the city. Older than the walls. From before the world learned to measure itself in stone and silver."

The children leaned forward. Even the ones who had been fidgeting went still.

"How old?" one of them asked. A girl with red hair and a face full of freckles.

"Old enough that no one remembers if it's true." Mother Gessa reached into a basket beside her and pulled out a small cloth bundle. "But that's the thing about old stories. They don't need to be true to matter. They just need to be remembered."

She unwrapped the cloth, revealing a candle. Plain wax, the kind you could buy in any market for a few coppers. She lit it with a taper from the fire, and the children leaned closer, as if the light gave them permission.

The children went quiet. Waiting.

Mother Gessa began to speak.

***

"Once, long before the Age of Grey, there was a wanderer named Vaeryn."

Selene pressed closer to the window, her breath fogging the glass. She wiped it away with her sleeve.

"He was born without a place," Mother Gessa continued. "No clan to claim him. No family to teach him his name. No city willing to call him their own. He wandered the dark places between settlements. The roads that led nowhere. The paths that people traveled only when they had no other choice."

The candle flame danced. The children leaned closer.

The boy with the cut on his cheek had stopped guarding his soup bowl. The red-haired girl had finally gone still, her restless legs quiet for the first time since Selene had started watching. Even the dark-haired boy who trusted nothing had edged forward, his scared eyes fixed on Mother Gessa's face.

But it was Kira who held Selene's attention.

The girl's soup bowl sat forgotten in her lap, her hands wrapped around it more from habit than hunger. Her blue eyes had gone wide, reflecting the firelight, and there was something in her face that Selene recognized. Not hope, exactly. Something more fragile than hope. The desperate wish that someone, somewhere, might actually care about the forgotten.

"He carried no weapon. Just a shard of starlight wrapped in cloth, pressed against his chest like a promise he'd made to someone he couldn't remember. And everywhere he went, he found people who'd been abandoned by the world. People who'd fallen through the cracks and been forgotten. People who were waiting to die because dying seemed easier than surviving."

Selene's hands curled into fists at her sides. She knew that feeling. That particular exhaustion that came when fighting felt pointless and giving up felt like relief.

But something else was happening too. Something she hadn't expected.

Mother Gessa's voice carried through the glass, muffled but warm, and Selene found herself leaning closer to the window. Not to see better. To hear better. The cadence of the old woman's words, the rise and fall of the telling, it was pulling at something buried so deep she'd forgotten it was there.

Her mother had told stories like this.

Not this story. Different ones. Tales about clever foxes and stubborn farmers, about girls who outsmarted wolves, and boys who found treasure in unlikely places. Selene couldn't remember the plots anymore, couldn't remember the endings. But she remembered the feeling. Curled up in blankets that smelled like woodsmoke and soap. Her mother's voice in the darkness, steady and sure. The absolute certainty that nothing bad could happen as long as the story kept going.

She hadn't thought about that in years. Had trained herself not to think about it. The before was a locked room she didn't visit because visiting meant remembering what she'd lost.

But Mother Gessa's voice kept threading through the window, and Selene's body was responding without her permission. Her shoulders had dropped. Her jaw had unclenched. She was breathing slower, deeper, the way she used to breathe when she was five years old and safe and her mother was saying *once upon a time* in the dark.

She hated it. Hated the softness creeping into her chest. Hated that a stranger's voice could reach past seventeen years of armor and find the child still hiding underneath.

But she didn't move away from the window.

“There was a girl in a village on the edge of the known world,” Mother Gessa said, her voice softening. “Her family had died in a plague, and the villagers had decided she was cursed. They left food outside her door but wouldn’t speak to her, wouldn’t touch her, wouldn’t acknowledge she existed except as a problem they were too afraid to solve. She was seven years old and so tired of being alone that she’d stopped eating the food they left. Just sat in the ruins of her home, small and quiet, waiting for the end.”

The younger of the two siblings made a small sound, something between a whimper and a breath. Her brother pulled her closer under the shared blanket, his jaw tight.

Kira’s arms tightened around her knees. Her eyes had gone bright in the firelight, wet at the edges, though no tears fell. She was holding herself perfectly still, the way children learned to hold themselves when feeling too much was dangerous.

Selene saw it through the window and felt her throat close.

Seven years old. Alone. Waiting.

Every child in that cellar knew what that felt like. Every single one of them had been that girl at some point, waiting in ruins for an end that seemed easier than surviving. That was why they were here. That was why Mother Gessa kept this place, kept the fire burning, kept the soup hot. Because she knew.

“Vaeryn found her there,” Mother Gessa continued. “Sitting in ash and silence. He sat with her. Didn’t speak at first. Just sat. Then he shared his bread. Told her stories about the places he’d been and the people he’d met. About a woman who’d survived a winter with nothing but determination and a broken knife. About a child who’d outrun slavers through a forest by being smaller and faster and more desperate than anyone thought possible.”

The fire cracked. A log shifted in the hearth.

“And when the villagers came to drive him away, he stood between them and the girl and said, ‘If you want to hurt her, you’ll have to go through me first.’ The villagers left. Vaeryn stayed. And the starlight at his chest grew a little brighter.”

"There was a man," Mother Gessa continued, "who'd been cast out of his clan for refusing to fight in a war he didn't believe in. He wandered the roads alone, starving, too proud to beg and too tired to care whether he lived or died. Vaeryn found him collapsed on a mountain path, more dead than alive, and carried him to shelter on his own back."

The children were rapt. Even the restless ones had gone still.

"Fed him. Stayed with him. Sat with him through the fever dreams and the shaking and the long nights when the man wanted to give up because living hurt too much. And when the man asked why, Vaeryn said, 'Because refusing to fight for something you don't believe in is the bravest thing a person can do. And brave people deserve to live.' The man lived. The starlight grew brighter."

Selene watched Kira's face through the dirty glass. The girl was absorbed in the story, her bowl of soup forgotten in her lap, her blue eyes fixed on Mother Gessa with an intensity that bordered on hunger.

Not hunger for food. Hunger for something else. Something that soup couldn't fill.

"Vaeryn didn't leave them," Mother Gessa said. "He stayed. He shared what little he had. He sat with them in the dark and reminded them that darkness wasn't forever. That morning would come if they could just survive the night. And when the monsters came, he stood between them and the people he'd chosen to protect."

"What kind of monsters?" one of the children whispered. The boy with dark hair and scared eyes. His voice was small, fragile, the voice of someone who already knew about monsters but needed to hear that someone else knew too.

Mother Gessa's face was gentle. Understanding. "The kind that are made of hunger. Made of shadow. Made of all the things people forget when they stop caring about each other. Made of greed and cruelty and the slow death of compassion in a world that rewards neither."

The fire cracked again. The candle flame bent as the children leaned closer, their breath pulling the air.

"They took the shape of wolves that walked on two legs. Of smoke that whispered lies about how much easier it would be to give up. Of cold that seeped into bones and made people forget they'd ever been warm. They came for Vaeryn because he was a reminder that compassion existed in a world that had decided compassion was too expensive to afford."

The red-haired girl had pulled her knees up to her chest, making herself small. The siblings were pressed so close together they looked like one person. Even the boy with the cut on his cheek had stopped pretending to be brave, his eyes fixed on Mother Gessa with naked fear.

They knew these monsters. Every child in that room had met them. Had felt the cold that made you forget you'd ever been warm. Had heard the whispers about how much easier it would be to give up.

Selene thought about Garnath. About the vendors who threatened children with rocks. About the woman who had told a starving girl to find somewhere else to die. About all the small cruelties that added up until the city itself felt like a monster made of hunger and shadow.

"There was a night," Mother Gessa said, "when the shadow-wolves cornered him in a canyon with a family he'd been protecting. Three children. Two parents. All of them starving. All of them exhausted. All of them ready to give up because giving up meant the pain would stop and the fear would end and they could finally rest."

The room had gone completely silent. Even the fire seemed to be listening.

Kira hadn't moved. Hadn't blinked. Her blue eyes were locked on Mother Gessa's face with an intensity that made something ache in Selene's chest. This wasn't just a story to her. This was a question. The only question that mattered when you were small and alone and waiting: would anyone come?

"The wolves circled. Patient. Knowing. Vaeryn stood at the front of the family, unarmed, holding nothing except that wrapped shard of light. And the wolves said, 'Give us the children. Let them go quietly. You can walk away. You don't have to die for people who aren't your blood. You don't have to suffer for strangers who would never do the same for you.'"

Selene's jaw tightened. She knew what the wolves were really saying. She'd heard versions of it her whole life. Don't care. Don't get involved. Don't risk yourself for anyone who can't pay you back.

"Vaeryn looked at the wolves. Looked at the children behind him. Looked at the shard of starlight in his hands. And he said, 'They don't have to be my blood to be worth protecting. They don't have to pay me back for me to stand in front of them. They just have to be people. And people deserve someone to stand between them and the dark.'"

Mother Gessa paused. The candle flame stood perfectly still.

The younger sibling was crying now, silent tears tracking down dirty cheeks. Her brother didn't try to stop her. He was crying too, though he was trying harder to hide it.

"The wolves attacked. Vaeryn stood. And in the end, when the morning came and the shadows retreated, the family was still alive. Still together. Still breathing."

"What happened to Vaeryn?" Kira's voice, barely above a whisper. The first words Selene had ever heard her speak.

The room held its breath. Every child leaning forward, needing to know. Needing to hear that the one who stood, the one who chose to protect, had survived. Had been okay. Had gotten the happy ending that none of them believed in anymore but still desperately wanted.

Mother Gessa's smile was sad. Knowing. The kind of smile that said she understood exactly why the question mattered.

"The story doesn't say. Some stories don't tell you the ending. They just remind you that someone stood. That someone chose to protect instead of walk away. That even in a world full of shadow-wolves, there are people who carry a little light with them wherever they go."

She reached into her basket again and pulled out a small candle, unlit, which she held out toward Kira.

"For you," she said. "To remind you that darkness isn't forever. That morning always comes, if you can just survive the night."

Kira took the candle with trembling hands. Held it like it was precious. Like it was the most valuable thing anyone had ever given her. Her eyes were wet now, though she still hadn't let the tears fall. Still holding on. Still surviving.

The other children watched, and in their faces Selene could see something shifting. Not hope, exactly. Hope was too expensive for children like these. But something. The memory that someone, somewhere, had once stood in front of the darkness. That it had happened at least once, even if it was just a story.

Selene pulled back from the window. Her throat was tight. Her eyes burned in a way she didn't want to examine.

Just a story. An old folk tale told to street children in a cellar. It didn't mean anything. It didn't change anything.

But she couldn't stop seeing Kira's face when she'd asked what happened to Vaeryn. Couldn't stop hearing the desperate hope in that whisper-soft voice.

Couldn't stop thinking about her mother's voice in the darkness, telling stories that she couldn't remember anymore.

***

The coins were nothing.

Three coppers, dull and worn, the kind of money that wouldn't buy much but might buy something. Selene fished them from her pocket without thinking about it, without examining why.

She set them on the windowsill, wedged into a crack where they wouldn't fall but would be visible to anyone who came up the cellar steps in the morning.

Not enough to matter. Just enough to notice.

She didn't know who would find them. Didn't know if they'd go to Mother Gessa or one of the children or some passerby who would pocket them and walk away. It didn't matter. The coins weren't the point.

She wasn't sure what the point was.

Selene walked back through Southside alone, her boots silent on cobblestones that had seen a thousand years of feet. The city was dark around her, darker than the cellar had been, and colder. No fire here. No stories. No one standing between the shadow-wolves and the children they wanted to devour.

Just Garnath. The city that ate its weak and called it natural order.

She thought about the story. About Vaeryn, whoever he was, whatever he'd been. A wanderer who found abandoned people and stood in front of them when the darkness came.

It was a fairy tale. The kind of thing people told children so they could sleep at night, so they could believe that someone would come and save them when the world turned cruel.

Selene had stopped believing in fairy tales a long time ago. Had learned, counting in the dark while the house burned, that no one was coming. That the only person who would save her was herself. That hope was a luxury she couldn't afford.

But she kept walking. And she kept thinking about a girl with blue eyes who looked like her and held a candle like it was precious. Who had asked, in a voice barely above a whisper, what happened to the man who chose to stand.

The story doesn't say.

She didn't know what that meant. Didn't know why it mattered. But she couldn't stop hearing it, couldn't stop feeling it lodge somewhere behind her ribs like a splinter she couldn't reach.

Selene reached the edge of the Merchant Quarter before she realized where she was going. She stopped, looked around, and found herself on a corner she didn't recognize, in a part of the city she had no business being in at this hour.

She'd walked in a circle. Or close to it.

The cellar was three blocks behind her. The window with the copper coins. The children inside, warm and fed and listening to stories about people who carried light.

She stood there for a long time, alone in the dark, not sure what she was feeling and not sure she wanted to know.

Then she turned and walked home.

Ten feet of distance between her and nothing at all.

CHAPTER 8: The Tightening

The checkpoint wasn't there yesterday.

Selene spotted it from a rooftop on the edge of the Narrows, three streets from their usual approach to the Merchant Quarter. Four Watchers in gray, a folding table with a ledger, and a line of irritated citizens waiting to explain why they needed to cross into the better part of the city.

"That's new," Mirael said, crouched beside her.

"That's the third new one this week."

They'd already rerouted twice. The crossing near the tanneries had sprouted a checkpoint four days ago. The bridge at the end of Candlemaker's Row had one now too, manned by a young officer Selene didn't recognize. The familiar faces were being rotated out, replaced by men who didn't know the rhythms of the district, who didn't know which bribes to take and which questions not to ask.

Men who were hungry to prove themselves.

"Harren's gone," Mirael said quietly. "I asked around. Transferred to the harbor watch."

Harren had been useful. Lazy, corrupt, and predictable. The kind of Watcher who understood that everyone had to eat, and that a few silvers bought more peace than a dozen arrests. He'd let them pass a hundred times without a second glance.

His replacement was a problem.

"The new one's named Aldric," Mirael continued. "Young. Ambitious. Keeps records of every face that passes his station."

"Of course he does."

Selene watched the checkpoint for another minute, cataloging. Two Watchers checking papers, one writing in the ledger, one standing back with his hand near his weapon. The line moved slowly. A woman with a basket of eggs was arguing about something, her voice carrying but her words lost to distance.

Then she saw something else.

Not Watchers. Paladins. Two of them, standing at the mouth of an alley across the square. Silver and white, the colors sharp against the gray stone. One was talking to a shopkeeper, gesturing, asking questions. The other was watching the crowd with the patient attention of a man who had all day and intended to use it.

"Paladins," Mirael breathed. "That's new too."

Selene didn't answer. She was watching the one asking questions. Middle-aged. Weathered face. The look of a man who'd been doing this work long enough to know what mattered and what didn't. He wasn't aggressive. Wasn't threatening. Just methodical. Patient. The kind of investigation style that actually got results.

The shopkeeper shook his head. The Paladin nodded, thanked him, moved to the next stall.

"They're asking about something specific," Mirael said. "Look at him. He's not fishing. He knows what he's looking for."

"Let's go."

"We go around," Selene said. "Through the Warrens."

"That adds an hour."

"Then we leave earlier."

Mirael didn't argue. She knew when Selene's voice meant negotiation and when it meant the conversation was over.

This was the second kind.

***

The Warrens route wasn't clear either.

They found that out the hard way, rounding a corner into a dead-end alley that should have been a shortcut, and finding four Watchers and a folding table blocking the only exit.

"Papers," the young one said. Aldric. Had to be. The one who kept records.

Selene felt Mirael tense beside her. They had papers. Good ones. But papers got looked at, and looks got remembered, and remembered faces became targets.

"Just passing through," Selene said. "We'll go around."

"Papers first." Aldric didn't raise his voice. Didn't need to. The three Watchers behind him had their hands on their weapons, casual but ready. "New regulations. Everyone gets documented."

No choice. Selene handed over their papers. Watched Aldric study them with the careful attention of a man who intended to remember every detail.

"Selene," he read. "And Mirael." He looked up, comparing faces to names. "Where are you coming from?"

"The Narrows."

"Where are you going?"

"Does it matter?"

"Everything matters now." He said it without malice, almost apologetically. Just a man doing his job. That made it worse somehow. "Occupation?"

"Private work."

"What kind of private work?"

"The kind that's private."

One of the Watchers behind Aldric shifted his weight. A small movement, but deliberate. A reminder that they could make this harder if they wanted to.

Aldric just wrote something in his ledger. Took his time about it. Let them stand there while the ink dried, while the other Watchers looked them over, while the alley felt smaller and smaller around them.

"You can go," he said finally, handing back the papers. "But I'd find a different route next time. This one's going to be watched for a while."

They walked past him without answering. Selene could feel his eyes on her back, cataloging. Adding her to whatever picture he was building.

"He's going to remember us," Mirael said quietly when they were clear.

"They all are. That's the point."

***

Davresh kept them waiting.

That was new too. Davresh never kept them waiting. Davresh understood that their time was money, that delays meant risk, that a contractor who wasted a professional's evening didn't stay a contractor for long.

But tonight they sat in the back room of a wine shop on Coppersmith Street, watching candles burn down and listening to the sounds of the tavern through thin walls. Laughter. Argument. Someone singing badly. The ordinary noise of Garnath pretending everything was fine.

When Davresh finally appeared, he looked like he hadn't slept in days.

"Sorry," he said, sliding into the chair across from them. "Complications."

"We've been here an hour."

"I know. I'm sorry." He rubbed his face with both hands, the gesture of a man who was trying to scrub away exhaustion and failing. "Everything's complicated right now."

Selene waited. Davresh would talk when he was ready, and pushing him would only make him defensive.

"The Merchant's Row job," he said finally. "It's off."

Mirael's expression didn't change, but Selene saw her fingers tighten on the edge of the table. That job was supposed to pay for the next two months. Food. Lodging. The bribes that kept them invisible.

"Off," Selene repeated. "Why?"

"Client pulled out."

"Clients don't pull out. Clients need things done. That's why they're clients."

Davresh looked away, toward the wall, toward the door, toward anywhere that wasn't Selene's face. "This one did."

"Davresh."

"Your names are getting expensive." He said it quietly, almost apologetically. "Word came down. You're too hot right now. Anyone who works with you is taking on risk they didn't sign up for."

"Word came down from where?"

"I don't know. I don't want to know." He finally met her eyes, and what Selene saw there wasn't greed or calculation. It was fear. "Look, I've been good to you. Both of you. Fair cuts, no games. But I have a family. I have people who depend on me not getting my throat cut in an alley."

"We've never brought trouble to your door."

"The trouble's coming whether you bring it or not." He leaned forward, lowering his voice even though the room was empty. "Someone's asking questions. Not Watchers. Someone else. Someone with enough reach to make the Guild nervous, and the Guild doesn't get nervous about much."

Selene felt Mirael's eyes on her. Felt the question neither of them would ask out loud.

"What kind of questions?"

"About you. Your work history. Your patterns. Where you sleep, where you eat, who you talk to." Davresh shook his head. "I don't know who's asking. I just know everyone's suddenly very interested in not being the one who answers."

He stood, leaving a small purse on the table. Lighter than it should have been.

"That's for the Thornway job. The one that actually happened." He paused at the door, not quite looking back. "Find somewhere else to be for a while. Somewhere far from Garnath. I'm serious."

Then he was gone, and the candle guttered in the draft from the closing door.

***

The Veiled Lantern was quieter than usual.

Selene noticed it the moment they stepped through the door. The common room was half-empty, the usual crowd of merchants and minor nobles thinned to a scattering of nervous men drinking faster than they should. The working men and women who normally circulated through the room were absent, tucked away in back rooms or simply not working tonight.

Viena met them at the foot of the stairs, which was unusual. She normally let her people handle the initial approach, stayed in her office like a queen holding court. But tonight she was downstairs, dressed in wine-colored silk, her silver hair pinned up with jade combs. Watching the door like she'd been waiting for someone.

"My two favorite ghosts," she said. "I was wondering when you'd show up."

"We need to talk."

"I know." Viena gestured toward the stairs. "Upstairs. The walls are thinner than they look down here."

Her office was warm, a fire burning in the grate, but the warmth felt wrong somehow. Tense. Viena poured three glasses of wine without asking if they wanted any, handed two to them, and settled into her chair with the third.

"How bad is it out there?" she asked.

"You tell us. You hear everything."

"I hear less than I used to. That's part of the problem." Viena swirled her wine, watching the candlelight play through the dark liquid. "People are scared to talk. Scared to be seen talking. Scared to be the one who said something to someone who said something to someone else."

"Who's squeezing them?"

"Multiple someones. That's what makes this interesting." Viena took a long sip of wine. "The Guild's pulling back on independent contractors. Anyone too visible, too successful, too much of a target. They're cutting loose the people they can't protect to protect the people they can."

"We've noticed."

"I imagine you have. Your names have been coming up in conversations I don't want to be having." Viena set her glass down, her expression shifting from hostess to something harder. "There's a Paladin. Not the usual kind. This one's patient. Methodical. He's not trying to catch anyone in the act. He's building something. A case. A map. I don't know exactly what, but everyone he talks to gets nervous, and the people he talks to next get even more nervous."

Selene thought about the man in the square. Middle-aged. Weathered face. The patient attention of someone who had all day and intended to use every hour of it.

"What's his name?"

"I don't know. No one does. He doesn't announce himself. Just shows up, asks questions, leaves. But he's good. Better than good. The kind of investigator who actually solves things instead of just making arrests."

"What's he asking about?"

Viena looked at Selene directly. "You. Your work. Your history. Where you came from. How you survived those first years on the street." She paused. "He's not just interested in what you've done. He's interested in what was done to you."

The words landed strangely. Selene turned them over, tried to make them fit into a shape she understood.

"Why would a Paladin care about that?"

"I don't know. I don't know why any of this is happening. I just know it's happening, and you're at the center of it, and that makes you dangerous to be near." Viena stood, moving to the window, looking out at the street below. "The catacombs job is still available. Good money. Clean work, as these things go. And it would get you underground and out of sight for a while."

"We're not that desperate yet."

"Aren't you?" Viena turned back, her eyes sharp. "Your contracts are drying up. Your routes are closing. Someone is building a case against you, and someone else is watching you from shadows. How much worse does it need to get before you're desperate enough?"

Selene didn't have an answer.

***

The fight started on Candlemaker's Row.

Not deliberately. Not planned. It just happened, the way fights between people who know each other too well always happen. One wrong word leading to another leading to something that couldn't be unsaid.

"We should consider it," Mirael said. "The catacombs. Viena's right. We need to disappear for a while."

"We don't run."

"This isn't running. It's strategy. It's staying alive long enough to figure out what's happening."

"And if we go underground, we lose everything we have up here. Our routes. Our contacts. Our reputation." Selene kept walking, her pace faster than it needed to be. "We come back up and we're starting over. Worse than starting over. We're starting over with people remembering that we ran."

"We'd be alive to start over. That's the point."

"The point is we don't know what we're running from. We don't know who's asking questions or why. We don't know what the Paladin wants or what the Guild is afraid of. We're blind, and you want us to run blind into a hole in the ground and hope it works out."

"I want us to survive." Mirael grabbed her arm, stopping her in the middle of the street. "That's all I've ever wanted. Keeping us alive. Keeping us together. And right now, staying here feels like waiting to die."

Selene pulled her arm free. Harder than she needed to.

"Then go."

The words hung in the air between them. Cold. Final.

Mirael's face went still. Not angry. Something worse than angry. Hurt. Anger would have been easier to bear.

"What did you say?"

"If you think we're going to die here, then go. Find somewhere safer. I won't stop you." Selene heard herself talking and couldn't stop. "You've always been better at running than I am. At knowing when to cut your losses. So cut them. Walk away. You don't owe me anything."

"I don't owe you anything?" Mirael's voice was quiet now. Dangerously quiet. "Twelve years. Twelve years of watching your back, covering your mistakes, pulling you out of situations you should never have survived. And you're telling me I don't owe you anything?"

"I know how long it's been, Mirael. You don't have to keep counting."

The words landed like a slap. Mirael went still.

For a long moment, neither of them moved. The street was empty around them, the city going about its business somewhere else, leaving them alone with the damage.

"Don't ever tell me to leave again." Mirael's voice was ice now. Controlled. The regal bearing she wore like armor snapping back into place. "If you say that to me again, I won't forgive it."

She turned and walked away. Not running. Just walking. Controlled. Dignified.

Selene stood in the middle of Candlemaker's Row and watched her go.

She should have followed. Should have apologized. Should have said something, anything, to close the wound she'd just torn open.

She didn't.

***

She found Mirael again an hour later, sitting on a low wall near the harbor, watching the water.

Neither of them spoke. Selene sat down beside her, leaving a foot of space between them. The night was cold, the wind coming off the water sharp with salt and the smell of fish and tar.

They stayed like that for a long time. Not talking. Not touching. Just existing in the same space, which was harder than it should have been after what had been said.

It was Mirael who spotted him.

"Upper window," she said quietly. "Across the square. Don't look."

Selene didn't look. She shifted slightly, adjusting her position on the wall, and let her peripheral vision do the work.

A figure in shadow. Tall. Still. Watching them from a window three stories up, barely visible in the darkness except for the faint gleam of moonlight on something metal.

"Not the first time," Mirael said quietly.

"I know."

"Selene."

"I know."

They sat there, being watched, and didn't run. Didn't move. Just let whoever it was see them seeing him.

After a long moment, the figure withdrew from the window. Gone, as if it had never been there at all.

"We need to move," Selene said.

"Yes."

They walked back through the city together, not speaking, the foot of distance between them feeling like miles.

***

Their room at the Veiled Lantern was cold when they got back. The fire had burned down to embers, and the noise from the common floors below was muted, distant, the world continuing without them.

Mirael rebuilt the fire without a word. Selene stood by the window, looking out at the street below, watching for movement that shouldn't be there.

They didn't talk about the fight. Didn't apologize. Didn't pretend it hadn't happened. The words were still there, hanging in the air between them, and neither of them knew how to take them back.

Two beds. Ten feet apart.

Mirael climbed into hers without saying goodnight. Turned toward the wall.

The silence stretched. Selene watched the street, the fire, the shape of Mirael's back under thin blankets. The words from the fight still hung in the air, sharp and ugly.

"If we take Viena's catacomb job," Selene said quietly, "at least we won't have to worry about checkpoints anymore."

Silence.

"Just cave-ins. Flooding. Whatever's been living down there eating rats for the last hundred years."

A sound from Mirael's bed. Muffled. Almost a laugh.

"You're terrible at apologies," Mirael said into her pillow.

"That wasn't an apology. That was a tactical assessment."

"It was terrible."

"The catacombs or the apology?"

"Both."

Another silence. But different this time. The sharp edges slightly blunted.

"Go to sleep, Selene."

"You first."

Mirael's breathing slowed. Pretending to sleep. Selene knew the difference by now.

Selene stayed by the window.

She thought about the Paladin asking questions. The figure in the shadows. The contracts drying up. The routes closing. The net tightening from every direction at once.

She thought about Mirael's face when she'd said *Then go.* The way the words had landed. The damage they'd done.

She thought about Candlemaker's Row and didn't think about the cellar three blocks away where a girl with blue eyes was probably sleeping with a candle clutched in her hands.

The city was closing around them. The pressure was building. And now the cracks weren't just in the walls.

They were between them.

Selene stood by the window until the fire burned down again, watching the street, waiting for a shadow that didn't appear.

She didn't sleep that night.

Neither did Mirael.

CHAPTER 9: Outlets

Morning came gray and cold, the way mornings always came in Garnath.

Selene woke to the sound of Mirael moving around the room. Quiet footsteps. The soft clink of the water pitcher. The careful sounds of someone trying not to wake a person who was already awake.

She kept her eyes closed. Listened. Let the pretense hold for another minute.

"I know you're not sleeping," Mirael said.

Selene opened her eyes. Mirael was standing by the window, already dressed, her hair pinned back in the practical style she wore when they had work to do. She looked tired. The kind of tired that sleep didn't fix.

"How long have you been up?"

"A while."

Neither of them mentioned the night before. The fight. The words that still hung in the air between them, sharp-edged and unresolved. They'd been doing this for twelve years. They knew how to step around the broken glass.

Selene sat up, swung her legs over the edge of the bed. The floor was cold under her feet. Below them, the Lantern was quiet, the morning hours when the workers slept and the customers had gone home to their respectable lives.

"We need to talk about the job," Mirael said.

"I know."

"We're running out of options."

"I know."

Mirael turned from the window. Her face was carefully neutral, the regal mask she wore when she didn't want Selene to see what was underneath.

"Then let's talk about it. Somewhere else. Somewhere that isn't this room."

***

The Broken Oar sat three streets back from the harbor, wedged between a rope-maker's shop and a building that had been a warehouse once and was now just a place where rats lived better than most of Southside's residents. The sign above the door showed an oar snapped in half, the paint so faded you could barely make out the shape anymore. Nobody remembered why it was called that. Nobody cared.

Inside, the air was thick with pipe smoke and the smell of bodies that worked hard and washed rarely. The floor was sticky with decades of spilled ale. The bar was a single plank of driftwood, scarred and stained, held up by barrels that had seen better centuries. Behind it, a woman named Gerda pulled drinks with the mechanical efficiency of someone who'd stopped caring about customers twenty years ago and was just waiting for the building to fall down around her.

Midmorning crowd. The night shift coming off the docks, too tired to go home and too wired to sleep. A table of fishermen arguing about catch weights, their voices rising and falling in the eternal rhythm of men who'd been having the same argument for thirty years. Two old men by the fire, playing cards with a deck so worn the suits were mostly guesswork. A woman in the corner booth, head down on her arms, either sleeping or dead. Nobody had checked. Nobody would.

At the bar, three dockworkers hunched over their ales, talking low.

". . . fourth checkpoint this week. Fourth. Can't take a piss without some gray-coat asking where you're going."

"Heard they're looking for someone. Someone specific."

"They're always looking for someone. Doesn't mean they have to look at me."

"My cousin works the Narrows gate. Says they've got lists now. Actual lists. Names, descriptions, known associates. Like we're already guilty. Just haven't been caught yet."

"In this city? We are."

Selene and Mirael took their usual spot, backs to the wall, facing the door. The table was carved with initials and crude drawings and one very detailed anatomical suggestion that someone had spent real time on. Gerda brought wine without being asked and left without speaking. The transaction of regulars.

"Viena's job," Mirael said, once they were alone. "The Warrens."

"It's suicide."

"It's work. It's money. It's getting us out of sight while whatever this is blows over."

Selene drank. The wine was cheap and sour, the kind that burned going down and sat in your stomach like regret. "The Warrens are Guild territory. We go down there, we're walking into their house. Their tunnels. Their rules."

At the fishermen's table, the argument had shifted.

". . . telling you, the whole market's wrong. Used to be you could sell your catch same day, fair price, no questions. Now there's fees. Permits. Some Guild man standing there with his hand out before you can even unload."

"It's the same everywhere. My brother-in-law runs a cart in the Merchant Quarter. Says the protection money's doubled since spring. Doubled. And what's he getting for it? Same nothing as before, just costs more."

"City's eating itself. Always has been. Just doing it faster now."

"We're already playing by their rules up here," Mirael said. "At least down there, we'd have a purpose. A job. Something to focus on besides waiting for the next checkpoint to close."

"And if we get caught?"

"Then we don't come back up." Mirael's voice was flat. Matter-of-fact. "But we might not come back up anyway. Not the way things are going."

One of the dockworkers at the bar had turned around on his stool. Big man. Thick neck, thicker arms, the kind of muscles you got from hauling cargo twelve hours a day. He was staring at their table with the bleary focus of someone who'd been drinking since his shift ended at dawn.

Selene clocked him. Kept talking.

"We could leave," Mirael said. Quieter now. "Like Davresh said. Find somewhere else. Start over."

"We talked about this."

"We argued about it. That's not the same thing."

The dockworker stood up. His friends tried to pull him back. He shook them off and started walking toward their table, his gait the careful swagger of a man who knew he was drunk and was trying to hide it.

Here we go.

"The answer's the same," Selene said, not looking at him.

"Ladies." The dockworker stopped at their table, looming. Up close he smelled like fish guts and cheap beer and the particular sourness of a man who'd decided that whatever happened next was someone else's fault. "Drinking alone? That's no fun. Why don't you come sit with us? My friends are friendly."

"We're not alone," Mirael said, her voice cool. "We're with each other."

"That's what I mean." He grinned, showing teeth that had lost a few fights. "Two pretty things like you, sitting in a corner, whispering. What are you, sisters? Friends?" His grin widened. "Something else?"

"We're the kind of women who drink in peace," Selene said. "You should try it. The peace part."

"Aw, don't be like that." He put his hand on the table, leaning in. His breath was worse than his smell. "I'm just being friendly. This is a friendly place. Friendly city. Friendly people."

"You're in my way."

"What?"

Selene looked up at him, finally. Let him see her eyes. Let him see what was behind them. "Move."

Something in his expression flickered. The drunk confidence meeting something it didn't recognize. His friends at the bar had gone quiet. The fishermen had stopped arguing. Even the card players by the fire were watching now.

"I'm just talking," he said, but his voice had lost its swagger.

"And now you're done." Selene's hand moved to her belt, casual, almost lazy. Not drawing. Just resting. Just reminding. "Go back to your friends. Finish your drink. Tell them you tried and we weren't interested. Everyone keeps their teeth, and we all have a nice morning."

He should have walked away. Any sober man would have. But drunk pride was its own kind of stupid, and he had plenty of both.

"Frigid bitch," he muttered. And then he reached for her.

His hand closed around her wrist on the table. Big fingers. Strong grip. The kind of grab that was meant to pull her up, drag her somewhere, show her who was in charge.

Selene's dagger was in his hand before he finished the motion.

Not a slash. Not a threat. The blade punched straight down through the meat of his palm, pinning it to the table with a solid thunk that silenced the entire tavern.

He screamed. High and raw and shocked, the sound of a man who'd never had steel in his flesh before. His friends at the bar lurched up from their stools. One of them reached for something at his belt.

"Don't." Selene's voice was flat. She hadn't moved except for the strike. Her other hand was still wrapped around her wine cup. "He grabbed me. Everyone saw it. This is what happens."

The dockworker was whimpering now, staring at the blade through his hand, at the blood pooling on the scarred wood. His friends had frozen, calculating odds, measuring distances, deciding if their loyalty was worth bleeding for.

It wasn't. It never was.

"You crazy whore," one of them said, but he was pulling his friend's arm, trying to get him to move. "Pull it out, Dagen. Pull it out and let's go."

"I can't," Dagen gasped. "I can't, it's stuck, it's . . ."

Selene twisted the blade. Just slightly. Dagen screamed again.

"Next time a woman tells you to move," she said, "you move."

She pulled the dagger free in one clean motion. Dagen collapsed backward, clutching his ruined hand to his chest, blood streaming between his fingers. His friends caught him, hauled him upright, started dragging him toward the door.

"This isn't over," one of them spat. "We'll tell the Paladins. They're looking for people like you. There's a man, been asking questions all over the docks. Asking about women who carry blades and don't know their place."

"Tell him whatever you want." Selene wiped the blade on her sleeve, sheathed it. "Tell him I said hello."

The door slammed behind them. The tavern stayed silent for a long moment. Then, slowly, the noise resumed. The fishermen went back to arguing, quieter now. The card players went back to their game, not looking toward the corner. Gerda came over with a rag and wiped down the blood on the table without a word, without meeting Selene's eyes.

Just another morning at the Broken Oar. Just another incident that would find its way to someone's ear. Someone patient. Someone methodical. Someone building a case.

Mirael let out a breath. "That was . . ."

"Necessary."

"That is going to get back to people."

"It was always going to get back to people. At least now they know the cost." Selene picked up her wine, drank, set it down. Her hand was steady. Her heart was steady. The violence had come and gone like weather, leaving nothing behind. "He grabbed me."

"I know."

"He would have done worse."

"I know." Mirael's voice was quiet. "That's not what worries me."

Selene didn't ask what worried her. She already knew.

Mirael was quiet for a moment. When she spoke again, her voice had changed. Softer. More careful.

"What are we doing, Selene?"

"Drinking. Talking. Scaring dockworkers."

"I mean us. What are we doing? Where is this going?"

Selene's hand tightened on her cup. "It's going the same place it's always been going. Forward. One day at a time. One job at a time."

"That's not an answer."

"It's the only answer I have."

The silence stretched. Mirael looked down at her wine, then back up at Selene. Something in her expression shifted. A decision being made.

She reached across the table. Touched Selene's hand.

Just that. Just fingers on fingers. The lightest contact. The kind of touch that could mean nothing or everything, depending on what came next.

Selene went still.

"I'm not asking for anything," Mirael said quietly. "I'm just . . . I need to know you're still in there. That you still feel something. Anything."

Selene looked at Mirael's hand on hers. Pale fingers against scarred knuckles. The touch was warm. Gentle. Everything she couldn't let herself want.

She pulled away.

Not fast. Not cruel. Just a slow withdrawal, her hand sliding back across the table until the distance was restored. Ten inches. Same as always.

Mirael's face didn't change. But something behind her eyes went dark. A light going out.

"Right," she said. "Of course."

"Mirael."

"No, it's fine. I shouldn't have . . ." She picked up her wine, drank, set it down too hard. "I shouldn't have."

They sat in silence after that. The old men by the fire argued about fish prices. The woman in the corner booth snored softly. The world went on, ordinary and oblivious, while something small and fragile died in the space between them.

***

They walked back to the Lantern through streets that felt different in daylight. Busier. Louder. The city going about its business, buying and selling and surviving, the eternal machinery of Garnath grinding forward.

Mirael walked ahead, her spine straight, her shoulders tight. The regal bearing she used as armor, keeping the world at a distance. Keeping Selene at a distance.

They didn't talk.

At the Lantern, Mirael went upstairs without a word. The door to their room closed behind her. Not slammed. Just closed. Quiet and final.

Selene stood in the hallway, looking at the closed door.

She should go in. Should say something. Should try to fix whatever she'd broken at that table, with that pulled-away hand, with all the words she couldn't say and all the feelings she couldn't feel.

She didn't.

She turned and walked down the hall, past the private rooms, down the stairs to the second floor where Viena's workers plied their trade.

***

Not Lira this time.

Selene chose Maren. Tall, broad-shouldered, dark skin and darker eyes. A man who looked like he could take whatever she needed to give. She'd been with him before, once or twice, when the silence inside got too loud and she needed something harder to drown it out.

His room was at the end of the hall. Smaller than Lira's, but cleaner. A bed. A washstand. A window that looked out on nothing.

"You look like you're carrying something heavy," Maren said, closing the door behind them.

"I'm not here to talk."

"Fair enough."

He reached for her, slow and careful, the way you'd approach a wounded animal. Selene didn't want slow. Didn't want careful. She grabbed his shirt and pulled him in, her mouth finding his, her teeth catching his lower lip hard enough to make him hiss.

He pulled back, surprised. "Rough day?"

"Rough everything."

Something shifted in his expression. Understanding, maybe. Or just professional calculation, adjusting to what the client needed. Either way, he stopped being gentle.

Good.

She shoved him toward the bed and he went, pulling her with him. They hit the mattress hard, a tangle of limbs and grabbing hands. Selene was on top, straddling him, yanking at the laces of his shirt while he worked at hers. The fabric tore somewhere. Neither of them cared.

His hands found her breasts, rough and demanding, the way she needed them to be. She ground down against him, feeling him harden through his trousers, feeling her own body respond with the mechanical efficiency of muscle memory. Wet where she was supposed to be wet. Ready where she was supposed to be ready. The body knew what to do even when the mind had checked out.

She unlaced him and took him in her hand. He groaned, his hips bucking up into her grip. She stroked hard, too hard maybe, but he didn't complain. Just reached between her legs and gave back what she was giving, his fingers rough and direct, finding the places that made her gasp.

"Inside," she said. "Now."

He didn't argue.

She rose up and sank down onto him in one motion, taking him to the hilt. The stretch was good. The fullness was good. Something to feel that wasn't the ache in her chest, the echo of Mirael's face when she'd pulled her hand away.

"You always this friendly?" Maren managed, his voice strained.

"You complaining?"

"Just making conversation."

"Don't."

She rode him hard, her hands braced on his chest, her hips snapping with a rhythm that was more violence than pleasure. Maren kept up, thrusting up to meet her, his hands gripping her hips hard enough to bruise. The bed creaked. The headboard knocked against the wall.

"At this rate," he gasped between thrusts, "you're going to owe me hazard pay."

"Bill Viena."

He laughed, breathless, and she almost smiled. Almost. Then she ground down harder and the laughter turned into a groan.

"Gods," he gasped. "Slow down, I'm going to . . ."

"Don't."

She clenched around him, deliberately, and watched his eyes roll back. But he held on, stubborn or professional or both, and kept moving. His thumb found the spot above where they were joined, circling with rough precision, and Selene felt the pressure building despite herself. Despite the emptiness. Despite everything.

She came with her teeth clenched, refusing to make a sound. The orgasm ripped through her like a blade, sharp and bright and gone too fast, leaving nothing behind. She kept moving through it, kept riding him, until Maren grabbed her hips and held her down and spent himself inside her with a groan that the whole floor probably heard.

"Next time," he managed, still catching his breath, "warn a man."

"Where's the fun in that?"

Silence.

Just breathing. Just the creak of the bed settling. Just two bodies pressed together, slick with sweat, hearts pounding from exertion rather than connection.

Selene climbed off him and sat on the edge of the bed, her back to him. She could feel his release sliding down her thigh. Feel the ache in muscles she'd pushed too hard. Feel absolutely nothing in the place where feeling was supposed to live.

"That was . . ." Maren paused, catching his breath. "You wore me out."

She didn't answer.

"Whatever you're running from," he said, "I hope you find it. Or it stops chasing you. Whichever."

Selene stood. Found her clothes. Dressed without looking at him, without speaking, without acknowledging that anything had happened between them except a transaction. She left coins on the washstand. More than she owed. Less than she'd taken.

The door closed behind her.

The ache was still there. The silence inside. Nothing had changed.

Nothing ever changed.

***

Two floors up, Mirael sat on the edge of her bed and listened.

The walls in the Veiled Lantern were thin. That was the point, Viena always said. Thin walls meant no pretending. Everyone heard everything, and everyone learned to keep their mouths shut about what they heard. A house built on mutual silence.

Mirael had never found it funny.

She heard them now. Through the floor, through the beams, through the particular acoustics of a building designed to carry sound. The rhythmic creak of bedsprings. The knock of a headboard against a wall. And voices. Maren's low rumble. Selene's sharp responses.

She couldn't make out the words. She didn't need to.

The creaking got faster. Louder. More desperate. Mirael stared at the wall and counted the cracks in the plaster and tried to think about anything else. The Warrens job. The checkpoints. The figure watching from windows. Anything but the sounds filtering up from below.

A groan. Deep. Male. Loud enough to hear clearly.

Then silence.

Mirael closed her eyes. Her hands were shaking. She pressed them flat against her thighs and willed them to stop.

She should leave. Should walk out, find a tavern, drink until she couldn't hear anything anymore. Should do something, anything, besides sit here and wait for Selene to come back smelling like sweat and sex and someone who wasn't her.

She didn't move.

She never did.

***

Mirael was sitting on her bed when Selene came back to the room.

Not reading. Not writing. Just sitting, her hands folded in her lap, her eyes on the door. Waiting.

Selene stopped in the doorway.

Their eyes met. Something passed between them, wordless and heavy. Mirael's expression didn't change. Didn't accuse. Didn't plead. Just looked at her with eyes that had seen too much and understood all of it.

"Feel better?" Mirael asked. Her voice was steady. Too steady.

"No."

"I didn't think so."

Selene walked to her bed. Sat down. The ten feet between them felt like miles.

"Mirael, I . . ."

"Don't." Mirael held up her hand. "Don't apologize. Don't explain. I've heard the explanations. I know what you'd say." She paused. Her voice cracked, just slightly, before she controlled it. "I just need to not hear it right now."

Selene nodded. There was nothing else to do.

Mirael stood and walked to the small desk in the corner where she kept her journal. She sat down, opened the leather cover, and began to write. The scratch of the quill was the only sound in the room.

Selene watched her for a moment. Watched the way Mirael's hand moved across the page, quick and certain, the words flowing out of her like blood from a wound. She didn't ask what Mirael was writing.

She already knew it was about her.

She lay back on her bed and stared at the ceiling and listened to the scratch of the quill. Her hand found the edge of the blanket, gripped it, knuckles going white. She didn't know why. Didn't know what she was holding onto.

She didn't sleep for a long time.

CHAPTER 10: The Narrowing

Selene woke up sore in places she'd forgotten she had.

She sat up slowly, wincing. Her thighs ached. Her hips ached. There was a bruise on her left side she didn't remember getting, and her lower back felt like someone had used it for target practice.

Mirael was already awake, sitting by the window with a cup of something hot, watching her with an expression that was trying very hard to be neutral and failing completely.

"Don't," Selene said.

"I didn't say anything."

"You were thinking it."

"I was thinking that you're moving like an old woman this morning." Mirael took a sip of her drink. "I was also thinking that perhaps you brought this on yourself."

"I don't remember asking for commentary."

"And yet here it is, free of charge." Mirael's mouth twitched. Almost a smile. Almost. "How was Maren?"

"Functional."

"That good?"

Selene stood up, slowly, and immediately regretted it. Every muscle in her legs screamed. She'd ridden him like she was trying to break something, and apparently her body had decided to break first.

"You could have warned me," Mirael said, still watching. "I would have stuffed wool in my ears."

"You could have left."

"And miss the performance? The headboard alone deserves applause. I'm surprised it's still attached to the wall."

"Are you done?"

"Almost." Mirael set down her cup. "You're limping."

"I'm not limping."

"You're definitely limping. It's a very specific limp. The limp of a woman who forgot she's not twenty anymore and tried to prove something to someone who didn't need convincing."

Selene grabbed her trousers from the chair and pulled them on, ignoring the way her body protested every movement. "I hate you."

"No you don't."

"I hate you specifically right now, in this moment."

"That's fair." Mirael stood, stretched, moved toward the door with the easy grace of someone who hadn't spent the previous evening trying to fuck her feelings into submission. "Get dressed. We need to check the Thornway passage. I heard they've put up new notices."

"What kind of notices?"

"The kind with seals on them. The kind that mean someone's been busy with paperwork while you were busy with Maren."

Selene threw a boot at her. Mirael caught it, laughing, and ducked out the door before Selene could find the other one.

***

Three days after the Broken Oar, Selene learned what paperwork could do that blades couldn't.

The Thornway passage was closed. A notice had been nailed to the gate, the kind of official script that meant someone with a seal had signed something. New regulations. Transit permits required. Applications available at the Harbor Authority, processing time four to six weeks.

"Four to six weeks," Mirael read aloud. "For a passage we've used twice a month for three years."

"They're not trying to stop us." Selene studied the notice, looking for cracks, finding none. "They're trying to slow us down. Make us visible. Make us apply for things."

"Make us put our names on paper."

"That too."

An old woman pushed past them, muttering about the inconvenience. A merchant with a handcart full of cloth was arguing with someone who looked official, waving his hands, his voice rising. The official just pointed at the notice and shrugged. Rules were rules.

"This used to be a free passage," the merchant was saying. "My father used this passage. His father before him. Now I need a permit? Now I need to wait six weeks?"

"Four to six," the official corrected. "Could be four."

"Could be never! You think my cloth will wait six weeks? You think my buyers will wait?"

The official shrugged again. He'd probably heard this argument a dozen times today. Would hear it a dozen more before sunset. None of it would change anything.

They tried the Candlemaker's route instead. Same notice. Different gate. Same seal at the bottom, the same processing time, the same polite suggestion that law-abiding citizens had nothing to fear from proper documentation.

By midday they'd found four more closures. The net wasn't made of checkpoints anymore. It was made of paper and patience and the slow grinding machinery of bureaucracy that didn't need guards because it had something better: time.

***

Davresh wouldn't see them.

That was new. In twelve years, Davresh had always seen them. Even when the jobs were thin, even when the heat was high, even when smarter men would have pretended not to know their names. His door had always opened.

"He's not in," said the boy at the counter. Fourteen, maybe. Thin as a stick and twice as nervous, the kind of apprentice who'd been told exactly what to say and nothing else.

"He's always in." Selene kept her voice level. Her legs still ached from yesterday, and standing here arguing with a child wasn't helping. "Tell him it's about the Thornway permits. Tell him we need routes."

"He's not in."

"Tell him."

The boy's eyes flicked to the back room. Just for a second. Just long enough.

"He said to tell you he's not in. Specifically. He said you'd come, and he said to tell you he's not in, and he said . . ." The boy swallowed. "He said to tell you he's sorry. But he's not in."

Selene looked at the back room door. She could hear someone breathing on the other side. Could picture Davresh standing there, ear pressed to the wood, waiting for them to leave.

She thought about walking through it anyway. Thought about the look on his face, the fear she'd see there, the way he'd flinch when she asked him why.

She didn't.

Some doors, once you kicked them open, stayed broken.

"Tell him we understand," Mirael said, her voice carefully neutral. "Tell him we hope his health improves."

They left. The boy watched them go with the relieved expression of someone who'd expected violence and received mercy instead.

Outside, the street was busy with midday traffic. Carts and pedestrians and the eternal noise of a city that didn't care about their problems. Selene leaned against a wall and tried to look like she wasn't resting her legs.

"You're still limping," Mirael observed.

"I'm not limping."

"You're favoring your right side."

"I'm leaning. There's a difference."

"There really isn't." Mirael's mouth twitched again, but the humor didn't reach her eyes. "That's three contacts in two days. Davresh. Mikkel at the fish market. The woman who runs the south gate laundry."

"I can count."

"They're all scared, Selene. And not of us. Of being seen with us."

"I know."

"Something changed. Something more than the checkpoints, more than the permits. Someone's making it expensive to know us."

Selene didn't answer. She was thinking about the dockworker at the Broken Oar. The threat he'd made. The man asking questions.

A patient man with money and time and no reason to rush. Building a case brick by brick.

***

The money came out on the table that night, spread across the scarred wood in neat stacks while the fire crackled and the noise from the Lantern's lower floors drifted up through the boards.

Mirael counted. She always counted. It was one of her rituals, one of the ways she kept control when everything else was spinning loose. Neat stacks. Careful tallies. Numbers that didn't lie even when people did.

"Fourteen days," she said when she was done. "If we eat light and nothing breaks and no one demands a bribe we can't refuse. Fourteen days."

"And if something breaks?"

"Ten. Maybe less."

Selene stared at the stacks. Fourteen days. Two weeks. Not enough time to wait out the permits, not enough time to find new routes, not enough time for the heat to die down and the doors to open again.

"The catacombs job," she said.

Mirael's hands went still on the coins. "You said it was suicide."

"I said infiltrating the Warrens was suicide. Viena's job isn't the Warrens proper. It's the edges. The old tunnels. Get close enough to see what the Guild is doing down there, then get out."

"Intel gathering."

"Someone wants to know what the Guild is up to. What they're moving, what they're protecting, what's worth putting that many men underground." Selene shrugged. "Viena didn't say who. The client's paying extra to stay anonymous."

"That doesn't worry you?"

"Everything worries me. But anonymous money spends the same as any other kind."

"And the pay?"

"Enough to buy us three months. Maybe four, if we're careful."

Mirael was quiet for a long moment. Her fingers traced the edge of a coin stack, straightening what was already straight.

"Someone with money wants information on the Guild," she said slowly. "Someone who won't show their face. Someone who's willing to pay two smugglers to crawl into the dark and spy on the most dangerous organization in Garnath." She looked up. "That doesn't sound like a job. That sounds like someone moving pieces on a board."

"Maybe. Or maybe it's just a merchant who got squeezed and wants leverage. Or a noble with a grudge. Or someone planning a move and needing to know what they're moving against."

"Or someone who wants us specifically. Someone who knows we're desperate and knows we'll take work others won't."

Selene didn't answer. She'd thought the same thing. The timing was too convenient. The money too good. The anonymity too careful. It felt like bait.

But bait only mattered if you had other options.

"You hate underground," Mirael said finally. "You hate enclosed spaces. You hate anywhere you can't see the sky."

"I hate starving more."

"Do you?"

The question hung there. Selene didn't have an answer that wasn't a lie.

"We don't have to decide tonight," Mirael said. "We have fourteen days. Things could change."

"Things are changing. That's the problem."

Mirael gathered the coins, stacked them neatly in their leather pouch, tucked them into the hidden pocket in her travel bag. Ritual complete. Control maintained. The numbers didn't lie, but they didn't help either.

"I'm going to the market tomorrow," she said. "Early. See if any of our old contacts will talk. Maybe someone's heard something we haven't."

"I'll come with you."

"No." Mirael's voice was firm. "You'll stay here. Rest. Stay out of sight." She paused. "Your face is too well known right now. The incident at the Oar is still fresh. Let me be the one who moves."

Selene wanted to argue. Wanted to say that splitting up was dangerous, that Mirael shouldn't be alone, that staying behind felt like hiding.

She didn't say any of it.

"Fine. I'll stay."

"Thank you."

Mirael went to bed without another word and turned toward the wall. Her breathing slowed into the rhythm that meant she was done talking, done planning, done holding herself together for the night.

Selene stayed up, watching the fire die down to embers. The tunnels kept pushing into her thoughts. The darkness. The weight of stone overhead. Fourteen days of money and no good options.

***

Mirael left before dawn.

Selene heard her moving in the dark, the soft sounds of someone dressing quietly, trying not to wake a person who was already awake. The door opened. Closed. Footsteps faded down the hall.

She should sleep. She knew she should sleep. But the room felt wrong, somehow. Too quiet. Too still. Like the air itself was holding its breath.

She got up. Lit a candle. Looked around.

Everything was where it should be. Their bags by the door. The coin pouch in Mirael's hiding spot. Clothes folded on the chair. Water pitcher on the stand. Nothing moved, nothing taken, nothing disturbed.

Except.

The window latch was open.

She'd checked that latch before bed. She always checked. It was habit, survival instinct, the kind of thing you did without thinking when you'd spent your life sleeping in places where unlocked windows got you killed.

It had been latched. She was certain.

The latch showed no damage. No scratches from a tool, no splinters from force. Someone had lifted it from outside, looked in, and closed it again without latching it properly. Someone careful. Someone skilled.

She crossed to the window. Looked out at the alley below. Shadows and garbage and the faint gray of approaching dawn. The alley was empty.

But on the windowsill, barely visible in the candlelight, there was a mark. A scrape in the grime. The kind of mark a boot might leave if someone had crouched there, balanced on the narrow ledge, looking in.

Watching.

Selene's hand went to her belt. Found nothing. Her daggers were across the room, with her clothes, because she'd been in bed, because she'd thought she was safe, because she'd gotten careless.

She made herself breathe. Made herself think.

Watchers didn't climb. They came with ledgers and questions and official authority. Paladins announced themselves. Knocked on doors. Believed in process.

Whoever had been on that ledge was something else entirely.

She thought about the silhouette she'd seen days ago, in the courtyard near the checkpoints. The shape that had been there and then wasn't, gone before she could get a clear look. Like smoke. Like something that existed just outside the corner of her eye.

He'd found them.

Whoever he was. Whatever he wanted. He knew where they slept now. Knew their window. Knew how to get close without being seen.

And he'd wanted her to know he knew.

The unlatched window wasn't carelessness. It was a message.

I was here. I can come back.

Selene closed the window. Latched it. Checked it three times.

Then she sat on her bed with her daggers in her lap and waited for morning

***

Mirael came back at midday with nothing.

"Everyone's scared," she said, dropping onto her bed. She looked exhausted. Worn thin in a way that sleep wouldn't fix. "The fishmonger pretended not to recognize me. The woman at the south gate literally turned and walked away when I approached. Even old Gerren, who's known us for years, just shook his head and closed his stall."

"Did anyone talk?"

"One. A boy who runs messages for the harbor merchants. He didn't know much, but he'd heard things." Mirael pulled off her boots, rubbed her feet. "There's a list. An actual list, with names on it. Anyone who does business with the people on that list gets a visit. Someone who isn't a Watcher. Someone who asks questions and doesn't write anything down and makes it very clear that cooperation is in everyone's best interest."

"Did he describe this someone?"

"Older. Well-dressed. Patient." Mirael looked up. "He said the man never threatens. Never raises his voice. Just asks questions and waits, and somehow by the time he leaves, people have decided they don't want to know us anymore."

Weston. Had to be. Building his case one conversation at a time, one closed door at a time, one ruined relationship at a time.

"There's more," Mirael said. "The boy mentioned something else. Someone else. He said there's been another man asking about us. Not the patient one. This one doesn't ask questions. He just . . . appears. Watches. Leaves before anyone can get a good look at him."

Selene's hand tightened on her dagger.

"The boy said people are more scared of that one. The patient man wants information. The other one . . ." Mirael paused. "The boy said it feels like he's waiting for something. Like he's already decided what he's going to do, and he's just waiting for the right moment to do it."

"The window," Selene said.

"What?"

"The window latch was open this morning. After you left. Someone had been on the ledge. Looking in."

Mirael went pale. "Why didn't you tell me?"

"I'm telling you now."

"Selene, if someone knows where we sleep . . ."

"They already knew. This was just them letting us know they knew." Selene stood, walked to the window, looked out at the alley that suddenly felt less like an escape route and more like a hunting ground. "We have two people looking for us now. One's building a case. The other one's building something else."

"What do we do?"

Selene turned back to the room. To Mirael, pale and tired and scared in a way she was trying not to show. To the neat stacks of coins that bought them fourteen days. To the walls that had felt safe yesterday and felt like a trap today.

"We go talk to Viena," she said. "And this time, she answers our questions."

***

Viena was in her office when they arrived, a small room at the back of the Lantern's ground floor where she conducted business that couldn't happen in public. Ledgers on the desk. A lockbox in the corner. The smell of ink and old paper and the faint sweetness of the perfume she wore to mask the smell of the trade she ran.

She looked up when they entered, and something in her expression shifted. The wariness of someone who'd been expecting this visit and dreading it.

"The job," Selene said without preamble. "We need to know more."

"I told you what I know."

"You told us what you wanted us to know. That's not the same thing."

Viena leaned back in her chair. Studied them both with eyes that had seen too much and calculated too quickly. "What do you want to know?"

"How did this job come to you?"

"A messenger. Young man, well-dressed, no name given. He delivered a letter with the terms and a purse with the first payment. Said his employer valued discretion and would pay well for it."

"You didn't find that suspicious?"

"Everything in this city is suspicious. That doesn't make it false." Viena shrugged. "The money was real. Gold, not promises. That's more than most clients offer."

"Who's the employer?"

"I don't know."

"Guess."

"I don't guess. I deal in information, and I don't have any." Viena's voice hardened. "The letter was unsigned. The messenger wouldn't answer questions. The payment came from no bank I could trace. Whoever this is, they know how to stay hidden."

Mirael stepped forward. "The payment structure. How does it work?"

"Half up front, already paid to me. Half on completion, delivered the same way. If you don't come back, I keep the first half for my trouble."

"And if we come back with nothing? No intel, no information?"

"Then you don't get the second half. But you don't owe anything either. The job is results-based, not effort-based."

Selene and Mirael exchanged a look. That was unusual. Most clients wanted results or nothing. This one was paying them to try, regardless of outcome. That kind of generosity usually meant the job was worse than it sounded.

"Who benefits if we disappear underground?" Selene asked.

Viena's expression flickered. Just for a moment. Just enough.

"I don't know what you mean."

"Yes, you do. Someone's squeezing us. Checkpoints. Permits. Our contacts won't talk to us anymore. And suddenly there's a job that takes us out of sight, into tunnels where accidents happen and bodies don't get found." Selene leaned on the desk. "Who benefits?"

"A lot of people would benefit from you disappearing. You've made enemies. That's not news."

"But this job appeared right when we needed it most. Right when our options were running out. That's convenient."

"Convenient for you, maybe. I'm just the broker." Viena met her eyes. "I didn't set you up, Selene. I've known you twelve years. If I wanted you dead, I'd have done it already."

"Maybe you're being used too."

The silence stretched. Viena looked away first.

"Maybe I am," she said quietly. "But the money's still real. And you still need work."

***

They spent the next two days trying to trace the client.

Mirael worked the financial angle. She talked to money-changers, bankers, anyone who might have handled gold moving through unusual channels. She called in favors. She spent coin they couldn't afford to spend. She hit nothing but walls.

"Whoever they are, they know how to move money," she reported on the second evening. "The gold Viena received was clean. No marks, no mint stamps that traced to any specific source. Could have come from anywhere. Could have come from nowhere."

"So we can't follow the money."

"The money doesn't want to be followed."

Selene worked the street angle. She watched the Lantern, looking for anyone watching back. She asked careful questions in careful places. She tried to find the well-dressed messenger Viena had described.

Nothing. The man had appeared, delivered his message, and vanished. No one remembered seeing him before. No one remembered seeing him since.

"It's a dead end," Selene admitted. "Whoever set this up, they're good. Better than us."

"That should worry us more than it does."

"It worries me plenty. But worried doesn't pay the rent."

They sat in their room that night, the door locked, the window checked three times and spread their gear across the beds. If they were going into the tunnels, they were going prepared.

***

"Signal system," Selene said, holding up a small brass whistle. "Three short bursts means trouble. One long means fall back to the last junction. Two long means abort, get out however you can."

"And if we get separated?"

"We don't get separated. We stay within sight of each other at all times. If something happens and we can't, we rally at the Candlemaker's Row entrance. Wait until dawn. If the other person doesn't show . . ."

She didn't finish the sentence. She didn't need to.

"Supplies," Mirael said, all business now. "Rope. Two hundred feet, in case we need to climb or descend. Candles, thirty, plus flint and steel. Chalk for marking passages we've been through. Food for three days, water for two. We'll have to find more down there if it takes longer."

"It won't take longer. In and out. We get close enough to see what the Guild is moving, we document it, we leave."

"And if the Guild sees us first?"

"They won't."

"Selene."

"They won't. We're not going into the Warrens. We're skirting the edges. The old tunnels the Guild sealed off years ago. They don't patrol them because they don't need to. We stay quiet, we stay careful, we get what we need, and we get out."

Mirael didn't look convinced. She checked her pack again, counting items she'd already counted twice. Her ritual. Her control.

"Payment," she said. "Half is already with Viena. If we don't come back, she keeps it. If we do come back, she holds it until we deliver the intel and the second half arrives."

"And if the second half doesn't arrive?"

"Then we have half and a grudge. Better than nothing and a grave."

Selene nodded. It wasn't perfect. Nothing about this was perfect. But it was the best they could do with what they had.

"Contingencies," she said. "If something goes wrong. Really wrong. If one of us doesn't make it back."

Mirael's hands went still on her pack.

"Then the other one gets out," Selene continued. "Doesn't wait. Doesn't look back. Gets out, gets the money from Viena, and disappears. New city. New name. New life."

"I'm not leaving you down there."

"If I'm dead, I won't care. And if I'm captured, you can't help me. The only thing you'd accomplish is dying too."

"And if you're the one who makes it back? If I'm the one who doesn't?"

Selene didn't answer for a long moment. The fire crackled. Somewhere below them, the Lantern went about its business, oblivious.

"Then I get out," she said finally. "And I don't look back."

It was a lie. They both knew it was a lie. But some lies were necessary.

"Mother Gessa," Mirael said. "Someone should know we're going. In case we don't come back."

Selene nodded slowly. She'd been thinking the same thing. Not for Gessa's sake, but for the girl in the cellar. The one she'd left bread for and walked away from. The one she'd been avoiding thinking about ever since.

"I'll go tonight," she said. "Before we leave."

"You want me to come?"

"No. This one's mine."

***

Mother Gessa's cellar was warm and smelled like bread and tallow candles. Selene stood in the doorway, watching the old woman move between sleeping children, adjusting blankets, checking foreheads, doing the quiet work of someone who'd made caring for strays into a calling.

Kira was in the corner. The same corner she'd been sleeping in since she'd found her way to Gessa's, weeks ago. She had a candle burning beside her pallet, even though the cellar was already lit. Her candle. The one she'd been clutching when Selene found her.

The girl looked up when Selene approached. Blue eyes, wary and watchful. The look of a child who'd learned that adults meant trouble more often than help.

"You," Kira said. It wasn't a greeting. It wasn't an accusation. Just recognition.

"Me."

Selene didn't know what to do with her hands. Didn't know where to stand. She'd killed men without hesitation, navigated the most dangerous parts of Garnath without fear, and here she was, paralyzed by a child who barely came up to her chest.

"You brought me here," Kira said. "Then you left."

"I did."

"Why?"

"Because you needed somewhere safe. And I'm not safe."

Kira considered this. Her fingers found the edge of her blanket, worrying the fabric the way children did when they were thinking hard about something.

"Mother Gessa says you're a smuggler."

"Mother Gessa talks too much."

"She says you help people sometimes. When you feel like it."

"Do I?"

"She says you helped her once. Got medicine for the children when the fever came through. Didn't ask for payment."

Selene remembered that. Three years ago, maybe four. A sickness had swept through the Narrows, killing the weak and the young. She'd stolen the medicine from a merchant's warehouse because it was easier than watching children die. She hadn't thought anyone remembered.

"That was a long time ago."

"She remembers." Kira's eyes were steady on hers. Too old for her face. Too knowing. "She says you're not as bad as you pretend to be."

"She's wrong."

"Maybe." Kira shrugged, a surprisingly adult gesture. "Why are you here?"

Selene crouched down, putting herself at eye level with the girl. It felt strange. Vulnerable. She couldn't remember the last time she'd made herself small for anyone.

"I'm going away for a while. Underground. Into the tunnels beneath the city."

"The catacombs?" Kira's eyes widened slightly. "The other children say there are monsters down there. Dead things that walk."

"There are no monsters. Just people. People are worse."

"I know." Said simply. Said like a fact she'd learned the hard way.

Selene felt something twist in her chest. This girl. This stupid, stubborn, too-smart girl who'd survived on the streets alone, who'd stolen from the wrong people and nearly died for it, who looked at the world with eyes that had already seen too much.

"I might not come back," Selene said. "The tunnels are dangerous. Things could go wrong."

"Okay."

"If I don't come back, Mother Gessa will take care of you. You'll be safe here."

"I'm always safe." Kira's voice was flat. "Until I'm not."

"That's . . . that's not . . ." Selene stopped. She didn't know how to do this. Didn't know how to promise things she couldn't guarantee, comfort someone who'd learned that comfort was usually a lie.

"Why are you telling me this?" Kira asked. "We don't know each other. You helped me once. That doesn't make us anything."

It was true. It was completely true. And it shouldn't have stung the way it did.

"I don't know," Selene admitted. "I just . . . I wanted you to know. That someone was thinking about you. Before they went into the dark."

Kira was quiet for a long moment. Her fingers had stopped worrying the blanket. She was looking at Selene like she was trying to solve a puzzle.

"My mother used to say that," she said finally. "Before she died. That she was thinking about me. That even when she wasn't there, she was thinking about me." She paused. "It didn't help."

"No. I don't imagine it did."

"But she said it anyway."

"Yeah."

"So you're saying it too."

"I guess I am."

Another silence. Then Kira did something unexpected. She reached out and touched Selene's hand. Just for a second. Just her small fingers brushing Selene's scarred knuckles.

"Don't die in the tunnels," she said. Then, quieter: "I don't like it when people don't come back." Selene didn't know what that meant. Didn't know why it made her throat tight.

"I'll try not to."

"Good." Kira pulled her hand back, tucked it under her blanket. "You can go now. I need to sleep."

"Right. Of course."

Selene stood. Felt like she should say something else. Didn't know what.

"Selene," she said instead. "My name. It's Selene."

Kira looked up at her. Something shifted in those blue eyes. Not warmth, exactly. But something.

"I know," she said. "Mother Gessa told me."

Then she turned toward the wall and closed her eyes, and Selene stood there for a moment longer before walking away, stepping back out into the cold night air, wondering why she felt like she'd just made a promise she didn't know how to keep.

***

Mirael was asleep when she got back to the Lantern. Or pretending to be. It was hard to tell the difference sometimes.

Selene checked the window, then the door. The window again because once was never enough.

"Well?" Mirael's voice, quiet in the dark.

"She's fine. Gessa knows we're going. If we're not back in a week . . ."

"She'll know what it means."

"Yeah."

Silence. Then:

"What was it like? Seeing her?"

Selene didn't answer for a long moment. She thought about blue eyes and small fingers and a girl who'd said "don't die in the tunnels" like she was giving an order.

"Strange," she said finally. "It was strange."

Mirael didn't ask anything else. She understood that some things didn't have words.

They lay in the dark, ten feet apart, and didn't sleep.

***

Morning came gray and cold, the way mornings always came in Garnath.

They left the Lantern at dawn, packs on their backs, blades at their belts, walking toward the Candlemaker's Row entrance that would take them underground. The city was just waking up around them, merchants opening stalls, workers trudging to their shifts, the eternal machinery of survival grinding forward.

No one looked at them. No one cared. Just two more women in a city full of people trying not to be noticed.

The net was closing. The walls were shrinking. And somewhere out there, two men were waiting, one with a ledger and one with something worse. But there was also someone else. Someone with money and patience and a plan they couldn't see. Someone moving pieces on a board.

And in a cellar on Candlemaker's Row, a girl with blue eyes was sleeping with a candle burning beside her, not knowing that the woman who'd bought her bread on the worst day of her life was walking into the dark and might not come back.

They were walking into a trap. They knew it. They were going anyway, because the alternative was staying still and being strangled slowly by permits and paperwork and the patient accumulation of evidence.

The tunnels meant moving. The dark meant a chance. That would have to be enough.

The entrance loomed ahead, a black mouth in the city's foundation. Cold air breathed up from below, carrying the smell of damp stone and old dust.

Selene adjusted her pack straps and stepped into the dark.

CHAPTER 11: The Descent

The darkness swallowed sound differently than she expected.

Above ground, noise scattered. It bounced off walls, split around corners, dissipated into open air. Down here, in the throat of the old tunnels, sound moved like water. It pooled in low places. It traveled along stone in ways that made distance impossible to judge. A drip from somewhere ahead could be ten feet away or a hundred.

Selene kept her breathing shallow. Listened to the tunnel breathe back.

The entrance had been exactly where Viena's contact said it would be. A drainage grate in the Candlemaker's Row district, rusted hinges shrieking when Mirael pulled it open. The smell hit them first. Damp stone and old rot and something chemical underneath, runoff from the tanneries that had been seeping into these tunnels for decades.

They'd descended a ladder into darkness. Twenty rungs down. Then thirty. The city sounds faded with each step until there was nothing but their own movement and the wet echo of their boots on stone.

That had been an hour ago. Maybe longer. Time moved strangely underground.

"Junction ahead." Mirael's voice was barely above a whisper. Even that felt too loud. She held the lantern low, shielding most of its light with her body, letting just enough escape to read the charcoal marks she'd been leaving on the walls. "Left branch should take us toward the Warrens. The old storage levels."

The Warrens. Guild territory. Where they kept the things they didn't want found.

Selene checked behind them. Nothing but darkness pressing in. The tunnel they'd come through was a black throat, patient and hungry.

"How much further?"

"Another quarter mile. Maybe less." Mirael consulted the rough map she'd assembled from three different sources, none of them complete. "The storage chambers should be past the second cistern. That's where the shipping manifests mentioned transfer points."

The job. Selene kept her mind on the job. Intel on Guild operations. What were they moving through these tunnels? Where was it going? Who was paying?

Information was leverage. Leverage was survival.

They moved.

The tunnel narrowed. Selene's shoulders brushed both walls. The ceiling dropped until she had to duck, then drop to a crouch, then crawl on hands and knees through a section where the stone squeezed tight as a fist. Old fear woke in her chest. The cupboard. The dark. The weight of the world pressing down. She breathed through it. Kept moving. The fear was seventeen years old and she'd learned to carry it without letting it carry her.

Mirael emerged first on the other side, holding the lantern while Selene pulled herself through. For a moment their eyes met. Something passed between them. Concern, maybe. Or just old habit wearing a familiar shape.

Then Mirael turned away and they kept walking.

The next stretch was darker. Mirael kept the lantern low, shielded, just enough light to see the ground immediately ahead. Anything more would announce their presence to anyone watching. The darkness pressed in from all sides, thick as wool.

Mirael bumped into Selene's back. Then again, a few steps later.

"I know you like touching me," Selene murmured without turning around, "but could we try not to fall on our faces before making it out alive?"

A pause. Then Mirael's voice, dry despite everything. "If I wanted to touch you, I'd pick somewhere with better lighting and fewer rats."

"Romantic."

"Practical."

They kept moving. The darkness swallowed the almost-smile on Selene's face before Mirael could see it.

***

The first storage chamber was empty.

Empty, but worked clean. The kind that cost time and hands. Selene ran her fingers along the walls, feeling for the marks that always got left behind. Scrapes where crates had been dragged. Discoloration where something had been stacked for years and then moved. Bolt holes in the floor where shelving had been anchored.

"They cleared it out," Mirael said. "Recently. Look at the dust patterns."

She was right. The floor was clean in paths, dirty in others. Boot prints visible in the thinner sections. Multiple sets, different sizes. Heavy traffic in the last few weeks.

"But cleared out to where?"

Mirael crouched, examining something on the ground. A scrap of paper, water-damaged and torn. She held it to the lantern light.

"Shipping notation. Partial route number." Her eyes moved across the fragment. "This is recent. Within the month."

Selene took it from her. The handwriting was cramped, efficient. Guild clerical work. She could make out numbers, abbreviations, what looked like a date.

"They're moving something. Something big enough to need multiple transfers."

"Or something they don't want traced."

They searched the chamber properly. Selene found more scraps in the corners where the cleaning had been rushed. Manifest fragments. Names she didn't recognize. Numbers that might be quantities, might be prices, might be coordinates. Nothing complete. Nothing damning. But pieces of a pattern.

Mirael sketched quick copies of everything, her charcoal moving fast across her own paper. Documentation. Evidence. Something to trade if they needed to.

"There's more ahead," she said. "The main storage should be deeper. Past the cistern."

She took the lead this time.

***

The screaming started three tunnels later.

Selene heard it before she could identify it. A sound that didn't belong underground. High, ragged, broken in the middle where breath ran out. Then silence. Then it started again, worse than before.

She grabbed Mirael's arm. They pressed against the wall, lantern extinguished.

The sound was coming from somewhere ahead and to the left. A side chamber, maybe. The acoustics down here made it hard to tell. But the quality of the scream was unmistakable. That wasn't pain from an accident. That wasn't someone who'd fallen or been crushed by shifting stone.

That was pain being administered, expertly.

They crept forward. The tunnel curved, and light leaked around the bend. Torchlight, flickering. Voices underneath the screaming, calm and conversational. Professional.

Selene eased her head around the corner.

The chamber was small. Maybe twenty feet across. Three men in Guild browns stood around a fourth man who'd been tied to a chair. The chair was bolted to the floor. Old bolts. This room had been used for this purpose before.

The man in the chair was maybe forty. Hard to tell through the blood and swelling. His shirt had been torn open. His hands were bound to the armrests, fingers splayed and held in place by leather straps.

One of the Guild men was holding a thin metal rod. A pin, really. Long and sharp. He was saying something Selene couldn't quite hear, his tone patient, almost bored. Then he slid the pin under the bound man's fingernail.

The scream that followed was inhuman. The kind of sound that came from somewhere deeper than the throat. The man thrashed against his bonds, chair legs scraping against stone, but there was nowhere to go. The straps held.

The Guild man waited until the screaming subsided into ragged sobbing. Then he asked his question again. Same patient tone. Same bored inflection.

The bound man shook his head. Said something. Pleading, from the sound of it.

The Guild man shrugged and reached for another finger.

Selene pulled back. Mirael was pressed against the wall beside her, face pale in the darkness. She'd seen it too.

"We can't," Mirael breathed. The words were barely audible. "Three of them. More nearby, probably. We'd die and he'd still be in that chair."

Selene knew she was right. The odds were clean and ugly. Three armed men. Confined space. She could take one before they knew she was there, maybe two. But tunnels carried sound, and sound brought bodies, and bodies meant dying tired instead of dying quick. The screaming started again. Louder this time. More desperate.

"There's a water trough," Mirael said. Her voice had gone flat. Detached. The voice she used when she was forcing herself not to feel something. "Against the far wall. I saw buckets."

Selene had seen them too. She knew what they were for. Hold a man's head under until his lungs burned and his body started shutting down. Pull him up just before he drowned. Let him gasp and choke and remember what breathing felt like. Then do it again.

They weren't just killing him. They were making him useful first. "We keep moving," Selene said.

"Selene."

"We keep moving."

She turned away from the light. Away from the screaming. Found the thread Mirael had left marking their path and followed it deeper into the dark.

Behind them, the sounds continued. Then stopped. Then started again, different now. Wetter. The man had stopped screaming words and started making other sounds. Animal sounds. The sounds of someone who'd stopped waiting for rescue and started hoping for death.

They walked until they couldn't hear it anymore. It took longer than it should have.

***

Neither of them spoke for a long time after that.

The tunnels pressed in. The darkness felt heavier. Selene's hands wouldn't stop shaking, a fine tremor she couldn't control. It wasn't fear. It was aftermath. Rage with nowhere to go.

She'd seen violence before. She'd committed violence before. But there was something about the patience of it. The methodology. The way the Guild man had asked his questions in that bored tone, like he was filling out paperwork instead of destroying a human being one nerve at a time.

This was what they did. This was what happened to people who got caught.

This was what would happen to her and Mirael if they failed tonight.

"The storage chamber should be close," Mirael said eventually. Her voice was still flat. Still detached. "Another hundred yards, maybe."

Selene nodded. Didn't trust her voice.

They moved.

***

The vault was impossible to miss.

Heavy iron doors, newer than anything else they'd seen down here. Reinforced with bands of steel and fitted with locks that would take hours to pick. Someone had invested serious coin in keeping this room sealed.

Through a gap where the doors didn't quite meet, Selene could see what was inside. Her breath caught.

Gold. Stacks of it. Coins piled in wooden chests, some of them overflowing onto the stone floor. Silver too, and gems that caught the torchlight and threw it back in colors she didn't have names for. Bolts of silk. Carved ivory. A small fortune in spices, the kind that cost more than houses in the districts where she'd grown up.

This wasn't smuggled goods. This was a treasury. The accumulated wealth of decades of Guild operations, hidden away where the tax collectors and the Trade Council and anyone else who might ask inconvenient questions would never find it.

Two men stood guard on either side of the doors.

Selene had seen big men before. Dock workers with shoulders like oxen. Enforcers who'd been bred for intimidation. But these two were something else. They made the doorframe look small. Their arms were thicker than Selene's thighs, and their hands could have palmed her entire head with room to spare.

They were also, she noticed, impressively hairy. Dark fur covered their forearms, crept up their necks, probably continued under their leather armor in ways she didn't want to imagine. One of them scratched absently at his chest, and the sound was audible from twenty feet away.

"Think they have to shave their backs before putting the armor on?" Selene whispered.

Mirael's lips twitched. The first sign of anything other than that flat detachment since the torture chamber. "Probably use a horse brush."

"Or just let it grow through the leather. Natural padding."

It wasn't funny. Nothing about tonight was funny. But they needed this. A moment of something that wasn't horror or fear or the weight of what they'd witnessed.

"We're not getting in there," Mirael said, sobering.

"Wasn't planning on it." Selene pulled back from the corner. "But now we know where the Guild keeps its real wealth. That's worth something."

They marked the location on Mirael's map. Another piece of intelligence. Another bargaining chip if they survived long enough to use it.

Deeper.

***

The storage chamber wasn't guarded by giants.

Selene saw the light first. A faint glow from around a corner, the kind of light that shouldn't exist this far underground. She grabbed Mirael's arm, pulled her back against the wall, extinguished their lantern with her palm. The darkness was immediate and total.

They waited. Listened.

Voices. Low, muffled by stone, but definitely voices. Two men, maybe three. The cadence of bored conversation. Regular guards, not the hulking treasury watchdogs.

Selene's hand found her knife. She felt Mirael's tension beside her, coiled and ready.

They crept forward. Inch by inch. The glow brightened as they approached the corner. Selene pressed herself flat against the wall and eased her head around just far enough to see.

A larger chamber. Actual torches mounted in iron brackets, throwing dancing shadows across stacked crates and barrels. Three men in the brown coats of Guild Watchers, sitting around an overturned crate playing cards. Their weapons leaned against the wall within reach but not in hand. Comfortable. Confident that no one would find them this deep.

Beyond them, more crates. Dozens of them. Marked with symbols Selene didn't recognize. Whatever the Guild was moving, this was a waystation. A transfer point.

She pulled back. Found Mirael's ear in the darkness.

"Three Watchers. Armed but relaxed. Cargo behind them."

"Can we go around?"

Selene thought about the tunnel layout. The map Mirael had pieced together. "Maybe. But we need to know what's in those crates."

"That's not the job."

"The job is intel. That's intel."

A pause. Then Mirael's breath against her cheek, resigned. "How do you want to do this?"

Selene considered. Three men. Confined space. No clean escape route if things went wrong. But they were comfortable. Not expecting trouble. That was an advantage.

"Wait here. If I'm not back in ten minutes, find another way."

She didn't wait for Mirael's answer.

***

The first Watcher died without knowing she was there.

Selene came up from behind, knife across his throat, hand over his mouth. The wet gurgle was quieter than conversation. She lowered his body to the ground, eased him between two crates where he wouldn't be immediately visible.

The second Watcher looked up at the wrong moment. His eyes went wide. His mouth opened to shout.

Selene's thrown knife caught him in the throat. He went down clawing at his neck, making sounds that weren't quite words. She was on him before he hit the ground, finishing what the throw had started.

The third Watcher was faster. He had his sword half-drawn when Selene reached him, managed to get it between them, managed to land a glancing blow across her ribs that would bruise ugly tomorrow. But he was panicked and she was calm. She got inside his guard, got her knife under his chin, felt the resistance and then the give.

He slid down the wall, leaving a dark smear on the stone.

Selene stood in the torchlight, breathing hard. Her ribs throbbed. Blood on her hands, her clothes, her face. She didn't bother figuring out how much was hers. Mirael emerged from the darkness. Her expression was careful. Neutral. The expression she wore when she was deciding whether or not to say something.

"Ten minutes," she said. "You had ten minutes."

"Didn't need them."

They moved to the crates. Selene pried one open while Mirael stood watch, knife in hand, eyes on the tunnels.

Inside: weapons. Good ones. Steel that gleamed in the torchlight, wrapped in oiled cloth. Swords, daggers, crossbow bolts. Military grade. Not the rough iron the Guild usually moved.

"Someone's arming for something," Selene said.

Mirael checked another crate. "Coin here. Silver. A lot of it."

A third crate held documents. Stacks of them, bundled and sealed. Selene broke one seal, scanned the contents. Shipping routes. Names. Dates. A map of the tunnel network that was more complete than anything Mirael had assembled.

"We need copies of this."

"We don't have time. Someone will check on these guards eventually."

"Then work fast."

They worked. Mirael sketching the map from memory, her hand moving in quick strokes. Selene copying names, dates, anything that looked important. The documents painted a picture of something larger than smuggling. Coordination between factions. Movement of resources toward a specific date.

Something was coming. Something the Guild was preparing for.

"Selene."

Mirael's voice had changed. Selene looked up.

Footsteps. Coming from the tunnel they'd used to enter. Multiple sets, moving fast.

"They know we're here."

Selene grabbed the documents she'd copied, shoved them into her belt. Left the rest. No time.

"The other tunnel. Move."

They ran.

***

The chase was a nightmare of darkness and stone.

Selene's lungs burned. The bruise on her ribs screamed with every breath. Behind them, torchlight bounced off the walls, getting closer. Voices shouting. Commands in the clipped efficiency of Guild enforcement.

Mirael led, her mental map guiding them through junctions Selene couldn't have navigated alone. Two turns, then a hard drop that turned their run into a controlled slide. Water at the bottom, ankle-deep, cold as death. They splashed through it, the sound echoing everywhere.

"This way." Mirael's voice was ragged. "There's a collapse point. Old section. They might not follow."

Or they might. But there were no better options.

The tunnel narrowed. Tightened. Selene felt the walls pressing in, felt the ceiling dropping, felt the old fear clawing at her chest. She forced it down. Kept moving.

Behind them, closer now. Torchlight catching up. Someone shouted something about corners, about cutting them off.

The passage opened into a larger space. A junction of some kind, multiple tunnels branching off in different directions. Old stone, crumbling in places. Wooden supports that had rotted to nothing, leaving the ceiling to sag under its own weight.

"Which way?"

Mirael spun, orienting herself. "I don't . . . this isn't on any map. We're past the surveyed sections."

The torchlight was almost on them. Selene could hear individual voices now, individual footsteps.

"Pick one."

"I don't know where they go."

"Pick one anyway."

Mirael pointed. The smallest tunnel, half-collapsed, barely large enough to squeeze through. "That one. If we can get through, they might not be able to follow."

They squeezed.

Selene went first this time, forcing her body through the gap, feeling stone scrape against her back, her chest, her face. The darkness was absolute. She couldn't see Mirael behind her, could only hear her breathing, feel her hand occasionally brushing Selene's boot.

The tunnel went on. And on. Getting tighter instead of looser. Selene's shoulders jammed. She twisted, forced herself forward, felt something tear. Kept going.

Behind them, muffled by stone, she heard the Watchers reach the junction. Heard them arguing about which way. Heard someone suggest they couldn't fit through the gap.

Then she heard nothing at all.

The tunnel opened. Suddenly, unexpectedly. Selene tumbled forward into empty space, hit stone hard enough to drive the air from her lungs. Mirael came through a moment later, landing on top of her in a tangle of limbs.

They lay there. Breathing. Listening.

No pursuit. No torchlight. Just darkness and silence and the sound of their own ragged breathing.

"This," Mirael said between gasps, "was a terrible idea."

"You mentioned that. Several times."

"We're lost. Completely lost. No map, no markers, no way back through Guild territory." Mirael pushed herself up, found the lantern, struck a match with shaking hands. "How exactly did you think this was going to end?"

"I'm sorry, was I supposed to learn tunnels at some cutpurse academy?" Selene sat up, wincing at the new collection of bruises. "Maybe you got that class. Along with your table manners and proper curtseying."

"I didn't go to finishing school."

"Could've fooled me. You hold a knife like you're worried about your table manners."

Mirael's mouth twitched despite herself. "I hold a knife like someone who knows which end goes in the other person."

"And yet here we are. Lost underground. Your map. Your research."

"Your stupid decision to kill three Watchers instead of going around them."

"They were between us and the intel."

"The intel we can't deliver if we die down here."

They glared at each other in the flickering lantern light. Then Selene snorted. Then Mirael's shoulders started shaking. It wasn't quite laughter. More like the sound pressure makes when it has to go somewhere.

"We're going to die in a hole," Mirael said. "And the last thing I'll hear is you making fun of my table manners."

"There are worse ways to go."

"Name one."

Selene thought about the man in the chair. The pins. The patient, bored questions.

"I can think of a few."

The almost-laughter died. They both remembered what they'd seen.

"Where are we?" Selene's voice came out hoarse.

Mirael held up the lantern, letting the light spread across their surroundings.

A chamber. Not the storage rooms they'd seen before. Something older. Something different.

The walls were carved clean. Deliberate. Someone had taken time down here. Patterns ran along the stone, worn smooth in places like hands had passed there. The ceiling arched high overhead, lost in shadows even the lantern couldn't reach.

And ahead, barely visible in the flickering light, three stone pedestals stood in a row.

Selene pushed herself up. Her whole body hurt. The bruise on her ribs had company now. But she was alive. They were both alive.

"We need to find another way out," Mirael said. "There has to be something on the other side."

"There has to be."

They started walking deeper into the chamber. Behind them, the tunnel they'd squeezed through held nothing but sealed stone and silence.

CHAPTER 12: The Chamber

The chamber was older than anything they'd seen.

Selene could feel it in the air. The weight of centuries pressing down, thick as the dust that coated every surface. The lantern light seemed weaker here, swallowed by shadows that didn't want to give way.

She moved toward the pedestals. The first, empty. The second, shattered. The third still held what it had been made to hold.

Two daggers lay crossed on its surface. Dark metal that seemed to drink the lantern light rather than reflect it. Even from ten feet away, Selene could see the craftsmanship. The balance. The way the blades caught what little light there was and held it like a secret.

"Those aren't Guild," Mirael said quietly. She'd moved closer, studying the daggers with the professional assessment of someone who'd handled a lot of weapons. "I've never seen metal like that."

Selene hadn't either. The blades were dark, almost black, but with a depth to the color that suggested layers rather than surface. Old steel. Older than the Guild, older than Garnath, maybe older than anything she had a name for.

Papers were scattered around the base of the pedestal. Yellowed with age, curling at the edges, covered in handwriting that made Selene's chest tighten before she understood why.

She knew that handwriting.

She'd seen it on the backs of recipes, on lists pinned to the kitchen wall, on the note her mother had left the morning of the fire telling her father she'd gone to market and would be back before noon.

"Selene." Mirael's voice had changed. Careful now. Watching.

"That's my mother's writing."

The words came out flat. Distant. Like someone else was saying them from very far away.

She crossed to the pedestal, stepping over scattered papers, and picked up the nearest one. The ink had faded but the words were still legible. Notes. Observations. A diagram of something she didn't recognize, labeled in her mother's careful hand.

The third set remains sealed. We've documented its location but accessing the chamber would require resources we don't have. Araveth believes the stories are myth. I'm not certain. The craftsmanship suggests otherwise.

Araveth. Her father's name. Written in her mother's hand, in a chamber that had been sealed for who knew how long.

They'd been here. Her parents had been here, in this exact room, studying these exact daggers. Before Selene was born, maybe. Before everything.

"There's more." Mirael had moved to the far side of the chamber, where papers had drifted against the wall. She was crouched down, sorting through them with quick, efficient hands. "Maps. More notes. It looks like they were researching something."

Selene should go look. Should help sort through whatever her parents had left behind. But she couldn't move. Couldn't stop staring at the daggers on the pedestal, dark and patient, waiting like they'd been waiting for a very long time.

"I'm going to touch them," she said.

"Selene, wait. We don't know what they'll do to you."

"I'm going to touch them."

Mirael stood. Crossed to the pedestal. Put herself between Selene and the daggers.

"Let me." Her voice was steady. Professional. The voice she used when she was about to do something she didn't want to do. "If something's wrong with them, better to find out with me than with you."

Selene wanted to argue. But Mirael was already reaching out, her fingers extending toward the nearest blade.

She touched the hilt.

The sound she made wasn't quite a scream. More like a gasp that got caught halfway out, strangled by surprise and pain. She jerked her hand back, cradling it against her chest.

"Mirael." Selene moved toward her.

"I'm fine." But her voice was tight, and when she uncurled her fingers, Selene could see the marks. Red welts across her palm and fingers, like she'd grabbed a heated brand. "Cold." Her voice was tight. "Not heat. Cold that burns. I've read about this. I didn't think it was real." The daggers sat on their pedestal, unchanged. Patient. Waiting.

Selene reached past Mirael.

"Don't." But Selene was already reaching.

Her fingers closed around the first hilt.

Warmth.

It wasn't heat. Nothing that burned. Just warmth, spreading up from the grip into her hand, her wrist, her arm. Like holding something that had been sitting in sunlight. Like coming home after a long winter night.

The dagger fit her hand like it had been made for her. The weight was perfect. The balance was perfect. Everything about it felt right in a way that nothing had in a very long time.

And then the name was there.

Vael'thera.

She didn't hear it. Didn't see it written anywhere. The word was simply present, filling a space in her mind she hadn't known was empty. It wasn't whispered or bestowed. Just there, like it had always been there and she'd only just noticed. The way you suddenly become aware of your own heartbeat in a quiet room.

She reached for the second dagger.

Nyrixel.

Same warmth. Same perfect fit. Same sense of a name sliding into place like a key into a lock she'd been carrying her whole life without knowing.

Vael'thera. Nyrixel.

She would never speak them. Not to Mirael. Not to anyone. They existed now in that private space behind her eyes where she kept the things that were only hers. The names her parents had called her before they died. The sound of her mother's laugh. The feeling of her father's hand on her head. And now these. Two more secrets to carry in silence.

The daggers were warm in her hands. Both of them. Waiting.

And then nothing.

***

"Selene!"

Hands on her shoulders. Shaking her. Hard.

"Selene, wake up. Wake up!"

She blinked. The chamber swam back into focus. Mirael's face was inches from hers, pale beneath the dust, eyes wide with something that looked like terror.

"What . . ." Selene's voice came out rough. Wrong. Like she'd been asleep for hours.

"You were gone." Mirael's hands were still gripping her shoulders, fingers digging in hard enough to bruise. "You touched those things and you just . . . stopped. Eyes open. Not moving. Not breathing." Her voice cracked. "I thought you were dead. I thought they killed you."

Selene looked down. The daggers were in her hands. She didn't remember picking up the second one. Didn't remember anything after the names had surfaced.

"How long?"

"I don't know. Minutes. It felt like hours." Mirael let go of her shoulders, stepped back, wrapped her arms around herself like she was trying to hold something in. "Your eyes were wrong. Dark. Like something was looking out through them that wasn't you."

Selene tested her grip on the daggers. Still warm. Still perfectly balanced. Still hers in a way she couldn't explain and didn't want to examine too closely.

"I'm fine."

"You weren't fine. You were somewhere else."

"I'm here now."

Mirael stared at her. The expression on her face was complicated. Fear, yes. But something else underneath it. Something that looked like grief.

"They didn't want me," she said quietly. "They burned me. But they . . . what? Welcomed you? Claimed you?"

"I don't know what happened." That was true. The missing time sat in her memory like a hole in fabric. She remembered the names. Remembered the warmth. Then nothing until Mirael's hands shaking her back to consciousness.

"Put them down."

"No."

The word came out before Selene could think about it. Automatic. Certain. And that certainty scared her more than the missing time, more than the names that had appeared from nowhere, more than Mirael's terrified face.

She didn't want to put them down. The thought of setting them aside, of walking away and leaving them on that pedestal, felt wrong in a way that made her stomach clench.

"They're just blades," she said. The words felt like a lie even as she spoke them. "Good ones. Old ones. But just blades."

Mirael didn't look convinced. But she didn't argue.

"We should take everything we can carry," Selene said. "The papers. Whatever else is here. We can sort through it later."

She slid the daggers into her belt. They settled against her hips like they'd always been there. Like they'd been waiting for exactly this shape to hold them.

Vael'thera on her left. Nyrixel on her right.

Names she would carry in silence for the rest of her life.

Mirael had already turned back to the scattered papers against the wall. Her movements were quick now. Urgent. Gathering documents, folding them, stuffing them into her pack.

Selene joined her, scooping up loose pages, trying not to look too closely at her mother's handwriting. There would be time for that later. Time to read every word, to understand what her parents had been doing here, what they'd been looking for.

Time to find out what had gotten them killed.

***

Mirael found the letter while Selene was on the other side of the chamber.

It was tucked between two pages of notes, sealed with wax that had cracked with age. The handwriting on the outside wasn't Selene's mother's. Someone else. Official and formal, the kind of handwriting that came from people who gave orders.

She broke the seal. Read the contents.

And went very still.

Names. Dates. A chain of command spelled out in cold, bureaucratic language. An order for elimination, signed and countersigned, referencing the Araveth research and the threat it posed to certain parties who preferred their secrets to stay buried.

Not an accident. Not a random fire. A sanctioned killing, approved by people who still held power. People whose names Mirael recognized from Guild ledgers, from Trade Council documents, from the web of corruption that ran through Garnath like rot through wood.

If Selene saw this, she would burn the city down to get to them.

And she would die doing it. Because these weren't street-level criminals or Guild enforcers. These were the people who owned the street-level criminals and Guild enforcers. The ones who never got their hands dirty because they had entire organizations to do it for them.

Selene would try anyway. Mirael knew her. Knew the cold fire that burned underneath all that emptiness. Give her a target and she'd become a weapon aimed at it, and she wouldn't stop until she hit it or it destroyed her.

Mirael folded the letter. Slipped it into the inner pocket of her jacket, the one she used for documents too important to lose.

"Find anything?" Selene's voice from across the chamber.

"More notes. Maps. Research." Mirael kept her voice steady. Kept gathering papers like nothing had changed. "Your parents were thorough."

"They were scholars before they were anything else."

They were targeted, Mirael didn't say. *They were murdered by people who are still alive. People you could reach if you knew where to look.*

She sealed the pocket. Kept the secret.

Later, when they were safe, when they were out of this hole, she would figure out what to do. Maybe she'd find a way to use the information without telling Selene. Maybe she'd find a way to take those people down quietly, without Selene throwing herself at them like a blade aimed at her own destruction.

Or maybe she'd just hold onto it. Keep it buried like those people had tried to bury Selene's parents. Protect Selene from the truth that would get her killed.

It wasn't right. Mirael knew that. But right and alive weren't always the same thing.

***

The rumble started deep in the stone.

Selene felt it before she heard it. A vibration running through the floor, up through her boots, into her bones. Dust sifted down from the ceiling in thin streams.

"That's not good." Mirael was already moving toward the far side of the chamber, where a second passage opened into darkness. "The supports are failing."

"We just got here."

"And now we're leaving. Move."

More rumbling. Louder this time. A crack appeared in the ceiling, running from one wall to the other like a wound opening. Stone groaned. Dust became a cascade.

Selene grabbed the last handful of papers within reach and ran.

The passage was narrow. Low. She had to duck to fit, Mirael right behind her, both of them moving as fast as the cramped space would allow. Behind them, the sound of collapse. Stone hitting stone. The chamber they'd just left, sealing itself shut with the finality of a tomb.

The passage twisted and climbed. Selene lost track of direction, of distance, of everything except the need to keep moving, to stay ahead of the collapse that was chasing them through the dark.

Then light.

Real light. Grey and pale, filtering down from somewhere above.

Daylight.

CHAPTER 13: Emergence

Dawn came grey and cold.

Selene squeezed through the crack in the foundation wall first, stone scraping against her ribs, her shoulders, every bruise she'd collected in the night screaming as she forced herself through. She tumbled into an alley between two buildings that had seen better centuries, hit the cobblestones hard.

Behind her, Mirael's breath came in sharp gasps. The crack was narrow, and Mirael was stuck halfway, one arm through, the rest of her wedged against crumbling stone.

"I can't . . ." Her voice was thin. Panicked.

Selene turned back. Reached through the gap. Found Mirael's hand and gripped it.

"I've got you. Exhale and push."

Mirael's fingers tightened around hers. Desperate. Trusting. For a moment they were just two women who'd kept each other alive for fourteen years, and nothing else mattered.

Mirael exhaled. Pushed. Selene pulled.

She came through in a scrape of fabric and skin, and they both collapsed against the alley wall, breathing hard.

The sky overhead was the color of dirty wool. The air tasted like rain and woodsmoke and the particular stench of Garnath waking up. Somewhere nearby, a cart rattled over cobblestones. A dog barked. The city was starting its day like nothing had happened. Like two women hadn't just crawled out of its bones carrying weapons that shouldn't exist.

Mirael's face was grey with dust, blood dried in a streak down her temple from a cut she'd gotten in the collapse. Her hands were shaking. The burn marks from the daggers' rejection had faded to angry red welts across her palms.

She kept flexing her fingers. Opening and closing them like she was checking they still worked. Like they belonged to someone else now.

They'd been underground all night. It felt like longer.

"We need to move," Mirael said. Her voice was hoarse. "We're exposed here."

"I know."

But neither of them moved. Not yet. The exhaustion was too heavy, pressing them down against the stones like gravity had doubled overnight.

Selene looked at the daggers at her hips. Drew one, just to feel it in her hand again.

Vael'thera.

The name surfaced unbidden, the way it had in the chamber. Private. Certain. Hers.

The blade caught the grey morning light, dark metal drinking the illumination rather than reflecting it. It was warm in her grip. Comfortable. Like it had always been there and she'd just been too distracted to notice.

"They burned me."

Mirael's voice was quiet. Flat.

Selene looked at her.

Mirael held up her hands, palms out. The welts had faded to pale pink but she studied them like they still held answers.

"I've been thinking about it," she said. "The rejection. There's nothing in any text I've read about relics choosing. But that's what it felt like. A choice."

Selene slid the dagger back into her belt. She didn't have an answer. Didn't want to think about what the answer might be.

"I don't know."

"That's not good enough."

"It's what I have."

Mirael stared at her. Something moved behind her eyes. Pain, maybe. Or something older than pain. Something that had been building for fourteen years and finally found a shape it couldn't ignore.

"We should find somewhere safe," Selene said. "Get cleaned up. Figure out what we actually brought back from down there."

She pushed herself to her feet. Her whole body screamed. Her ribs felt like someone had used them for drum practice. But standing was possible, and standing meant moving, and moving meant surviving.

Mirael didn't argue. She just pushed herself up and followed.

The silence between them was heavier than it had been in years.

***

They found a room.

Not the safehouse. That was burned, probably, or watched at minimum. Not Viena's either. Too obvious. Too many eyes that might talk for the right price.

This was a room above a tannery in the Narrows. The smell was appalling, which meant no one came here unless they had to. The owner asked no questions and accepted payment in coin that didn't clink too loudly.

Selene stripped off her ruined jacket, catalogued her injuries in the cracked mirror. Bruised ribs, probably cracked. Scraped hands. A gash on her shoulder she didn't remember getting. Nothing that would kill her. Nothing that would stop her.

The daggers sat on the bed beside her. She couldn't bring herself to put them further away.

Nyrixel.

The second name, surfacing like the first. She hadn't said either of them aloud. Wasn't sure she ever would. They existed in that space behind her eyes where she kept the things that were only hers.

In the corner of the room, Mirael was going through her pack. Sorting the papers they'd grabbed from the chamber. Her mother's research. Whatever else they'd managed to salvage before the ceiling came down.

And the letter.

Mirael's hands paused on her jacket. The inner pocket. The one she used for documents too important to lose.

The letter was still there. She could feel its weight like a stone against her chest.

***

Names. Dates. A chain of command.

Mirael had read it twice in the chamber, committing the details to memory even as she'd decided Selene could never see it. Now, in the thin morning light filtering through the tannery's grimy window, she read it again.

The handwriting was official. Formal. The kind that came from people who signed death warrants and then went home to dinner.

Re: Araveth inquiry. Assets confirmed. Research poses unacceptable risk to Council operations. Recommend permanent closure. Authorization granted.

That was it. Seventeen years of grief reduced to three sentences. A family burned because someone decided their questions were inconvenient.

And the names at the bottom. The signatures. People who still walked Garnath's streets. Still sat on councils. Still breathed.

If Selene saw this, she would hunt them. And they would kill her for it.

Mirael folded the letter. Unfolded it. Folded it again.

She deserves to know.

Knowing gets her killed.

The argument went in circles. Every time, it landed in the same place.

Right and alive weren't always the same thing.

***

Selene was asleep.

Not deeply. Never deeply. But enough that her breathing had steadied, her body finally surrendering to the exhaustion it had been fighting all night. The daggers were still on the bed beside her, close enough to grab. She'd positioned herself between them and the door without seeming to think about it.

Mirael watched her for a long moment. The sharp lines of her face, softened slightly by sleep. The scars she'd accumulated over seventeen years of surviving. The way her hand rested near the daggers even in unconsciousness, like some part of her was already learning to reach for them first.

Something had changed in that chamber. Something Mirael couldn't name and didn't want to examine too closely. The daggers had rejected her and claimed Selene, and that rejection felt like more than just metal being picky about who held it.

But that was a problem for later. Right now, there was a more immediate one.

The letter in her pocket. The names. The truth that would burn Selene alive if she ever found it.

Mirael crossed to the small fireplace. The tannery kept a fire going year-round, something about the curing process. The flames were low but steady, orange light flickering against soot-blackened stone.

She took out the letter.

Held it for a moment. Feeling the weight of it. The paper was old, edges soft with age, but the words were still clear. Still damning. Still capable of destroying everything.

Last chance, she told herself. *Last chance to do the right thing.*

But the right thing and the safe thing had stopped being the same thing a long time ago. Maybe they'd never been the same thing at all.

She fed the letter to the flames.

The paper caught immediately, edges curling black, the careful handwriting disappearing into ash and smoke. The names went first. Then the dates. Then the authorization that had murdered Selene's family seventeen years ago.

Gone.

Mirael watched until there was nothing left but grey ash mixed with the soot of a thousand other fires. No evidence. No proof. Nothing for anyone else to find and use against Selene.

Nothing for Selene to find and use against herself.

She looked down at her hands. Ash on her fingers. She didn't brush it off. The smell of burned paper clung to her sleeves, her hair. She'd carry that smell for days. Would smell it in her dreams.

Her hands trembled. Just once. She forced them still.

This was what they did. The people who signed that letter. The ones who decided what truths other people deserved to know. They made choices for everyone else and called it protection.

She'd hated them for seventeen years. Now she was one of them.

The weight in Mirael's chest didn't lift. If anything, it settled deeper. Became permanent.

She'd carry this for the rest of her life. The names. The truth. The choice she'd made to bury it.

And Selene would never know.

***

"Don't turn around."

Selene kept walking. Kept her pace steady. "How many?"

"Three. Maybe four. They picked us up at the last corner."

"Guild?"

"Guild. The way they're moving. Spread formation, watching the exits."

Selene's mind raced. They could try to lose them in the crowd, but the streets were thinning as they moved away from the main thoroughfares. They could double back, but that risked running into more of them.

The alley opened to their left. Narrow. Dark. The kind of space where things happened that nobody saw.

"In here," Selene said. "Better to face them than let them pick the ground."

Mirael didn't argue. They slipped into the shadows between buildings, moving fast, putting distance between themselves and the street. Behind them, footsteps quickened. The pretense of casual surveillance dropped.

Selene turned. Drew the daggers.

The motion was automatic. She didn't think about it, didn't plan it. Her hands just moved, and suddenly *Vael'thera* and *Nyrixel* were in her grip, warm and balanced and ready.

Four men entered the alley mouth. Big. Armed. The kind of muscle the Guild used for work that needed doing quietly. And Selene recognized one of them. The scarred face. The broken nose. He'd been in the tunnels. He'd been one of the ones chasing them through the dark.

"That's her," he said. "That's the one who killed Brennan."

They spread out. Professional. They'd done this before. Four against two in a confined space, and they had reach and numbers and probably backup a whistle away.

Selene should have been afraid. Should have been calculating odds, looking for escape routes, preparing to run.

Instead, she felt calm. Clear. Like the world had slowed down and she was the only thing still moving at normal speed.

The first man came at her fast. Knife in hand, going for her throat.

She moved.

Not the way she usually moved. Faster. Lighter. Like her body had forgotten it was supposed to be tired, supposed to be injured, supposed to be carrying the weight of a night spent crawling through collapsing tunnels. The daggers pulled her through the motion, or maybe she pulled them. She couldn't tell the difference.

Vael'thera opened his arm from wrist to elbow. He screamed. Dropped the knife.

The second man was already swinging. A club, heavy wood, aimed at her skull. Selene ducked under it, felt the wind of its passing, and *Nyrixel* found the soft space between his ribs. He folded. Didn't get back up.

Two down. Heartbeats. She'd taken two men down in heartbeats.

The scarred man hung back. Smart. He'd seen what she could do now. He was reassessing, recalculating, trying to figure out how two exhausted women had just become something else entirely.

The fourth man broke. Turned to run. Mirael's knife caught him in the back of the thigh and he went down hard, screaming, crawling toward the alley mouth.

That left the scarred one.

He looked at Selene. At the daggers in her hands, dark metal slick with blood. At the two men on the ground, one groaning, one silent. At his friend trying to drag himself away with a blade in his leg.

"What the hells are you?" he asked.

Selene didn't answer. She didn't know the answer. Ten seconds ago she'd been a tired smuggler with new weapons. Now she felt like something else. Something that had always been sleeping inside her and had just woken up.

The scarred man ran.

She let him go. Let him carry the story back to whoever had sent him. Let him describe what he'd seen. Let the fear spread.

"Selene." Mirael's voice, behind her. Quiet. Careful. "Your hands."

Selene looked down. The daggers were still in her grip. Still warm. Still perfectly balanced. The blood on them was already drying, darkening against the dark metal.

Her hands weren't shaking. They should have been shaking. After a fight like that, after killing a man, her hands always shook. But they were steady. Certain. Like the daggers had drained the tremor right out of her.

She knew this feeling. Had known it since she was seven years old, crouched in a cupboard while her world burned. The emptiness that came when feeling was too expensive. She'd built that hollow place herself, brick by brick, year by year.

The daggers fit there perfectly.

"I'm fine," she said.

"You're not fine. That was . . ." Mirael trailed off. Her mouth opened, closed. Tried again. "I don't know what that was. But it wasn't you."

"Better weapons."

"That wasn't better weapons. That was something else."

Mirael was looking at her strangely. Not with anger or confusion. With something worse.

Caution.

The kind of look you gave a dog you weren't sure was tame anymore.

It lasted half a heartbeat. Then Mirael's face shifted, smoothed, became familiar again. But Selene had seen it. And Mirael knew she'd seen it.

Neither of them said anything.

Selene slid the daggers back into her belt. The warmth of them settled against her hips. Comfortable. Right.

She didn't want to think about what had just happened. Didn't want to examine why she'd moved like that, felt like that, killed like that. The daggers were tools. Superior tools. That was all.

That had to be all.

"Come on," she said. "We still need to collect from Viena."

They left the alley. Behind them, one man dead, two wounded, one fled. The evening crowd on the main street hadn't noticed a thing.

Just another bit of violence in a city built on it.

***

Daven had been watching all day.

He'd picked up their trail at dawn, near the old cistern access points. He'd been waiting there since before first light. Not hunting. Waiting. Because the job those two women had taken was supposed to end one way, and he'd wanted to confirm it.

The catacombs were good at swallowing people. The Guild patrols, the unstable tunnels, the sections that hadn't been mapped in centuries. Send someone down there without backup, without Guild authorization, and the odds of them coming back up were slim. That was the point. That was why the job had been created in the first place.

A quiet solution to a seventeen-year-old problem.

The dock worker's daughter had seen something she shouldn't have, back when she was seven years old. She probably didn't even remember it. Probably had no idea why her family had burned or who had signed the order. But loose threads had a way of unraveling, and Serith didn't like loose threads.

So the job had appeared. Anonymous client. Untraceable gold. A task that would take her exactly where she needed to go to disappear forever.

Except she hadn't disappeared.

He'd seen them emerge at dawn. Covered in dust and blood, moving like everything hurt. Alive when they shouldn't be.

He'd followed them to a tannery in the Narrows, waited while they rested, then followed them again when they emerged at dusk.

He was three streets behind them when the Guild men made their move. Four enforcers. Confined alley. The kind of numbers that should have ended it.

It didn't end it.

He watched from a rooftop as she cut through them like they were standing still. And that was when he got his first clear look at what she was carrying.

Dark metal at her hips. Two blades. Old craft, the kind that didn't exist anymore. She moved with them like she'd been born wearing them, like they were part of her body instead of just weapons.

His stomach dropped.

He'd killed people. Lots of people. It was his job, and he was good at it. But watching her walk out of that alley with blood still drying on her sleeves and those blades riding her hips like they'd always been there, he felt something he hadn't felt in years.

Fear. The real kind. The kind that made you want to walk the other way and pretend you'd never seen anything.

He didn't walk away, though. He had a job too.

But he wanted to.

She'd found something down there. In the sections that had been sealed for centuries. The sections that certain people had been searching for, spending fortunes trying to locate, killing to keep secret.

Relics.

The trap hadn't just failed. It had backfired. Serith had tried to eliminate a loose thread and instead had handed her weapons that made her infinitely more dangerous.

Daven watched them disappear into the evening crowds.

Then he moved. Fast.

***

Serith's man found him before he found Serith's man.

The grey-haired courier appeared at Daven's elbow like smoke, falling into step beside him without breaking stride. That was how it worked. You didn't summon Serith's people. They found you when you had something worth hearing.

"The catacombs job," Daven said, keeping his voice low. "It failed."

"Failed how?"

"They're alive. Both of them. Came up this morning through an old foundation access near the harbor."

The grey-haired man's expression didn't change. But his pace slowed slightly. Processing.

"That's unfortunate."

"It gets worse." Daven kept walking, kept his eyes forward, just two men having a conversation on a busy street. "She found something down there. Weapons. Old ones. Dark metal, ancient craft. The kind of relics people have been looking for."

Now the grey-haired man stopped. Just for a heartbeat. Just long enough to tell Daven that this information had weight.

"She has them? On her person?"

"At her hips. Like she'd been carrying them her whole life."

Silence. The evening crowd flowed around them, oblivious. A cart rattled past, laden with the day's unsold goods. The ordinary sounds of Garnath settling into night, completely unaware that something had just shifted in the architecture of power beneath its streets.

"Serith will need to know," the grey-haired man said finally.

"That's why I found you."

"The original order was to let the tunnels take her. Let the dark do the work."

"The tunnels didn't handle it. And now she's armed with something that certain people have spent years trying to find." Daven met the man's eyes. "This isn't a loose thread anymore. This is a problem. An active one."

The grey-haired man nodded slowly. Already calculating. Already seeing the shape of what would come next.

"New orders will be issued within the day," he said. "The dark didn't take her. Now we do it ourselves."

"Meaning?"

"Meaning the dock worker's daughter just moved to the top of the list." The grey-haired man's voice was flat. Professional. The voice of someone who arranged deaths the way other people arranged furniture. "Serith doesn't like it when his solutions create bigger problems. He likes it even less when those problems arm themselves with relics from the sealed sections."

He turned to go. Paused.

"Find her. Track her. Don't engage, not yet. But don't lose her either. When the order comes down, it'll come down fast."

Then he was gone, slipping into the crowd like he'd never been there at all.

Daven stood in the fading light, thinking about dark metal and ancient craft and a woman who should have died in the tunnels but hadn't.

Serith had tried to solve a problem quietly.

He'd made it worse.

And now someone was going to have to clean up the mess the loud way.

CHAPTER 14: The New Weight

The daggers woke her.

Not with sound. Not with movement. Just presence. The weight of them against her hips, warm through the thin blanket, pulling her up from sleep the way a hand on her shoulder might have done.

Selene lay still. Stared at the water-stained ceiling of the room they'd rented after leaving the tannery. Three days since the catacombs. Three days since the alley. Three days of moving from place to place, never staying long enough for patterns to form.

Vael'thera. Nyrixel.

The names were always there now. Background noise. Like her own heartbeat.

Mirael was already awake. Sitting by the window, watching the street below. The burn marks on her palms had faded to pink scars, but she still flexed her fingers sometimes. Checking. Remembering.

"Anything?" Selene asked.

"Quiet. Too quiet."

That was the problem. After the alley, after four Guild men went down and one ran back to tell the story, there should have been retaliation. Should have been muscle on every corner, questions in every tavern, pressure until they surfaced.

Instead, nothing.

The Guild was thinking. And the Guild thinking was worse than the Guild acting.

Selene sat up. The daggers shifted with her, settling into place like they'd been waiting for her to move. She didn't remember putting them on before she slept. She didn't remember taking them off either.

"We need money," Mirael said without turning around. "We've been bleeding coin for three days. Safe houses aren't free."

"I know."

"Viena's holding the second half of the catacombs payment. We never collected."

"I know."

Mirael finally turned. Her face was careful. Neutral. The face she wore when she was choosing not to say something.

"You want to go back there," Selene said.

"I want to eat next week. The Lantern is the only place that will still do business with us right now."

She was right. The jobs had dried up completely since the catacombs. Word traveled fast in Garnath, and the word traveling now was that Selene and Mirael had kicked a hornet's nest and come out carrying weapons that made certain people very nervous.

No one wanted to hire contractors who brought that kind of attention.

"Tonight," Selene said. "After dark."

***

They moved through the day like ghosts.

Separate routes. Timed check-ins. The old patterns from years ago, when they were young and hunted and hadn't yet learned that being hunted never really stopped.

Selene found herself in the Merchant Quarter by midday, walking streets she had no business walking, just to see if anyone was watching. Testing the shape of the cage.

People looked at her differently now.

She noticed it in the way they stepped aside. Not the usual give-way that came with hard eyes and a confident walk. Something else. Something in the way she moved now, the way she scanned corners without thinking, the way her hands stayed loose and ready. The daggers were hidden under her coat, but the rumors weren't. Word had spread about the alley. About what she'd done to four Guild men with blades no one had ever seen before.

A fruit vendor she'd bought from for years wouldn't meet her eyes. A beggar who usually asked for coin pressed himself against the wall as she passed. A group of dockworkers stopped their conversation mid-sentence and didn't start again until she was a full street away.

She should have felt powerful. Should have felt satisfied that the city was finally seeing her clearly.

Instead, she felt the distance. The space that opened around her wherever she walked. The way the world was pulling back, making room for something it didn't want to touch.

By afternoon, she'd confirmed what she already suspected.

The Guild wasn't hunting them. The Guild was containing them. Cutting off their options, their contacts, their income. Letting them starve in place while the people upstairs decided what to do about the woman who'd killed their men with weapons that shouldn't exist.

Smart. Patient. Terrifying.

***

The Veiled Lantern looked the same as it always did.

Warm light. Muffled music. The smell of perfume and woodsmoke leaking out whenever the door opened. A place that sold pleasure and information in equal measure, and never confused the two.

Selene went in alone. Mirael waited outside, in an alley across the street where she could watch both doors.

They didn't discuss why. Didn't need to.

Viena was in her office. Ledgers open. Quill in hand. The picture of a woman managing a business, not running an intelligence network that touched half the city's underworld.

"You're still alive," Viena said without looking up. "I heard conflicting reports."

"The reports were optimistic."

"Apparently." Viena set down her quill. Studied Selene with eyes that calculated everything and gave nothing away. "The second half of your payment. That's why you're here."

"That's why I'm here."

Viena opened a drawer. Counted out coins. Slid them across the desk.

"The client never collected their copy of the intelligence," she said. "Never made contact again. Whatever they wanted from those tunnels, it wasn't the information you gathered."

Selene took the coins. Didn't count them. Viena didn't cheat.

"They wanted us dead," she said. "The job was designed to kill us."

"I've considered that possibility."

"And?"

Viena leaned back in her chair. "And if I were the suspicious type, I might wonder who has the resources to create an anonymous commission, the knowledge to know you'd take a job into the catacombs, and the motivation to want you gone without fingerprints."

"That's a short list."

"Very short."

They looked at each other. Neither said Serith's name. Neither needed to.

"You're radioactive," Viena said. Not cruel. Just fact. "I can still move information. I can still hold coin. But work?" She shook her head. "Not while the air is this hot."

"How long?"

"Until someone bigger blinks. Until the people watching you decide you're predictable instead of explosive." Viena's eyes were steady. "You survived the catacombs. Now survive this. Come back when the heat dies down."

Selene had expected this. Had known it was coming since the alley.

Still. Hearing it said out loud made it real.

"The back rooms," she said. "Are they still open to me?"

"The workers choose their clients." A pause. "But yes. The Lantern is still neutral ground. That hasn't changed."

"Good."

Selene turned to leave.

"Selene."

She stopped. Didn't turn.

"Be careful what you carry," Viena said quietly. One clipped sentence. Then nothing.

Selene walked out without answering.

***

The worker's name was Lira.

Dark hair. Soft hands. A voice like honey and smoke. She'd been at the Lantern for three years, and Selene had been with her before. Had chosen her because Lira didn't ask questions and didn't expect anything. Easier. Less complicated. Bodies that knew the routine.

Tonight she didn't want easy.

The room was small and clean. Candles on the windowsill. Sheets that smelled like lavender. Lira moved toward her with practiced grace, fingers already working at the laces of Selene's shirt.

Selene let her. Helped her. Pulled at Lira's clothes in return, the familiar urgency building, the old pattern asserting itself. This was what she came for. Release. Distraction. The temporary obliteration of thought.

Their clothes fell away. Skin against skin. Lira's mouth found her neck, her collarbone, working lower with confident patience.

And Selene felt . . . nothing.

Not arousal. Not anticipation. Not even the mechanical readiness that usually carried her through these encounters. Just emptiness where the wanting should have been.

She tried. Pulled Lira closer. Kissed her harder. Tried to force her body into responding the way it was supposed to, the way it always had.

Nothing.

Lira pulled back. Studied her face with eyes that had seen this before, probably. The clients who came looking for one thing and needed something else entirely.

"Hey," she said softly. "What do you actually want?"

Selene opened her mouth to say something. Anything. The words that would get this back on track, that would make her body cooperate, that would give her the release she'd paid for.

Nothing came out.

She closed her eyes. Felt the weight of everything she wasn't saying pressing against the inside of her chest. The catacombs. The daggers. Mirael's face when she looked at her now. The way the whole city had pulled back like she was something dangerous. The loneliness that had been building for seventeen years and had finally become too heavy to ignore.

"Just . . ." Her voice came out rough. Wrong. "Just shut up and hold me."

Lira didn't ask questions. Didn't comment. Just shifted on the bed, opened her arms, and let Selene curl into them.

It was awkward at first. Selene didn't know how to do this. Didn't know how to accept softness without trying to turn it into something else. Her body kept tensing, kept waiting for the next move, kept expecting this to turn into the transaction she'd come for.

But Lira just held her. Warm and patient and present. One hand stroking her hair. The other resting on her back.

Selene's mouth opened again. She wanted to say something. Wanted to explain why she was here, what she was feeling, what had scraped her so raw she couldn't even want properly anymore.

The words wouldn't come.

They never did.

She lay there in the candlelight, wrapped in a stranger's arms, and felt the first real thing she'd felt in days: the ache of wanting to be known and having no idea how to let it happen.

When she left, she didn't look back. Didn't know if she'd ever come back. Something had shifted, and the old pattern didn't fit anymore.

Mirael was where she'd left her. Leaning against the alley wall, arms crossed, face turned away from the Lantern's back door.

"Done?"

"Done."

Mirael's eyes flicked to Selene's throat, to the flush that hadn't quite faded. Then away. Her jaw tightened once, and she pushed off the wall without another word.

They walked in silence. The streets were darker now, the evening crowds thinning, the city settling into its nighttime rhythms.

Mirael didn't ask what had happened inside. Didn't look at her with questions or judgment.

Just walked beside her. Close enough to touch. Miles away.

***

She saw Weston the next morning.

Not in the Narrows, where Paladins rarely bothered. In the Merchant Quarter, near the silversmith row where she had no business being. She'd been testing routes, looking for gaps in the net, and there he was.

Standing at the corner of two streets. Talking to a merchant. Taking notes in a small leather book.

He looked up as she passed.

Not at her face. At her hips. At the shape of the daggers under her coat.

His expression didn't change. No anger. No fear. Just the focused attention of a man cataloging something he'd have to deal with eventually. The look of someone who'd been watching a problem grow and had finally decided it was too big to ignore.

He opened his book to a page already marked with a ribbon. Wrote something down. Blotted the ink with the practiced motion of someone who'd done this a thousand times.

Closed the book.

Looked at her face now. Met her eyes across thirty feet of crowded street. Held her gaze for three heartbeats.

Then he turned and walked away.

No confrontation. No warning. No attempt to stop her or question her or do any of the things Paladins usually did when they spotted someone like her.

Just observation. Just record-keeping. Just the quiet acknowledgment that she had crossed some line that couldn't be uncrossed.

Selene kept walking. Kept her pace steady. Kept her hands away from the daggers even though every instinct told her to reach for them.

Behind her, Weston disappeared into the crowd.

She didn't tell Mirael about that either.

***

The next three days were worse.

Every contact they tried was closed. Every favor they called in was suddenly unavailable. Every safe house they'd used in the past decade had heard something, seen something, decided something that made them shake their heads and close their doors.

Maren was the worst.

She'd fenced goods for Selene and Mirael for six years. Had always met them in her back room, offered tea, haggled like it was a game they both enjoyed. Now she wouldn't even open the door all the way. Just a crack. Just wide enough to pass coins through.

"I'm sorry," she said. Her voice was thin. Scared. "I'm sorry, I can't. You understand. You have to understand."

"Maren . . ."

"Please don't come back. Please." The coins appeared in the crack. Payment for the last job, months overdue. "This is everything I owe. We're square. Please."

The door closed. Selene heard the bolt slide home. Then a second bolt. Then something heavy being dragged across the floor.

That was the shape of it now. People who'd known them for years treating them like plague carriers. Apologizing while they locked their doors. Paying debts just to sever the connection.

The net was tightening. Slowly. Patiently. The kind of squeeze that didn't need violence because it had time.

On the fourth day, Selene saw Daven.

Just a glimpse. A familiar shape on a rooftop three streets away, there for a heartbeat and then gone. Could have been anyone.

Could have been her imagination, frayed nerves finding threats in shadows.

But she knew.

He was tracking them. Had been tracking them since the catacombs, probably. Watching. Waiting. Reporting to whoever held his leash.

She didn't tell Mirael.

Instead, she went to Grey Temple.

***

The orphanage was quiet in the late afternoon. Most of the children were in the courtyard, supervised by one of Mother Gessa's helpers. Kira wasn't among them. Selene spotted her through a window, alone in the common room, drawing something on a scrap of paper with a stub of charcoal.

She didn't go in. Just watched.

Kira's face was pinched with concentration. Whatever she was drawing mattered to her. She kept erasing parts and starting over, tongue pressed between her teeth.

"She does that for hours sometimes."

Selene turned. Mother Gessa stood in the doorway, arms crossed, watching her watch Kira.

"I wasn't . . ."

"Yes, you were. It's fine." Gessa stepped out into the alley, pulling the door mostly closed behind her. "You're the only one who comes for her, you know. The coins. The watching from the rooftops. She notices." It wasn't a question.

"She needs shoes," Selene said. "Hers have holes."

"She has new shoes. I bought them with your coins." Gessa studied her with the calm assessment of a woman who'd seen every kind of trouble walk through her doors. "What do you want to know?"

Selene hadn't planned to ask. Hadn't planned to come here at all. But the words came out anyway.

"Where did she come from? Before here."

"The street. That's all she knows. She doesn't remember anything before it. No parents. No home." Gessa's voice was matter-of-fact. No pity. Just truth. "She'd been on her own for at least two years before someone brought her to me. Maybe longer. She doesn't know."

Two years. Maybe longer. On the streets before she was old enough to remember anything else. The killing years, when the city decided whether you lived or didn't.

"She survived," Selene said.

"She did. Barely. When she came to me she weighed less than a wet cat and flinched every time someone raised their hand." Gessa shook her head. "Started talking again after the first six months."

Started talking again. Which meant she'd stopped.

"What does she need?"

Gessa raised an eyebrow. "That's a strange question from a stranger leaving anonymous coins."

"I'm not a stranger."

"No. You're the woman from the rooftops. The one she watches for." Gessa's expression shifted, something hard coming into it. "She thinks you're magic. Thinks you appeared out of nowhere to save her that night in the market, and that means you'll always appear when she needs you."

"I'm not magic."

"I know that. She doesn't." Gessa leaned against the wall, suddenly looking tired. "What she needs is stability. Routine. The knowledge that tomorrow will look like today, and the day after that. She needs to stop expecting the world to burn down every time she closes her eyes."

Selene thought about the rented rooms. The moving every few days. The net tightening around her and Mirael, squeezing them smaller and smaller.

"I can't give her that."

"No. You can't." Gessa's voice wasn't cruel. Just honest. "But you can give her something else. You can let her see that surviving doesn't mean disappearing. That the hard ones don't always end up alone."

"And if they do?"

"Then at least she'll know it wasn't inevitable."

They stood in silence. Through the window, Kira finished her drawing and held it up, studying it critically. Then she crumpled it and started over.

"She draws the same thing every time," Gessa said. "A house. With a door. She's been drawing it for eight months and she's never satisfied."

Selene watched her start again. The careful lines. The concentration.

A house with a door.

Something she'd never had. Something she still believed she might.

"I have to go," Selene said.

"I know." Gessa didn't move from the doorway. "Come back when you can. She looks for you on the rooftops every morning. It would be good for her to know you're real."

Selene left without answering. Without looking back. Without letting herself think too hard about a seven-year-old girl drawing houses she'd never live in.

But she went.

That was something.

***

That night, in another rented room in another part of the city, Mirael sat on the edge of the bed and stared at nothing.

"The routes are gone," she said. "The contacts are gone. The jobs are gone." She looked up. "What do we do?"

Selene stood by the window. Watching the street. The old habit.

"We wait," she said. "We adapt. We find new routes, new contacts, new jobs."

"How? Everyone's afraid of us now."

“Then we find people who are afraid of something else more.”

Mirael was quiet for a long moment.

“You’re quieter lately,” she said finally. Not an accusation. Just an observation. “You used to talk more. Make jokes. Now you just . . . watch things.”

Selene didn’t have an answer for that. She wasn’t sure Mirael was wrong.

“I’m fine,” she said.

Mirael looked at her. The look lasted a long time. Measuring. Deciding whether to push or let it go.

She let it go.

“Get some sleep,” Mirael said, and lay down, turning toward the wall.

Selene stayed by the window. Watched the street. Felt the weight of everything she wasn’t saying pressing against the inside of her chest.

Somewhere out there, Daven was watching.

Somewhere out there, people were making decisions about her future.

She didn’t know what came next.

But she knew it was coming anyway.

CHAPTER 15: Mother Gessa's Second Story

Sometime in the night, Mirael had crawled into bed with her.

Selene woke to cold feet pressing against her calves, to the familiar weight of Mirael's body curled against her back, to the soft rhythm of breath against her shoulder blade. She didn't remember Mirael coming in. Didn't remember the mattress shifting or the covers lifting. Just this: warmth where there had been empty space, presence where there had been none.

She should have pulled away. Should have reminded Mirael of the unspoken rules they'd built over fourteen years. Ten feet of distance. Separate beds. The careful choreography of bodies that never quite touched.

Instead, she lay still.

Mirael's arm was draped across her waist, fingers curled loosely against her stomach. Her forehead rested between Selene's shoulder blades. Small. Trusting. The way she used to sleep when they were children, back when the world was simpler and the rules hadn't hardened into walls.

Selene closed her eyes.

Just this once. Just for a moment. She could allow this.

Outside, the city stirred toward dawn. Carts rattled in distant streets. A dog barked once and fell silent. The sounds of Garnath waking, indifferent to the two women tangled together in a rented room.

Mirael made a small sound in her sleep. Burrowed closer. Her cold feet found new territory on Selene's ankles, and Selene let her. Let the warmth build between them. Let herself pretend, just for these few stolen minutes, that this was something she could keep.

She didn't sleep that night. But she stayed.

***

Before Mirael woke, Selene slipped out of bed.

She moved carefully, extracting herself from Mirael's arms without disturbing her. Dressed in the grey light filtering through the shutters. Buckled the daggers at her hips. The familiar weight settled against her thighs, and she felt something ease in her chest. Armor back in place.

Mirael stirred but didn't wake. Her hand reached across the empty space where Selene had been, found nothing, and curled into a fist against the sheets.

Selene watched her for a moment. The lines of worry that had carved themselves into Mirael's face over the past weeks. The way her jaw stayed tight even in sleep. The grey in her hair that hadn't been there a year ago.

She left without waking her.

***

The streets were quiet in the early morning. Vendors setting up stalls. Dockworkers heading to the first shift. The city in that between-state when night hadn't quite surrendered to day.

Selene walked without direction. Past the fishmongers and the rope-makers. Through the narrow alleys where the sun never quite reached. Into the parts of Garnath where respectable people didn't go and everyone else pretended not to see each other.

She needed to think. Needed space that Mirael's presence didn't fill.

Three blocks into the Lowers, she felt him.

Daven. Following at a careful distance, keeping to the shadows, moving when she moved. Good at his job. Patient. The kind of predator who understood that rushing got you killed.

She didn't look back. Didn't let her pace change. Just noted his presence the way she noted the cobblestones under her feet and the weight of the daggers at her hips.

Near the old tannery, she turned into an alley. Waited. When he didn't appear at the entrance after thirty seconds, she climbed.

The rooftops were her territory. Had been since she was seven years old and the streets were full of things that wanted to hurt her. She moved across them now without thinking, jumping gaps that would have terrified her a decade ago, finding handholds in crumbling brick that only muscle memory recognized.

By the time she dropped back to street level four blocks away, Daven was gone. Lost in the maze of rooftops and alleys she'd been navigating since before he'd known her name.

She found herself near Grey Temple without meaning to be.

The old building squatted at the edge of the Lowers like something that had grown there instead of being built. Walls stained with decades of soot. Windows that let in light but not much hope. The kind of place that existed because children kept appearing and someone had to do something with them.

Mother Gessa's orphanage.

Through one of the windows, Selene could see figures moving. Small shapes gathering. Children settling onto the floor in the common room, cross-legged and expectant.

Storytime.

She hadn't planned this. Hadn't meant to come here. But her feet had carried her anyway, and now she stood in the shadow of the building across the street, watching through dirty glass as the children arranged themselves around an old woman in a worn grey dress.

Kira was there. Third row, near the wall. Her dark hair still tangled, her clothes still slightly too big. But she was sitting straighter than she had a month ago. Eating better. The coins Selene had been leaving were doing their work.

Through the glass, Mother Gessa began to speak.

***

Selene couldn't hear the words from outside. Just the rhythm of them, rising and falling like tide against stone. But she could see Kira's face, and that was enough.

The girl was transfixed. Leaning forward, lips slightly parted, eyes fixed on Gessa with the intensity of someone watching the only light in a dark room. Whatever story this was, it mattered to her.

Selene moved closer. Found a spot near a side door where the sound carried better.

" . . .and so Vaeryn returned to the village he'd left twenty years before. He'd gone to fight in someone else's war, and the war had changed him. Broken things inside that didn't heal right. Made him into someone his own mother wouldn't recognize."

Gessa's voice was rough with age but steady. The kind of voice that had told a thousand stories and would tell a thousand more.

"He found his family's house. Stood outside the gate. Watched his sister hanging laundry, his nieces and nephews playing in the dirt. Children he'd never met, born while he was bleeding in foreign mud."

Kira's hands were clasped in her lap, knuckles white.

"He could have walked through that gate. Could have said his name and watched their faces change. But he didn't. Because he knew what he'd become. The things he'd done to survive. The blood on his hands that no amount of washing would clean. He couldn't bring that into their home. Couldn't let it touch them."

A small boy in the front row raised his hand. "Did they ever find out he was there?"

Gessa's face softened. Saddened. "He stayed in that village for eleven years. Worked as a laborer. Lived in a room above the tavern. Every day he watched them from a distance. When bandits came, he was there in the dark to make sure they didn't come back. When the harvest failed, coin appeared on their doorstep. When his sister's husband died, he dug the grave himself, at night, so she wouldn't have to pay for it."

Silence in the room. Even the youngest children felt it.

"What happened to him?" Kira's voice. Small but steady.

"He died in that tavern room. Alone. And when they found his things, there was a letter. It explained who he was. What he'd done. Why he'd stayed away." Gessa let the words settle. "His sister read it and wept. Not because he was gone. Because he'd been there the whole time, and she'd never known."

Gessa looked at the children.

"Stories don't tell us how to live. They tell us how to feel about living. Vaeryn's story is sad. But it is also true in the way that matters most. Sometimes love means staying close to someone who can't see you anymore. Sometimes the bravest thing is watching over people who don't know you're there."

Storytime ended. The children scattered, some to chores, some to play, some to the quiet corners where children went when stories hit too close to home.

Kira didn't move. She sat against the wall, arms wrapped around her knees, staring at nothing.

Selene pushed open the side door and went in.

***

The common room smelled like porridge and woodsmoke. Gessa looked up when Selene entered, nodded once, and turned back to collecting cushions. No questions. No commentary. Just the acceptance of a woman who had seen everything and judged nothing.

Selene crossed the room to where Kira sat.

The girl looked up. Her eyes widened, and something flickered across her face. Surprise. Hope. The careful wariness of someone who had learned not to trust good things.

"You came inside," Kira said.

"I did."

"You don't usually."

"No."

Kira unfolded slowly, like a plant reaching toward unexpected sunlight. "Mother Gessa said you might. Someday. She said you were working up to it."

Selene didn't know what to say to that. Hadn't known she was working up to anything. "Are you hungry?"

Kira's stomach answered before she could. A small growl that made her cheeks flush.

"Come on," Selene said. "I know a place."

***

The "place" was a baker's stall three streets away. Not much to look at, just a wooden cart with a canvas awning and an old woman who made meat pies that tasted like someone's grandmother had blessed them personally.

Selene bought two. Handed one to Kira. Watched her eat.

The girl devoured the first half in seconds, then caught herself and slowed down. Forcing herself to savor it. The discipline of someone who had learned that food wasn't guaranteed and the next meal might be a long time coming.

"You don't have to ration it," Selene said. "I'll buy you another if you want."

Kira looked at her. Measuring. Deciding whether to believe her.

"Why?" she asked.

"Why what?"

"Why do you keep coming? Why do you leave coins? Why did you save me that night in the market?"

Selene took a bite of her own pie. Chewed. Swallowed. Bought time.

"I don't know," she said finally. Honest, because Kira deserved honest. "I saw you, and I recognized something."

"What?"

"Myself. When I was your age."

Kira considered this. Turned it over like a coin she wasn't sure was real.

"Were you hungry too?"

"Always."

"Were you scared?"

"Every day."

"Did someone help you?"

Selene thought of Rook. The grey eyes and the iron grip and the voice that called her Shadow. The four months that had taught her everything and the empty room that had taught her even more.

"Someone tried," she said. "It didn't last."

They walked in silence after that. Through the back alleys and side streets, away from the main thoroughfares where Daven might be watching. Kira led without being asked, taking them through gaps in fences and under broken boards, moving through the city's hidden geography with the confidence of someone who had mapped it for survival.

They ended up in a narrow alley between two abandoned buildings. Clean enough. Quiet. A place where the world felt smaller and safer.

Kira sat against the wall. After a moment, Selene sat beside her.

"This is where I used to sleep," Kira said. "Before Mother Gessa."

"It's well hidden."

"I found it by accident. Was running from some older boys." She pulled her knees up, wrapped her arms around them. "It's still mine. I come here when I need to think."

"And you're showing it to me."

Kira shrugged. Small shoulders moving under too-big clothes. "You showed me something too. That morning. When you bought that bread and left it where I could find it." She looked at Selene sideways. "I thought you were magic."

"I'm not."

"I know. Mother Gessa told me. She said you're just a person who decided to care at the right moment."

Selene didn't have an answer for that.

They sat in comfortable silence. The alley walls blocked out most of the city sounds, creating a pocket of stillness in the middle of Garnath's chaos. Kira's breathing slowed. Steadied. The tension she carried in her small frame began to ease.

"The story today," Selene said finally. "About Vaeryn. It bothered you."

Kira nodded. Didn't look at her.

"Why?"

A long pause. Then: "Because he stayed. Even when they couldn't see him anymore. Even when it hurt." Her voice was very quiet. "Most people don't stay."

Selene felt something twist in her chest. A recognition that went deeper than words.

"No," she said. "They don't."

"Will you?"

The question hung in the air. Simple and devastating.

Selene looked at the girl beside her. The dark hair and the wary eyes and the stubborn set of her jaw. A child who had survived things no child should survive. Who was still surviving them, every day, in a city that didn't care whether she lived or died.

"I don't make promises," Selene said. "I learned a long time ago that promises break."

Kira's face didn't change. She'd expected that answer. Had probably heard versions of it her whole short life.

"But," Selene continued, "I'm here now. And I keep coming back. That's the closest thing to a promise I know how to give."

Kira was quiet for a long moment. Then she leaned sideways, just slightly, until her shoulder touched Selene's arm.

"Okay," she said.

They stayed like that until the shadows started to lengthen. Two people who had learned the same lessons from different teachers, sitting in comfortable silence in a hidden alley that belonged to a child who had nothing else to call her own.
When Selene finally stood to leave, Kira looked up at her.

"Selene." She said it like she was checking if it still fit. If the woman attached to it was still the same one who'd given it.

"Still me."

"Good."

Kira tested the word. "Selene." She nodded. "I'm Kira. But you already knew that."

"I did." Selene paused at the alley entrance. Looked back at the small figure still sitting against the wall. "You remind me of a firefly, you know that? Small and bright and hard to catch."

Kira's face split into a smile. The first real smile Selene had seen from her. It transformed her whole face, made her look like the child she was instead of the survivor she'd had to become.

"I like that," she said. "Firefly."

She said it again, quieter. Testing the shape of it. Like she was memorizing something she'd been waiting her whole life to own.

"Take care of yourself, Firefly."

Kira looked up. "You'll come back?"

Selene almost smiled. "That's not a promise. It's just true."

She left before she could say anything else. Before the warmth in her chest could become something dangerous.

***

Mirael was awake when she got back.

Sitting at the small table by the window. Not eating. Not reading. Just sitting. Her hands flat on the table, her shoulders rigid, her eyes fixed on the door as if she'd been waiting for hours.

She probably had.

"Where were you?" Mirael's voice was carefully controlled. The kind of calm that came before storms.

"Walking."

"For five hours?"

Selene closed the door behind her. Crossed to the washbasin. Started cleaning the street dust from her hands. "I needed to think."

"You needed to think." Mirael's chair scraped against the floor as she stood. "You slipped out while I was asleep. You didn't leave a note. You didn't tell me where you were going. And you needed to think."

"Yes."

"Where did you go?"

Selene dried her hands. Didn't turn around. "Grey Temple."

The silence that followed was worse than shouting.

"Grey Temple," Mirael repeated. "So it wasn't the Lantern this time."

Selene's shoulders tightened. "Don't."

"Don't what? Don't notice? Don't care?" Mirael's laugh was brittle. "I've been not-noticing for years, Selene. Every time you come back smelling like someone else's sheets. Every time you slip out after dark and think I'm too stupid to know where you're going."

"That's not . . ."

"And now there's a child. A little girl you visit in secret. A little girl whose name I only know because I followed you once and hated myself for it."

Selene turned. Faced her.

Mirael looked exhausted. Worn thin. The woman who had crawled into bed with her last night, seeking warmth, had been replaced by someone holding herself together with nothing but anger and will.

"I can't keep doing this," Mirael said. "I can't keep watching you pull away. I can't keep waking up alone and not knowing if you're coming back."

"I always come back."

"Do you? Do you really?" Mirael's voice cracked. "Your body comes back. Your hands come back. But you? You've been leaving for years, Selene. Piece by piece. And I keep trying to hold onto what's left, and it keeps slipping through my fingers."

"Don't give me that shit."

Mirael flinched. "Excuse me?"

"You heard me." Selene's voice went flat. Hard. The voice she used on jobs, on threats, on people she wanted to stop talking. "Don't stand there acting like I'm doing something to you. I went for a walk. I saw a kid. That's it."

"That's not it and you know it."

"Then tell me what it is, Mirael. Tell me what crime I committed by leaving this room for five fucking hours."

Mirael's jaw tightened. "I want you to talk to me. I want you to tell me what you're feeling instead of disappearing to strangers for whatever it is you can't get from me."

"Kira's not a stranger."

"She is to me!" Mirael's voice rose. "Fourteen years, and you've never let me meet her. You take strangers to bed. You take a seven-year-old into your heart. And I get what? I get to wait. I get to watch you walk out the door and wonder which version of soft you're giving away tonight."

"It's not the same."

"You're right. It's worse." Mirael's voice cracked. "The Lantern I understood. Bodies are easy. But her? You're gentle with her. You're present with her. You have that in you, and you've never once . . ."

She stopped. Couldn't finish.

Something snapped in Selene's chest. The cold place where she kept things locked away cracked open, and what came out was ugly.

"At least they don't look at me like I'm failing them," she said. "At least they don't pretend it's something it isn't. The Lantern is honest. Kira is honest. You're the only one who keeps wanting me to be something I told you I'm not."

Mirael went white. "That's not fair."

"No? You want to compare them? Fine. Let's compare. They don't ask for pieces of me I don't have. They don't look at me like I owe them something I never promised. The workers leave when it's done. Kira just wants me to show up. Neither of them watches me with that look in their eyes, waiting for me to turn into whatever the hell they wanted me to be."

"I never asked you to be anything."

"Bullshit." Selene's hands were shaking now. She hid them behind her back, pressed them against the wall. "You've been asking since the day we met. You just do it quiet. With looks. With sighs. With crawling into my bed and putting your cold feet on me like that's supposed to mean something."

"It does mean something."

"To you. Not to me."

The words hung in the air. Selene watched them land. Watched Mirael's face crumble and rebuild itself, watched the tears gather and refuse to fall.

"I've been here for fourteen years," Mirael said. Her voice was shaking. "I chose you. Over and over. Through the jobs that almost killed us. Through the daggers that chose you instead of me.

Through every night you spent with someone else while I slept alone on the other side of a wall."

"I am so fucking tired of hearing about fourteen years!" The words ripped out of Selene before she could stop them. "You think I can't count? You think I don't know how long it's been? You throw that number at me like it's supposed to mean something, like I'm supposed to fall down and thank you for it."

"I'm not asking you to thank me."

"Then stop acting like it bought you a claim on me."

"I'm not . . ."

"You are. You want credit for staying? Congratulations. You're still here. That's it. That's all it is. I didn't put a collar on you. I didn't ask you to crawl after me." Selene's voice was rising now, the street coming out, the ugly words she'd learned before she'd learned anything else. "I never asked you to stay."

The silence that followed was absolute.

Selene opened her mouth. To take it back. To say something that would undo the last five minutes, the last five sentences, the look on Mirael's face.

Nothing came out.

She hated herself for needing words she didn't have.

Mirael's face went blank. The anger drained out of her, replaced by something worse. Something empty.

"No," she said quietly. "You didn't."

She crossed to the door. Picked up her coat from the hook.

"Mirael . . ."

"Don't." Her voice was flat now. Dead. "Don't you fucking dare say my name like that. Not after this."

She left without looking back.

Selene stood alone in the empty room. Listened to the footsteps fade down the stairs. Heard the front door close, then nothing.

The room was cold. Her hands were still shaking. She pressed them against her thighs until they stopped.

She sat on the edge of the bed where Mirael had slept. Where they had tangled together in the dark, before dawn, before any of this.

Her hands didn't shake anymore. They never did for long.

But something in her chest felt like it was breaking anyway.

***

Across the city, in a place Selene would never think to look, Mirael sat alone.

The Gilded Sparrow wasn't the kind of establishment that catered to people like her. Crystal chandeliers. Linen tablecloths. The soft clink of silver against porcelain and the murmur of conversations held by people who had never worried about where their next meal was coming from.

She'd found a table in the back corner. Shadows. Privacy. A single candle flickering between her and the rest of the room.

The wine was too expensive. She ordered it anyway. Let it sit in front of her, dark red in a glass that probably cost more than a week's lodging.

Her journal was open on the table.

The pages were worn soft from years of handling. Ink and confession and the things she couldn't say out loud. She'd started it the night Selene promised to stay. Had written in it almost every day since.

The pen moved across the page. Steady. Controlled. The way she kept everything controlled, except when she couldn't anymore.

Around her, the restaurant hummed with the sounds of people who belonged here. Couples leaning close. Families celebrating. The easy laughter of lives that hadn't been carved out of Garnath's gutters.

Mirael didn't belong here. But she couldn't go back to that room. Not yet. Not while the words were still fresh, still bleeding.

The candle guttered. She watched the flame struggle and recover.

She took a sip of the wine. It tasted like money and regret.

The pen kept moving. Page after page. Things she had never said. Things she didn't know how to say. Things she had always assumed Selene would just feel, would just know, without being told.

Maybe that was the problem.

She closed the journal. Pressed her palm flat against the leather cover, feeling the weight of all those years underneath her hand.

Somewhere across the city, Selene was sitting alone in a cold room, and Mirael was sitting alone in a warm one, and the distance between them had never felt larger.

She opened the journal again.

The candle flickered. The restaurant murmured. Mirael wrote until her hand cramped, and then she wrote some more.

Some things were easier on paper.

Some things were only possible there.

At the bar, a man in a merchant's coat glanced her way. Held the look a moment too long. Then turned back to his drink like he hadn't.

Mirael didn't notice.

CHAPTER 16: The Safehouse Fire

The room was wrong.

Selene lay on her back, staring at the ceiling she couldn't see. No breathing from the other side of the room. No rustle of blankets. No warmth radiating from a body that had shared her space for longer than she'd lived with her parents.

She turned onto her side. The mattress felt too wide. She turned onto her back. Her skin itched like something was crawling underneath it.

I never asked you to stay.

She sat up. Swung her legs over the edge of the bed. Pressed her palms against her eyes until colors bloomed in the dark.

She'd meant the words to wound. Had watched them land. Watched Mirael's face go still in that particular way that meant the blow had found bone. And she hadn't taken them back. Hadn't even tried. Had just stood there like a coward while Mirael grabbed her bag and walked out the door.

Selene stood. Her feet found her boots without asking permission. Her hands buckled her belt, checked her knives, settled the daggers against her hips. The weight of them was familiar now, almost comforting, and she hated that she'd started thinking of them that way.

She couldn't stay here. Couldn't lie in this bed that still smelled like Mirael's hair and pretend she was going to sleep. Couldn't sit with her own cruelty bouncing off the walls until dawn.

The door closed behind her, and Garnath swallowed her whole.

***

She walked fast, the way she always did when her mind was eating itself.

The Merchant Quarter was dead at this hour, shuttered storefronts and hired guards who watched her pass with bored suspicion. She cut through the alley where she'd killed her first man at nine, the one who'd grabbed her arm and called her pretty, and the memory didn't even slow her down anymore. Just another landmark in a city built from her own violence.

Her boots struck the cobblestones hard enough to jar her knees. Good. The impact gave her something to feel besides the gnawing in her chest.

I never asked you to stay.

True. Technically true. She hadn't asked. Hadn't needed to.

Mirael had just . . . stayed. Through the warehouse fire when they were twelve. Through the lean winters when they'd split a single potato and called it dinner. Through every close call and bad job and narrow escape. Through Selene taking strangers to bed and coming home smelling like other people's skin. Through all of it.

And tonight Selene had taken all of that and thrown it back in her face like it meant nothing.

Because she was angry. Because Mirael had pushed. Because the words were there, loaded and ready, and Selene had never learned how to leave weapons unfired.

She crossed the bridge where the beggars slept in shifts, stepping over bodies wrapped in rags. One of them stirred, looked up at her with cloudy eyes, then settled back down. Even the desperate knew when someone wasn't worth begging from.

The city at night had its own sounds. Distant laughter from taverns. A woman screaming somewhere, could be pleasure, could be pain, could be both. Dogs fighting over something dead in an alley. The constant drip of water from gutters that never fully dried.

Selene walked through it all and heard none of it.

She was thinking about Mirael's hands. The way they'd shaken when she grabbed her bag. The way her voice had cracked on the word "stay." The way she'd looked at Selene like she was seeing something she'd always known was there but had hoped she was wrong about.

If someone can leave you, they will.

Rook had taught her that. Four months of "watch the shoulders, little shadow," and then an empty room and six days of checking the stairs before she understood he wasn't coming back. She'd been nine. Old enough to learn, young enough that the lesson had carved itself into her bones.

Mirael had never left. Not once in all these years. Not even when Selene had given her every reason to.

And tonight Selene had finally told her the truth she'd been choking on: she'd never asked for any of it. The loyalty. The devotion. The way Mirael looked at her like she was something worth staying for.

She didn't deserve it.

The smell hit her before she saw the glow.

Selene stopped mid-stride, her head snapping up. Smoke. Not cookfire smoke, not torch smoke. This was thicker, blacker, wrong in a way that made her stomach clench before her mind caught up.

She turned toward it and saw the orange bleeding across the rooftops three districts over.

Their district.

She ran.

***

The streets blurred past. She knocked a drunk into a wall and didn't stop to apologize. She vaulted a cart that someone had left blocking an intersection, her hands hitting the wood and her body following in a motion so practiced she didn't have to think about it.

The smoke got thicker as she got closer. She could taste it now, ash and char and something chemical underneath. Her eyes started to water. She didn't slow down.

An old man stumbled out of a doorway in his nightclothes, gawking at the glow in the sky. Selene shoved past him. A woman carrying a child pressed against a wall to let her through, eyes wide with fear that had nothing to do with Selene.

She turned the corner onto their street and the heat hit her like a fist.

The building was a torch.

Flames poured from every window, three stories of fire eating everything she and Mirael had built. The roar of it filled her ears, a deep constant thunder that drowned thought and swallowed words. She could feel the heat on her face from thirty feet away, pressing against her skin like hands trying to push her back.

Her feet kept moving.

"Hey!" Someone grabbed her arm. A neighbor, one of the old men who sat on stoops and watched the street like it was theater. "You can't go in there, girl. It's gone."

Selene shook him off and kept moving.

Twenty feet. The heat was a wall now. She could feel her clothes getting hot, could smell her own hair starting to singe. The front door was a rectangle of solid flame, the frame buckling inward, the wood turning to charcoal before her eyes.

She went for the side alley. The window to the back room, the one with the loose latch she'd been meaning to fix for months.

The alley was an oven. She made it ten feet before the heat drove her back, her lungs refusing to pull air that felt like it was burning on the way down. She retreated, tried again, got five feet closer before a section of the wall collapsed outward in a shower of sparks and burning timber.

She threw herself backward. Hit the ground hard, her shoulder taking the impact, her head cracking against cobblestones. Something hot landed on her arm and she slapped it away, smelling burned cloth and the sharper smell of burned skin underneath.

Hands grabbed her, pulled her up, pulled her back. The old man again, and someone else, a woman with soot on her face and tears cutting tracks through the grime.

"It's gone," the woman said. "There's nothing you can do."

Selene shoved them away. Stood there in the mouth of the alley, breathing hard, watching the flames eat the window she'd been trying to reach.

The back room. The loose floorboard. Everything they'd saved for years, every coin scraped and hidden against the day things got worse.

Gone.

She ran the inventory the way she'd been taught. Coin cache: gone. Tunnel maps: gone. Backup weapons: gone. The bolt-hole address book: gone. Every redundancy, every exit strategy, every piece of margin they'd scraped together over the years. All of it was fuel now.

They still had the apartment. They still had the clothes on their backs and whatever Mirael had in her bag.

They had nothing else.

***

The crowd had grown while she'd been trying to die in an alley.

Neighbors spilled out of adjacent buildings, some in nightclothes, some half-dressed, all of them watching with that particular mix of horror and fascination that fire always drew. Bucket brigades had formed, chains of people passing water hand to hand, sloshing half of it on the street in their panic.

It was useless. The building was too far gone, the fire too hot, the water too little. But they kept trying anyway, because standing still felt like giving up.

Selene found herself in line without deciding to join. Her hands passed buckets, wood to wood to wood, the water inside sloshing against her wrists. The rhythm was something to hold onto. Something to do while her mind went somewhere else.

The building screamed as it died. That was the only word for it. The beams groaning, the walls cracking, the fire roaring its triumph over everything it touched. Every few minutes something collapsed inside and a new column of sparks shot toward the sky, orange and gold against the black, almost beautiful if you didn't think about what it meant.

The front room went first. Selene watched through the flames as the ceiling sagged, then fell, taking everything beneath it. The table Mirael had built from scrap lumber. The chairs they'd found on the street and repaired. The rug that had been a gift from Viena years ago, when gifts from Viena still came without conditions.

All of it, fuel now.

"Bucket's empty." The woman next to her was staring at her with hollow eyes.

Selene looked down. She'd been passing air for the last three rounds, her hands going through the motions while her mind was somewhere in the flames.

She stepped out of the line. No one noticed.

The front of the building collapsed with a sound like a giant taking a step. The crowd screamed and scattered, the bucket line breaking apart, people running in every direction. A burning beam crashed into the street and rolled, scattering sparks like seeds.

Selene didn't move. She stood there and watched the place she'd built fall into the flames and disappear.

"Selene!"

She turned. Mirael was shoving through the crowd, her face wild, her satchel bouncing against her hip. She wasn't looking at the fire. She was looking at Selene.

They collided in the street. Mirael's hands grabbed her arms, not checking for injury, just holding on. Her breath came in ragged gasps, her chest heaving against Selene's.

"You're here." Not a question. Something else.

"I was walking. Saw the smoke."

Mirael's grip tightened. For a moment Selene thought she might say something about the fight. About the words that had driven her out. About everything that had broken between them in that room.

She didn't.

"The back room," Mirael said instead. "The floorboards . . ."

"Gone."

Mirael's face crumpled for a moment. Just a moment. Then she straightened, jaw tightening, and turned to face the fire.

They stood side by side and watched it burn. The distance from the fight was still there, Selene could feel it like a wall between them. But this was bigger than the fight. This was everything they'd built turning to ash while they watched.

The second floor collapsed. They didn't flinch.

***

"Did you see them get out?"

The voice came from somewhere to Selene's left. A woman, middle-aged, wearing a shawl over her nightdress. She was talking to a man Selene vaguely recognized from three doors down.

"Who?"

"The two that lived there. The ones who kept to themselves." The woman's voice dropped, but not enough. "You know the ones."

The man grunted. "Saw one of them running up just now. The dark-haired one." He jerked his chin toward Selene and Mirael.

"Shame about the building. Though I can't say I'm surprised."

"No?"

"You live like that, eventually someone catches up with you."

Selene's hands curled into fists at her sides.

"What do you mean, live like that?" The man sounded curious now, the way people got when gossip turned interesting.

"Oh, you know." The woman's voice was thick with implication. "Two women, no men around. Coming and going at all hours. Visitors in cloaks who never showed their faces. Guild business, I heard. Or worse."

"I heard they killed someone," another voice chimed in. Younger, male, someone Selene couldn't see. "That dark-haired one. Cut a man's throat in an alley for looking at her wrong."

"Wouldn't surprise me. Cold eyes, that one. Like a snake."

Selene took a step toward them.

Mirael's hand closed around her wrist. Hard.

"Don't."

"They're standing right there talking shit about us while our place burns."

"I know." Mirael's grip didn't loosen. "And if you go over there and make a scene, you give them something real to talk about. You give Weston something to write down. You make us look guilty of whatever they're already convinced we did."

“I don’t care what they think.”

“Yes, you do.” Mirael pulled her back, putting her body between Selene and the gossips. “You care because if they think you’re dangerous, they won’t deal with you. They won’t sell to you. They won’t warn you when the Paladins are coming. You care because this city runs on reputation and you can’t afford to torch yours while our building is still burning.”

The words landed like cold water.

Selene stood there, muscles tight, staring past Mirael’s shoulder at the woman in the shawl. The woman who was still talking, still spreading poison, still enjoying someone else’s tragedy like it was theater put on for her benefit.

“I hate this city,” Selene said.

“I know.”

“I hate every single person in it.”

“I know.” Mirael’s hand was still on her wrist. “Hate them tomorrow. Right now we need to be smart.”

The gossips moved on eventually, drifting toward some other cluster of neighbors to share their theories. Selene watched them go and memorized faces.

She’d remember. She always remembered.

***

“Your building?”

Selene turned. Weston was picking his way through the debris toward them, his armor reflecting the firelight in orange and red. Two younger Paladins flanked him, trying to establish order in the chaos, pushing people back from the fire line.

“Back,” one of them shouted at a man who’d gotten too close. “Everyone back. The structure’s not stable.”

As if to prove the point, something crashed inside the building. A section of the second floor gave way, falling through to the first with a thunder of breaking wood. Sparks exploded outward, and Weston threw up an arm to shield his face.

He recovered quickly. Crossed the last few feet to where Selene and Mirael stood.

“Your building?” he asked again, lowering his arm. His voice was loud enough to carry over the roar.

Selene didn’t answer. He already knew.

“Where were you when it started?”

“Out.”

“Out where?”

A beam collapsed somewhere behind them. The crowd screamed. Weston didn’t flinch.

“Walking.” Selene kept her voice flat. “Couldn’t sleep.”

“At this hour?”

“I keep odd hours.”

Weston’s eyes moved to Mirael. “And you?”

“The Gilded Sparrow.” Mirael’s hand went to her satchel, a reflexive gesture Selene had seen a thousand times. “I left a few hours before.”

“Left from where?”

Mirael hesitated. Selene felt her own jaw tighten.

“Our other place,” Mirael said. “We have a room elsewhere.”

“But this building. You used it too.”

It wasn’t a question. Weston already knew the answer. Had probably known for months, had probably written it down in that ledger he carried everywhere, had probably filed it away with all the other pieces of Selene’s life he’d been collecting.

“We used it,” Selene said. “Now we don’t.”

Weston produced his ledger. Wrote something in that small, precise hand. A burning chunk of debris crashed into the street ten feet away, and he stepped aside without looking, without breaking the rhythm of his writing.

“Anyone else live in the building?”

“Three other tenants.” Selene watched the fire over his shoulder. The roof was starting to sag. “Drinn on the ground floor. Couple named Vass on the second. Old woman named Hetta in the back.”

“We’ve found them. Minor injuries. They got out.”

Something loosened in Selene's chest. She hadn't realized she'd been carrying it.

"Any threats recently?" Weston looked up from his ledger. His eyes caught the firelight and held it. "Anyone who'd want to see you displaced? Enemies with a grudge?"

The question hung between them. Sparks swirled through the air like drunk fireflies.

"No one specific." The lie came easily. It always did.

"You're sure about that?"

"I'm sure I'm not going to stand here answering questions while everything I own turns to ash."

Weston studied her for a long moment. Behind him, the roof finally gave way, folding inward with a groan that sounded almost human. A column of sparks shot toward the stars. Someone in the crowd was sobbing.

"The Guild's been busy lately," Weston said. His voice was almost conversational. "Lot of fires. Lot of accidents. Lot of people finding themselves suddenly without options."

"Is that so."

"It is." He tucked the ledger away. "Funny how certain names keep showing up in the margins. Patterns form when you write things down."

Selene said nothing. Let the fire speak for her.

"Do you have somewhere to go?" The question was almost gentle. Almost human. "I can arrange something. Temporary shelter, if you need it."

Selene felt Mirael's hand find her elbow. Light pressure. *Don't.*

"We'll manage," Mirael said.

Weston nodded slowly. His eyes stayed on Selene.

"I'm sure you will." He turned to go, then paused. Looked back over his shoulder. "Be careful out there. This city eats people who run out of options."

He walked away before Selene could respond. Not that she would have. Not that she had anything to say that wouldn't make things worse.

She watched him go, coordinating his men, directing the bucket brigades, doing the boring necessary work of containing disaster. He didn't look back again.

***

The fire burned itself out near dawn.

Selene stayed the whole time. She watched the building sag and collapse, watched the flames shrink to embers, watched the smoke thin from black to grey to white. Mirael stayed with her, silent, their shoulders almost touching but never quite making contact.

When there was nothing left but a skeleton of charred beams and glowing coals, Selene finally moved.

"Let's go."

They picked their way through the debris. The street was scattered with ash and broken glass, scraps of fabric that had blown out windows, a single boot that had belonged to someone on the second floor. The air tasted like char and ruin.

The crowd had thinned to nothing. A few neighbors still stood in clusters, talking in low voices, but most had gone back to their beds, their curiosity satisfied, their theories firmly in place. Old Drinn sat on a stoop across the street, his hands wrapped in cloth, staring at the ruins with empty eyes. The couple from the second floor had disappeared. Old Hetta was nowhere to be seen.

Weston was still there, directing two Paladins who were marking off the area with rope. He glanced at Selene as she passed but didn't say anything. Just wrote something in his ledger and went back to work.

She could feel his eyes on her until they turned the corner.

***

The walk to the brothel apartment took forever and no time at all.

They moved through streets that were waking up, merchants opening shutters, carts rattling toward the market square. The world going on like nothing had happened. Like everything Selene had built hadn't just turned to ash.

Mirael walked close enough that their arms brushed with every step. She hadn't said anything since the fire died. Neither had Selene.

What was there to say?

I'm sorry about the fight felt hollow now. The words that had seemed so important a few hours ago had been swallowed by the fire, reduced to the same ash as everything else. The back room. The loose floorboard. The table Mirael had built. The walls that had held a thousand conversations, a thousand silences, a thousand moments of just existing together in a space that belonged to no one but them.

Gone. All of it.

And Selene still couldn't give Mirael the apology she deserved. The words existed. She knew their shapes. But they wouldn't come out, wouldn't form on her tongue, wouldn't bridge the distance that had opened between them.

Some things were easier to burn than to fix.

The brothel was quiet when they arrived. The night's business long finished, the morning's not yet begun. They climbed the back stairs to the apartment, and Mirael unlocked the door with the key around her neck.

The room looked the same as when they'd left it. Their bed. Their things. But it felt different now, smaller somehow, the walls closer together than she remembered.

Mirael caught sight of herself in the small mirror by the washstand and stopped. Her face was grey with ash, her hair matted with soot, dark streaks running down her neck where sweat had cut channels through the grime. She looked like something the fire had spit out.

Selene didn't need a mirror to know she looked the same. She could smell herself. Smoke and char and burned cloth, the sharp chemical edge of things that weren't meant to burn.

Mirael moved to the copper tub in the corner without saying anything. Started working the pump, water splashing against metal, steam rising as the heated reservoir did its work. The brothel had its luxuries. Hot water was one of them.

"We need to think about the tunnel maps," Selene said. She leaned against the wall, arms crossed. "I had most of them memorized, but the newer routes . . ."

"I know some of them." Mirael kept pumping. The tub was filling slowly. "The one behind the tannery. The drainage access near the fish market."

"That's not enough."

"It's a start."

The water steamed. Mirael tested it with her fingers, adjusted something, kept filling.

"The coin is the real problem," Selene said. "We had maybe six months of margin under those boards. Now we're back to job-to-job."

"We've worked job-to-job before."

"We were younger. Stupider. Had less to lose."

Mirael turned off the pump. The tub was three-quarters full, steam curling off the surface. She started unbuttoning her shirt, fingers clumsy with exhaustion.

"We still have contacts," she said. "Viena's not passing work, but she hasn't cut us off completely. Maren's scared, but scared people come back around when they need something. We're not starting from nothing." The shirt fell to the floor. Mirael stepped out of her trousers, kicked them aside. Her skin was pale where the soot hadn't reached, grey everywhere else. She climbed into the tub with a small sound of relief, the water swallowing her up to her shoulders.

Selene watched her sink into the heat. Should have felt awkward, probably. Didn't. They'd shared tighter spaces than this. Had slept pressed together for warmth in winters that would have killed them separately. Had seen each other in every state a body could be in.

Mirael tipped her head back, eyes closed, and let the water hold her weight.

Selene could wait. Could sit on the bed and take her turn when Mirael was done. That was the smart play. The distance from the fight was still there, still real, and sharing a bath felt like pretending things were fine when they weren't.

But her skin itched with ash. Her lungs still burned with smoke. And the water looked warm, and Mirael looked small, and something in Selene's chest wouldn't let her stay on the other side of the room.

She unbuckled her belt. Set the daggers on the washstand where she could reach them. Pulled her ruined shirt over her head and stepped out of her trousers.

Mirael opened her eyes when the water shifted. Didn't say anything. Just moved forward to make room.

Selene lowered herself into the heat and felt something in her spine unlock. The water was almost too hot, the kind of temperature that hurt before it helped. She settled against the back of the tub, her knees bent to fit, and let her eyes close.

For a long moment, neither of them spoke.

Then Mirael's hand found a cloth somewhere, and she reached across and started wiping the ash from Selene's shoulder. Gentle. Methodical. Working in small circles the way she did everything, patient and thorough.

Selene should have stopped her. Should have said something like *I can do it myself* or *you don't have to.* The words were there, waiting.

She didn't say them.

She took the cloth instead, when Mirael's arm got tired. Returned the favor. Traced the line of Mirael's collarbone, the curve of her neck, the places where soot had settled into skin. Watched the water turn grey with everything the fire had left on them.

Mirael's breath caught once. Just once. She didn't say anything about it, and neither did Selene.

This wasn't forgiveness. Wasn't apology. Wasn't pretending the fight hadn't happened or that the words hadn't landed exactly where they'd been aimed.

This was just two people in a tub, washing a fire off each other because no one else was going to do it.

Selene told herself that. Told herself it was practical. Efficient. One tub, two bodies, limited hot water.

Mirael's eyes said she knew better. But she didn't push. Didn't ask for more than what was being offered. Just sat in the water and let Selene's hands move over her skin and memorized every second of it like she was writing it down somewhere Selene would never find.

The water cooled eventually. The grey settled to the bottom of the tub. They climbed out, dried off with the same towel because neither of them thought to grab a second one, and dressed in clean clothes that smelled like nothing at all.

Mirael sat on the edge of the bed. Her hair was damp, her face scrubbed clean, and she looked younger than she had in years. She looked at Selene like she wanted to say something.

She didn't.

Selene sat down next to her. Close enough that their shoulders touched.

"We should sleep," she said.

"I know."

Neither of them moved.

"I'm not going anywhere," Selene said. The words came out before she could stop them. The same words Mirael had said to her twelve years ago, in front of another fire, when they'd lost everything for the first time.

Mirael's hand found hers. Squeezed once.

"I know," she said again. Softer this time.

They fell asleep like that, sitting up, shoulders pressed together, hands intertwined. The sun climbed higher outside the window. The city went on without them.

CHAPTER 17: Threads

Selene woke with Mirael's weight against her shoulder and no idea how long she'd been asleep.

The light through the thin curtains was wrong. Too bright. Too high. Midmorning, maybe later. They'd slept sitting up against the headboard, hands still loosely intertwined, and at some point Mirael had slumped sideways until her head found the hollow of Selene's neck.

She looked peaceful. Younger than she had any right to look after the night they'd had. Her breathing was slow and even, her face slack, the tension lines around her eyes smoothed away by exhaustion.

Selene couldn't stand it.

The softness. The way Mirael's hair smelled like smoke and soap and something underneath that was just her. The weight of her, warm and trusting and fragile in a way that made Selene want to put her fist through the wall.

She'd said the words. Last night, in the grey space between exhaustion and sleep, she'd said them: *I'm not going anywhere.* And she'd meant it. Had felt it in her chest like a stone dropping into water.

But the water was still now, and all she could feel was the need to move. To do something. To stop sitting here in this borrowed room in this borrowed life while whoever had burned their safehouse walked around breathing.

She untangled her hand from Mirael's. Slow. Careful. Slid sideways until Mirael's head dropped to the pillow instead of her shoulder.

Mirael stirred. Made a small sound. Didn't wake.

Selene watched her for a moment longer than she should have. Then she stood, dressed in silence, and buckled the daggers at her hips.

***

"Where are you going?"

Mirael's voice was sleep-rough, muffled by the pillow. She hadn't opened her eyes.

"Looking for work." The lie came easy. They always did. "Stay here. Rest."

"I can come with . . ."

"No." Too sharp. Selene softened it, or tried to. "You need sleep. I'll see what I can shake loose. Be back in a few hours."

She was out the door before Mirael could argue.

Mirael listened to her footsteps fade down the stairs. The silence that followed was louder than the door closing had been.

She didn't believe the lie. Looking for work. Right. Selene's body had been coiled tight as a spring from the moment she woke up. That wasn't the posture of someone going to shake hands and make deals.

But Mirael was tired. Bone-tired. And she'd learned, over the years, that some doors Selene had to walk through alone.

She reached under the pillow and pulled out her journal. The leather was worn smooth from years of handling, the pages swollen with ink and memory. Everything she'd never been able to say out loud lived in these pages. Every fear. Every hope. Every moment she wanted to keep forever.

She opened it to a blank page. Stared at it.

What was there to write? That Selene had said the words and meant them? That for one moment, in the dark before dawn, Mirael had let herself believe things could be different?

She closed the journal without writing anything. Held it against her chest like a shield.

Some things were too fragile to put into words. Even here. Even in the only place that was truly hers.

***

The hallway was quiet. The brothel slept during the day, its workers recovering from the night's business, and Selene's boots on the stairs were the loudest sound in the building. She moved fast, taking the back exit into the alley, already running through the list in her head.

Not work. She wasn't looking for work.

She was looking for the people who'd burned twelve years of her life to the ground.

And when she found them, she was going to ask questions. And then she was going to make sure they never burned anything again.

***

The Sprawl woke up ugly, the way it always did.

Street vendors shouting over each other. Kids running errands for coin. Drunks sleeping off the night in doorways while stray dogs pissed on their boots. The smell of cooking meat and rotting garbage and the river that ran through everything like an open sewer.

Selene moved through it with her head down and her shoulders set. She knew how to work the Sprawl. Had grown up in it, learned its rhythms, knew which questions to ask and who to ask them to. On a good day, she could work a lead for hours, building a picture piece by piece until she knew exactly who she was looking for and exactly where to find them.

Today wasn't a good day.

Today she kicked over rocks and didn't care what crawled out.

"Who was working the docks two nights ago? South end, near the old customs house."

"Heard there was a fire in the Narrows. Anyone talking about who might've been responsible?"

"Two guys, Guild-marked, seen near the Kellman district the night before last. I want names."

She wasn't subtle. Wasn't patient. Wasn't careful. The people she talked to noticed. Some of them would remember. Some of them would talk to the wrong people about the woman with the daggers asking too many questions too loudly.

She didn't care.

An old woman selling fish heads watched her pass, eyes narrow and knowing. "Looking for trouble, that one," she muttered to the man beside her. Loud enough for Selene to hear. "Trouble usually finds people like her."

Selene kept walking.

A boy, maybe twelve, followed her for half a block before she turned and stared at him. He held up his hands, grinning. "Just seeing if you wanted a guide, lady. You're walking like you're lost."

"I'm not lost."

"Sure." He backed away, still grinning. "But someone's gonna tell someone what you're asking about. That's how it works down here. Nothing's free. Not even questions."

She knew that. Had known it since she was younger than him. Today she didn't care.

The trail came together faster than it should have, which should have been a warning. Two names: Garrett and Polk. Low-level Guild muscle, the kind who got paid to break things and not ask why. They'd been seen near the safehouse the evening before the fire, asking questions about who lived there, how often they came and went.

They were working today. Muscle for a card game in a back room off Fisher's Lane. Should be wrapping up around midday.

Smart move: Wait. Watch. See who they reported to. Follow the chain up.

Selene's move: Go there now. Catch them on the way out. Get answers.

She didn't think about the fact that she was outnumbered. Didn't think about the fact that she had no backup, no exit plan, no one who knew where she was. Didn't think about Mirael waking up alone in that borrowed room, waiting for her to come back.

She just moved.

***

Fisher's Lane was a piss-soaked alley that dead-ended at a collapsed warehouse. The card game ran out of a basement room with one entrance and no windows. Selene found a spot across the street where she could watch the door and waited.

She wasn't good at waiting. Not today.

Her ribs ached from hitting the cobblestones last night. Her arm still stung where the ember had burned through her sleeve. Every few minutes she caught herself grinding her teeth and had to consciously relax her jaw.

The door opened. Two men came out, squinting in the daylight. One was thick, running to fat, with the kind of hands that had broken a lot of bones. The other was leaner, meaner, with a scar running from his left eyebrow into his hairline.

Garrett and Polk. Had to be.

They turned toward the dead end, probably taking a shortcut through the collapsed warehouse. Selene followed.

The smart thing would have been to call out. Stop them in the open. Ask questions where someone might hear, where witnesses would make them careful.

Instead she waited until they were in the shadows of the collapsed building, out of sight of the street, and then she drew her daggers and stepped into the light.

"Which one of you wants to talk first?"

They turned. The fat one, Garrett, had his hand on a cudgel before he'd finished turning. The lean one, Polk, just smiled.

"The fuck are you?"

"The woman whose life you burned two nights ago."

Recognition flickered in Polk's eyes. "Shit. You're the one they were talking about. The snake."

"I prefer my name." Selene rolled her wrists, feeling the weight of the daggers. "Who gave the order?"

"Piss off."

"Wrong answer."

Garrett moved first. He was faster than he looked, the cudgel coming around in a wide arc aimed at her skull. She ducked it, stepped inside his reach, and put a dagger through his throat before she'd made a conscious decision to do it.

Blood sprayed across her face. Hot. Copper-smelling. Garrett's eyes went wide with surprise and then empty with death, and he dropped like a sack of meat.

Shit.

She'd meant to wound him. Meant to make him talk. The blade had found his throat on instinct, muscle memory taking over before her brain caught up.

Too fast. Too fucking fast.

Polk was staring at his partner's body with something between fear and calculation. His hand had found a knife somewhere, a blade about as long as his forearm, and he was holding it like he knew how to use it.

"Who gave the order?" Selene asked again. Her voice sounded strange. Too calm. "Tell me and you walk away."

"You just killed Garrett."

"Garrett made a choice. Make a better one."

Polk's eyes flicked to the alley entrance. Measuring distance. Calculating odds.

"It came from above," he said. "That's all I know. Someone up the chain wanted you exposed. Wanted to see what you'd do when you lost your bolt-hole."

"Someone has a name."

"Not one I know." His grip shifted on the knife. "I just do what I'm told. Same as anyone."

"And what were you told?"

"Watch the building. Report who came and went. Then clear out before midnight." He shrugged, trying for casual and missing by a mile. "Didn't know they were going to torch it. That's above my pay grade."

"Who do you report to?"

"Territory runner. Mid-level. Answers to someone higher."

"A mid-level didn't order a fire like that on his own."

"Probably not." Polk's smile was thin and mean. "But that's all you're getting from me, snake. Kill me or let me go."

The smart move was to let him go. Follow him. Use him to find the runner, and use the runner to find whoever was really pulling strings.

But she could still smell Garrett's blood. Could still feel the way the dagger had punched through his throat like it was nothing. And Polk was smiling at her like he knew exactly how fucked up she was right now, like he could see the cracks in her armor and was already planning how to exploit them.

"One more question," she said. "There was a man. Watching me for weeks before the fire. Dark hair. Forgettable face. He work for your boss too?"

Something shifted in Polk's expression. Not recognition exactly. More like a door closing.

"I don't know anything about that."

"You're lying."

"Kill me or let me go." He said it again, slower this time, like he was explaining something to a child. "Those are your options."

Selene's hands were shaking. She could feel it in her grip on the daggers, a fine tremor running through her fingers. Exhaustion. Adrenaline. The smoke in her lungs that hadn't fully cleared.

She should let him go. She should be smart.

Polk saw the shake in her hands and made his decision. The knife came up fast, a hard thrust aimed at her gut, and she reacted without thinking.

Sidestep. Parry. The knife scraped along her ribs instead of punching through them, opening a line of fire along her side, and then her dagger was in his chest and he was falling and it was over.

"Fuck." She stumbled back, hand going to her ribs. The wound was bleeding freely, soaking through her shirt, and it hurt in a way that told her it was deep. "Fuck. Fuck."

Two bodies at her feet. Nothing to show for it. A title she already knew, and a hint that whoever was watching her wasn't Guild. Not directly.

She'd come here for answers and left with a knife wound and a higher body count.

This was stupid. This was the kind of stupid that got people killed.

She wiped the daggers clean on Polk's shirt and sheathed them. Pressed her hand against her ribs and tried to breathe through the pain.

She needed to move. Needed to get out of here before someone came looking for Garrett and Polk. Needed to find somewhere to patch herself up before she bled through her shirt and left a trail even a blind man could follow.

She needed to not have done any of this.

Too late for that.

***

From the shadow of a doorway across the street, a man with a forgettable face watched her limp out of the alley.

He didn't follow. Didn't need to. He knew where she lived. Knew where she'd go. Had been watching her for weeks now, learning her patterns, her weaknesses, the cracks in the armor she didn't know she had.

Today she'd shown him something new. The woman with the daggers, the one who moved like smoke and killed like winter, was compromised. Sloppy. Emotional.

Interesting.

He waited until she'd turned the corner, then slipped into the alley she'd left. Two bodies. Guild muscle, from the look of them. She'd done the work quickly, but not cleanly. One of them had gotten a blade into her.

He crouched beside Polk's body. Checked the wounds. Read the story they told.

She was good. But she wasn't thinking straight. And people who weren't thinking straight made mistakes.

The kind of mistakes that could be exploited.

He stood, wiped his hands on his coat, and walked away. There was a report to make. A shadow to speak to.

The woman with the daggers was cracking.

The shadow he reported to would want to know.

***

The safehouse was gone, so she found an empty room in a building that was more hole than wall and did what she could with what she had.

The wound was worse than she'd hoped and better than she deserved. Deep enough to need stitching, not deep enough to have hit anything vital. She'd taken worse. She'd also taken it smarter, with backup, with someone to watch the door while she worked.

Today she had a dirty needle, thread stolen from a tailor's shop three years ago, and her own shaking hands.

"Shit." The needle went through skin and she bit down on a scream. "Shit. Shit."

This was her punishment. Not the wound itself but the doing of it. Sitting alone in a collapsed building, stitching herself back together because she'd been too proud and too angry and too fucking stupid to bring Mirael along.

She'd done this to herself. That was the worst part. She'd walked into that alley knowing the odds were bad and her head wasn't right and she did it anyway because she needed to hurt something. Needed to feel like she was doing something instead of just sitting in that room with Mirael's warmth against her shoulder and the memory of the words she'd said.

I'm not going anywhere.

She'd meant it.

She'd also left. First chance she got.

The stitching was rough, uneven, the kind of work that would scar ugly. Good enough. She tied it off, pressed a relatively clean rag against it, and sat there for a while just breathing.

Mirael was going to be furious.

No. Mirael was going to be hurt. That was worse.

Selene could handle fury. Could match it, meet it, let it burn itself out. But hurt was different. Hurt was quiet. Hurt was Mirael looking at her with those eyes that saw too much and saying nothing because there was nothing left to say.

She should stay here. Wait until dark. Come up with a better lie.

Instead she stood, gathered what was left of her dignity, and started the long walk back.

***

The apartment door opened and Mirael was on her feet before Selene had cleared the threshold.

"Where have you been?"

"I told you. Looking for work."

"For six hours?"

Had it been six hours? Time had gotten away from her somewhere between the killing and the stitching.

"It's a tough market."

Mirael's eyes were already moving, already cataloging. The blood on Selene's shirt that she'd tried to hide. The way she was holding her left arm close to her body. The pallor of her skin.

"You're hurt."

"I'm fine."

"You're bleeding through your shirt."

Selene looked down. The rag had slipped. The blood was spreading, a dark stain against the fabric, impossible to explain away.

"It's nothing."

"That's not nothing." Mirael crossed to her in three steps, hands already reaching for the hem of her shirt. "Let me see."

"Mirael . . ."

"Shut up and let me see."

The shirt came up. The stitching was visible, black thread against red-raw skin, the wound still seeping.

"Who did this?"

Selene didn't answer.

"Who. Did. This."

"Doesn't matter. They're dead."

Mirael's hands had stopped moving. She was staring at the wound, at the rough stitches, at the evidence of violence that had nothing to do with looking for work.

"What did you do?" Her voice was very quiet.

"Found two of them. Guild muscle. They were at our place the night before."

"You went after them."

"Yes."

"Alone."

"Yes."

Mirael stepped back. Her hands fell to her sides. She looked at Selene the way you look at something that's broken beyond repair.

"You said you were looking for work."

"I know what I said."

"You lied to me."

"Yes."

The word hung in the air between them. Selene watched Mirael's face cycle through something. Hurt, anger, exhaustion, back to hurt. It settled into a kind of stillness that was worse than any of them.

"Did you get what you needed? Did they tell you who ordered it?"

"One of them said a name. Doesn't lead anywhere useful."

"So you killed them."

"They didn't give me a choice."

"Bullshit." The word cracked like a whip. "You went there to kill them. You weren't looking for answers. You were looking for someone to hurt."

Selene's jaw tightened. The denial was right there, waiting to be spoken.

She couldn't say it. Couldn't lie about that too.

"I needed to do something."

"You needed to do something." Mirael repeated it like she was tasting the words, testing their weight. "You needed to do something, so you left me here. Told me you were looking for work.

Went off alone against Guild muscle with no backup and no plan and almost got yourself gutted."

"I handled it."

"You handled it." Mirael's voice was rising now, not to a shout but to something sharper. "You handled it. Look at yourself. Look at that fucking wound. You handled nothing. You got lucky."

"I killed them both."

"And what did that get you? What do you have now that you didn't have this morning?"

Nothing. The answer was nothing, and they both knew it.

"I couldn't just sit here." The words came out harder than she meant. "I couldn't just sit in this room and wait and pretend everything was fine while whoever did this walks around breathing."

"So you went out and made yourself feel better by killing two men who probably didn't even know why they were watching us."

"They knew enough."

"Did they? Or did you just need someone to bleed?"

Selene's hands curled into fists at her sides. The wound in her ribs screamed at the movement.

"I did what I had to do."

"You did what you wanted to do. There's a difference." Mirael turned away, walked to the small table where Selene's things were laid out, picked up the medical kit she kept there. "Sit down. Those stitches look like shit."

"I can . . ."

"Sit the fuck down, Selene."

She sat.

Mirael knelt in front of her. Her hands were steady as she pulled out the small knife she used for this, the clean thread, the curved needle. She'd done this before. They'd both done this before, for each other, more times than either of them wanted to count.

"Shirt off."

Selene pulled it over her head. The movement made the wound scream, and she felt fresh blood seep through the rough stitches.

Mirael's face didn't change. She leaned in close, examining the damage, and Selene could smell her. Soap and sleep and something underneath that was just Mirael. The same smell from this morning, when they'd been tangled together. When things had almost felt like they could be okay.

"This is going to hurt."

"I know."

The knife slid under the first stitch. Cut. Mirael pulled the thread free with steady fingers, her touch clinical even though her jaw was tight with anger.

Another stitch. Another. Selene watched Mirael's hands move over her skin and felt something twist in her chest that had nothing to do with the wound.

These hands had held her last night. Had washed ash from her shoulders. Had intertwined with hers in the dark while they both pretended sleep would come.

Now they were fixing what Selene had broken. Again.

"The muscle's not torn," Mirael said. Her voice was flat. Professional. "Just the skin. You're lucky."

"I know."

"You don't know shit."

The needle went in. Selene bit down on the inside of her cheek and tasted blood.

Mirael worked in silence after that. Stitch after stitch, neat and even, the way she did everything. Her hands were gentle even when her eyes were hard. Muscle memory. Years of patching each other up after jobs went wrong.

But this was different. This wasn't a job. This was Selene choosing violence over partnership, choosing rage over reason, choosing to walk out the door alone when Mirael was right there, willing to follow her anywhere.

The needle pierced skin again. Selene watched Mirael's face and saw the hurt underneath the anger. The exhaustion underneath the hurt.

She'd done that. All of it. In one stupid, reckless morning.

The stitching was almost done when Mirael finally spoke again.

"Last night meant something to me." Mirael's voice was quiet now. Flat. "Did it mean anything to you?"

Selene stared at the wall. Didn't answer.

"You said you weren't going anywhere. Those exact words. And then the first thing you did this morning was leave me here and go off to get yourself killed."

"I wasn't trying to get killed."

"Then what were you trying to do?"

The needle pierced skin. The thread pulled tight.

"I don't know." The truth, finally. "I don't know. I woke up, and I couldn't . . . I couldn't just lie there. Couldn't be still. Couldn't think about anything except finding whoever did this and making them pay."

"And what about me?"

"What about you?"

"I was there too." The needle stopped. Mirael's hands were shaking now, just slightly. "I lost it too. The safehouse was ours, not yours. Those years were ours. And you didn't even think to include me. Didn't even think I might want to help. Might want to be beside you when you found them."

"I didn't want you there."

"I know." Mirael's voice cracked on the second word. "That's the problem, Selene. I know."

She finished the stitching in silence. Tied it off. Pressed a clean bandage against the wound and taped it down. Her hands were gentle, the way they always were when she was taking care of something broken.

Selene watched her work and felt something in her chest that might have been shame.

"I've followed you for years," Mirael said finally. She wasn't looking at Selene. Was looking at her own hands, at the blood under her fingernails. "Through everything. Every bad job and close call and door that closed in our faces. I followed you because I believed in us. In what we were building."

"Mirael . . ."

"But I can't follow someone who doesn't want me beside her." She looked up. Her eyes were red but dry. "I can't be your partner if you won't let me be your partner. I can't keep giving you everything I have and watching you walk out the door like none of it matters."

"It matters."

"Does it? Because from where I'm standing, it looks like I'm just someone you come back to when you're done doing whatever you actually care about."

The words hit like a fist. Harder than the knife had.

"That's not . . ."

"Then tell me what it is. Tell me why you lied. Tell me why you'd rather bleed out in an alley alone than let me watch your back."

Selene opened her mouth. Nothing came out.

She didn't know. That was the truth. She didn't know why she'd done it, couldn't explain the thing inside her that made her push away anyone who got too close. Couldn't explain why Mirael's warmth against her shoulder had felt like a trap she needed to escape. Couldn't explain why hurting was easier than being held.

"I don't know how to be different." The words were barely a whisper. "I don't know how to be what you need."

Mirael looked at her for a long moment. Something passed across her face. Grief, maybe, or the death of something she'd been holding onto.

"I know," she said finally. "That's the worst part. I know."

She stood. Walked to the bed. Sat down on the edge with her back to Selene and pulled her journal from under the pillow.

She didn't open it. Just held it in her lap, her hands resting on the worn leather cover, her shoulders curved inward like she was trying to make herself smaller.

Selene watched her and felt the distance between them like a physical thing. Three feet of floor. Might as well have been miles.

She should say something. Apologize. Cross the room and take Mirael's hands and promise to be better.

The words wouldn't come. They never did.

Instead, she sat there, stitched and bandaged and hollow, and watched the light fade through the thin curtains.

Neither of them spoke.

Neither of them slept for a long time.

She could kill men in alleys, and yet, she couldn't cross three feet of floor.

CHAPTER 18: The Following

Three days of nothing.

Selene sat on the edge of the bed and counted what they had left. Coin enough to pay Viena for another week. Enough to eat, if they were careful. Enough to survive.

Not enough to rebuild.

Most of the catacombs payout had been in the cache. The rest had gone to food, bribes, and keeping Viena paid. Smart operators kept reserves in a secure location, separate from where they slept, accessible but hidden. Twelve years of careful saving. Gone in a single night of flame and smoke.

Mirael was already dressed, already packed, journal already in her bag. She'd been awake when Selene had opened her eyes. Maybe she'd never slept at all.

They hadn't talked. Not really. Not since the night Selene came back bloody and Mirael had stitched her up with steady hands and furious eyes. Three days of functional exchanges. Pass the bread. I'm going out. The door's locked.

Three days of Selene going out to find work and coming back with nothing.

Word traveled fast in the Sprawl. The woman with the daggers had killed two Guild men in an alley. Left bodies where anyone could find them. Sloppy. Emotional. Unpredictable.

Nobody wanted to hire unpredictable.

"Something came through." Mirael's voice was flat. She wasn't looking at Selene. "Harrick's crew needs extra hands for a job tonight."

Harrick. Third-rate operator who worked the kind of jobs no one else would touch. Three months ago, Selene would have laughed at the offer.

"What's the work?"

"Escort. Moving something from the warehouse district to the docks. They're not saying what."

Which meant it was bad. Stolen goods, maybe. Or something worse.

“Pay?”

“Enough to cover another week. Maybe two if the job goes clean.”

Low pay for high risk. The kind of work that came to people who’d burned their options.

Selene stood. “I’ll take it.”

“We’ll take it.” Mirael’s jaw was tight. “I’m not letting you walk into Harrick’s mess alone.”

There was a time when that would have sounded like partnership. Now it sounded like supervision.

Selene didn’t argue.

***

The preparation ritual was the same as it had always been. Check the daggers. Test the edges. Make sure the sheaths were seated properly. Belt buckled. Knives in place.

But the silence was wrong.

Usually they talked through jobs. Angles of approach. Exit routes. Who watched which direction. Contingencies for when things went sideways, because things always went sideways eventually.

Today there was nothing. Just the sound of leather and metal and two people who’d forgotten how to speak to each other.

Selene caught Mirael watching her. Not the soft look she’d grown used to over the years. Something colder. Evaluating. Like she was making calculations Selene couldn’t see.

“What?”

Mirael looked away. “Nothing.”

It wasn’t nothing. But Selene didn’t push. Didn’t have the right.

They finished in silence. Moved to the door. Mirael’s hand found the frame and stopped.

“I don’t know if I can follow you.”

Selene turned. Mirael wasn't looking at her. Was looking at her own hand on the doorframe, at the grain of the wood, at anything except Selene's face.

"Not after what you did. Not after watching you throw away everything we built because you needed something to hurt."

"Mirael . . ."

"Don't." The word was sharp. "Don't say my name like that. Like you're going to explain. Like there's some reason that would make it okay."

Selene's mouth closed. She didn't have a reason. Not one that would matter.

"Then don't follow." The words came out before she could stop them. Flat. Defensive. Wrong.

Mirael's head came up. Her eyes were hard in a way Selene hadn't seen in years. The softness was gone like it had never existed.

"You think I stay because I have nowhere else to go?"

Selene didn't answer.

Mirael stepped away from the door. Toward her. Each step deliberate.

"I know the name of every contact we've ever worked with. Every favor owed. Every debt unpaid. I know which Guild lieutenants are skimming from their bosses and which Paladins take bribes to look the other way."

She let that land. Selene felt something cold settle in her stomach.

"I know where three bodies are buried that would end careers if they surfaced. I know secrets that people would kill to keep quiet. I know who's sleeping with who, who's stealing from who, who's planning to move against who."

Mirael's voice was low. Controlled. More dangerous than shouting.

"I've spent twelve years building a network you don't even see. Because you don't have to. Because I handle it. Because I've been protecting you from threats you never even knew existed."

Selene's hands had gone still at her sides. She'd never heard Mirael talk like this. Had never seen this face, this posture, this cold precision.

"You think you're the dangerous one?" Mirael almost smiled. Almost. "You're a blade, Selene. Sharp and certain and terrifying when you need to be. But blades don't aim themselves. I find the work. I read the angles. I keep us breathing between the blood." She was close now. Close enough that Selene could see the years in her eyes. The exhaustion. The anger. Something else underneath that looked like desperation.

"I could walk out this door and have a new life inside a month. I have favors to call. People who'd take me on without asking questions. I could disappear so completely you'd never find me, no matter how hard you looked."

The cold in Selene's stomach spread. But not for the reasons Mirael thought.

Mirael kept listing exits like prayers. Like if she said them out loud, they'd become true.

If they were true, she wouldn't need to say them.

"I stay because I choose to." Mirael's voice cracked. Just slightly. "Not because I need you. Because I want you."

But that wasn't what Selene saw.

She saw a woman who had wrapped her entire existence around a partnership that couldn't give her what she needed. A woman whose network existed because Selene was the blade. Whose purpose had calcified around keeping Selene alive. Who didn't know who she was outside that orbit anymore.

Mirael wasn't showing her teeth.

She was showing her cage.

"Get your shit together." Mirael's voice was hard again. Controlled. "I mean it. Stop shutting me out. Stop running off to bleed alone. Stop pretending you don't need anyone."

She stepped closer. Close enough that Selene could feel the heat of her.

"Because if you keep doing this, you really will find yourself alone. And we both know you can't do this without me."

The words landed. But not the way Mirael meant them to.

Selene heard: *I've made myself indispensable. I've built my whole life around making sure you can't function without me. And now I need you to need me back.*

That wasn't love. That was survival dressed up as devotion.

And the worst part was, Selene understood it perfectly. She'd done the same thing with violence. Made herself essential through the only skill she had.

They were both cages. Just different shapes.

"I know," Selene said. Two words. All she could manage.

Because she did know. She knew Mirael's value. Knew her importance. Knew everything she'd built and carried and sacrificed.

But she couldn't give her what she wanted. Not the way she wanted it.

Mirael stared at her. Waiting for more.

It didn't come.

Something shifted in Mirael's face. Not disappointment. Recognition. The slow understanding that Selene was never going to say the words she needed to hear.

"That's it? That's all you have?"

"I don't know how to be what you need." The truth. Finally. "I can try to be a better partner. I can try to stop shutting you out. But I can't . . ." She stopped. Couldn't say the rest.

I can't love you the way you want. I can't give you my heart. I don't know if I have one to give.

Mirael's jaw tightened. "Trying would be new."

Not acceptance. Not forgiveness. Just acknowledgment that Selene had offered something, even if it wasn't enough.

She picked up her bag. Adjusted her knife.

"I'll watch your left."

She walked out the door.

Selene stood there. Not relieved. Sick.

She'd just watched Mirael lay herself bare. Show her teeth. Show her desperation. And all Selene had felt was the noose tightening around her neck.

If I fail, she falls. If I leave, she collapses. If I die, she has nothing.

That wasn't partnership. That was a trap they'd built together without realizing it.

She followed Mirael out. Because that's what she did. That's all she knew how to do.

But something had changed. Something had closed.

She'd let this get too close. Let the lines blur. Let Mirael's need become a weight she couldn't carry.

She wouldn't make that mistake again.

***

The job was exactly what Selene expected. Bad.

Harrick's crew was six people including them, moving wooden crates from a warehouse to a waiting boat. The crates were heavy and unmarked and nobody asked what was inside. That was the job. Don't ask. Don't look. Just carry and collect.

It went sideways around midnight.

Someone had talked. Or someone had been watching. Either way, there were men waiting at the docks who weren't supposed to be there, and suddenly the night was full of shouting and steel.

Selene moved on instinct. The daggers found her hands without conscious thought. A man came at her, and she opened his throat. Another grabbed for one of the crates, and she put a blade through his eye.

But she was watching Mirael.

Not with warmth. With clarity.

She saw Mirael position herself at the edge of the fight, never in the center, always where information flowed fastest. Saw her direct Harrick's men with quick gestures, keeping the chaos organized. Saw the knife work when it came, precise and economical, nothing wasted.

Twelve years. Selene had never really seen her work. Had been too busy being the blade to notice the hand.

But now she saw something else too.

Mirael's eyes kept finding her. Checking. Making sure Selene was still standing.

Not watching the fight. Watching Selene.

Her whole purpose has calcified around keeping me alive.

The thought made something in Selene's chest go cold.

The fight ended. Bodies on the dock. Crates secured. Coin changed hands in an alley two blocks away.

They walked back toward the apartment in silence.

Selene kept her distance. A few feet more than usual. Enough to be noticed.

Mirael noticed.

Halfway there, she stopped.

"I'm going to the market. We need supplies."

Translation: *I need space. I need to not be near you right now.*

Good. Selene needed the same thing.

"Okay."

Mirael looked at her for a long moment. Whatever she saw made her mouth tighten.

Then she walked away, the bag with the journal over her shoulder.

Selene watched her disappear into the early morning crowd.

She should go back to the apartment. Rest. Think about what came next.

Instead, she walked.

***

She didn't plan to end up at Mother Gessa's.

But her feet knew the way, and by the time she realized where she was going, she was already there.

The house was quiet in the early morning. Most of the children still asleep. Gessa probably in the kitchen, doing whatever it was that kept a place like this running.

Kira was in the yard.

She was trying to hang a wet shirt on the line, but she was too short to reach properly. The shirt kept slipping, and she kept jumping to catch it, her small face screwed up in frustration.

Selene watched from the gate. Something in her chest loosened. Just slightly.

"Need help?"

Kira spun around. Her face broke into a grin when she saw who it was.

"You came back!"

"Said I would."

"People say things." Kira shrugged, already turning back to the laundry. "Doesn't mean they do them."

Six years old. Already knew that much about the world.

Selene walked over and took the shirt from her hands. Hung it on the line without effort.

"Show-off," Kira muttered.

"Height advantage."

"That's cheating."

"That's life."

Kira made a face at her, but she was smiling. She picked up another wet thing from the basket. Some kind of rag. Held it up toward Selene expectantly.

They worked in silence for a while. Selene hanging, Kira handing things up. The rhythm was easy. Undemanding.

No negotiations. No leverage. No teeth.

"You look sad," Kira said eventually.

"I'm not sad."

"You look like something." She considered. "Tired maybe. Gessa looks like that sometimes. When the money's bad."

"Money's fine."

"Then what?"

Selene hung another shirt. Stared at the line instead of at Kira.

"Someone's mad at me. Someone I work with."

"Did you do something bad?"

"I did something stupid."

"That's different." Kira nodded like this made perfect sense. "Did you say sorry?"

"It's more complicated than that."

"Grown-ups always say that." Kira handed her another rag. "Usually it's not."

Selene almost smiled. "This time it is."

"Why?"

Because Mirael wants something I can't give her. Because I'm a cage she built around herself. Because every time I try to care about her the right way, I feel like I'm drowning.

"Because I'm not good at being what people need."

Kira thought about this. Her small face was serious.

"Gessa says you can't make people happy. You can only not make them sad on purpose."

Selene blinked. "That's . . . actually pretty smart."

"She says it when the big kids fight." Kira shrugged. "I think it means you shouldn't be mean just because you can."

Something in Selene's chest shifted.

You shouldn't be mean just because you can.

She hadn't been mean to Mirael. Not on purpose. But she hadn't been kind either. Had just . . . existed alongside her without ever really seeing what it cost her.

"What if you're not mean, but you're not nice either?" Selene asked. "What if you just . . . don't know how to be what someone wants?"

Kira considered this with the gravity of someone being asked to solve a difficult puzzle.

"Then you try anyway," she said finally. "Even if it's wrong. Trying is better than not trying."

"What if trying makes it worse?"

"At least they know you tried." Kira looked up at her. "Some people don't even do that. Some people just leave."

The words hit harder than they should have.

Some people just leave.

Selene thought about her parents. About Rook. About everyone who'd walked away without trying.

She thought about Mirael, who'd stayed for twelve years. Who'd tried every single day, in her own way, even when Selene made it hard.

And she thought about herself. The walls she'd built. The distance she'd maintained. The way she kept everyone at arm's length because it was safer than letting them in.

She wasn't mean.

But she'd never really tried either.

"Hey." Kira tugged at her sleeve. "You're thinking too hard. Your face went all weird."

Selene looked down at her. This small, serious child who'd already learned that the world was cruel and had decided to be kind anyway.

"When did you get so smart?"

"I was always smart." Kira grinned. "You just didn't notice."

For the first time in days, Selene felt something that wasn't pressure or guilt or fear.

It was something warmer. Something simpler.

This. This was where her heart could breathe.

Not with Mirael, where every emotion came wrapped in obligation and history and the weight of what they owed each other.

Here. With a six-year-old who just wanted someone to come back when they said they would.

"I'm going to teach you how to move quiet next week," Selene said. "Like I promised."

"I know." Kira's grin widened. "You already said."

"I'm saying it again."

"Okay." She handed Selene the last piece of laundry. "You should come back more. Even when you don't have to teach me stuff. Gessa likes you. She says you're good under all the sharp."

"Good under all the sharp?"

"Her words." Kira shrugged. "I think she means you're not as scary as you look."

Selene hung the last piece. Looked at the line of wet clothes moving slightly in the morning breeze.

"I should go."

"Back to the person you made sad?"

"Back to work."

Kira nodded. Then, without warning, she stepped forward and hugged Selene's leg. Quick. Fierce. Over before Selene could react.

"Don't be a leaver," Kira said. "I don't like leavers."

Selene's throat tightened.

"I won't."

"Promise?"

She shouldn't. She'd just spent five minutes explaining why promises were weapons people used to hurt you. Why asking for them was dangerous. Why giving them was worse.

But Kira was looking at her with eyes that had already learned too much about leavers. And Selene found she couldn't add herself to that list. Not even hypothetically.

"I promise."

Kira studied her face for a moment. Whatever she saw satisfied her.

"Okay. See you next week."

She picked up the empty basket and headed toward the house without looking back.

Selene watched her go.

***

The walk back to the apartment was quiet.

The city moved around her. Same streets. Same crowds. Same noise.

But something was different.

Not better. Just clearer.

She thought about Mirael. The teeth she'd shown. The desperation underneath. The cage they'd built together without meaning to.

She couldn't give Mirael what she wanted. That hadn't changed. Probably never would.

But Kira was right. Trying was better than not trying. Even if it was wrong. Even if it made things worse.

Not trying was just another kind of leaving.

And Selene was tired of being a leaver.

The apartment door was closed when she reached it. She stood outside for a moment. Gathering herself.

Not for what she was about to offer.

For what she was about to take away.

Then she went in.

Mirael was there. Sitting on the bed. The journal was closed in her lap. Her eyes were red.

She looked up when Selene entered. Guarded. Waiting for whatever came next.

Selene closed the door. Leaned against it. Let the silence stretch for a moment.

"I talked to someone today," she said. "A kid I know. She said something that made sense."

Mirael didn't respond. Just watched.

"She said trying is better than not trying. Even if you do it wrong." Selene paused. "So I'm going to try. To be better at the partnership. At not shutting you out. At not running off alone when things get hard."

Something shifted in Mirael's face. The beginning of hope.

Selene killed it.

"But I need you to hear something. And I need you to really hear it, because I'm only going to say this once."

Mirael went still.

"This is a partnership." Selene's voice was calm. Tired. Absolute. "This is not a romance. This will never be a romance."

The words landed. Hard.

"I can give you my back in a fight. I can give you loyalty. I can give you work and honesty, and whatever version of friendship I'm capable of." She held Mirael's gaze. "I cannot give you my heart. Not like that."

Mirael's face had gone pale.

"I should have said this a long time ago. Should have drawn this line before we built twelve years on a foundation I knew was cracked." Selene's throat was tight, but her voice stayed even. "That's on me. I let it stay unclear because it was easier. Because I didn't want to lose what we had."

She pushed off the door. Stood in the middle of the room. Nowhere to hide.

"If you stay, you stay knowing this doesn't change. There's no 'someday.' There's no 'maybe if I wait long enough.' This is what I am. This is all I have."

Mirael's hands had curled into fists in her lap. Her jaw was clenched so tight Selene could see the muscle jumping.

"And if that's not enough . . ." Selene made herself say it. "I understand. If you need to leave, I won't chase you. I won't blame you. You deserve more than what I can give, and we both know it."

Silence.

The kind that pressed against the walls and made the room feel smaller.

Mirael's voice came out rough. Barely above a whisper.

"You're serious."

"Yes."

"This isn't . . . this isn't you pushing me away because you're scared. This isn't something I can wait out."

"No."

Mirael closed her eyes. Her shoulders curved inward. For a long moment she just sat there, breathing, her hands still clenched around nothing.

When she opened her eyes again, something had changed. The hope was gone. In its place was something harder. Colder. The face of a woman who'd just watched a door close that she'd been trying to open for twelve years.

"Then I stay," she said. Her voice was flat. "Because the alternative is worse. Because I don't know who I am without this, and that's my problem, not yours."

It wasn't acceptance. It wasn't forgiveness.

It was a choice made with open eyes and a closed heart.

Selene nodded once.

"I'm going to sleep."

She moved to the chair by the window. Not the bed. She'd earned that distance now. Claimed it.

Mirael watched her settle. Her face was blank. Controlled. The mask of someone who'd just learned how to stop hoping.

"Thank you," she said quietly. "For finally being honest."

It didn't sound like gratitude. It sounded like she was dying.

Selene turned her face toward the wall. Listened to the sound of the journal opening behind her. The scratch of quill on paper.

Mirael writing it down. All of it. The words Selene had finally said. The door that had finally closed.

Selene's hands were shaking. She pressed them flat against her thighs and willed them to stop.

Don't be a leaver.

She wouldn't be. Not to Kira. Not to that small, fierce thing that didn't ask her to be more than she was.

That was where her heart would stay.

She listened to Mirael write until the scratching stopped. Listened to the bed shift as Mirael lay down. Listened to her breathing slow into something like sleep.

Then she closed her eyes.

The rest was just survival.

CHAPTER 19: The Contract

The apartment felt different now.

Same walls. Same window. Same bed where Mirael slept alone while Selene took the chair. But the air had changed. Cleaner, maybe. Colder, definitely.

Outside, Garnath was already grinding. Cart wheels on cobblestone. A fishmonger's call from two streets over. Somewhere a dog barked and was silenced. The city didn't care what happened inside these walls. It never did.

Selene watched the morning light crawl across the floor and waited for the discomfort to arrive.

It didn't.

Mirael was already awake. Already dressed. Moving through the room with crisp efficiency, gathering supplies, organizing gear. Every motion precise. Professional. The way she moved before a job with a client she didn't like but needed to impress.

She was performing.

Selene recognized it because she'd seen Mirael do it a thousand times for other people. The regal bearing. The measured speech. The careful distance that said *I am here to work, not to feel.*

Mirael thought this would teach Selene something. Would make her realize what she'd lost. Would show her the cost of drawing that line.

It didn't.

Selene watched her move through the morning routine and felt . . . relief. This was easier. This was cleaner. No more navigating the weight of someone else's wanting. No more feeling Mirael's eyes on her and knowing she was failing just by existing.

Partnership. That's what this was now. Clean lines. Clear expectations.

Selene told herself it was better this way.

She meant it.

***

"We need to count what's left."

Mirael's voice was flat. Not angry. Not hurt. Just . . . empty. The voice she used with clients who didn't deserve warmth but still required service.

Selene sat at the small table while Mirael laid out the coin. Copper. Some silver. A few bits of gold that caught the light like accusations.

"The catacombs job paid well," Mirael said, not looking at her. "But most of it went into the cache."

The cache that burned. Twelve years of careful saving, gone in a single night of smoke and flame.

"This is what we have." Mirael gestured at the spread. "Enough for three weeks. Maybe four if we're careful. Enough to work. Not enough to rebuild."

She delivered the information like a report. Facts without feeling. The performance of a partner who was only a partner now.

Selene looked at the money and saw their future laid out in metal. Not broke. Not starving. Just . . . stopped. Treading water with no shore in sight.

"Then we work," she said. "Same as always."

"Same as always."

Mirael began gathering the coins. Efficient. Mechanical. Waiting for Selene to say something about how cold she was being.

Selene didn't.

She was fine with this. More than fine. This was what she'd asked for. What she'd demanded. A partnership without the weight of wanting.

If Mirael had hoped her coldness would wake Selene up to what she'd thrown away, she was going to be disappointed.

Some things couldn't be rebuilt. Selene had made peace with that a long time ago.

***

The knock came midmorning.

Selene's hand found her dagger before she was fully standing. Old habits. The kind that kept you alive in Garnath.

Mirael moved to the side of the door, out of direct line. Also old habits. The choreography of survival, practiced until it was instinct.

"Who is it?"

"Weston."

Selene's jaw tightened. She looked at Mirael. Mirael's face gave nothing away. Professional. Detached. Still performing.

"I'm alone," Weston added through the wood. "No backup. No uniforms. Just . . . just talk. Please."

That last word. *Please.* It didn't belong in a Paladin's mouth. Not when talking to someone like her.

Selene opened the door.

He looked worse than the last time she'd seen him. Older. Worn thin in a way that had nothing to do with age. The shadows under his eyes said he hadn't slept well in days. Maybe weeks.

"May I come in?"

"No."

He nodded. Didn't argue. Like he'd expected that and had decided not to waste energy fighting it. He pulled out a small notebook. Flipped to a page already covered in tight handwriting.

"Then we'll do this here." He scanned the page. "Three nights ago. Between second and third bell. Where were you?"

"Working."

"Where?"

"Dockside. Cargo escort."

"Anyone who can confirm that?"

"The client. Harrick's crew."

Weston made a note. "And the night of the Meridian Street fire?"

"Home. Asleep."

"Anyone who can confirm that?"

Selene's jaw tightened. "My partner."

"Who lives with you. Who depends on you." Weston's voice was flat. Professional. "The magistrates won't count that."

"Then they won't count it."

He turned a page. “A man named Garrett was found dead in an alley off Coppersmith Row six days ago. Knife work. Professional. You know anything about that?”

Selene kept her face still. Garrett. The Guild muscle she’d killed looking for information about the fire. The one she’d killed too fast, before he could talk.

“No.”

The lie came easy. They always did.

“His partner Polk was found three streets over. Same night. Same wounds.” Weston looked up from his notes. Met her eyes. “Someone’s been asking questions about you, Selene. Asking hard. And the people who might have answers keep turning up dead.”

Selene said nothing. Let the silence sit.

Weston’s eyes moved to her side. The place where her shirt pulled slightly, where she’d been favoring her ribs without thinking about it.

“That injury,” he said. “When?”

Selene didn’t flinch. “Last week. Job went sideways.”

“What job?”

“Cargo escort. Dockside. Someone got greedy.”

Weston wrote it down. His pen paused for half a second, then kept moving.

“The wounds on Polk were defensive. Someone fast. Someone trained.” He closed the notebook. “Same week. Same neighborhood. Same knife work.”

“Lots of knife work in this city.”

“There is.” Weston tucked the notebook into his coat. “Garrett and Polk were Guild muscle. Low level. Disposable. The kind of men someone uses and throws away.” He met her eyes again. “I don’t know what happened in that alley. Maybe I don’t want to know. What I do know is that everything else, the fire, the witnesses, the pattern, that’s a frame. Someone’s building a case against you, and they’re good at it.”

“Then why are you here asking questions you already know the answers to?”

Weston's jaw worked. He looked past her, into the apartment, then back at her face. The weight in his eyes was almost unbearable to look at.

"Because I have to. Because the evidence exists whether I believe it or not. Because I've got a file on my desk with your name on it, and that file gets thicker every day." His voice was quiet. Stripped of authority. Just a tired man saying true things. "I've been holding the line. Pushing back on the reports. Asking for more time, more investigation. But the evidence keeps coming. Witnesses. Bodies. A pattern that points at you no matter which way I turn it."

"And you're warning me. Why?"

"Because I still think there's something worth saving here." He held her gaze. "I don't know what it is. I don't know why. But eighteen years in this job, you learn to trust your gut, and my gut says you're not what they're painting you as."

Selene didn't know what to do with that. Didn't know how to hold something that felt almost like faith from a man who wore a uniform.

"So what happens now?"

Weston tucked the notebook back into his coat. Something closed behind his eyes.

"Now I do my job. I file my report. I present what I have, and what I have is enough to compel." He stepped back from the door. "There will be a summons. Maybe a week from now, maybe less. Formal questioning. A trial path. I'll be the one who comes for you, because I'd rather it be me than someone who doesn't care about the truth."

"And if I run?"

"Then they send people who don't ask questions first. And I can't protect you from that." He turned to go, then stopped. Looked back over his shoulder. "This is the last time I can come to you like this. Off the books. Man to woman instead of Paladin to suspect. After this, it's all official. All recorded. All leading somewhere neither of us wants to go."

"Why tell me any of this?"

"Because someone should." He walked away. Didn't look back again.

Selene closed the door. Leaned against it.

"He's trying to save you," Mirael said. Her voice was still flat. Still professional. But something flickered underneath. "He's risking his career to give you warning."

"I know."

"Do you know why?"

Selene thought about it. A Paladin with eighteen years of service, throwing himself against the machine for a woman who'd never given him a reason to care.

"No," she said. "I don't."

Outside, the city kept moving. It always did. Garnath didn't pause for questions or complications. It ground forward, day after day, wearing down everyone who lived inside it.

***

The job came through Viena's network. Escort work. Moving cargo from the warehouse district to a merchant ship at the eastern docks.

The pay was low. The scrutiny was high. The kind of job that came to people who'd burned their better options.

Selene took it anyway.

"This is beneath us," Mirael said as they prepared. Not complaining. Just stating fact. Her voice still flat. Still performing the role of partner-without-feeling.

"Everything's beneath us right now. Until it isn't."

Mirael checked her knife. Checked her bag. Straightened her clothes. Every motion controlled. Deliberate. A woman going through the mechanics of work without any of the warmth that used to come with it.

She was waiting for Selene to comment on how cold she was being. Waiting for Selene to miss what they'd had. Waiting for some crack in the wall.

Selene didn't give her one.

"Let's go. Cargo won't move itself."

***

Across the city, in a room that smelled of old paper and older money, a contract changed hands.

The paper was stamped twice. No names. Just marks. The payment had been split into three purses, delivered by three different couriers, so no single man could be traced back to the order.

The man who received it didn't speak. Didn't need to. The instructions were clear enough. The target's description. Her patterns. Her known associates. The places she frequented, the routes she traveled, the blind spots in her awareness.

"She's dragging heat into lanes that used to stay quiet," said the man behind the desk. Guild sigils on his collar. Authority in his voice. "Two bodies in the open, and now every knife in the Sprawl thinks it can act without permission."

The operative read the contract once. Committed it to memory. Set the paper down.

"Timeline?"

"Soon. But clean. No witnesses. No questions. Make it look like the city did what the city does."

A nod. Nothing more.

The operative left the way he'd come. Silent. Efficient. Already planning.

He had a job to do.

***

The cargo job went smoothly. Too smoothly, maybe. The kind of easy that made Selene's teeth itch.

The warehouse district smelled like tar and rotting fish and the particular desperation of men who loaded ships for coin that wouldn't last the week. Garnath's bones showed here, where the pretty facades gave way to function. Cracked stone. Rusted iron. The constant groan of rigging and the shouts of foremen who'd long since stopped caring about anything but weight and time.

They walked the crates from warehouse to dock. Watched the longshoremen load them onto a ship that flew no flag Selene recognized. Collected their pay from a man who wouldn't meet their eyes.

"Something's wrong," Mirael said as they walked away from the docks.

"Something's always wrong."

"No. Something specific. That job was too clean. No Guild interference. No Watchers asking questions. No complications."

Selene had noticed the same thing. Had been trying not to think about it.

"Maybe we got lucky."

"We don't get lucky. We get by. Anything more than that is suspicious."

They took the long way home. Through the market district, where the crowds would swallow them. Where anyone following would have to work for it.

The market was loud. Chaotic. Bodies pressing against bodies, voices competing for attention, the smell of fish and bread and unwashed humanity mixing into something that was uniquely Garnath.

A man bumped into Mirael. Hard. His shoulder caught her bag, twisting the strap, and for one terrible moment the flap came open and the journal slid halfway out.

Mirael grabbed it. Shoved it back inside. Clutched the bag against her chest like someone had tried to take her heart.

The man kept walking. Didn't look back. Probably didn't even notice what he'd almost done.

"It's fine," Selene said. "Just the crowd."

But Mirael wasn't listening. She was staring at the bag in her hands. At the journal that had almost spilled into the mud and the feet of strangers.

"Mirael."

"Everything's in here." Mirael's voice was strange. Hollow. The mechanical coldness cracking to show something raw underneath. "Fourteen years. Everything I couldn't say out loud. Everything I . . ."

She stopped. Closed the flap. Tightened the strap until it pressed against her body.

"It's fine," Selene said again.

"It almost wasn't."

They walked the rest of the way in silence. But something had changed. Mirael's hand never left the bag now. She kept it close, kept checking it, kept adjusting the strap like she could feel phantom hands trying to take it.

The journal wasn't just a book anymore.

It was everything she'd poured into something that couldn't reject her. Fourteen years of wanting and hurting and hoping, all bound in leather and paper.

And now she knew it could be taken.

***

In an alley three streets away, a man with no name worth remembering watched them disappear into the crowd.

He was the kind of man cities produced by the thousands. Thin. Hungry. Face like every other face in the Sprawl, forgettable before you'd finished looking at it. The kind of man who begged when begging worked and stole when it didn't. The kind of man people stepped over in gutters without wondering if he was sleeping or dead.

Nobody would remember him. That was the point.

He'd been told to watch. To wait. To find the right moment.

The bag. That's what mattered. The leather satchel the quiet one carried. He'd seen her clutch it just now, seen the way she held it like it contained something precious.

He didn't know what was inside. Didn't care. Didn't need to.

He'd been promised coin. Enough to eat for a week. Maybe more if he was quick and clean.

Wait for the right moment. Grab and run. Meet at the broken fountain on Ravel Street. Third bell. Get paid.

Simple.

He'd done worse for less. He'd do worse again.

He scratched at the sores on his arm and kept watching.

***

The orphanage was quiet when she arrived. She'd stopped pretending these visits were accidents. The house was quiet in the late afternoon. Most of the children napping or doing chores. The smell of bread baking somewhere inside. Normal. Safe. Everything the rest of Garnath wasn't.

Kira was in the yard, sitting on an overturned bucket, drawing shapes in the dirt with a stick.

Selene leaned against the gate and watched.

Something in her chest loosened. Just slightly. Just enough to notice.

"You're staring."

Kira hadn't looked up. Six years old and already aware when someone was watching her. Garnath taught that early.

"Just thinking."

"About what?"

"About you." Selene walked into the yard. Crouched down to Kira's level. "Can I ask you something?"

Kira finally looked up. Her face was serious. Guarded. The face of a child who'd learned that questions from adults usually meant trouble.

"Depends."

"Smart answer." Selene almost smiled. "When I'm not around . . . when you're here, or on the streets, and someone bothers you. A bigger kid. Someone mean. What do you do?"

Kira's brow furrowed. She thought about it with the gravity of someone being asked to solve a difficult puzzle.

"Depends on who," she said finally. "Some of them, you can talk to. Make them laugh or give them something and they go away."

"And the ones you can't talk to?"

"Run." Kira shrugged like this was obvious. "I'm small. I'm fast. Most of them get bored."

"And if you can't run?"

Kira's face changed. Something harder underneath. Something that had already learned things a six-year-old shouldn't have to learn.

"Then you make it hurt to hold you. Bite. Scratch. Go for eyes. Scream until someone comes or they let go." She looked down at her stick. "Mother Gessa says fighting is wrong. But she's never been small in a city that doesn't care."

Selene felt something twist in her chest. Recognition. Memory. A girl who'd learned the same lessons in the same streets, twenty years ago.

"You're smart," she said. "Smarter than I was at your age."

"You were my age once?"

"Hard to believe, I know."

Kira almost smiled. Almost. "Did you fight?"

"Still do."

"Did you win?"

"I'm still here. That's the only winning that counts."

Kira considered this. Nodded like it made sense.

"Will you show me?" she asked. "How to fight better? So I don't always have to run?"

Selene hesitated. Teaching meant commitment. Teaching meant coming back. Teaching meant being the kind of person someone counted on.

But Kira was looking at her with those eyes. Those too-old, too-careful eyes that hadn't given up on hoping even though hoping was dangerous.

"Maybe," Selene said. "If I come back."

"Will you come back?"

"I'll try."

"That's what people say when they mean no."

"That's what people say when they mean they don't know yet." Selene stood. "But I came back today. And the time before. That count for anything?"

Kira thought about it.

"Yeah," she said finally. "That counts."

Selene hesitated. Then: "If you're ever in real trouble. The kind where running isn't enough. There's a place called the Veiled Lantern. Dockside, near the fish market. Ask for Viena. Tell her you know me."

Kira's eyes went wide. "What kind of place?"

"The kind you don't go to unless you have to. But Viena's good people, in her own way. She'll find me. Or she'll keep you safe until I can get there."

"Where's your room?"

Selene blinked. The question was so practical, so street-smart, that it caught her off guard.

"Back stair. Past the kitchen. Second door on the left."

Kira nodded once, filing it away.

"Why are you telling me this?"

Because the world breaks children, and I can't always be there. Because I was your age once, with nowhere to go and no one to ask. Because some things should have been said to me and weren't.

"Because you should know," Selene said. "Just in case."

Kira nodded. Serious. Filing it away the way street children filed away everything that might keep them alive.

"The Veiled Lantern. Viena. Dockside." She looked up at Selene. "I don't forget places. People lie, places don't."

"Good girl."

***

The operative watched from a rooftop two buildings away.

The wind carried the smell of blade oil and old leather. He didn't move. Didn't shift. Just watched.

He'd been tracking her for three days now. Learning her patterns. Her routes. Her blind spots.

She was good. Better than most. Aware of her surroundings in a way that made her hard to follow.

But she had patterns.

The brothel where she did business. The apartment where she slept. The orphanage she visited.

He could have taken her twice already. Clean angles. Easy kills.

He hadn't. Not yet.

She was at Gessa's place again. Talking to a child in the yard.

He filed it away. Kept watching.

***

The apartment was dark when Selene returned.

Mirael was at the table, writing by candlelight. The journal was chained to her now, the bag strap looped around her wrist even as she wrote. She hadn't done that before. Before the market. Before she'd felt it almost slip away.

She looked up when Selene entered. Her face was controlled. Professional. Still performing.

But something was different in her eyes. Fear, maybe. The new understanding that the one thing she had left could be taken.

"Where were you?"

"Walking."

"You always say that."

"It's always true."

Mirael's jaw tightened. She wanted to push. Wanted to crack the wall and find something worth fighting for underneath. But that wasn't what they were anymore.

Partners. Just partners.

She went back to writing.

Selene moved to the chair by the window. Watched Mirael's hand move across the page. Watched the way she kept the bag close, kept her wrist through the strap, kept her body between the journal and the door.

"You're being careful with that now," Selene said. "The bag."

Mirael's hand stopped. She didn't look up.

"It almost fell in the market. Into the mud. Into the crowd."

"I remember."

"Everything's in here." Mirael's voice was quiet. Not cold anymore. Cracked. "Fourteen years of . . . of everything. If I lost it . . ."

She didn't finish. Didn't have to.

Selene wanted to say something. Wanted to offer comfort or reassurance or something that would help.

But she'd drawn the line. She'd made the rules. And reaching across now would only make things worse.

"Get some sleep," she said instead. "We have work tomorrow."

Mirael nodded. Closed the journal. Ran her thumb along the spine once, the way she always did. Then she wrapped it in the cloth she kept for this purpose, placed it under her pillow, and adjusted it until it sat exactly right. The same position. The same angle. Every night.

Selene had never noticed before. Now she couldn't stop noticing.

She settled into her chair. Closed her eyes.

Outside, Garnath breathed its slow, grinding breath. Distant shouts. A woman's laughter cut short. The creak of cart wheels on cobblestone that never stopped, not even at night. The city didn't sleep. It just changed predators.

Somewhere in the dark, three different ones were circling.

A Paladin running out of time.

A hungry ghost who would do anything for coin.

And someone else. Someone patient. Someone who watched and waited and chose not to strike.

Selene felt the weight of all of it pressing down. The sense that something was coming. Something she couldn't see yet. The city knew. It always knew before the people in it did.

But she was tired. And tomorrow would bring more work, more questions, more survival.

She'd deal with it then.

She always did.

CHAPTER 20: The Theft

The morning came gray and wet.

Rain had fallen sometime in the night, and Garnath wore it like a second skin. Water pooled in the broken cobblestones, turned the gutters into rivers of filth, made the city smell like rot and rust and the particular misery of people who couldn't afford to stay dry.

Selene watched the light crawl through the window and listened to Mirael move through the apartment behind her.

Mirael was packing the journal. The same ritual as every morning since the market, but slower now. More careful. She ran her thumb along the spine before wrapping it in cloth, the gesture so familiar Selene could have done it blindfolded.

Selene turned back to the window. Some things were easier not to watch.

"We have work," Selene said without turning around.

"I know."

"Viena's contact. The message run to the merchant quarter."

"I know."

Mirael's voice was flat. Professional. Still performing the role of partner-without-feeling, three days later. Still waiting for Selene to crack. Still not understanding that Selene was fine with this, that the distance was easier, that the absence of wanting was a relief rather than a punishment.

But underneath the performance, something else now. Something brittle. The journal had become her anchor, and anchors only mattered when you were afraid of drifting away.

"We should go. Before the streets get too crowded."

"I'm ready."

Selene turned. Mirael stood by the door, bag on her hip. "Then let's go."

***

Garnath in the morning was a machine grinding to life.

Carts rattled over wet stone. Shopkeepers threw open shutters and cursed the rain. A fishmonger's cart had overturned on the corner of Haller Street, and the driver was screaming at a boy who'd run into him while two street dogs circled the spilled catch, waiting for their moment.

The city didn't pause for small disasters. It flowed around them and kept moving.

Selene walked half a step ahead of Mirael, eyes scanning the crowd out of habit. Looking for faces that appeared twice. For hands that moved wrong. For the particular stillness of someone waiting for something.

She saw nothing. Felt everything.

The itch between her shoulder blades that said someone was watching. The prickle at the back of her neck that had kept her alive for twenty-three years in this city. Garnath was full of eyes, and some of them were pointed at her.

But she couldn't find them. Couldn't pin down the source.

"Something wrong?" Mirael asked.

"No."

Yes. Something was wrong. Something had been wrong for days, maybe weeks. The sense of a net tightening. Of pieces moving in the dark. Of machinery grinding toward a conclusion she couldn't see.

But she couldn't point to it. Couldn't name it. So she said nothing and kept walking.

***

In an alley three streets behind them, the man with no name scratched at the sores on his arm and watched.

He'd been following them since they left the apartment. Keeping distance. Staying in the crowds. Just another face in the river of bodies that filled Garnath's streets every morning.

The woman with the bag. That's what mattered.

Today was the day. Had to be. He couldn't afford to wait anymore.

The coin he'd been promised would feed him for a week. Maybe two if he was careful. And he was always careful. That's how you survived in the Sprawl. You took what you could get, and you didn't ask questions.

Wait for the right moment. Grab and run. Meet at the broken fountain on Ravel Street. Third bell.

Simple.

He'd done worse for less.

The two women turned onto Merchant Way, and he followed.

***

The message run took them through the merchant quarter, past the guild halls and the counting houses, through streets that smelled like money and ambition instead of fish and desperation.

Different city here. Same rules underneath.

Selene delivered Viena's message to a man in a silk coat who pretended not to know what she was talking about, then slipped three silver coins into her palm when no one was looking. Mirael waited outside, bag clutched tight, eyes moving.

"Done," Selene said when she emerged. "Easy money."

"Too easy."

"You keep saying that."

"Because it keeps holding true."

They took the long way back. Through the market district again, because crowds meant cover. Because being lost in a sea of bodies was safer than being visible on an empty street.

The market was louder today. Some kind of festival preparation, banners going up, vendors shouting over each other, more bodies than usual pressing through the narrow lanes. Selene had to fight for every step.

Too many bodies. Too much noise.

The crowd pressed in from all sides, and Selene felt the familiar itch crawl up her spine. Vulnerability. Exposure. The feeling of being watched by eyes she couldn't find.

She turned to check on Mirael.

Lost her.

Just for a moment. Just long enough for the crowd to surge and swallow the space between them.

"Mirael?"

Then she heard the scream.

***

It happened fast.

Too fast to stop. Too fast to do anything but watch.

A body hitting Mirael from behind. Hard. Professional. A shoulder driven into her spine, a hand grabbing the strap, a knife flashing in the gray light.

The strap didn't break. It was cut.

Mirael went down. Knees hitting cobblestone. Hands reaching for something that was already gone.

She hit the ground and kept reaching. Fingers clawing at wet stone, at the legs of strangers, at nothing.

The thief was already running. Male. Thin. Forgettable. Moving through the crowd like water, the bag clutched to his chest, disappearing into the sea of bodies that parted for him and closed behind him.

And Mirael was screaming.

Not words. Something rawer than words. Something that came from the place where she'd been storing everything she couldn't say, everything she couldn't give, everything she'd poured into pages because pages couldn't reject her.

Three days of careful coldness shattered. Three days of professional distance gone in a single breath. Just raw, animal grief pouring out of her throat in a sound that made the crowd around her step back.

"SELENE!"

But Selene was already moving.

***

The crowd parted for her because something in her face made people step aside. Or maybe it was the way she moved, all predator, all purpose, a blade cutting through flesh.

She didn’t think about Mirael on the ground behind her. Didn’t think about the sound she’d made, the way her hands had kept reaching for something that wasn’t there. Didn’t think about anything except the thin figure disappearing into the chaos ahead.

The thief was fast. Knew the streets. Knew the alleys and the shortcuts and the places where the crowd thinned enough to run.

But Selene knew them better.

Twenty-three years. Every alley. Every rooftop. Every broken fence and collapsed wall and drainage tunnel that could be a shortcut if you were desperate enough.

She ran.

Through the market. Past a fishmonger who cursed as she knocked his display. Under a banner that tangled in her hair and tore free. Into the maze of alleys that led toward the eastern slums.

Garnath blurred around her. Wet stone. Running gutters. The smell of piss and rotting vegetables and the particular desperation of a city that had been grinding people to nothing for three hundred years.

The faces of people who didn’t care. Who would never care. Who looked away from violence because violence was the city’s native language and they’d learned long ago that watching could make you a participant.

The thief glanced back. Saw her gaining.

His face was thin and desperate and forgettable. Hollow cheeks. Sores on his neck. The kind of face Garnath stamped out by the thousands. Nobody. Nothing. A ghost who’d been dead long before someone cut his throat.

He ran faster.

Selene ran faster still.

Her lungs burned. Her legs screamed. The wound in her side, weeks healed but never quite right, pulled with every stride.

She didn’t slow down.

Two streets. Three. The crowds thinning. The buildings getting older, more broken, leaning into each other like drunks holding each other up. The slums opening ahead like a wound in the city's side.

He was heading somewhere specific. She could see it in the way he moved, the certainty underneath the panic. He had a destination. A meeting point. Someone waiting.

Ravel Street. The broken fountain. Third bell.

She knew. She'd read his instructions in his body before she'd known there were instructions to read.

She pushed harder. Closed the gap. Three steps behind now. Two. Close enough to hear his ragged breathing. Close enough to see the sweat soaking through his shirt. Close enough to smell his fear.

Almost.

Almost.

The thief ducked into an alley. Selene followed, one step behind, hand reaching for his collar.

The alley opened into a small square. A broken fountain in the center, dry for years, the statue of some forgotten saint long since stolen for scrap.

Third bell was just striking somewhere in the distance.

The thief stopped running.

Because he'd already arrived.

And something was wrong.

***

Selene smelled it before she saw it.

Smoke. Oil. The thick, greasy stench of something burning that shouldn't be burning.

The alley opened into a small square. A broken fountain in the center, dry for years, the statue of some forgotten saint long since stolen for scrap.

The fire was in the fountain basin. Roaring. Too big, too hot, too deliberate. Someone had poured oil, lots of it, and set it ablaze.

The thief was in the fire.

He was still moving. Barely. His arms twitching, his legs kicking weakly, his mouth open in a scream that had already burned away to nothing. His throat had been cut first, she could see that much, but whoever had done it hadn't waited for him to die before they'd started burning.

And beside him, in the flames, something else. Leather curling. Pages blackening. The shape of a book being swallowed by fire.

Mirael's journal. It had to be.

"No."

Selene lunged forward. The heat hit her like a wall. She staggered back, threw up an arm to shield her face. The fire was too hot, too big, the oil still feeding it.

She looked for something, anything. A stick. A pole. A way to reach in and grab it.

Nothing.

She tried again. Got closer this time, close enough to feel her eyebrows singeing, close enough to see the pages turning to ash one by one. Her hand reached out.

The heat drove her back.

"No. No, no, no."

She circled the fountain. Looking for an angle. A gap in the flames. Somewhere the fire burned lower.

There wasn't one.

The oil had been poured deliberately. Evenly. The whole basin was an inferno, and anything inside it was fuel.

She found a broken board in the alley mouth. Ran back. Tried to hook the journal, to drag it out, to do something.

The board caught fire in seconds. She dropped it, cursing.

The thief had stopped moving.

The journal was still burning.

Selene stood there, heat washing over her face, and watched.

Whatever was burning had already gone past saving. Leather blackened and curled. Pages turned to ash. Fragments floated up on the hot air and disappeared into the grey sky.

She couldn't reach it.

She could only watch it die.

Movement.

At the edge of the square. A figure stepping back into shadow.

Selene's head snapped around. Her eyes found him before he disappeared completely.

Daven.

She knew him. Had seen him before, in the spaces between jobs, in the corners of rooms where people like her weren't supposed to notice people like him. Guild adjacent. Watcher connected. The kind of man who moved between factions like smoke, never quite belonging to any of them.

He was watching her. Had been watching the whole time. Standing in the shadows while she tried to save something that was already gone.

Their eyes met.

He smiled.

Not a gloating smile. Not triumphant. Something worse. Something that said: *This is exactly what was supposed to happen. And there's nothing you can do about it.*

Then he was gone. Melted back into the alley like he'd never been there at all.

Selene took a step toward where he'd been. Stopped.

The fire was still burning. The journal was still dying. And chasing a shadow through the slums wouldn't bring back what was already ash.

But she'd remember that face. That smile.

She'd remember.

When the flames finally began to die down, there was nothing left. Just char. Just bones. Just the greasy residue of oil and flesh and paper.

She stepped closer. Knelt at the edge of the basin, still warm, still smoking.

Reached into the ashes.

Found nothing. Char. Fragments that crumbled when she touched them. Nothing recognizable. Nothing to prove what had burned.

But what else could it have been?

Gone. It had to be gone.

She sat back on her heels. Read the scene.

Someone had been here. Waiting. The thief had been expected. The fire had been prepared. The oil, the timing, the precision of it. This wasn't random violence. This was an execution.

And Daven had been watching.

She didn't know if he'd done it himself. Didn't know if he'd ordered it. But he'd been here, standing in the shadows, watching her try to save something that was already gone. And he'd smiled.

That smile said he knew exactly what was happening. Said this was going according to plan.

But why? Why steal a journal? Why burn it? What could Mirael have possibly written that was worth this much planning, this much cruelty?

She didn't have answers. Just questions. Just ash. Just the memory of a face in the shadows.

She stood up. Her hands were black with soot. Her face felt tight from the heat.

She didn't feel anything else yet.

That would come later.

The grief would come later.

The rage was already here.

Voices at the edge of the square. Someone had seen the smoke. Someone had called for authority.

Two figures in Paladin gray entering through the alley she'd come from. And behind them, moving slower, notebook already in hand, a face she recognized.

Weston.

His eyes found the fire first. The body. The remains of something that had been a person an hour ago. Then his eyes found her.

Standing at the edge of the fountain. Hands black with ash. Face red from heat. Looking like exactly what she was: someone who'd been here when it happened.

He opened his notebook. Started writing.

Something snapped in Selene's chest.

"Don't."

Weston looked up.

"Don't look at me like that." She took a step toward him. The two Paladins tensed, hands moving toward their weapons, but Weston held up a hand and they stopped. "Don't write in your little book like I did this. Like I'm the one who burned a man alive in a fountain."

"I'm not writing that you did anything." Weston's voice was calm. Tired. "I'm writing what I see."

"And what do you see?"

"You. Here. Again." He closed the notebook but didn't put it away. "A body. A fire. And you standing in the middle of it with ash on your hands."

"We were robbed." The words came out hard and fast. "Someone stole from my partner. In the market. I chased him. He ran here. When I arrived, he was already burning. Someone was waiting for him. Someone set this up."

"Who?"

Selene hesitated. Daven's face flashed in her mind. The smile. The shadow melting back into the alley.

"I don't know."

"You don't know." Weston's voice wasn't accusatory. Just flat. Just noting another gap in a story full of gaps.

"I saw someone. Watching. He was gone before I could . . ."

"Description?"

"Male. Average height. Dark hair. The kind of face you forget."

Weston wrote it down. They both knew it was useless. Half the men in Garnath matched that description.

"What was stolen?"

"A journal. My partner's journal."

"Why would someone steal a journal?"

"I don't know." And that was true. She didn't know. Didn't understand why anyone would go to these lengths for Mirael's private thoughts.

Weston studied her face for a long moment. She couldn't read what he was thinking. Couldn't tell if he believed her or was just filing away more evidence for the case he was building.

"This wasn't my fault." Her voice cracked. She hated that it cracked. Hated that she sounded like she was pleading. "Someone robbed us. I tried to stop it. I was too late. That's all this is."

"I believe you."

She went still. She hadn't expected them.

"You . . . what?"

"I believe someone robbed you. I believe you chased them. I believe you arrived here after the killing, not before." Weston tucked the notebook into his coat. "But it doesn't matter what I believe. It matters what the evidence says. And the evidence says you were present at another death. Another fire. Another scene that doesn't add up."

"So what happens now?"

"Now I do my job." He turned to the two Paladins, started giving orders about the body, the fire, the scene. Then he looked back at her. "Go home, Selene. Take care of your partner. The summons is coming. Maybe tomorrow. Maybe the day after. But it's coming, and there's nothing either of us can do to stop it now."

She wanted to argue. Wanted to fight. Wanted to make him understand that she was the victim here, not the criminal.

But she saw his face. Saw the weight he was carrying. Saw a good man being crushed between what he believed and what the evidence demanded.

She walked away.

Didn't look back.

But she felt him watching her leave. Felt the case building behind her like a wall she couldn't climb.

***

The walk back took forever.

The city moved around her the way it always did. Carts and bodies and the endless noise of Garnath being Garnath. Nobody looked at her twice. Nobody cared that her hands were black with ash, that her face was tight from heat, that she was walking like someone carrying a body.

She passed the fishmonger she'd knocked into. He cursed at her again. She didn't hear him.

She passed the alley where she'd almost caught him. Where her fingers had been inches from his collar. Where another half-second would have been enough.

She passed children playing in a gutter, kicking something dead between them. She passed a woman crying in a doorway. She passed two men fighting over a coin purse, blood on the cobblestones, neither of them winning.

Garnath. Just Garnath. The city that ground people down and didn't care. The city that had been doing this for three hundred years and would keep doing it for three hundred more.

The market came back into view.

Mirael was where she'd left her.

Not standing. Not sitting. Kneeling. Still kneeling on the wet cobblestones in the middle of the lane, people flowing around her like water around a stone. Her hands were still out in front of her. Still reaching for something that wasn't there. Still frozen in the moment of loss.

She hadn't moved. The whole time Selene had been running, chasing, watching, failing, Mirael had been kneeling here with her hands out. Waiting for Selene to bring it back. Waiting for it to not be real.

Selene stopped in front of her.

Mirael looked up.

Her face was wrong. Not the professional coldness. Not the performance. Something underneath that, something that had been hiding behind the mask for fourteen years and was now exposed and bleeding.

Her eyes were dry. That was the worst part. Not crying. Past crying. The kind of devastation that went so deep tears couldn't reach it.

"Did you . . ."

Selene shook her head.

"It's gone."

Two words. Simple. Final.

Mirael's mouth opened. Closed. Opened again.

"What do you mean it's gone?"

"Burned. Someone was waiting. The thief, the journal, all of it. Burned."

"No."

"Mirael . . ."

"No." Mirael's hands dropped to the cobblestones. Pressed flat against the wet stone like she was trying to hold herself to the earth. "No. No, you're wrong. You missed something. It's not . . . it can't be . . ."

"I saw it burn. I tried to get it out. I couldn't."

"Then go back. Go back and look again. Maybe there's something left, maybe . . ."

"There's nothing left."

Mirael's face crumpled. Not all at once. Slowly. Like something collapsing from the inside.

Her mouth opened, and the sound that came out was not a scream.

It was worse than a scream.

It was the sound of fourteen years dying. Every word she'd ever written. Every feeling she'd ever hidden. Every piece of herself she'd given to those pages because she couldn't give them to Selene.

Gone.

All of it.

Gone.

The sound went on and on, and Selene stood there and let it wash over her because there was nothing else to do. No comfort to offer. No words that would help. Just the raw fact of loss, pouring out of Mirael's throat in a sound that made people turn away.

When the sound finally stopped, Mirael was curled on the cobblestones. Knees to chest. Arms wrapped around herself. Shaking.

Selene crouched down. Put a hand on her shoulder.

"We need to go."

Mirael didn't respond.

"We can't stay here. People are watching. We need to go home."

Home. The apartment that wasn't safe. The place where Mirael had spent every night for three days wrapping and unwrapping a journal that no longer existed.

"Mirael. We have to move."

Slowly, Mirael uncurled. Let Selene help her to her feet. Let Selene guide her through the crowd, one arm around her shoulders, holding her up because her legs didn't seem to remember how to work.

They walked home in silence.

The city ground on around them.

It didn't care.

It never did.

***

The apartment felt emptier than it had that morning.

Same walls. Same window. Same bed. But something was missing now. Something that had filled the space without Selene realizing it was there.

Mirael sat on the edge of the bed. Staring at nothing. Her hands were in her lap, fingers moving like they were searching for something to hold.

Selene stood by the window. Watched the street below. Watched the city keep moving like nothing had happened.

The question had been building since the fountain. Since she'd seen Daven's face in the shadows. Since she'd realized this wasn't random, wasn't coincidence, wasn't just bad luck in a city full of bad luck.

"What was in it?"

Mirael didn't look up. "What?"

"The journal. What was in it?" Selene turned from the window. "Someone went to a lot of trouble to steal it. Hired a thief. Set a trap. Burned a man alive to cover their tracks. That's not something you do for nothing. That's not something you do for just . . . thoughts."

Mirael's hands stopped moving.

"What was in it, Mirael?"

"Nothing."

"Don't lie to me. Not now."

"I'm not lying." Mirael's voice was hollow. Empty. The voice of someone who'd poured everything out and had nothing left. "It was just . . . me. That's all. Fourteen years of me. Things I thought. Things I felt. Things I couldn't say out loud."

"Things about what? About who?"

Mirael finally looked up. Her eyes were red-rimmed but dry. Past tears. Past everything.

"About everything. About the work. About the Guild. About . . ." She stopped. Swallowed. "About you."

Selene felt something twist in her chest. "About me."

"About us. About what we are. What we aren't. What I wanted us to be." Mirael's laugh was bitter, broken. "Fourteen years of wanting something I was never going to get. Fourteen years of writing it down because I couldn't say it. And now it's gone, and it doesn't matter anymore, does it? It's ash. It's nothing. Just like everything else."

"Someone wanted it badly enough to kill for it."

"Then they wasted their time." Mirael's voice cracked. "There was nothing in there worth killing for. Just a stupid woman writing stupid things about a stupid hope that was never going to come true. They burned it. Good. Let them read smoke. Let them choke on ash. There's nothing left."

She believed it. Selene could see that. Mirael believed the journal had burned. Believed whoever had taken it had destroyed it along with the thief and any evidence of what had happened.

She didn't know someone had been watching. Didn't know the fire was theater. Didn't know that somewhere in this city, her fourteen years of secrets were sitting in someone else's hands.

Selene didn't tell her.

What would be the point? The journal was gone either way. Burned or stolen, it was out of their reach. Telling Mirael it might still exist somewhere would only make it worse. Would give her hope when there was no hope to give.

Better to let her grieve for something destroyed than torture herself wondering who was reading her heart.

"I'm sorry," Selene said.

The words felt hollow. Useless. But she said them anyway.

Mirael didn't respond. Just sat there on the edge of the bed, hands empty, eyes empty, everything empty.

After a while, she lay down. Curled on her side. Facing the wall.

She didn't reach for the pillow. Didn't check for something that wasn't there anymore. Didn't go through the ritual that had defined her nights for fourteen years.

The ritual was dead.

The journal was dead.

Something in Mirael had died with it.

Selene sat in her chair by the window and let the night come. Let the city change predators. Garnath breathed its slow, grinding breath outside, the same as it always did.

Somewhere out there, a man with a forgettable face had stood in the shadows and smiled while she failed. Whoever he was, whatever he wanted, he'd gotten it. The journal was ash. The thief was bones. And Daven had walked away clean.

She didn't know why.

But she knew his face now.

And faces could be found.

CHAPTER 21: The Ashes

Selene woke in the chair by the window.

Gray light. Morning, probably. The kind of light that didn't commit to anything, just filled the room with the absence of dark and called it day.

She hadn't meant to sleep. Hadn't thought she could. But somewhere between watching the street and watching nothing, her body had made the decision for her. Now her neck ached and her back was stiff and her hands still smelled like ash.

She looked at the bed.

Mirael hadn't moved.

Still curled on her side. Still facing the wall. Still wearing the same clothes she'd worn yesterday, when she'd knelt on cobblestones in the middle of a market and screamed without words.

The apartment was quiet.

Not the comfortable quiet of two people who didn't need to talk. This was something else. Something hollowed out. The space where sound should be, emptied of everything that used to fill it.

Selene realized what was missing.

The ritual.

Every morning for as long as they'd lived together, Mirael had performed the same series of sounds. The soft rustle of cloth. The creak of leather. The small, private moment of thumb against spine. Checking. Always checking. Making sure the journal was still there, still real, still hers.

Now there was nothing to check.

The sounds were gone because the ritual was gone because the journal was gone because everything Mirael had poured into those pages for fourteen years was ash in a fountain basin on Ravel Street.

Selene sat in the chair and listened to the silence and understood, for the first time, how much space that ritual had occupied. How much of their life together had been built around it without her noticing.

She'd resented it, sometimes. The way Mirael guarded those pages. The way she wrote instead of speaking. The way she kept pieces of herself locked away in leather and cloth and wouldn't share them no matter how many years passed.

Now the resentment felt stupid. Small. The kind of thing you only recognize as petty when it's too late to take it back.

Mirael had been holding herself together with that journal.

And now she wasn't holding herself together at all.

***

An hour passed. Maybe two.

Selene didn't move from the chair. She watched the street below, watched the city wake up, watched Garnath begin its endless grinding. A cart rattled past, driver cursing at his mule. Two women argued over the price of something Selene couldn't see. The same noise as yesterday. The same indifference.

Eventually, Mirael stirred.

Not waking. She probably hadn't slept. Just moving because a body could only stay still for so long before it demanded something. She uncurled slowly, like it hurt, and sat up on the edge of the bed.

She didn't look at Selene. Didn't look at anything.

"There's water," Selene said. "And some bread from yesterday."

Mirael didn't respond.

"You should eat something."

Nothing.

Selene got up. Found the bread. Brought it over. Held it out like an offering to someone who'd forgotten what offerings were for.

Mirael looked at it. Looked through it. Her hands stayed in her lap.

"I'm not hungry."

"You haven't eaten since yesterday morning."

"I know."

Her voice was flat. Empty. Just sounds shaped into words because that's what mouths did when they had to respond. There was nothing behind them. No feeling. No fight. Just the mechanical process of being alive without wanting to be.

Selene set the bread down on the bed beside her. Mirael didn't touch it.

"We need to work," Selene said.

Mirael looked at her then. First time since yesterday. Her eyes were dry. Red-rimmed but dry. Past tears, past grief, past everything that made a person feel human.

"Work," she repeated. Like the word was in a language she'd forgotten.

"We're low on coin. The cache burned. What we have won't last more than a few weeks."

"Okay."

"So we need to take a job. Today. Something."

"Okay."

She wasn't agreeing. Wasn't disagreeing. Just making sounds. Selene could have said anything and gotten the same response. We need to burn down the Paladin barracks. Okay. We need to walk into the harbor and drown. Okay.

This wasn't Mirael being difficult. This wasn't even Mirael being broken in a way that could heal.

This was Mirael ceasing to exist.

The body was present. The person who'd lived in it had gone somewhere Selene couldn't follow.

***

Selene left her in the apartment.

She didn't want to. Didn't feel right about it. But staying wouldn't help, and they needed money, and someone had to keep moving or they'd both end up frozen in that room waiting for something that wasn't coming.

The street was cold. Gray sky pressing down like a hand on the city's throat. Garnath in winter was a different animal than

Garnath in summer. Meaner. Less forgiving. The kind of cold that got into your bones and made everything harder.

Selene walked and tried to think about anything except Mirael's face.

Failed.

She kept seeing it. The hollowness. The absence. The way her eyes had looked at the bread like it was something from another world, another life, another person's problem.

Fourteen years.

That's how long Mirael had been writing in that journal. Fourteen years of thoughts and feelings and the things she couldn't say out loud. All of it gone. All of it ash.

And Selene had stood there watching it burn.

She'd tried to save it. She had. She'd reached into the flames until the heat drove her back, tried to hook it with a burning board, circled the fountain looking for an angle that didn't exist. But trying wasn't the same as succeeding, and the journal had burned anyway, and now Mirael was empty and Selene couldn't fill her back up no matter how much bread she offered.

That was the worst part, maybe.

Not the failure. She was used to failure. You didn't survive twenty-three years in Garnath without learning how to swallow failure and keep moving.

The worst part was knowing that nothing she did now would help.

Mirael's pain wasn't a problem she could solve. Wasn't an enemy she could kill. Wasn't a lock she could pick or a guard she could avoid or a score she could settle. It was just there, massive and immovable, and all Selene could do was watch it crush someone she cared about.

Cared about.

She tested the words in her mind. Rolled them around. Tried to figure out if they were true or just habit.

She'd drawn the line. Told Mirael it had to stop. The wanting, the hoping, the things that bled through when they were too close. She'd said partnership only, and she'd meant it, and she still meant it.

But caring about someone wasn't the same as wanting them.

You could care about a partner. Could want them safe, want them functional, want them to stop looking like their soul had been scooped out with a spoon. That wasn't love. That was just basic human decency. The minimum you owed someone you'd shared ten years of your life with.

Wasn't it?

Selene walked faster. The questions were useless. The questions were a distraction from the fact that she needed money and work and something to focus on that wasn't the hollow in Mirael's eyes.

She went to find Tomas.

***

Tomas ran a message service out of the back of a tannery in the Sprawl. Legitimate enough to have a ledger, dirty enough to be useful. Selene had done work for him for years. Quick jobs, clean pay, no questions.

He was behind his usual table when she walked in. Looked up. Saw her face.

And flinched.

Small. Quick. Most people wouldn't have noticed. But Selene noticed everything, and what she noticed was Tomas looking at her like she'd brought a plague into his shop.

"Selene." His voice was careful. Measured. "Wasn't expecting you."

"I need work."

"Yeah, I figured." He glanced at the door behind her. Then at the window. Then at his hands. Anywhere but her face. "Thing is, nothing right now."

"Nothing."

"Quiet week."

"It's never a quiet week."

"This week it is."

Selene moved closer. Not threatening. Just present. Close enough to see the sweat starting on his forehead, the way his fingers were tapping against the table, the particular nervousness of a man who wanted to be somewhere else.

"Tomas. What's going on?"

"Nothing's going on."

"You've had work for me every week for four years. Now suddenly nothing. The day after half the city saw me chasing a thief through the market and showing up at a burning body."

He looked up then. Finally. And she saw it in his eyes.

Fear.

Not fear of her. Fear of something else. Something that scared him more than she did.

"I was told not to talk to you."

The words hung in the air like smoke.

"By who?"

"Didn't say. Didn't have to."

"What does that mean?"

"Means someone suggested it would be better if I kept my distance from you for a while." Tomas's voice dropped. Quieter now. Almost apologetic. "Not a threat. Not exactly. Just a . . . suggestion. The kind of suggestion you don't ignore if you want to keep working in this city."

"Who makes suggestions like that?"

"People who can make them stick." He stood up. Moved toward the back room. "I'm sorry, Selene. I am. You've always been good business. But I'm not dying for you. Nobody is."

He disappeared through the door.

Selene stood in the empty shop and listened to the sound of a tannery doing what tanneries did and tried to understand what had just happened.

***

She tried two more contacts.

Vela, who ran protection money for a string of gambling dens. She was always looking for muscle, always had work, always paid on time.

Vela's man at the door told Selene she wasn't there. Selene knew he was lying. She could see Vela's shadow behind the curtain, very deliberately not moving.

Then Garrett's old partner, a man named Holt who'd taken over after Garrett's death. He should have been angry at Selene. Should have wanted revenge. Instead, he just looked scared.

"Can't help you," he said. "Don't come back."

Three contacts. Three walls.

Something was happening. Something she couldn't see. The city was closing around her like a fist, and she didn't know why or who was doing it or how to make it stop.

She walked home through streets that felt different now. Watched everyone. Trusted no one. Felt the old familiar itch between her shoulder blades, the sense of eyes she couldn't find.

The itch had been there for weeks. She'd ignored it. Pushed through it. Told herself she was being paranoid.

Now she wasn't so sure.

She was passing a stationer's shop when she stopped.

The window display was cluttered with paper and ink and wax seals, the tools of merchants and clerks and people who had lives worth documenting. In the corner, stacked in a neat pile, were journals. Leather-bound. Different sizes, different colors, but all the same basic thing.

Empty pages waiting to be filled.

Selene stood there for a long time, looking at them.

It was stupid. She knew it was stupid. You couldn't replace fourteen years with a blank book. You couldn't give someone back the words they'd lost by handing them a place to put new ones. Grief didn't work that way. Loss didn't work that way.

But she didn't know what else to do.

She couldn't find work. Couldn't find answers. Couldn't fix whatever was broken in Mirael's head or her heart or wherever the damage had landed. She couldn't do anything that mattered.

But she could do this. One small, stupid, probably useless thing.

She went inside.

The shopkeeper was an old man with ink-stained fingers who didn't ask questions about why a woman who looked like Selene would want a journal. He just took her coin and wrapped it in paper and handed it over like it was any other transaction.

The journal was smaller than Mirael's had been. Different leather, darker. But it was real and it was something and maybe that was enough.

Or maybe it was nothing.

She'd find out soon enough.

***

The apartment was the same when she returned.

The apartment looked exactly as she'd left it. Mirael sat on the edge of the bed, staring at nothing, hands empty in her lap.

Mirael had moved at some point. The bread was gone, at least. That was something.

Selene set the wrapped journal on the table. Didn't say anything about it yet. First things first.

"No work," she said. "Nobody's talking to me. Something's wrong."

Mirael didn't look up. Didn't respond.

Selene sat down in the chair by the window. Looked at the woman she'd shared a decade with. Tried to find some trace of the person she knew in the hollow shell on the bed.

"Mirael."

Nothing.

"Mirael, I need you to hear me."

"I hear you."

"Something is happening. The fire, the journal, the way people are shutting us out. It's connected. It has to be."

"Okay."

"Does that mean anything to you? Do you understand what I'm saying?"

Mirael finally looked at her. Slowly. Like turning her head required effort she barely had.

"I understand. Someone wanted the journal. Someone got it. Someone is making sure you can't figure out who." Her voice was flat. Reciting facts like they were distant history instead of present danger. "It makes sense. In a horrible, obvious way. It all makes sense."

"Then help me. Talk to me. Tell me what was in that journal that someone would do all this to get it."

"I told you. Me. Fourteen years of me."

"That's not an answer."

"It's the only answer I have." Mirael's eyes drifted back to the wall. "Whoever wanted it, they have it now. Or they burned it. Either way, it's gone. Either way, I'm empty. What difference does it make what was in it?"

"It makes a difference because someone is hunting us."

"Then let them."

The words fell like stones into water. Selene felt them land somewhere in her chest, cold and heavy.

"What did you just say?"

"Let them hunt. Let them find us. Let them finish it." Mirael's voice didn't waver. Didn't crack. Just kept going, flat and hopeless and terrifyingly calm. "What's left to protect? The journal's gone. The money's gone. You don't want me the way I want you. I'm sitting in this room waiting for nothing, hoping for nothing, and I'm tired, Selene. I'm so tired."

"Don't."

"Don't what? Don't tell the truth? Don't admit that I've been holding on by my fingernails for years and now there's nothing left to hold?"

"Don't give up."

"Why not?" For the first time, something flickered in Mirael's eyes. Not hope. Something darker. "Give me one good reason."

Selene opened her mouth. Closed it.

What was she supposed to say? I need you? That was true but it wasn't enough. We've survived worse? They hadn't. Not like this. There's still a chance? A chance for what?

"Kira," she said finally.

Mirael blinked.

"Kira. At the orphanage. She's six years old and she looks at me like I'm the only thing standing between her and the dark." Selene leaned forward. "You think I can keep showing up for her if I'm burying you? You think Mother Gessa lives forever? You think that girl has anyone else?"

"She has you."

"She has us. Both of us. That's what we promised."

Mirael looked at her. Really looked, for the first time since the market. And Selene saw something shift behind her eyes. Not hope. Not yet. But something that wasn't complete surrender.

"I can't feel anything," Mirael said quietly. "I keep waiting for the grief to come, and it doesn't. There's just . . . nothing. Like someone carved out everything that made me a person and left the rest behind."

"I know."

"Do you? Do you know what it's like to have everything you couldn't say destroyed by someone you never saw for reasons you don't understand?"

Selene thought about her own past. The cupboard. The darkness. The things she'd lost before she was old enough to understand what losing meant.

"Maybe not exactly. But I know empty. I know the place you go when there's nothing left and you have to keep going anyway." She reached out. Touched Mirael's hand. First real contact since the line she'd drawn. "You don't have to feel anything right now. You just have to stay."

Mirael looked at their hands. Didn't pull away. Didn't lean in.

"Stay," she repeated.

"Stay. That's all. Stay alive, stay here, stay with me until we figure out what's happening. Can you do that?"

A long silence.

"I don't know."

It wasn't a yes. But it wasn't a refusal either.

Selene took it.

She got up. Went to the table. Picked up the wrapped parcel she'd set there when she came in.

"I got you something."

Mirael looked at the package. Didn't reach for it.

Selene brought it over. Sat down on the bed beside her. Held it out.

"It's not . . . I know it's not the same. It can't be the same. But I thought maybe . . ."

She didn't know how to finish the sentence. Didn't know what she'd thought, exactly. That blank pages could replace fourteen years of words? That leather and paper could fill the hole that had been carved out of Mirael's chest?

Stupid. It was stupid. She knew it was stupid.

But she'd bought it anyway, and now she was holding it out like an offering to someone who'd forgotten what offerings meant.

Mirael took the package. Slowly. Like it might bite.

She unwrapped it. The paper fell away, revealing the journal underneath. Smaller than her old one. Darker leather. Different.

Mirael stared at it.

For a long moment, nothing happened. She just looked at it, this small bound book full of empty pages, and Selene couldn't read her face at all.

Then Mirael's hands started shaking.

"I can't."

"Mirael."

"I can't." Her voice cracked. First real emotion since the market, and it wasn't gratitude. It was something rawer. Harder. "Do you understand? I can't just . . . start over. I can't just write new words like the old ones didn't matter. Like fourteen years of my life didn't just turn to ash."

"That's not what I meant."

"What did you think would happen?" Mirael looked at her, and there were tears now. Finally. Spilling down her cheeks like something had broken loose. "Did you think I'd just open it up and start writing again? 'Day one of my new journal, everything's fine now'?"

"No. I just thought . . ."

"You thought you could fix it. You thought if you found the right thing to give me, the right words to say, you could make it better." Mirael's laugh was bitter, broken, wet with tears. "That's what you do, isn't it? Fix things. Solve problems. Find the angle."

Selene didn't say anything. Couldn't.

"Some things can't be fixed, Selene. Some things just stay broken."

Mirael set the journal down on the bed between them. Carefully. Like it was something fragile, something that might shatter if she held it too hard.

She didn't throw it. Didn't push it away. Just set it down and looked at it with tears running down her face and something in her eyes that might have been grief finally arriving.

"I'm sorry," Selene said. "It was stupid."

"It wasn't stupid." Mirael wiped her face with the back of her hand. "It was . . . you. Trying. In the only way you know how."

"Is that a good thing or a bad thing?"

"I don't know." Mirael looked at the journal again. Reached out. Touched the cover with one finger. "Ask me in a year. If we're still alive."

She didn't pick it up. Didn't open it. But she didn't push it away either.

It sat there between them, full of empty pages waiting for words that might never come.

Then Mirael's hand moved. Slowly. Like she wasn't sure she wanted to know what she'd find.

She opened the cover.

And went still.

Selene's handwriting. Rough. Unpracticed. The letters uneven, like someone who wrote so rarely that each word cost her something.

Fourteen years burned. I know.

These pages *don't* know what *they're* waiting for. Neither do I.

But *I'm* still here.

Mirael's breath caught. Her fingers traced the words, the indentations where the charcoal had pressed too hard, where Selene had gripped it like a weapon because that was the only way she knew how to hold anything.

"When did you . . ."

"Before." Selene's voice was rough. "I didn't know if you'd ever open it. But I wanted something to be there if you did."

The tears came again. Different this time. Not grief. Something else.

Mirael reached for her.

Selene hesitated. One breath. Two.

Then she let herself be pulled in. Let Mirael's arms wrap around her. Let her face press into Mirael's shoulder.

She didn't cry. Selene never cried.

But she stayed.

***

Evening came slowly.

The gray light turned grayer, then darker, then disappeared altogether. Selene lit a single candle because they couldn't afford more and because the darkness felt appropriate somehow. A city outside the window full of lights they couldn't share. A room full of shadows they couldn't escape.

Mirael had retreated to the bed again. Not sleeping. Just lying there with her eyes open, watching the ceiling like it might tell her something if she looked long enough.

Selene sat by the window and tried to put the pieces together.

The theft. The fire. The contacts shutting her out. The sense of being watched that had been growing for weeks.

It wasn't random. Couldn't be random. Random didn't feel like this.

Someone had hired a patsy to steal the journal. Someone had been waiting at the fountain to . . . what? Take it? Burn it? Why burn the thief too? Why make it so theatrical, so public, so impossible to miss?

And Daven.

She kept coming back to that. The figure in the shadows. The smile. The way he'd melted back into the alley like he'd never been there.

She didn't know him. Not really. She'd seen him before, in the spaces between things, the corners where people like her weren't supposed to notice people like him. But she didn't know who he worked for. Didn't know what he wanted. Didn't know why he'd been there watching her fail.

He'd smiled.

That was the part that stuck with her. Not malice, exactly. Something worse. Satisfaction. The look of someone watching a plan unfold exactly as intended.

She'd been part of someone's plan. The theft, the chase, the fire. All of it choreographed. And she'd played her role perfectly, arriving exactly where she was supposed to, exactly when she was supposed to, too late to change anything.

The thought made her stomach clench.

She wasn't used to being the one who was managed. She was the one who managed others. Read people, anticipated moves, stayed three steps ahead. That was how she survived.

Now she was behind. Playing catch-up. Dancing to music someone else was writing.

She hated it.

***

The knock came just before full dark.

Soft. Patient. Not the kind of knock that came with violence behind it.

Selene was on her feet before the sound finished, one hand finding the knife she kept in her boot, body angled toward the door without blocking the window.

"Selene." Mirael's voice, flat but alert. She'd sat up on the bed. "Who?"

"Stay there."

Selene moved to the door. Didn't open it. Listened.

Breathing on the other side. One person. Waiting.

"Who is it?"

"Weston."

The name went through her like cold water. She'd been expecting it. Dreading it. Knowing it was coming ever since he'd seen her at the fountain with ash on her hands.

She opened the door.

He looked worse than she'd ever seen him. Tired in a way that went deeper than sleep. The kind of exhaustion that came from carrying something too heavy for too long.

He was alone. No Paladins flanking him. No official formation. Just a man in a gray coat standing in a dark hallway with a notebook he wasn't holding.

"Can I come in?"

"No."

He nodded. Like he'd expected that. "Then I'll say it here. We need to talk. Officially. Tomorrow morning. You know where."

"Am I under arrest?"

"Not yet. Not tonight." He paused. Chose his next words carefully. "This is the last courtesy I can offer you. If you run, I can't help you. I won't be able to protect you from what comes next."

"And if I don't run?"

"Then maybe we can figure out what's actually happening before it's too late."

Selene studied his face. Looking for the lie. The trap. The angle.

She didn't find one.

That was almost worse. Because it meant he was telling the truth, and the truth was that he was trying to help her, and good men trying to help had a way of dying in Garnath.

"Why?" she asked. "Why warn me? Why come alone?"

"Because I've been building a case against you for weeks, and every piece of evidence falls into place too perfectly." His voice dropped. "I've seen frame jobs before. This one's better than most. But it's still a frame job, and I want to know who's holding the brush."

"You believe me?"

"I believe the evidence is lying to me. That's not the same thing as believing you." He stepped back. Started to turn away. Stopped. "Tomorrow morning. Early. If you're not there, I have to assume you're guilty and act accordingly."

He walked away. His footsteps faded down the stairs.

Selene closed the door. Leaned against it.

Her mind was already racing. Calculating.

Running was an option. It was always an option. She knew the routes out of the city, the places to disappear, the ways to become nobody in a crowd of nobodies. She'd done it before. Could do it again.

But running meant leaving Mirael. And Mirael couldn't run. Could barely stand. Could barely exist. If Selene disappeared into the night, Mirael would be alone in this apartment with nothing but empty hands and a future that had stopped meaning anything.

Running meant leaving Kira. The Kettle. The promise they'd made to a girl who'd already lost too much.

Running meant confirming the guilt she didn't have. Making herself prey instead of problem. And Weston was right about one thing: if she ran, he'd have to chase. And Weston didn't stop. She'd seen his files, seen his patience, seen the cold, relentless machinery of a man who believed in the law deeply enough to follow it wherever it led.

If she ran, she'd be running forever.

If she stayed, she might die anyway.

But at least if she stayed, she'd know why.

And there was something else. Something in Weston's face when he'd talked about the evidence. Frustration. Confusion. The look of a man who'd found an answer that didn't match the question.

He didn't understand what was happening either.

Maybe that was worth something. Maybe together they could see something neither of them could see alone.

Or maybe she was walking into a trap that would close around her and never open.

She thought about the fountain. The fire. The smile in the shadows.

Someone was orchestrating this. Someone who understood systems and timing and the way people moved through a city like pieces on a board. Someone who'd been three steps ahead since before Selene knew there was a game.

She couldn't fight what she couldn't see.

But Weston could see things she couldn't. Had access to records, reports, the machinery of law that Selene had spent her whole life avoiding.

Maybe that was the play. Use Weston's eyes while she still had the chance. Figure out who was moving the pieces. Then decide what to do about it.

It was a terrible plan. But it was the only one she had.

***

She looked at Mirael.

Still sitting on the bed. Watching her. The first spark of something other than emptiness in her eyes.

"That was Weston."

"I heard."

"He wants me to come in tomorrow. Officially."

"I heard that too."

"If I go, I might not come back."

Mirael was quiet for a long moment. Then: "If you don't go?"

"Then I run. We run. And we keep running until they catch us or we die somewhere else."

"Is that what you want?"

Selene thought about it. Really thought about it.

"No. I want to know who's doing this. I want to find the man who stood in the shadows and smiled while everything burned. I want answers."

"Then go."

"If I go, you're alone."

"I'm already alone." Mirael's voice cracked. First emotion she'd shown in hours. "I've been alone for years, Selene. Even when you were right beside me. At least this way, one of us might find out why they want you dead." Selene crossed the room. Sat down on the bed. Close but not touching.

"When this is over," she said, "we're going to visit Kira. Both of us. We're going to sit in the kitchen at the Kettle and drink whatever terrible tea Mother Gessa makes and watch that girl practice the footwork you're going to teach her."

"I told her I'd show her how to walk quiet. That's not the same as teaching."

"Keep telling yourself that."

Mirael was quiet. Then, very softly: "That's the first time you've talked about the future since . . ."

"Since I drew the line."

"Yes."

"I know." Selene stood up. Moved back to the window. "Get some sleep. Tomorrow's going to be hard for both of us."

She didn't watch Mirael lie down. Didn't need to. She heard the bed creak, heard the breathing slowly even out, heard the particular sound of someone not sleeping but trying to.

Outside, Garnath breathed its slow, grinding breath. Lights flickered in windows. Predators changed shifts with prey. The city that had been consuming people for three hundred years continued its work, indifferent to the small dramas playing out in the rooms above its streets.

Tomorrow, Selene would walk into the Paladin station and sit across from a man who wanted to arrest her.

Tomorrow, she would find out how much trouble she was really in.

Tonight, she sat in the chair by the window and watched the dark.

Somewhere out there, a man with a forgettable face was sleeping well.

She hoped he enjoyed it while he could.

CHAPTER 22: The Arrest

The morning came whether she wanted it to or not.

Selene stood by the window and watched the gray light spread across Garnath like a stain. The city was waking up. A cart rattled past below. Someone shouted something she couldn't make out. Another day grinding into motion, indifferent to what it would cost her.

Behind her, Mirael sat on the edge of the bed.

The new journal was beside her. Still wrapped in its paper. Still untouched. Selene didn't know if that was grief or rejection or something else entirely, and she didn't have time to figure it out.

"I'm going."

Mirael didn't look up. "I know."

"Weston said morning. I don't want to give him a reason to come here."

"I know."

Selene turned from the window. Looked at the woman she was leaving behind. Mirael's hands were in her lap, fingers still, face empty. The hollowness from yesterday hadn't lifted. If anything, it had settled deeper, like water finding the lowest point.

"If I don't come back . . ."

"Don't." Mirael's voice cracked on the word. First sign of anything beneath the surface. "Don't say that. Just . . . come back."

"I'll try."

"Try harder."

Selene crossed the room. Stopped in front of her. For a moment, she didn't know what to do with her hands. Touch her? Leave her alone? The line she'd drawn was still there, still necessary, but it felt cruel now in a way it hadn't before.

She settled for resting her palm on Mirael's shoulder. Brief. Firm. The kind of touch that said I'm here without promising anything more.

"Stay inside. Don't answer the door for anyone."

"What if it's you?"

"I'll knock three times. Pause. Then twice more."

Mirael nodded. Still didn't look up.

Selene left before she could change her mind.

***

The street hit her like cold water.

Garnath in the early morning was a different beast than Garnath at night. Less dangerous, maybe, but more indifferent. The city didn't care that her stomach was in knots. Didn't care that every step she took was carrying her toward something she couldn't undo.

She started walking.

The Paladin station was in the administrative quarter, near the guild halls and the merchant courts. A long walk from the apartment. Too much time to think. Too much time for her mind to tear itself apart.

She made it three blocks before the doubts started screaming.

What was she doing? Walking into a cage. Handing herself over to people who'd been trying to catch her for most of her life. Trusting a man she barely knew because he'd looked tired and said things that sounded like truth.

She could still run.

The thought kept circling back, no matter how many times she pushed it away. She could still turn around. Right now. This corner, left instead of right. Into the Sprawl, through the back alleys, out through the harbor district. She knew people. She knew routes. She knew how to disappear.

Mirael couldn't run. But Mirael wasn't safe with her anyway. Maybe Mirael would be safer without her. Maybe the headhunter would lose interest if Selene vanished. Maybe the Guild would forget.

She kept walking.

Her feet knew the way even when her head didn't want to go. Left on Tanner Street. Right on the merchant road. Straight through the morning crowds, faces blurring past, nobody looking at her twice because why would they? She was just another body in the river of bodies that filled this city every day.

She made it six more blocks before she stopped.

A corner. A crossroads. Left toward the station. Right toward the harbor. Straight ahead toward the market district, where she could lose herself in the crowd and think, just think, just have a moment to figure out if this was the right choice or the last mistake she'd ever make.

She stood there.

People flowed around her. A merchant cursed at her for blocking the path. A child ran past, laughing at something. The city moved and breathed and didn't care that she was frozen in the middle of it, unable to make her feet go forward.

What was waiting for her at that station?

Weston. A man who believed in process. A man who'd spent weeks building a case against her and then warned her it was coming. A man who'd said I believe you and I have to arrest you in the same conversation.

Was that enough? Was believing her enough to matter?

And what was waiting for her on the street?

Contacts who wouldn't talk. Doors that were closed. A headhunter who was always three steps ahead. A Guild that had already signed her death warrant. A partner who couldn't run and couldn't fight and couldn't do anything except sit on a bed and stare at a journal she couldn't bring herself to open.

If she ran, she was prey. Forever. Running until she died tired in some alley, killed by someone she never saw coming.

If she ran, she confirmed everything they said about her. Guilty. Criminal. Worth killing.

If she ran, she never found out who was doing this. Never found the face in the shadows. Never got answers. Never got revenge.

The face. The smile. The way he'd stood there watching while everything burned.

That was what decided it.

Not Weston. Not the promise of protection. Not even Mirael or Kira or the weight of everything bearing down on her.

The smile.

Someone had watched her fail and smiled. Someone had orchestrated all of this and stood in the shadows to enjoy it. Someone out there thought they'd won, thought she was already dead, thought she was nothing but a loose end being quietly tied off.

She wanted to see that face again. Wanted to watch it change when it realized she wasn't dead yet.

And she couldn't do that if she was running.

Her feet started moving again. Toward the station. Toward the cage.

Not surrender. Not trust. Just the cold, clear knowledge that the only way out was through.

***

The Paladin station was a gray stone building in the administrative quarter. Official. Imposing. The kind of architecture designed to make people feel small before they even walked through the door.

Selene stood outside and looked at it.

She'd passed this building a hundred times. Always on the other side of the street. Always with her head down, her face unremarkable, her presence unremarkable. The kind of woman nobody remembered because she'd made it her life's work to be forgettable.

Now she was walking in the front door.

Her hand found the handle. Cold iron. Real. Final.

She thought about Mirael. Sitting on the bed. Waiting.

She thought about Kira. At the Kettle. Not knowing any of this was happening.

She thought about the man in the shadows. Smiling.

She pushed the door open.

***

The inside of the station was exactly what she expected. Stone floors. Stone walls. The smell of old paper and older sweat.

Guards in gray uniforms moving through corridors, carrying documents, carrying weapons, carrying the weight of a system that had been grinding people into dust long before Selene was born.

She approached the front desk. A man in clerk's robes looked up.

"I'm here to see Inspector Weston. He's expecting me."

The clerk's eyebrows rose slightly. He checked a ledger. Found something.

"Name?"

"Selene."

He made a note. Gestured to a guard. The guard approached.

"This way."

No roughness. No hostility. Just procedure. Just the machinery of law doing what machinery did.

She followed.

Through corridors. Past doors. Past rooms where people in gray asked questions and people not in gray tried to answer them. The station was alive with the business of judgment, and she was walking into its heart.

The guard stopped at a door. Knocked once. Opened it.

"She's here."

Weston's voice from inside: "Send her in."

The guard stepped aside. Selene walked through.

***

The room was small. A table. Two chairs. A window too high to see out of, letting in gray light that didn't illuminate anything. No papers. No notebook. Nothing official.

Weston sat on the far side of the table. He looked worse than last night. Dark circles under his eyes. A tension in his shoulders that said he'd been carrying something heavy for too long.

"Close the door."

Selene closed it. Stood there.

"Sit."

She sat. The chair was hard. Uncomfortable. Designed that way.

For a long moment, neither of them spoke. They just looked at each other across the table, two people who had no reason to trust each other trying to figure out if they had any other choice.

"Thank you for coming," Weston said finally.

"I almost didn't."

"I know." He leaned back in his chair. "I could see it in your face last night. The calculation. The part of you that wanted to run."

"The part of me that's kept me alive this long."

"And yet here you are."

"Here I am."

Another silence. Weston rubbed his eyes with the heels of his hands. The gesture was tired, human, nothing like the composed investigator she'd seen at crime scenes.

"I'm going to tell you some things," he said. "Things I shouldn't tell you. Things that could end my career if anyone found out I said them."

"Why?"

"Because I need to know what you know. And you're not going to trust me enough to share unless I give you something first."

Selene waited.

Weston folded his hands on the table. "I've been building a case against you for weeks. You know that. Every piece of evidence points at you. The safehouse fire. The bodies in the alley. The burning at the fountain. Every time something goes wrong in this city, you're standing in the middle of it."

"I didn't . . ."

"I know." He cut her off. Not aggressive. Just certain. "I know you didn't. That's the problem."

Selene frowned. "I don't understand."

"The evidence against you is perfect. Too perfect." Weston's voice dropped. "I've been doing this job a long time. I know what real evidence looks like. It's messy. Incomplete. Full of gaps and contradictions. Real criminals make mistakes. Real cases have holes."

"And mine doesn't."

"Your case is immaculate. Every witness statement exactly where it needs to be. Every piece of physical evidence perfectly preserved. Every document filed correctly, processed correctly, pointing at exactly the right conclusion." He shook his head. "It's constructed. Built piece by piece."

"Someone's framing me."

"Someone's doing more than that." Weston leaned forward. "Someone is using the system. Not fighting it, not bribing it. Using it. They understand how information flows through this building. How paperwork moves. How cases get built and processed and prioritized. They're feeding evidence into the machine and letting the machine do the work."

Selene felt cold. "Who?"

"I don't know. But I know what they're not." Weston held up a finger. "They're not Guild. The Guild is sloppy. Political. They bribe officials and threaten witnesses and leave fingerprints everywhere because they don't care who knows. This is different. This is surgical. Patient. The work of someone who thinks in systems."

"A professional."

"More than professional. An artist." Weston's jaw tightened. "I've seen frame jobs before. This is the best one I've ever seen. Whoever's doing this, they're not just trying to get you arrested. They're building something airtight. Something that will hold up in trial. Something that will get you convicted and executed without anyone ever asking the wrong questions."

Selene thought about the fountain. The fire. The thief burning in the basin while she stood there helpless.

"The knife," she said quietly.

Weston looked at her. "What?"

"You're describing a knife. Something sharp. Precise. Designed to cut clean."

"Yes. That's exactly what this is." He paused. "But that's not the only thing I found."

"What else?"

Weston reached into his coat. Pulled out a folded piece of paper. Set it on the table between them but didn't open it.

"Your name appeared on a list three days ago. A Guild list. Internal. Not supposed to exist, officially, but we both know better."

"What kind of list?"

"Authorization for removal." Weston's voice was flat. "No body vote. No formal process. Just a name and a date and a notation that says 'sanctioned.'"

Selene's stomach dropped. She'd known the Guild had problems with her. Had known she'd made enemies, stepped on territories, taken jobs that other people wanted. But this was different. This was formal. This was the Guild deciding she wasn't worth the trouble of keeping alive.

"So the Guild wants me dead."

"The Guild has approved your death. But I don't think they're the ones framing you." Weston tapped the paper. "The frame job and the sanction feel separate. Different patterns. Different methods. The frame is precise, patient, long-term. The sanction is blunt, political, recent." He paused. "But I could be wrong. Someone inside the Guild could be running the knife. Someone smart enough to make it look like outside work."

"Two different problems."

"Two different death warrants. Probably." Weston met her eyes. "You have a knife and a hammer both coming for you. The knife is surgical, building a case that will kill you legally. The hammer is the Guild, who'll kill you in an alley if the knife takes too long. Whether they're working together or just happening at the same time, I can't tell you."

Selene sat with that. Two separate forces. Both wanting her dead. Both working toward the same end through different means.

"Are they connected?"

"Maybe. The Guild could have hired the knife. Contracted an outside professional to do the frame job while they handle the street-level removal. That would explain why both are happening at once."

"Or?"

"Or the knife has their own reasons, and the Guild sanction is just coincidence. Or cover. Someone else wants you dead, and they're using the Guild's decision as camouflage." Weston spread his hands. "I don't know which it is. That's why I need to know what you know."

Selene looked at the paper on the table. The list with her name on it. The formal acknowledgment that she'd been marked for death by people who would never face consequences for it.

"What do you want from me?"

"Tell me what happened at the fountain. Tell me what you saw. Tell me anything that might help me understand who's holding the knife."

She could lie. Could give him nothing. Could sit in silence and let him arrest her and hope that custody was enough protection.

But he'd given her something. Two death warrants. The shape of what was hunting her. More than anyone else had given her in weeks.

She decided to give him something back.

"The theft wasn't random," she said. "The target was specific. My partner's journal. Something she'd been writing in for fourteen years."

Weston's eyes sharpened. "What was in it?"

"I don't know. She never told me. But someone wanted it badly enough to plan this whole thing around getting it."

"Go on."

"The thief was a tool. Desperate. Forgettable. The kind of person you use once and throw away. He didn't choose the meet point. Someone else did. The broken fountain on Ravel Street."

"How do you know?"

"Because it was perfect. Perfect for a chase. Perfect for me to follow. Perfect for me to arrive exactly when I was supposed to." Selene's voice hardened. "I was herded. Every step of that chase, I was going exactly where someone wanted me to go."

Weston nodded slowly. "And when you got there?"

"The fire was already burning. The thief was already dead. Throat cut, then burned. Theatrical. Designed to be seen." She paused. "And someone was watching."

"Watching?"

"In the shadows. At the edge of the square. A man. I didn't see him until it was too late. He was just . . . standing there. Watching me try to save something that was already gone."

"Did you get a look at him?"

Selene's hands tightened on the edge of the table. "I told you what he looked like. But there's one thing I didn't mention."

"What?"

"He smiled."

Weston was quiet for a long moment.

"The knife," he said finally. "That's the knife. Patient. Precise. Watching his work unfold."

"He wanted me to see him. Wanted me to know I'd been played." Selene's voice was steady, but something cold was moving beneath it. "He's not just trying to kill me. He's enjoying it."

"Do you know who he is?"

"No. But I've seen him before. In the spaces between things. The edges of rooms. He moves like smoke. Belongs everywhere and nowhere."

"A professional."

"A ghost."

Weston picked up the paper from the table. Folded it again. Put it back in his coat.

"The Guild sanctioned your removal. But they didn't orchestrate this. They don't have the patience or the precision." He stood up. "Someone else is hunting you. Someone who understands systems better than the system understands itself. Someone who's been ahead of you from the beginning."

"A headhunter."

"The best I've ever seen evidence of." Weston's voice was heavy. "I don't know who hired them. I don't know why. But I know they're not done. The frame is still being built. The knife is still cutting."

He moved around the table. Selene tensed, but he stopped a few feet away.

"I have to arrest you now."

She'd known it was coming. Still felt it land somewhere in her chest, heavy and cold.

"I know."

"But I want you to understand something." Weston's voice dropped. "This might be the safest place for you right now."

Selene looked up at him. "A cell?"

"In custody, you're in the system. Official. Documented. There's a record of you being here, being processed, being held." He met her eyes. "They can't disappear you. Can't stage another accident. Can't have you killed in an alley and call it random violence."

"You're arresting me to protect me."

"I'm arresting you because the evidence demands it. But yes." He pulled cuffs from his belt. "This is the only shield I can offer. In here, you're visible. Out there, you're prey."

"And what about the trial?"

"I'm going to push for one. Hard. Proper process. Full examination of evidence." Weston held out the cuffs. "Under scrutiny, the frame falls apart. The knife can't work in daylight. If I can get you to trial, the whole thing unravels."

Selene looked at the cuffs. Cold iron. The weight of everything she'd spent her life avoiding.

"How long?"

"A day. Maybe two. Then it goes above me."

"And if someone above you doesn't want a trial?"

Weston's face hardened. Something flickered behind his eyes that Selene hadn't seen before. Not anger. Determination.

"Then we'll both find out what this system really is."

She held out her wrists.

The cuffs closed around them. Cold. Final.

“I’ll do everything I can,” Weston said quietly. “That’s all I can promise.”

“I know.”

He led her to the door. Opened it. Nodded to the guard outside.

“Processing. Then holding cell. Standard procedure.”

The guard took her arm. Not rough. Just firm.

Selene looked back at Weston. He was standing in the doorway, watching her go, something heavy in his face.

“Find them,” she said. “Before they finish what they started.”

The guard pulled her forward. The door closed behind her.

***

Processing was efficient.

They reached for her weapons. The first guard’s hand closed on *Vael’thera*’s hilt.

He screamed. Jerked back. His palm was already blistering, the skin going white with cold burns.

“What the hells . . .”

“I’ll do it.” Selene’s voice was flat. She drew the daggers herself, slowly, and set them on the table. The guards stared at them like they might bite. “You’ll need gloves. Or a cloth. They don’t like being touched.”

They found a cloth. Wrapped the blades without touching them. Put them in a box with her name on it.

Selene watched them go. Felt the warmth leave her hands. Felt the names retreat to that silent place behind her eyes.

They asked her questions. Name. Age. Address. Occupation. She gave them answers. Some true. Some less true. They didn’t seem to care either way.

They walked her through corridors. Down stairs. The light getting dimmer. The air getting colder. The weight of stone pressing down from above.

The holding area was in the basement. A row of cells carved into the bedrock. Iron doors with small windows. The smell of damp and despair and people who had been here too long.

They stopped at a cell. One of the guards unlocked the door. The other removed her cuffs.

"In."

She went in.

The cell was small. Stone on every side. A bench built into the wall. A bucket in the corner. A window too high and too small to show anything except a rectangle of gray.

The door closed behind her.

The lock turned.

And just like that, she was contained.

***

She stood in the center of the cell for a long time.

This was new.

She'd been in bad situations before. Cornered. Trapped. Outnumbered. But there had always been a way out. A door to kick down. A window to climb through. A guard to bribe or threaten or kill.

Not here.

Here there was just stone and iron and the weight of the system pressing down on her from all sides. The machinery of law, finally doing what it had been trying to do her whole life: putting her in a box and keeping her there.

She couldn't run.

For the first time in her life, running was not an option. The walls were too thick. The door was too strong. There was no angle to work, no leverage to find, no way out except through a process she didn't control.

She was at someone else's mercy.

She sat down on the bench. Hard stone. Cold.

Two death warrants. That's what Weston had said. A knife and a hammer.

The knife was patient. Precise. Building a frame that would hold up in court. Playing a long game she didn't understand.

The hammer was the Guild. Blunt. Political. They'd signed off on her death because she was inconvenient, because she'd made enemies, because it was easier to remove a problem than solve it.

One wanted her convicted. One wanted her dead in a ditch. Both would get what they wanted if she couldn't find a way out of this cell.

But Weston thought custody would protect her. Thought the walls that trapped her would also shield her. Thought being in the system was safer than being outside it.

Maybe he was right.

In here, she was visible. Documented. A person on a ledger, subject to process and procedure. They couldn't disappear her without questions.

Out there, she was nobody. A body waiting to happen. One more death in a city that produced them by the hundreds.

Maybe the cage was better than the street.

Or maybe she was just telling herself that because the alternative was admitting she had no control at all.

She leaned back against the stone wall. Closed her eyes.

Mirael was in the apartment. Alone. Surrounded by emptiness, waiting for a knock that might never come.

Kira was at the Kettle. Safe, for now. Not knowing that the people who'd promised to protect her were both in cages of different kinds.

And somewhere out there, a man with a forgettable face was sleeping well. Satisfied. Certain that his plan was working.

She thought about his smile.

She thought about what she would do to it when she got out of here.

If she got out of here.

Tomorrow, Weston would push for a trial. Tomorrow, he'd try to give her a chance.

Tomorrow, someone would try to stop him.

She didn't know who. Didn't know how. But she knew the knife wouldn't let her reach a courtroom. Knew the hammer wouldn't wait for due process. Knew that whatever protection these walls offered, it came with an expiration date.

One day. Maybe two. That's what Weston had said.

After that, it went above him.

She opened her eyes. Looked at the small rectangle of gray light above her. Watched it dim as the sun moved somewhere she couldn't see.

The light faded. The rectangle went from gray to dark gray to nothing.

Somewhere in the building above her, a door slammed. Footsteps. Voices she couldn't make out. The machinery of law, still grinding, indifferent to the woman in its belly.

She pulled her knees up. Wrapped her arms around them.

The cold crept in from the stone beneath her.

She waited.

CHAPTER 23: The Witness Falls

The cupboard was dark.

She couldn't see anything. Couldn't move. The walls pressed in on every side, close enough that her shoulders touched wood when she breathed, close enough that her knees were jammed against her chest and her neck bent at an angle that would hurt for days.

Boots on the floor outside.

Heavy. Slow. The rhythm of men who had all the time in the world because no one was going to stop them.

She held her breath. Made herself small. Made herself nothing. If she was quiet enough, still enough, maybe they'd forget she was there. Maybe they'd leave. Maybe she'd wake up and her mother would be making breakfast and her father would be reading by the window and none of this would be real.

The boots stopped.

Right outside the cupboard door.

She could hear breathing on the other side of the wood. The creak of leather as someone shifted their weight. Her own heart slamming against her ribs so loud they had to hear it too, had to know she was in here, had to know.

The door rattled.

She screamed.

***

Selene woke with the scream still in her throat.

Stone ceiling above her. Gray light through a small window. Cold seeping up through the bench beneath her, through her clothes, into her bones.

Not the cupboard. The cell.

She sat up. Her hands were shaking. She pressed them flat against the stone bench, let the cold steady her, let the present replace the past.

It had been years since she'd had that dream. She'd thought she was past it. Thought she'd buried it deep enough that it couldn't reach her anymore, couldn't drag her back to that dark space where a little girl waited for men to decide if she lived or died.

But the cell had found it. Had dug it up like a dog finding old bones.

The same helplessness. The same walls pressing in. The same boots on stone somewhere above her, moving with purpose, deciding things she couldn't control.

Her parents had died while she hid in a cupboard.

She'd heard the sounds. The shouts. The wet noise of blade meeting flesh. Her mother's voice, cut short. Her father's body hitting the floor.

She'd survived because she was small and quiet and good at being nothing. Because the men with boots hadn't thought to check the cupboard. Because luck, or fate, or whatever cruel force governed the universe had decided she got to live while everyone she loved got to die.

She'd told herself she'd buried it. Left it behind in a burning house in a life that no longer existed.

But it was still there. Under everything.

She was still that girl. Still hiding. Still listening to boots and hoping they'd pass her by.

The only difference was the size of the cupboard.

She made herself breathe. In. Out. Slow.

The dream faded. The present settled back into place. She was in a cell in a Paladin station, waiting for a man named Weston to decide her fate. Not a cupboard in her childhood home, waiting for soldiers to find her.

Different. This was different.

She had to believe it was different.

She stood. Walked to the small window. Too high to see out of, but she could see the light changing. Morning, probably. Another day in a cage.

Above her, the station was waking up. She could hear it through the stone. Boots on floors. Voices. The rhythm of authority doing what authority did: grinding forward, indifferent to the woman in its basement.

Boots on stone.

She closed her eyes. Pushed the thought away.

A slot in the door opened. A bowl slid through. Porridge, probably. She didn't look at it. Didn't eat. Her stomach was a knot of something that wasn't hunger, and food wouldn't help.

She waited.

That was all she could do now. Wait and wonder if Weston had found what he was looking for. Wait and wonder if trial meant freedom or just a different kind of death. Wait and listen to the building breathe above her, full of people who wanted her gone for reasons she still didn't fully understand.

The morning stretched. The light in the window shifted. The porridge went cold in its bowl.

Then footsteps. Different from before. Purposeful. Coming closer.

A key in the lock. The door swinging open.

Weston stood in the frame.

He looked worse than yesterday. Dark circles deeper. Lines around his mouth that hadn't been there before. But something in his eyes had changed. Not hope, exactly. Resolve. The look of a man who'd made a decision and was going to see it through no matter what it cost.

"Get up," he said. "We're moving."

Selene stood. "Trial?"

"I'm pushing for one. Today. Before this goes any higher up the chain." He stepped back to let her through. "I found something last night. Not proof, but enough to ask questions they don't want asked."

"What kind of questions?"

"The kind that make powerful people nervous." He gestured down the corridor. "Come on. Stay close."

No cuffs this time. She noticed that. He was treating her like a person being escorted, not a prisoner being transported. It meant something. She wasn't sure what.

They walked.

***

The station was different in daylight.

Stone corridors that had felt like a throat swallowing her now opened into wider spaces. Offices with open doors. Clerks carrying ledgers. The business of judgment, visible and ordinary.

Other Paladins passed them. Some nodded to Weston. Some didn't. Some looked at Selene with curiosity. Others with something colder.

She felt the tension in the building like a change in pressure before a storm. Something was wrong. Something beneath the surface, invisible but heavy.

"Where are we going?" she asked quietly.

"My office. I need to prepare the formal request for trial." Weston's voice was low, meant only for her. "Once it's filed, they can't make you disappear. There'll be a record. A process. People watching."

"And if someone doesn't want that process?"

"Then we'll find out soon enough."

They passed a door marked EVIDENCE. Selene's eyes caught on it. Held for half a second longer than they should have.

Her daggers were in there. Her lockpicks. The tools that made her who she was. Confiscated, catalogued, locked away behind a door that probably wouldn't hold her for more than thirty seconds if she had the right motivation.

Weston noticed her looking. Said nothing.

They kept walking.

***

The voice came from behind them.

"Weston."

They stopped. Turned.

A man stood in the corridor. Paladin gray, like Weston. But younger. Harder. The kind of face that had never softened with doubt, never creased with questions about whether orders were right or just convenient.

Selene recognized the type. She'd seen it in Guild enforcers, in street muscle, in every organization that valued obedience over thought. The new generation. Polished and empty, believing in nothing but the chain of command.

"Varek," Weston said. His voice was careful. Measured.

Varek walked closer. Not hurrying. Taking his time. Other Paladins in the corridor had stopped what they were doing. Watching. Waiting.

"Where are you taking the prisoner?"

"Formal questioning. Preparation for trial."

"Trial." Varek smiled. It didn't reach his eyes. "There's not going to be a trial."

The words landed in the corridor like stones dropped into still water. Selene felt the ripples spread outward, felt the watching Paladins shift their weight, felt something change in the air between one breath and the next.

Weston's face didn't move. But his eyes changed. Understanding settling in like cold water.

"On whose authority?"

"The kind that doesn't need to explain itself to you."

"I see." Weston's voice stayed level. "And who gave that authority? Who decided that due process doesn't apply to this case?"

"You're asking questions above your rank."

"I'm asking questions a Paladin should ask. Questions about justice. About law. About what we're actually supposed to be doing here."

Varek's hand moved to his belt. To the blade hanging there. The gesture was casual, almost lazy. Like he was just resting his hand. But Selene saw it for what it was.

Weston saw it too.

His eyes dropped to the weapon. When he spoke again, his voice was quieter. Different.

"Why are you armed, Varek?"

A pause. Heavy.

Selene understood then. Weston had come for a custody transfer. A walk to his office. Paperwork and process. He'd followed protocol. He'd trusted the system.

He wasn't armed.

Weston's belt was bare. Varek's wasn't.

Varek had known what this morning was going to be.

"You came here to kill me," Selene said. Not a question. Just recognition.

Varek didn't answer. Didn't need to.

Other Paladins in the corridor were frozen. Watching. Some of them confused, some of them scared, some of them just waiting to see which way the wind would blow.

Weston turned his body. Put himself between Varek and Selene. Physically. A wall of flesh and gray cloth and stubborn, stupid principle.

"Step aside, Weston." Varek's hand closed around the hilt of his blade. "This doesn't have to include you."

"She's entitled to due process. That's the law."

"The law is what we say it is."

"No." Weston's voice was steady. Certain. The voice of a man who'd spent his whole career believing in something and wasn't going to stop now. "The law is what protects people from men like you. It's what separates us from . . ." He stopped. Started again. "The moment we decide we're above it, we become the thing we're supposed to fight."

"Poetry." Varek drew his blade. The steel caught the light from a high window. "Too bad pretty words don't stop steel."

"I have evidence this case was manufactured. Evidence of a frame job. Evidence that someone is using this institution as a weapon." Weston didn't move. Didn't flinch. "I'm going to ask questions in a proper forum. I'm going to demand answers. And if you kill me here, in front of witnesses, you're going to prove everything I suspected."

"Maybe. But you'll still be dead."

Weston didn't have an answer for that. Or maybe he did and it didn't matter anymore.

Selene wanted to move. Wanted to grab Weston, pull him aside, do something. But her body wouldn't respond. Her legs had turned to stone. Her arms hung at her sides like they belonged to someone else. All that training, all those years of learning to act when others froze, and now she was the one who couldn't move.

She was frozen, watching two men face each other in a corridor while the world held its breath.

"Last chance," Varek said. "Step aside."

Weston looked at him. Really looked. And Selene saw something shift in his face. Not fear. Something sadder. Recognition of what the institution he'd served had become. What the new generation believed. What his whole career had been building toward.

"No," he said quietly. "I don't think I will."

Varek moved.

***

It happened fast.

Faster than Selene could track. Faster than thought.

The blade came up. Varek stepped forward. Weston raised his arm to block, nothing but flesh and cloth against steel.

The blade went in below his ribs. Once. A grunt of impact. Then again, higher, between the bones of his chest, and Selene heard the sound it made going in, a sound she'd heard before but never like this, never standing useless while it happened to someone who was dying for her.

Weston staggered. Grabbed Varek's arm. More reflex than intent, his body trying to hold itself together while everything fell apart inside.

Blood spread across his gray coat. Dark against the fabric. Too much, too fast.

Varek pulled the blade free. Stepped back. Clinical. Professional. The work of a man who'd done this before.

Weston didn't fall. Not yet.

He turned his head. Found Selene's eyes. Found her standing there, frozen, useless, watching him die.

And she saw something in his face that she'd remember for the rest of her life.

Not fear. Not pain. Not even regret.

Relief.

His mouth opened. Blood on his lips.

"RUN, Selene!" The words came out broken, wet. "Get out of here!"

Then his legs gave out and he fell.

***

The silence lasted forever.

One heartbeat. Two. The corridor held its breath.

Blood spread on stone. Slow. Patient. Finding the cracks between the flagstones.

Weston's hand twitched once against the floor. Then went still.

Selene couldn't move. Her body had forgotten how. She stood there and watched a good man bleed out on a corridor floor because he'd tried to do the right thing.

His eyes were still open. Still looking at her. Already empty.

The whole world had stopped. Every Paladin frozen. The machinery of the institution grinding to a halt because something had just broken that couldn't be fixed.

Then the silence broke.

"MURDERER!"

A young Paladin, face white with horror, pointing at Varek. His voice cracking on the word.

It was like a spell shattering. Suddenly everyone was moving at once.

Two Paladins tackled Varek. A third joined them. He fought, blade swinging, but they bore him down with weight and numbers.

Someone was screaming for restraints. Someone else was screaming for a healer, too late, too late.

The corridor erupted into chaos. Running footsteps. Shouted orders that contradicted other orders. The institution tearing itself apart in real time, loyalty fracturing along lines nobody had seen until the blade came out.

Selene stood in the middle of it.

Nobody was looking at her.

They were looking at the body. At the murderer being wrestled to the ground. At the blood spreading across the stones they'd walked on every day thinking they were the good ones, the righteous ones, the ones who served justice.

RUN, Selene.

His voice in her head. His last words. The gift he'd given her with his dying breath.

She tried to run.

Her legs didn't work right. The first step was a stumble, her body catching up to commands it had stopped receiving somewhere between the blade and the floor. The second step was better. The third was almost normal.

She ran.

***

Not toward the exit. Toward the evidence room.

The door was ajar. Someone had fled in a hurry when the shouting started, left it swinging open behind them. A ring of keys still hung from the lock, swaying slightly. She slipped inside, pulled the door most of the way closed, scanned the shelves.

Her belongings were in a box on a high shelf. Her name on a tag. She dragged a stool over, climbed, pulled the box down. It clattered against the shelf below. Too loud.

She froze. Listened.

Footsteps in the corridor. Someone running past. Not stopping.

The box opened. Her hands were shaking.

Daggers first. She grabbed them, and her fingers betrayed her. One slipped from her grip, clattered against the floor. She stared at it for a second. Hadn't dropped a blade since she was twelve years old.

The familiar leather found her palm when she picked it up. The familiar weight. She forced her hands to close around the grips. Wasn't whole without them. Hadn't realized how naked she'd felt until she was armed again.

But her hands were still shaking.

Lockpicks. Boot knife. The small pouch of coins they'd found on her.

She left the rest. Didn't matter.

Outside, the chaos was still building. She could hear it through the walls. Voices raised in anger, in accusation, in the particular panic of people who'd just watched their world crack open.

She cracked the door. Checked the corridor. A clerk hurried past, ledger clutched to his chest, not looking anywhere but straight ahead.

She stepped out. Walked like she belonged. Like she'd been sent to fetch something. Like she was supposed to be here.

A Paladin rounded the corner ahead of her.

She didn't hesitate. Turned left into a service passage. The kind of route servants and clerks used, not Paladins. Kept walking. Didn't look back.

The passage led to stairs. The stairs led to a door. The door led to an alley behind the station.

Cold air hit her face. Gray light. Garnath, going about its business, oblivious to what had just happened inside.

She walked.

Didn't run. Running drew attention. Running marked you as prey.

Behind her, the Paladin station was still in chaos. Varek was being restrained somewhere inside. Weston's body was cooling on a stone floor. The fractures that had been invisible for years were finally showing through.

She kept walking.

***

Three blocks away, she ducked into an alley and stopped.

Her back hit the wall. Her legs wouldn't hold her anymore. She slid down until she was sitting on cold stone, knees pulled up, daggers in her hands.

The shaking started in her hands and spread.

She didn't know why. Death wasn't new to her. She'd caused it. Watched it. Walked away from it a hundred times. This shouldn't be different. Shouldn't affect her.

But her hands wouldn't stop shaking.

RUN, Selene.

She kept hearing it. The wet, broken sound of his voice. The way he'd found her eyes before he fell. The way he'd used his last moment to give her a chance instead of asking for help, begging for his life, doing any of the things a dying man should do.

He'd stepped between her and a blade. Unarmed. Knowing what would happen.

Why?

She was just a case to him. A problem. A name in a file. He'd spent weeks building evidence against her, hunting her through paperwork and procedure, doing his job the way he'd always done his job.

And then he'd died for her.

Because she was entitled to due process. Because the law mattered. Because some things were worth dying for even if the person you were dying for wasn't worth anything at all.

It didn't make sense. She didn't want it to make sense.

But Weston was dead and she was alive and that meant something. That created a debt she couldn't pay, couldn't ignore, couldn't pretend didn't exist.

She owed him.

The thought made her angry. She didn't want to owe anyone. Didn't want to carry a dead man's sacrifice like a weight around her neck. Didn't want to feel the particular kind of guilt that came from being the reason a good person died.

But she felt it anyway.

She'd survived the cupboard because she was small and quiet and good at being nothing. She'd survived this because a man she barely knew decided she mattered more than his own life.

The same feeling. The same sick weight in her chest. Her mother, and now this.

She sat in the alley and didn't know what to do with any of it.

***

The shaking stopped eventually.

The cold helped. The stone beneath her, leaching heat from her body, forcing her to focus on something physical instead of the images playing on repeat behind her eyes.

She made herself think.

Weston was dead. That couldn't be changed. But what he'd died for, what he'd been trying to expose, that was still there.

Someone had manufactured a case against her. Someone had signed her death warrant with the Guild. Someone had orchestrated all of this, moving pieces on a board she couldn't see, playing a game she didn't understand.

The knife. That's what Weston had called it. Surgical. Patient. Someone operating between systems.

And the hammer. The Guild sanction. Blunt. Political.

Varek was just a tool. Someone had given him orders. Someone above him, someone who'd decided that due process was inconvenient, that a trial was a risk, that it was easier to kill a good man in a corridor than to let the truth come out.

The corruption ran deeper than one young Paladin with a blade.

She didn't know how deep. Didn't know who was pulling the strings. Didn't know why someone had gone to all this trouble just to kill her.

But she knew where to start.

A man with a forgettable face. A smile in the shadows. Someone who'd watched her fail and enjoyed it.

She didn't have a name yet. She'd find one.

She stood up. Legs steadier now. Hands still.

Weston had given her something with his death. Not just escape. Direction.

She couldn't pay back what she owed him. Couldn't bring him back, couldn't undo the blade, couldn't change the fact that a good man had died for a system that didn't deserve him.

But she could find the people responsible.

She stepped out of the alley.

First: Mirael.

Then: the man with the smile.

***

The knock came out wrong.

Three times. Pause. Twice more. Her hands still weren't working right. The rhythm was off, the spacing uneven. But it was close enough.

The door opened.

Mirael stood there. Still hollow. Still empty. The same woman Selene had left when she'd walked out the door to turn herself in.

But something changed in her face when she saw Selene.

The emptiness cracked. Something sharper underneath. Not concern, exactly. Recognition. The look of someone who'd seen enough death to know what it left behind.

"Selene."

Selene stood in the doorway. Couldn't make herself move. Couldn't make herself speak. All those words, all those explanations, all that weight she'd been carrying since a good man fell in a corridor and told her to run.

She opened her mouth.

Nothing came out.

Mirael's eyes moved over her face. Reading something there. Something Selene couldn't hide, couldn't control, couldn't turn into the flat mask she wore for the rest of the world.

"Shit," Mirael said quietly. "What happened?"

Selene stepped inside.

The door closed behind her.

CHAPTER 24: Aftermath

Selene woke in the chair by the window.

She hadn't meant to sleep. The chair was hard, angled wrong, designed for sitting and not much else. But exhaustion didn't care about comfort. At some point in the night, her body had simply stopped asking permission.

Gray light filtered through the grimy glass. Morning. The city already grinding to life outside, carts rattling, voices rising, Garnath doing what Garnath always did. The world hadn't paused because a good man died in a corridor. It never did.

Her neck ached. Her hands still felt wrong, like they belonged to someone else. She flexed her fingers, counting each one as it moved, waiting for the familiar certainty to return.

It didn't.

A tremor ran through her left hand. Small. Quick. Gone before she could pin it down.

She made a fist. Held it until her knuckles went white. When she opened her hand again, it was steady.

Good enough.

Mirael was awake.

She sat on the edge of the bed, eyes on Selene. Had been watching for a while, from the stillness of her posture. Neither of them had slept much. The room still held the shape of last night's silence, the weight of questions unanswered.

Last night came back in pieces. The door closing behind her. Mirael's face. The two words that had hung in the air between them.

What happened?

Selene hadn't answered. Couldn't. Her mouth had opened and nothing had come out, and after a while Mirael had stopped waiting for words. She'd just watched Selene cross to the window and sit in this chair, and then she'd lain down on the bed without turning away, and the silence had stretched until it became its own kind of answer.

Mirael hadn't pushed. Hadn't pried. Hadn't done any of the things she usually did, the questions that weren't really questions, the observations designed to crack Selene open whether she wanted to be cracked or not.

She'd just let the night drown whatever needed drowning.

Now Mirael stood. Crossed to the small stove in the corner. Started water for tea.

She didn't look at Selene. Didn't ask anything. Just moved through the motions, giving her space while being present. The new journal still sat on the bed where it had been since Selene gave it to her. Untouched. Unopened.

Selene watched her move. Recognized what she was doing.

"You're handling me."

Mirael's hands didn't stop. "You needed it."

The water took its time heating. Selene sat in the chair and listened to it, the small sounds of normalcy that meant nothing and everything at the same time. When the tea was ready, Mirael brought it over. Placed it in Selene's hands without ceremony.

Selene wrapped her fingers around the cup. Warm. Something to hold onto.

"Weston's dead."

The words fell out. Flat. Simple. Like stating the weather or the time of day.

Mirael sat across from her on the room's only other chair. Waited.

"A Paladin killed him. Younger. Name was Varek."

Selene took a drink. The tea burned her tongue. Good. Something to feel that wasn't the emptiness.

"Weston didn't have a weapon. Policy."

Something shifted in Mirael's face. Not grief. Something harder.

"He followed the rules," she said quietly. "And they killed him for it."

Not a question. Just recognition.

Selene stared at the cup. Couldn't look at Mirael. Couldn't watch her face process what she was hearing.

"He stepped between us."

The words came in pieces. Not a story. Just fragments, falling out of her in the wrong order because the right order didn't exist anymore.

"He knew. He knew what was going to happen.

"He told me to run."

Mirael didn't interrupt. Didn't reach for her. Didn't do any of the things that would have made Selene stop talking.

"He said my name. Like it mattered."

Silence. The tea cooling in her hands.

"I don't know why he did it."

That was the part she couldn't make fit. The part that kept circling back no matter how many times she tried to put it away. A man she barely knew. A man who'd been building a case against her for weeks. A man who had every reason to let her die and no reason at all to step between her and a blade.

But he had.

And now he was dead and she was alive and none of it made any sense.

Selene stood. Couldn't sit anymore. The chair felt like a cage. She went to the window, checked the street below. Old habit. Threat assessment. Looking for faces that didn't belong, patterns that meant danger.

Nothing. Just Garnath waking up. Just people who didn't know or care that the world had changed.

She pulled out her daggers. Checked them. Clean. Sharp. The leather grips familiar against her palms. Something to do with her hands while her mind refused to settle.

Mirael watched but didn't comment.

"I need to check on Kira."

The thought surfaced from somewhere beneath the numbness. The girl at Mother Gessa's. The firefly she'd promised to protect.

"Is she safe there?"

"For now." Selene turned the blade, watching light catch the edge. "But if they're watching me. If they followed me there before . . ."

Her jaw tightened. Another person she could get killed. Another life tangled up in whatever web she'd stumbled into.

"Does anyone know about her?" Mirael's voice was quiet. Careful. "Anyone connected to this?"

Selene made herself think. Really think, past the exhaustion and the hollow ache behind her ribs.

The visits to the Kettle. She'd always been careful. Always watching for tails, for eyes that lingered too long. Mother Gessa kept her secrets. The other children didn't know Selene's name, just that she came sometimes and brought small things and talked to the girl with the quick hands.

"No. She's invisible. To anyone looking for me."

"Then she's safer than either of us."

Selene didn't like it. Didn't like Kira being out there, alone, without her watching. The protective instinct was irrational and she knew it. Going to her now would only paint a target on her back.

But knowing that didn't make it easier.

"I'll check on her. After. When this is done."

The promise sat heavy in her chest. Another debt. Another person counting on her to survive long enough to keep her word.

Mirael let the silence hold for a moment.

Selene's hands stopped moving on the dagger.

"There's something I didn't tell you," she said. "About the fountain. When the thief burned."

Mirael went still. Waiting.

"There was a man. Watching from the shadows. He saw me try to save it. Saw me fail." Selene's jaw tightened. "And he smiled."

"Who was he?"

"I don't know. Just his face. Built to be forgotten."

The kind of face that slid out of memory the moment you looked away. She'd seen it once, clearly, in the moment before Mirael screamed. A face designed to disappear.

"But someone knows."

She started pacing. Small room. Three steps and turn. Her body needed movement even if her mind couldn't find direction.

"The contacts who shut me out. Tomas. Vela. Holt."

Names she'd trusted. People who'd sold her information for years, taken her coin, kept her secrets. All of them suddenly deaf and blind the moment she needed them.

"Someone told them to stop talking. That means someone gave the order.

"I need to find out who."

Mirael: "They won't talk to you."

"No." Selene stopped by the window again. Stared at the street without seeing it. "They won't."

The silence stretched. Mirael understanding what she wasn't saying.

"I know people."

Selene turned.

"People who don't know your name. Don't know your face." Mirael was standing now, the hollowness still there in her eyes but something else underneath. Something harder. "From before. The journal years."

Ten years of contacts, informants, whisper-traders. All of them connected to Mirael, not to Selene. A separate network that had never touched her work.

"Let me ask. Let me be useful."

Selene's first instinct was no. Keep her safe. Keep her hidden. Don't let her anywhere near the thing that had already tried to kill them both.

"If they connect you to me . . ."

"Then what?" Mirael's voice was flat. "I'm already in danger. I've been in danger since they took the journal."

She crossed her arms. The gesture was familiar, the stubborn set of her shoulders that Selene had seen a thousand times before.

"At least this way I'm doing something besides waiting to see if today's the day someone kicks in the door."

Selene studied her. The woman who couldn't get out of bed two days ago. The woman who'd asked what the point was, who'd looked at her with empty eyes and talked about letting them finish it.

That woman was still there. The hollowness hadn't gone anywhere.

But she was standing now. Asking to help. Reaching for something that looked almost like purpose.

"Careful. Questions only. Nothing that points back here."

"I know how to be invisible." A ghost of something crossed Mirael's face. Not quite a smile. "You taught me."

"If something goes wrong. If you think you're being followed."

"The Broken Wheel. Back entrance. I know."

Selene hesitated. The next words tasted wrong in her mouth.

"I won't be shadowing you."

Mirael looked up. Surprised.

"If they're watching for me, if they know my face, I'll lead them straight to you." Selene's jaw tightened. "You're safer alone."

It was true. She hated that it was true. Every instinct she had screamed at her to follow, to watch, to be close enough to intervene if things went sideways. But instinct was the enemy of strategy, and strategy said: two people moving separately were harder to track than two people moving together.

"The knock," Selene said. "If I'm not here when you get back. Three, pause, two. Like always."

Mirael nodded.

"Today?"

"Today."

Mirael moved to get dressed. Purpose in her steps for the first time since the fire. Selene watched her pull on clothes, check her reflection, transform herself into someone ordinary. Someone forgettable.

At the door, Mirael paused. Didn't turn around.

"Be here when I get back."

Not a request. Not quite an order. Something in between.

"I will."

The door closed.

***

Selene stood in the empty room.

She should follow. Every part of her wanted to follow. Shadow Mirael through the streets, keep her in sight, be close enough to put a blade in anyone who looked at her wrong.

Instead she stayed.

She went to the window. Watched the street until Mirael's figure disappeared around a corner, swallowed by the morning crowd.

Kira was safe because nobody knew she existed. The best protection Selene could give her was distance.

Mirael was out there because she refused to stay hidden. Because she needed to do something, be something, even if that something was dangerous.

Two people she couldn't afford to lose. Two different kinds of risk.

Somewhere out there, a man with a forgettable face was still breathing. Still watching. Still playing a game she didn't understand.

She thought about Weston's eyes. The last thing she'd seen before he fell. Not fear. Not pain.

Relief.

She still didn't understand it. Maybe she never would.

But she could find the man who made it necessary.

She turned from the window. Pulled out her daggers. Started checking the edges, the balance, the familiar weight in her hands. Steady now. No tremors.

The city outside was a grid. Streets were sightlines. Crowds were cover. Every building was either an exit or a trap.

And somewhere in that grid, a man with a forgettable face thought he'd won.

She'd find him. She'd watch the smile leave his face.

That would have to do.

For now.

CHAPTER 25: The Name

The waiting was the worst part.

Selene sat by the window. Not moving. Not pacing. Pacing could be seen from the street, and anyone watching would know someone was inside, someone nervous, someone worth watching back.

So she sat.

The chair was hard. Her back ached from sleeping wrong the night before, from the cell before that, from days of running and hiding and never quite resting. Pain was familiar. She ignored it.

Mirael had been gone for three hours.

Or four. Selene had been counting at first, tracking the minutes by the angle of light through the grimy window, but somewhere around the second hour she'd lost the thread. Started over. Lost it again.

She checked her daggers. Drew them halfway, checked the edges, slid them back. The leather grips were warm from her body heat. She'd done this twice already. Maybe three times. She wasn't sure.

The walls pressed in. She could feel them, even when she wasn't looking at them. The air too still. The silence too thick.

A door slammed somewhere in the building.

Selene's hand went to her blade before she could stop it. She listened. Footsteps in the hall. Heavy. Male. Moving away.

Not Mirael. Not a threat. Just someone else living their life in this rotting building, unaware that a woman two floors up was counting the seconds until she found out if she'd sent her partner to die.

She made herself let go of the dagger. Made herself breathe.

In. Out. Slow.

Her left hand trembled. Just slightly. Just enough to notice.

She pressed it flat against her thigh. Held it there until the trembling stopped. Until the hand was hers again, obedient, controlled.

The new journal sat on the bed. Untouched since yesterday. A reminder of everything that had been taken, everything that couldn't be replaced.

Selene looked away.

***

Four hours.

Maybe five.

The light had shifted. Morning becoming afternoon, the shadows changing their angles, the city outside continuing its indifferent grind. Carts rattled past. Voices rose and fell. Dogs barked. Children shouted.

None of it meant anything. All of it could mean something.

She parsed the sounds automatically. Separating threat from noise. Footsteps that lingered from footsteps that passed. Voices that carried tension from voices that carried nothing.

Everything was fine.

Everything was wrong.

Mirael should have been back by now. She'd said a few hours. She'd said she knew people who would talk to her. She'd said she could be invisible.

But invisible people still died. Invisible people still made mistakes. Invisible people still asked the wrong question to the wrong person and ended up in an alley with their throat opened, and no one knew until the smell drew the rats.

Selene shut the thought down.

It came back.

She saw it: Mirael walking through the Lowers, asking questions, getting answers. Someone noticing. Someone following. Mirael not noticing because she was good but not that good, because no one was that good, because even Selene missed things sometimes and Mirael wasn't Selene.

A hand over her mouth. A blade across her throat. A body going limp.

Stop.

Selene stood. Couldn't sit anymore. The room was strangling her. She was trapped in here by her own logic, by the correct decision to stay hidden while Mirael did the work, and she hated every second of it.

She went to the door. Pressed her ear against the wood. Listened.

Nothing. Just the building breathing. Just silence where there should be footsteps.

Her hand found the latch. Cool iron under her palm.

She could go out. Could find Mirael. Could shadow her from a distance, make sure she was safe, be close enough to put a blade in anyone who touched her.

And lead them straight to her if anyone was watching.

Selene took her hand off the latch.

She went back to the window.

Sat down.

Started counting again.

***

She hadn't eaten.

The thought surfaced from somewhere practical, somewhere that still tracked things like food and water and the body's requirements for functioning. She'd had tea this morning. Nothing else. Yesterday had been . . . she couldn't remember. A piece of bread maybe. Something hard and stale from Mirael's bag.

It didn't matter. She wasn't hungry. Hunger was just another signal she could ignore. Her mind tried to show her a body. She refused to look.

She wasn't dead.

She was fine.

She was late.

Five hours. Six. The light was wrong now, afternoon bleeding toward evening, and Mirael should have been back hours ago and she wasn't and that meant something was wrong because people who were fine came back on time and people who were late were late because something had stopped them.

Selene's hands wanted to shake. Both of them now. She pressed them together, interlaced the fingers, squeezed until the knuckles went white.

The Broken Wheel. She'd given Mirael a fallback location. If something went wrong, if she thought she was being followed, she'd go there instead of coming back here.

Maybe she'd gone there.

Maybe she was sitting in the back of a tavern right now, waiting for Selene to show up, wondering why she hadn't come.

Or maybe she was dead.

Or captured.

Or worse.

Selene stood.

She grabbed her cloak from the hook by the door. Threw it over her shoulders. Her daggers were already in place, boot knife already strapped, everything ready because she was always ready, because the moment you weren't ready was the moment you died.

Her hand found the latch again.

Three taps.

She froze.

Pause.

Two more.

The knock pattern. The right pattern. The one Mirael knew, the one that meant safe, the one that meant alive.

Selene opened the door.

***

Mirael stood in the hallway.

Pale. Tired. Dark circles under her eyes that hadn't been there this morning. Her hands hung at her sides, fingers curled slightly, like they'd forgotten how to relax. But standing. Breathing. Whole.

Selene's hands wanted to shake so badly she had to grip the door frame to stop them.

She checked the hall. Empty. No one following. No one watching.

"Get inside."

Mirael stepped through. Selene closed the door behind her. Checked the latch. Checked it again.

When she turned around, Mirael had already sat down on the bed. Still wearing her coat. Too exhausted to take it off. Her boots were wet. She'd been walking for hours.

Neither of them spoke for a moment.

"You're late."

"I know."

Two words. No explanation. Selene should push, should demand to know what happened, but the relief flooding through her chest was making it hard to think. Relief and something else. Something that felt too much like fear.

She didn't do fear. Not like this. Not over someone else.

She sat down in the chair by the window. Put distance between them. Let the room settle.

"It took longer than I expected." Mirael's voice was raw. Scraped thin from talking to too many people who didn't want to talk. "People are scared."

"Scared of what?"

"You. What's happening around you." Mirael looked up. "They know something's moving. They don't know what, but they feel it. Like animals before a storm."

Selene waited. Mirael needed to get there at her own pace.

"I found someone. Old contact. Owes me from before."

"And?"

Mirael pulled her coat tighter. Not cold. Just holding herself together.

"There's a man. Doesn't work for the Guild. Doesn't work for anyone you'd recognize."

"Then who?"

"Old money. The kind that makes taverns go quiet when someone says their name."

A pause. Mirael looking at her, something heavy in her expression.

"He's called Daven."

The name landed like a stone in still water.

Daven.

Selene held it in her mind. Turned it over. Felt the weight of it.

A forgettable face finally had a name.

"What else?"

"He's a fixer. Patient. Professional. Works the spaces between organizations."

"Not Guild."

"No. Something older. Something that was here before the Guild mattered."

That fit. Surgical. Outside the system. Operating between the cracks.

"The Guild has its own contract on you," Mirael said. "That's separate. That's the hammer."

Two death warrants. Two different hands holding them.

"But Daven . . ." Mirael hesitated. "He's not political. He's not business."

"Then what is he?"

Mirael looked at her. Something shifting in her expression. Reluctance. Or maybe just exhaustion making the words harder to find.

"He's been asking about you. Not what you've done. Where you came from."

Selene went still.

"Seventeen years back. A house that burned after someone saw too much. A family that didn't survive."

The words hit her somewhere old. Somewhere she didn't let anyone touch. Somewhere she'd bricked up so long ago she'd almost forgotten the door existed.

"Why?"

"She didn't know. But he knows you survived something. Something you weren't supposed to survive."

The walls pressed close. Selene could feel her heartbeat in her throat, steady and slow, and that was wrong because her heart should be racing but her body had learned a long time ago to stay calm when everything was falling apart.

A loose end. That's what she was to him.

Not a target. Not a threat. Just something that should have been finished a long time ago.

"So this isn't about what I've done."

"It wasn't." Mirael's voice was careful now. Watching Selene for cracks. "You were just a loose end. Not worth the trouble."

"Until the daggers."

Mirael nodded slowly. "Until the daggers. Now you're a loose end holding something they want back."

The blades at her belt. The ones that had felt like luck when she'd taken them. The best score of her life, that's what she'd thought. The kind of find that changed things.

Not luck. A trigger.

"So he needs me dead and the daggers recovered."

"That's what it sounds like."

Two birds. One contract. She'd painted a target on her own back the moment she'd touched those blades. Taken something that mattered to someone who had the resources to send a man like Daven to get it back.

And now that he was looking, he'd found something else. Something older. A loose thread from seventeen years ago that someone had decided needed cutting.

Selene turned back to the window. The light was fading. Evening coming on. The city going gray and soft at the edges.

She didn't think about the cupboard. Didn't let herself go there.

But the fact that someone else knew. That someone had been looking. That all those years of burying the past hadn't been enough.

That changed things.

"So I have two things hunting me," she said.

"Yes. The Guild contract is business. Territory. You stepped on the wrong toes."

"And Daven?"

"Daven is something else. Someone wants you specifically. Has wanted you since before you were worth wanting."

Selene thought about the smile at the fountain. The way he'd watched her fail. Not a professional watching a target. Something more personal. Something that looked like enjoyment.

"He liked it," she said. "When I lost."

"Then he's not just doing a job."

No. He wasn't.

He was finishing something. Something that had started when she was seven years old, hiding in the dark, listening to her parents die.

"Where does he operate?"

"The Lowers, mostly. Warehouse district. But he moves."

"Does he know I'm looking?"

"Not yet. But he will. The moment you start asking, he'll know."

"Good."

Mirael looked at her. Surprised.

"I want him to know. I want him looking over his shoulder."

"That's not careful."

"No." Selene touched the hilt of her dagger. The one that had started all of this. "It's not."

***

Evening now.

The room had gone dark around them. Neither of them had moved to light a candle. The gray light from the window was enough to see by, and darkness felt safer. Darkness felt like cover.

Selene had a name. A location. A target.

The Guild was still out there. The hammer. That was later.

But Daven was something else. Daven was personal. Daven was connected to everything she'd spent seventeen years trying to bury.

Right now, she had a knife to find.

"You should eat something." Mirael's voice was quiet in the dark.

"So should you."

Neither of them moved.

Somewhere in the Lowers, a man named Daven was still breathing. Still thinking he'd won. Still waiting for the loose end to unravel on its own.

He didn't know she was coming.

He would soon.

Selene sat in the dark and let the name settle into her bones. Felt it take root. Felt it become something solid, something real, something she could aim at.

Daven.

The knife. The personal one. The one who smiled when she failed. The one who'd been waiting seventeen years for a reason to finish what someone had started in a burning house when she was too small to stop it.

Now she had a name.

That was all she'd ever needed.

CHAPTER 26: Ground Chosen

The backroom smelled like old beer and older secrets.

He'd been waiting for an hour. Maybe longer. Time didn't move right in places like this, windowless rooms where the Guild conducted the business that never made it into ledgers. He sat with his back to the wall, watching the door, counting the cracks in the ceiling because counting was better than thinking.

He knew why he was here.

He'd known for weeks. Ever since the first polite summons, the ones he'd answered with excuses. *She's harder to track than expected. She's gone to ground. Give me more time.*

Time had run out.

The door opened. A man stepped through. Gray hair cropped short. Scarred hands that had done work similar to his own, once, before age and rank had moved him to different duties. He carried no weapons visibly, but that meant nothing. Men like this were never unarmed.

He sat across the table. Didn't offer a name. Didn't need to.

"You know why I'm here."

"Yes."

"Then you know how this conversation ends."

Silence. The candle on the table flickered. Somewhere above them, the tavern continued its noise, laughter and arguments and the clink of cups. Normal sounds. Ordinary life happening while something else took shape in the dark below.

"The contract has been open for six weeks," the man said. "That's longer than any contract you've ever held."

"She's difficult."

"She's one woman."

"She's not like the others."

The man's expression didn't change. Didn't need to. The disappointment was already there, baked into the lines around his mouth, the flatness of his eyes.

"You're supposed to be the best we have."

He didn't answer. There was nothing to answer. The statement was true and the failure was his and no amount of explanation would change either of those facts.

"We've given you time," the man continued. "More than anyone else would get. More than you probably deserve, given how long you've been making excuses."

"I haven't been making excuses."

"Then what would you call it?"

He thought about the question. Really thought about it, because the answer mattered more than the man across from him would ever understand.

What would he call it?

Hesitation. That was the honest word. The word he'd never say out loud because saying it would be the same as dying. The Guild didn't tolerate hesitation. The Guild didn't care why a contract stayed open. The Guild only cared that it closed.

"I've been careful," he said instead. "She's aware. More aware than anyone I've tracked in years. She knows when she's being watched. She knows when something's wrong."

"And?"

"And rushing gets contractors killed. I've seen it happen."

The man leaned back. Studied him with eyes that had seen this conversation a hundred times before, with a hundred different contractors making a hundred different excuses for a hundred different failures.

"The Guild doesn't care about your caution. The Guild cares about results."

"I understand."

"Do you?"

The question hung there. Heavy. The kind of heavy that came with consequences attached.

"People are asking questions," the man said. "Important people. The kind who wonder why our best can't handle a single woman who's been making problems for months. The kind who start to wonder if maybe our best isn't what he used to be."

There it was. The threat underneath the words. Not stated directly because it didn't need to be. He'd been in this business long enough to hear what wasn't said.

Finish her, or we finish you.

Not quickly either. The Guild made examples of contractors who failed. Made sure everyone saw what happened when the work didn't get done. Slow deaths. Public enough that the message spread. Private enough that no one could prove anything.

"When?" he asked.

"Soon."

"How soon?"

"Before the week ends. Sooner if you can manage it."

Four days. Maybe five. After six weeks of delays, he had less than a week to do what he'd been avoiding since the contract first landed in his hands.

"And if she's still difficult?"

The man stood. The conversation was over. Had been over before it started, really. Everything else was just formality.

"Then I suggest you become more difficult than she is."

He left without another word. The door closed behind him. The room went quiet except for the muffled sounds of the tavern above, ordinary life continuing as if nothing had changed.

Everything had changed.

***

He sat alone in the dark for a long time.

The candle burned lower. Wax pooled on the table, spreading slowly, finding the grooves in the wood. He watched it without seeing it, his mind somewhere else, running through the same calculations he'd been running for weeks.

She was good. That was the problem. Better than most contractors he'd faced, and he'd faced plenty over the years. Quick. Careful. Patient when patience served her and explosive when it didn't. The kind of fighter who adapted mid-strike, who read opponents like text on a page and adjusted before they knew they'd been read.

None of it was instinct. That was the thing. Instinct was sloppy, reactive, full of holes. What she had was drilled. Burned in until it became reflex. Someone had corrected her mistakes until she stopped making them.

He'd studied her. Watched her work from a distance, cataloging her patterns, her tells, the small habits that everyone had whether they knew it or not. The way she checked corners. The way she positioned herself in crowds. The way she never stopped moving with her back to an open lane.

This was how it was supposed to look. This was what the work produced when it was done correctly.

That was also why he hadn't moved yet.

Because knowing someone that well meant knowing how hard they'd be to kill. And she would be hard. Harder than anything he'd done in years.

He let himself think about it. Really think, in the privacy of this room where no one could see the doubt on his face.

Would she make him pay for it?

Part of him thought it was wasteful. Work like hers didn't grow on trees. The Guild spent years producing assets who moved like that, and most of them washed out or died before they were useful. Ending her felt like burning a library because someone didn't like what was written inside.

But that wasn't his call. The Guild didn't ask what he thought was wasteful. The Guild asked for results.

Yes. The answer was yes, because it had to be yes, because the alternative was his own death and he wasn't ready for that yet. He had years left. Work left. A life that wasn't much but was still his, still something he wanted to keep.

So yes. He could do it.

The question was how.

***

He needed ground.

That was the first rule of any contract. Choose the terrain. Make the environment work for you instead of against you. Never fight on someone else's terms if you could possibly avoid it.

She'd been moving through the Lowers lately. Hunting something. He'd caught whispers, fragments, the kind of intelligence that drifted through the Guild's networks without anyone quite knowing where it came from. A name she was chasing. A man called Daven.

He didn't know who Daven was. Didn't care. What mattered was that she was focused on something else, her attention pointed in a direction that wasn't him.

Good. Let her hunt. Let her find what she was looking for. Let her spend herself on whatever vendetta was driving her.

When she was done, when she was tired, when the adrenaline faded and the exhaustion set in.

That's when he'd be there.

But where?

He closed his eyes. Mapped the city in his head, the way he'd done a thousand times before. Streets and alleys, rooftops and sewers, the places where shadows gathered and the places where light made you vulnerable. Garnath was a maze if you didn't know it. He knew it.

The Merchant Quarter.

The answer came to him the way answers always did when he stopped chasing them. The old district, near the eastern wall. Good streets. Clean sightlines. Multiple exits if things went wrong, and things always went wrong eventually.

He'd walked those streets enough to know them in his sleep. Knew which alleys dead-ended and which ones cut through. Knew where the guards patrolled and when. Knew the rhythm of the place, the way it breathed, the patterns that repeated day after day.

If he was going to do this, he was going to do it there.

***

He checked his blades.

Old habit. The kind that stayed with you long after you stopped thinking about it. Steel sliding free of leather, edges catching the candlelight, the familiar weight in his hands that meant safety and danger in equal measure.

The same blades he'd carried for twenty years. Good steel. Well-maintained. The kind of weapons that didn't fail you when failure meant dying.

She had her daggers. The ones that had gotten her into this mess in the first place. He'd seen them from a distance once, watched her use them on a practice target when she thought she was alone. Fast. Precise. The kind of bladework that came from years of training, not just instinct.

Someone had taught her well.

He slid the blades back into their sheaths. Stood. The chair scraped against the stone floor, loud in the empty room.

Time to scout the ground.

***

Garnath at night was a different city than Garnath by day.

The crowds thinned. The honest people went home, locked their doors, pretended the darkness didn't exist. The ones who remained were the ones who belonged to it, the ones who did their work in shadows because shadows were safer than light.

He moved through the streets like one of them. Just another body in the dark. Another face that no one would remember tomorrow.

The Merchant Quarter was quieter than the Lowers but not dead. Taverns still glowed. Voices still carried. The occasional patrol of city guards moved through, torches flickering, more interested in being seen than in seeing anything.

He avoided them out of habit. Found the alleys he remembered. Checked the sightlines, the exits, the places where someone could wait without being noticed.

Good ground. The kind of ground that favored patience over speed. The kind where knowing the terrain meant everything.

She'd come through here eventually. She had to. The Lowers connected to the Merchant Quarter in three places, and two of them were too public, too watched. The third was the route anyone with training would take.

He'd been in this work long enough to recognize discipline when he saw it.

He found his spot. A recessed doorway with good shadows, a clear view of the junction where the alley met the street. Close enough to strike, far enough to see her coming.

Now he waited.

Not tonight. She was still hunting, still focused on whatever ghost she was chasing. He could hear it in the way talk died when certain names came up. The way runners moved like they were being timed. Someone was moving with purpose, disturbing the patterns.

But soon.

A day. Maybe two. She'd finish her hunt or give up, and then she'd move through the city again, and then she'd pass through the Merchant Quarter because it was the smart route, the safe route, the route anyone with her training would choose.

And he'd be here.

***

He walked home through empty streets.

The city settled around him, quieting by degrees, the last of the tavern noise fading as he moved into the darker districts where no one went unless they had to. His footsteps were the only sound. His shadow the only movement.

She was out there somewhere. Sharpening herself for a kill. Thinking she was the hunter, not the prey.

She didn't know.

Didn't know that the Guild had stopped being patient. Didn't know that their best contractor had been given an ultimatum. Didn't know that someone was watching her patterns, studying her movements, choosing the ground where she would die.

Four days.

He'd use them well. Scout the terrain again tomorrow. Watch her from a distance if he could, track her progress on whatever hunt she was running. Wait for the moment when her guard dropped, when exhaustion won out over alertness, when she made the small mistake that everyone made eventually.

Then he'd close the distance.

Then he'd finish it.

The contract would close and she'd be dead and he'd go back to being what he'd always been. The Guild's best. A man who didn't hesitate. A professional who did the work no matter what the work required.

He told himself that.

He almost believed it.

The city swallowed him whole, and he disappeared into the dark.

The ground was chosen. The rest would follow.

CHAPTER 27: No Answers

Three days of hunting, and it ended in a warehouse that smelled like fish rot and old tar.

Selene crouched on the rooftop across the street, watching the building breathe. One guard at the front door, picking at his nails with a knife. Two more inside, based on the shadows that passed the grimy windows. And somewhere in there, a man with a forgettable face who had smiled while her world burned.

Daven.

She'd learned his patterns. Learned when he arrived, when he left, who came to see him and how long they stayed. Mirael's intel had been good. The warehouse was his base of operations, the place where he conducted business that never made it into ledgers.

Tonight, that business ended.

She hadn't slept properly in days. Hadn't eaten much either. Her body ran on anger and cold tea and something harder than either. The exhaustion was there, waiting at the edges, but she wouldn't let it in. Not yet. Not until this was done.

The guard at the front yawned. Scratched himself. Looked up at the sky like he was checking for rain.

Amateur.

***

The skylight hinges were rusted, but she'd oiled them two nights ago. They opened without a sound, just a whisper of metal on metal that got lost in the creak of the old building settling.

She dropped through. Caught a beam. Swung down to a stack of crates and landed in a crouch, silent as dust falling.

Dark inside. The kind of dark that had weight to it, pressing against her eyes until they adjusted. Crates everywhere, stacked high, creating corridors and dead ends. The smell was worse in here. Fish and tar and something else underneath. Something copper. Old blood, maybe. Or just her imagination filling in details that fit.

Voices deeper in. Two men talking. One of them laughed at something. Casual. Bored.

She moved through the shadows. Patient. No rush now that she was inside. The anger was cold, controlled, a blade she'd sharpened over days of watching and waiting. Not a fire. Fires made you stupid. This was ice. This was certainty.

A guard passed within arm's reach. Didn't see her. Didn't feel her. Kept walking toward the front of the building, oblivious.

She let him go. He wasn't the one she wanted.

***

Lantern light bled from under a door at the back. She pressed her ear to the wood and listened.

One voice now. His.

She recognized it before she consciously placed it. The fountain. The way he'd stood there watching her fail, watching Mirael scream, watching everything fall apart with that smile on his face.

Something twisted in her chest. Not fear. Something older than fear. Something that remembered a cupboard and boots on stone and a night when she'd learned that the world had teeth.

He was talking to someone. Giving instructions. His tone was flat, professional, the voice of a man discussing inventory or weather. Something in his voice scraped something old. The cupboard. The boots. The smell of smoke and the sound of adults making choices she couldn't stop. No proof. Just her nervous system insisting there was a connection.

She pulled her daggers.

The weight of them settled into her palms. Familiar. Perfect. The leather grips warm against her skin, the balance so precise it felt like the blades were extensions of her hands rather than separate things.

She opened the door.

***

Two men inside.

The first was muscle. Big. Broad shoulders, thick neck, the kind of body that was used to intimidating people. He sat on a crate near the door, a club leaning against his leg, a half-eaten apple in his hand.

He saw her first.

His eyes went wide. The apple dropped. His hand reached for the club.

Selene's dagger took him through the eye.

The blade went in so smoothly she almost didn't feel it. No resistance. No scrape of bone. Just the soft wet give of something that used to be a person and was now just meat.

The muscle's head snapped back. His body followed, toppling off the crate, legs kicking once, twice, then going still. The club clattered to the floor. The apple rolled into a corner, forgotten.

She pulled the blade free. Brain matter clung to the edge for a moment, gray and pink and glistening, then slid off like water. The steel was clean before she'd finished the motion.

That wasn't normal. She knew that wasn't normal.

Later.

Daven looked up from his table.

***

He sat at a scarred wooden desk, papers spread in front of him, a quill in his hand. Like a clerk. Like an accountant tallying figures at the end of a long day. Behind him, a second lantern hung from a hook, casting his shadow long and thin across the wall.

For one second, his face was naked. Surprise. Maybe fear. The mask stripped away by the speed of what had just happened.

Then the smile came back.

The same smile. The one from the fountain. The one that said he knew things she didn't, and always would.

"You're persistent." His voice was calm. Almost admiring. He set down the quill like they had all the time in the world. "I wondered when you'd find me."

Selene didn't respond. She crossed the room. Slow. Deliberate. Her boots made no sound on the stone floor.

“Took longer than I expected, honestly.” He leaned back in his chair. Made no move toward the knife on his belt. Too smart for that. Or maybe he just wanted to see what she’d do. “The girl from the fountain. The one who was supposed to be easy.”

Six feet away. She stopped.

“You know why I’m here.”

“I can guess.” His eyes flicked to the body by the door. The muscle, still leaking from the socket where his eye used to be. “You’ve improved. Or those blades aren’t what they appear to be.” She didn’t take the bait. Didn’t ask what he meant.

“You think killing me changes anything?” He was still smiling. Still calm. Like death was an abstract concept that happened to other people. “I’m just a hand. Cut it off, another grows back.”

“Then I’ll cut that one too.”

He laughed. Short. Genuine.

“I believe you would.”

She moved.

***

The dagger wanted this.

That was the thought that flickered through her mind as the blade came around. Not that she wanted it, though she did. The dagger itself. Eager. Hungry. Like the steel had been waiting for this moment since she’d first wrapped her fingers around the grip.

The balance did the rest. Weight and edge and geometry that didn’t forgive mistakes.

She barely felt resistance.

The edge opened Daven’s throat from ear to ear in a single stroke. Too deep. Too clean. The kind of wound that shouldn’t come from one motion, one blade, one human arm behind it. She’d cut throats before. She knew what it felt like, the drag of steel through muscle and cartilage, the work required to sever everything that needed severing.

This wasn’t that.

This was butter. This was paper. This was nothing at all.

Blood sheeted down his chest. Not spraying, not yet. The cut was so complete that his body hadn't caught up with what had happened. Then his heart beat once more, and the spray began.

It hit her across the face. Warm. Thick. The copper smell of it filling her nose, her mouth, painting her skin in someone else's dying.

Daven fell back in his chair. His hands came up to his throat. Instinct. Pointless instinct.

There was nothing to hold together. The wound gaped red and wet across his neck, a second smile to match the one he'd worn at the fountain. His fingers slipped in his own blood, trying to close something that would never close.

He tried to scream. What came out was a wet gurgle that died halfway up his throat.

She'd taken his smile from him. Given him a new one.

For one perfect second, Daven was just a man realizing he'd finally met something he couldn't charm his way out of.

Then something shifted in his eyes. The fear drained out. And he laughed.

The sound was wrong. Wet. Bubbling. Air escaping through places air was never meant to escape. But it was still a laugh. She could see it in his eyes, in the way his shoulders shook, in the bloody froth that formed at the corners of that gaping wound that used to be his throat.

He was laughing at her.

Dying faster than anyone should die, blood pouring out of him like water from a split skin, and he was laughing.

His mouth moved. Lips trying to form words. The vocal cords were gone, sliced clean through, but he tried anyway. She could read the shapes his mouth made.

"Your . . . fath . . ."

Something snapped inside her.

She grabbed his jaw. Wrenched it open. Her other hand moved before she knew what she was doing, the dagger sliding into his mouth, finding the root of his tongue and cutting.

He made a sound. Not a scream. Not a laugh. Something worse. Something that came from a place beyond either.

The tongue came free in a wet, ragged chunk. She pulled it out and threw it on the floor. Meat. Just meat now.

"Don't you fucking talk about my father."

Her voice didn't sound like hers. Too raw. Too young. The voice of a girl in a cupboard, not a woman with a blade.

She brought her boot down on the tongue. Ground it into the stone. Felt it squelch and flatten under her heel.

Daven watched. Eyes wide now. The amusement finally, finally gone. Replaced by something she'd wanted to see since the fountain.

Fear.

Real fear. The kind that came when you realized you weren't the predator anymore.

But it didn't last. Even now, even with his tongue on the floor and his throat opened to the spine, something shifted in his eyes. The fear faded. And the smile came back.

He tried to laugh. Couldn't. Tried to mouth something else. More blood. More bubbles. More of that horrible drowning sound.

His lips moved. She could read the shape. The same shape. Over and over.

Saw. Saw. Saw.

Then his body betrayed him completely.

The gurgle became a long, slow, wet exhale that seemed to go on forever, his chest deflating, his hands sliding away from the ruin of his throat, his head tipping back until he was staring at the ceiling.

The smile stayed.

Even in death, even with his throat opened to the spine, even with his tongue ground into the floor, even with his blood soaking into his clothes and pooling beneath the chair in a steady patter, he was smiling.

He found it funny. That was the thing she couldn't escape.

He died thinking she'd already lost.

***

Selene stood over him. Watching.

Blood dripped from her face. She could feel it cooling, thickening, starting to crust at the edges. His blood. The blood of the man who had smiled at the fountain, who had known something about her father and died laughing because she would never know what.

Your father saw . . .

Saw what? What did he see? What was worth seventeen years of loose ends and burning houses and hired killers?

She'd never know now.

She wiped her face with the back of her hand. It didn't help. Just smeared the blood around, painted her skin in streaks of red and brown.

The dagger was clean.

She looked at it. Really looked. The blade gleamed in the lantern light, perfect and unmarked, as if she hadn't just used it to nearly decapitate a man. No blood. No residue. Nothing.

The other dagger, the one she'd put through the muscle's eye, was the same. She'd felt the brain matter slide off, but the steel showed nothing. Just that perfect, hungry shine.

She understood now why someone wanted them back. These weren't just weapons. They were something else. Something that made killing too easy, too clean, too absolute.

Something that probably shouldn't exist.

She sheathed them anyway. They were hers now. Whatever they were.

***

She searched the room.

Papers on the desk. Ledgers. Names and dates and numbers that meant nothing to her. Contracts. Payments. A web of transactions that probably added up to something important if you knew how to read them.

She didn't.

Nothing about her. Nothing about her parents. Nothing about a fire seventeen years ago or a child who was supposed to die but didn't.

If there were answers here, Daven had kept them in his head. And she'd spilled his head across the floor along with everything else.

She went through his pockets. Coins. A key to something. A folded note with an address she didn't recognize.

Nothing useful. Nothing that explained anything.

The muscle had even less. No papers. No notes. Just a purse with a few copper pieces and a charm against bad luck that hadn't worked very well.

She stood in the middle of the room, surrounded by blood and bodies and the smell of death, and felt nothing at all.

***

He was just a tool.

The thought came to her as she stared at his body. The smile frozen on his face, the throat gaping, the blood still dripping in that steady patter that was starting to slow as the pool spread wider.

Just a tool. Like her. Like the muscle on the floor. Like everyone who did this kind of work.

Someone like Daven had been there seventeen years ago. Different face, same hands. The kind of man who showed up when money changed hands and questions weren't asked. Her parents had died to hands like his. And now those same hands had reached for her.

He hadn't known why. Probably hadn't cared. Just did the work. Collected the payment. Smiled while other people's worlds burned.

And now he was dead, and the person who'd paid him was still out there.

She'd killed her only lead.

The anger was gone. Spent. There was nothing left but the emptiness and the smell of blood and the weight of the daggers at her belt.

Your father saw . . .

She'd spend the rest of her life wondering what came next. That was the punishment. Not his death. His silence.

He'd won. Even dying, he'd won.

***

She cleaned herself as best she could. Found a bucket of water in the corner, probably for washing fish guts off crates. Cold. Stale. It did the job.

The blood came off her face, her hands, her arms. Turned the water pink, then red, then something darker. She scrubbed until her skin felt raw, until she couldn't smell copper anymore, until she looked almost human again.

Her clothes were ruined. Nothing to be done about that. She'd burn them later.

She took one last look around. The bodies. The blood. The papers that told her nothing.

The lantern still burned. It would burn down eventually. Someone would find this place in a day or two. By then, she'd be gone.

The daggers rested at her belt. Perfect. Deadly. Hers.

For now.

She left the way she came. Rooftop. Skylight. Silent.

The guard at the front was still picking at his nails. Still oblivious. She thought about killing him. Decided it wasn't worth the effort. He'd find out what happened to his boss soon enough.

The city swallowed her whole.

***

Garnath at night was indifferent to death.

Selene walked through empty streets, past closed shops and dark windows, past drunks sleeping in doorways and rats bold enough to watch her pass without flinching. The city didn't care that she'd just killed two men. Didn't care that one of them had died laughing at her. Didn't care that she was walking home with someone else's blood drying in her hair and answers she'd never get rotting in a warehouse.

Daven was dead. The knife was gone.

But the Guild contract was still open. The hammer was still out there somewhere, waiting.

And somewhere, behind all of it, someone who had wanted her dead since she was seven years old was still breathing, still pulling strings, still smiling in whatever shadows they called home.

She hadn't won. She'd just removed one piece from the board.

Tomorrow, she'd figure out what was left. Find a way forward. Keep moving, because moving was all she knew how to do.

Tonight, she walked home through the dark and tried not to think about what her father saw.

She didn't succeed.

CHAPTER 28: The Shape of It

She woke to Mirael's eyes.

Not the ceiling. Not the wall. Mirael, sitting in the chair by the window, watching her with the kind of stillness that meant she'd been watching for a while. The morning light caught the edges of her face, turned her expression into something unreadable.

Selene didn't move. Didn't speak. Just lay there, letting her body remember how to be awake, letting the room come into focus around her.

The hearth. Cold now. The clothes she'd burned in it while it was still dark reduced to ash and char and the faint smell of smoke that clung to everything.

Mirael had seen her do it. Had watched from the bed without a word while Selene fed fabric into the flames, watched the blood turn black and curl and disappear. Hadn't asked. Hadn't moved. Just watched.

She was still watching.

Selene sat up. The blanket fell away. Her hands were clean. She'd scrubbed them raw last night.

They still felt like they were covered in blood.

Mirael's face did something complicated. A shift in the muscles around her eyes, the corners of her mouth. Not fear. Not anger. Something worse.

Recognition.

Like she was seeing someone she'd hoped she'd never meet.

One breath. Two. The silence stretched between them, heavy and full of things that didn't need saying.

"Oh, Selene." Mirael's voice was quiet. Barely above a whisper. "What did you do?"

Not accusation. Not judgment. Just knowing. The kind of question that already had its answer written in the ashy air.

Selene opened her mouth. Closed it. Her throat felt thick, clogged with words that wouldn't form.

What would she even say? I killed him. He laughed. I cut out his tongue. He died smiling. I ground what was left of his voice into the stone floor and told him not to speak my father's name.

"He's dead."

That was all she could manage. Two words. Flat. Empty.

"I know." Mirael didn't move. Didn't blink. "That's not what I'm asking."

Selene looked away. At the wall. At her hands. At the ashes in the hearth that used to be evidence.

"He tried to say my father's name."

Silence.

"And?"

"And I stopped him."

More silence. The kind that filled the space between them like water, pressing in from all sides.

Mirael didn't ask how. She didn't need to. Selene could feel her reading it. In the set of her shoulders. In the way she couldn't hold eye contact. In the rawness of her hands and the hollow behind her eyes.

Some things didn't need words.

Mirael stood. Crossed to the bed. Sat on the edge, close enough to touch but not touching.

"You came back."

"Yes."

"You're still here."

"Yes."

"Then we deal with what comes next."

No lecture. No comfort. No reaching for something that wouldn't help. Just forward motion. Just the next step.

That was Mirael. That was why they worked.

Selene should have felt something. Relief that Mirael wasn't running. Gratitude for the steady presence, the lack of flinching. Something warm, something human.

She felt tired. That was all. Bone-deep tired, the kind that sleep didn't touch.

Daven was dead. The knife was gone.

And she had nothing to show for it except a half-word she'd never finish hearing.

Saw.

She pushed it away. It didn't stay pushed. It never would.

Her father. Whatever he saw. Whatever got him killed, got her mother killed, got her shoved into a cupboard while the world outside burned.

She'd spent seventeen years not knowing. Seventeen years of silence where answers should have been. And last night, for one moment, she'd been close. Close enough to taste it. Close enough to watch it die in Daven's throat along with everything else.

Your father saw . . .

What? What did he see? What was worth all of this?

She'd never know now. She'd made sure of that.

The anger came back, distant and cold. Not at Daven. At herself. At the girl who'd cut out a man's tongue because she couldn't bear to hear her father's name in his mouth. The girl who'd chosen silence over answers.

She'd do it again. That was the worst part. Given the same moment, the same choice, she'd do exactly the same thing.

Some lines you didn't let people cross. Even if it cost you everything.

***

Kira.

The thought surfaced without warning, sharp and clear.

Three days since Weston died. Three days since everything tilted sideways and started sliding toward something Selene couldn't see the bottom of.

Kira was still out there. Still invisible. Still protected by the distance Selene had put between them.

She thought about the girl's face. The way she'd looked at Selene in Mother Gessa's cellar, all those months ago. Hungry and scared and trying so hard not to show either. A child pretending to be harder than she was.

Selene had been that child once. Hiding in cupboards. Learning that the world had teeth. Learning that the people who were supposed to protect you could disappear in a single night, leaving nothing but smoke and silence.

She didn't want that for Kira. Didn't want her to learn the lessons Selene had learned. Didn't want her hands to know the weight of a blade, her dreams to fill with blood, her heart to calcify into something that could cut out a man's tongue and feel nothing but tired afterward.

Kira deserved better. Deserved a life that didn't look like Selene's.

That was the one thing Selene could give her. Distance. Safety. A future that didn't have this shape.

She held onto that thought. A small, cold comfort in a morning full of ash.

***

Mirael was watching her again.

Not obviously. Not with that first piercing attention. Just glances. The way you watched someone you were worried about but knew better than to crowd.

Selene looked at her. Really looked. The lines of her face. The gray in her hair. The steadiness in her hands as she held her cup of tea.

This woman had taken her in. Had shared her space, her bed, her silence. Had seen Selene come home covered in blood and hadn't flinched. Had asked the question that mattered and accepted the answer that didn't explain anything.

What did that cost? What did it take to love someone like Selene?

She didn't know. Wasn't sure she wanted to.

"Thank you." The words came out rough. Unpracticed.

Mirael looked up. Raised an eyebrow.

"For what?"

"For not asking."

A pause. Something moved behind Mirael's eyes. Something soft that she usually kept hidden.

"You'll tell me when you're ready. Or you won't. Either way, you're still here."

Selene nodded. Didn't trust her voice to say anything else.

***

The morning passed in fragments.

Mirael made tea. Selene drank it without tasting it. They didn't talk about last night. Didn't talk about much of anything. The silence between them wasn't comfortable, but it wasn't hostile either. It was the silence of two people who understood that some things needed time to settle before they could be touched.

Selene's hands were steady. That was something.

But there was a tremor somewhere deeper. In her chest. In her gut. The place where she kept the things she didn't look at.

Last night, she'd looked. Last night, something had cracked open and spilled out before she could stop it.

Don't you fucking talk about my father.

Her voice hadn't sounded like hers. Still didn't, in memory. Too raw. Too young. The voice of a seven-year-old girl who'd hidden in a cupboard while her world burned.

She didn't know who that was. Didn't want to meet her again.

***

"The Guild contract is still open."

Mirael said it like she was reading from a list. Practical. Factual. The next problem on the pile.

"I know."

"The knife is gone. The hammer is still out there."

"I know."

Mirael was quiet for a moment. Then: "What do you want to do?"

Selene stared at the wall. At the cracks in the plaster, the water stains, the places where time had worn the surface thin.

"One threat at a time. That's how you survive."

"Is that an answer?"

"It's the only one I have."

Mirael nodded. Let it rest.

***

She couldn't stay in this room. The walls were too close. The smell of smoke was too thick. The silence was too loud.

She needed air. Movement. Something that wasn't the inside of her own head.

"I'm going out."

Mirael looked up from where she sat. Reading now. Or pretending to. "Where?"

"I don't know. Just out."

A pause. Something passed across Mirael's face. Concern, maybe. Or the shadow of it.

"Be careful."

"I always am."

The words felt hollow. Both of them knew it.

Selene dressed. Clean clothes. Dark colors. She strapped on the daggers, felt the weight of them settle against her hips. Familiar now. Almost comforting.

She didn't think about what they'd done last night. What she'd done with them.

At the door, she paused. Looked back.

Mirael was watching her again. That same quiet attention. That same knowing in her eyes.

"Come back."

Not a question. Not a command. Something in between.

"I will."

She left before she could see whether or not Mirael believed her.

***

Garnath in daylight was a different city.

The same streets that felt like hunting grounds at night became ordinary under the sun. People buying bread. Children running errands. Guards standing at corners, looking bored. The sounds of commerce, of life, of a city that didn't care what had happened in a warehouse last night.

No one knew. No one cared. The city digested violence and kept moving. That was how it worked. That was how it had always worked.

Selene walked without direction at first. Just moving. Just breathing. Letting her feet carry her through the familiar maze of streets and alleys, letting the motion burn off some of the tension that had knotted itself into her muscles.

She ended up in the Merchant Quarter. Habit. The route she'd taken a hundred times before, burned into her body's memory until she didn't have to think about it.

The streets here were cleaner. Wider. Better maintained. This was where the money lived. The kind that hired people like Daven to solve problems. The kind that never got its hands dirty but always knew where the blood came from.

She'd walked this route a hundred times. Knew every corner, every alley, every shortcut.

Today it felt different.

Heavier. Like the air itself had weight.

She told herself it was exhaustion. Just exhaustion. The aftermath of too little sleep and too much death. Her body was tired. Her mind was tired. Everything felt harder than it should.

That was all.

***

Something prickled at the back of her neck.

Not a sound. Not a sight. Just awareness. The animal part of her brain waking up, sniffing the air, tasting something wrong.

The feeling of being watched. The feeling of being measured.

She'd felt it before. Knew what it meant.

Her pace didn't change. Her hands didn't move toward her blades. Nothing in her posture shifted, nothing that would tell a watcher she'd noticed.

But inside, something woke up. Something that had been sleeping through the grief and the hollow and the bone-deep tired.

She was being hunted.

***

She checked the street without appearing to check.

Rooflines. Doorways. Windows. The mathematics of ambush. All the places she would hide if she were the one watching. All the angles that offered advantage.

Nothing visible. Nothing obvious.

That was worse. That meant whoever was watching knew what they were doing. Knew how to stay hidden. Knew how to wait.

She kept walking. Slower now. Reading the terrain the way she'd been taught, all those years ago. Looking for the shape of the trap before she stepped into it.

The alley ahead. The junction where three streets met. The recessed doorways with good shadows.

She knew this place. Knew how she would use it if she were hunting someone.

Someone else knew too.

***

This was chosen ground.

The thought arrived cold and clear, cutting through the fog of exhaustion.

Someone had picked this spot. Scouted it. Decided that this was where it would happen.

And she'd walked right into it.

Turn back? They'd know she'd made them. Know she was aware. That changed the calculation, made her unpredictable, but it also meant running. And she didn't know what was behind her.

Keep walking? She was entering a kill box. The street ahead funneled. Got tighter. Fewer exits.

Classic setup. Whoever planned this knew what they were doing. Knew her routes. Knew her patterns. Knew where she'd be and when.

That wasn't amateur work. That wasn't desperate.

That was Guild.

***

She should have known. Should have expected this.

The knife was gone, but the hammer was always coming. The Guild didn't forgive. Didn't forget. Didn't stop until the contract was closed or the contractor was dead.

She'd just thought she'd have more time. More space to breathe. A few days to recover, to plan, to figure out what came next.

She was wrong.

Her hands wanted to reach for the daggers. She didn't let them. Not yet. Not until she knew what she was facing.

The street narrowed ahead. The shadows deepened.

She kept walking.

***

She felt him before she saw him.

Not movement. Not sound. Just pressure. The way air changed when someone who knew how to kill entered a space. A weight that hadn't been there before, a presence that pushed against her awareness like a hand pressing on her chest.

She'd felt it before. In training. In the field. The sense of another predator nearby, watching, waiting, measuring.

Never quite like this.

This was different. Heavier. Older. The presence of someone who had been doing this longer than she'd been alive.

She stopped.

The street was quiet. Too quiet. The ordinary noise of the city felt far away, muffled, like someone had wrapped the world in cloth.

Ahead, a shadow separated from a doorway.

A man. Older. Gray at the temples. Built like someone who'd spent a lifetime using his body as a weapon. Nothing wasted. Nothing soft. Every line of him purpose and patience and the kind of stillness that came from absolute certainty.

He didn't rush. Didn't posture. Just stepped into the light and waited.

Like he had all the time in the world.

Like he'd been waiting for this moment for weeks.

Selene's hands found her daggers. The weight of them settled into her palms, familiar and strange all at once. The same blades that had opened Daven's throat. The same blades that had cut out his tongue.

Across the street, the man watched. Patient. Professional.

Something flickered in his eyes. Recognition, maybe. Or something colder.

She didn't know his name. Didn't know his face.

But she knew what he was. What this was.

The hammer had finally fallen.

CHAPTER 29: The Professional

The Merchant Quarter was dead at this hour.

No haggling voices. No cart wheels grinding against cobblestones. No bodies pressing together in the narrow lanes between stalls. Just empty canvas awnings snapping in the night wind and shadows pooling thick where the torches had burned down to nothing.

Three days of killing anyone the Guild sent after her and waiting for them to send someone better. Tonight, they had. The man from the doorway. Gray at the temples. Still patient. Still waiting.

She'd felt him since the Thornway crossing. Not Daven's sloppy surveillance. Not the muscle the Guild kept throwing at her like bodies could solve the problem. Something else. Someone who knew how to move through a city without disturbing it. Someone patient.

Selene was done being patient.

Her ribs ached where Daven's blade had caught her. The cut on her shoulder had reopened twice since she'd stitched it closed. Her knuckles were split, her left knee was swelling, and somewhere under her collarbone was a bruise that made it hurt to breathe.

She didn't care.

The cloth merchant's stall was just ahead. Empty now, canvas tied down, wooden frame creaking in the wind. She'd passed it a thousand times since she was a child. It meant nothing to her anymore.

She stopped in the center of the lane. Right under the creaking frame. Didn't reach for *Vael'thera*. Didn't slip into the shadows the way every instinct told her to.

She just stood there. Let the cold wind bite at her wounds. Let whoever was watching get a good look.

"I know you're there." Her voice came out raw. Tired. She didn't try to hide it. "I'm done walking. If you're here to kill me, do it while I'm still standing."

The shadows didn't answer.

But they shifted.

And something stepped out of the darkness ahead.

Her hand found the hilt at her hip. The familiar weight of the dagger met her palm, still carrying the warmth of her body from hours of use. The motion was automatic, muscle memory carved into bone by years of practice. She didn't draw. Not yet. Drawing meant committing, and she was so fucking tired of committing.

Another one. Another Guild knife in the dark. Another body she'd have to make.

"I know you're there," she said. Her voice came out flat. Exhausted. Not the careful calm she usually projected, just the empty sound of someone who'd stopped caring about appearances. "Just come out. I don't have the energy for games."

Silence.

Then movement. A figure detaching from the shadows between two stalls, stepping into the faint moonlight that bled through the gaps in the awnings above. Tall. Broad-shouldered. Dressed in dark clothes that swallowed what little light there was. A mask covered everything below the eyes.

Guild. Had to be. The stance was too controlled, the movements too deliberate for street muscle. This was someone who'd been trained. Someone who'd done this before. Someone who moved like killing was as natural as breathing.

Not like the others. Not like the hard men with their numbers and their confidence. This was different.

"They finally sent someone competent," Selene said. She didn't bother with the false calm anymore. Let him hear how tired she was. Let him think it made her weak. "I was starting to feel insulted."

The figure didn't respond. Just watched her with eyes she couldn't read in the darkness. Something about the way he held himself felt wrong. Not threatening. Just . . . familiar in a way her muscles recognized and her mind refused to name.

She pushed the feeling aside. She'd been fighting for three days straight. Everything felt familiar. Everything felt wrong. Her brain was making connections that didn't exist because it was too exhausted to think clearly.

"So how do you want to do this?" She spread her hands slightly, showing him she hadn't drawn yet. "You attack, I defend, one of us dies in this alley? Or do we skip the part where you pretend you have a choice and get to the fucking point?"

He moved.

Fast. Faster than she'd expected. Faster than anyone she'd fought in years. The blade in his hand was already cutting toward her before she'd finished processing that he'd drawn it. She twisted, felt the edge whisper past her cheek, close enough to taste the steel. Her daggers were in her hands now, both of them, dark metal warm against her palms, instinct overriding everything else.

She parried his second strike. The impact shuddered up her arm, harder than it should have been, sending pain lancing through the shoulder she'd stitched closed twice already. He was strong. Stronger than his lean frame suggested. And he moved like water, each attack flowing into the next without pause or hesitation.

She'd fought Guild killers before. This was different.

He was a master.

His third strike opened a cut across her forearm. Shallow but bleeding. His fourth drove her back two steps. His fifth nearly took her throat out, and only a desperate twist saved her from dying right there in the market where she used to steal bread as a child. Warmth bloomed along her neck. When she touched it, her fingers came away with a smear of red. He'd missed. Barely.

Her body was screaming at her. Three days of fighting. Three days of wounds and exhaustion and running on anger instead of sleep. And now this. Now the best the Guild had to offer, moving like death itself, giving her nothing.

She tried to create distance. He didn't let her. Every time she found a gap, he was already there, shutting it down. Every angle she tried to exploit, he'd closed before she could commit. He was reading her like a book. Anticipating her movements before she made them.

And his footwork. Gods, his footwork was wrong. Familiar-wrong. Like she'd seen it somewhere and couldn't remember where. The way he pivoted on his back foot, the angle he kept his shoulders, the economy of motion that wasted nothing.

She knew this style. She knew it because someone had drilled it into her muscles when she was nine years old and desperate to learn.

The thought flickered and died. She didn't have time for thoughts. He was pressing her now, driving her back toward the cloth merchant's stall, cutting off her angles of escape. His blade caught the moonlight and she saw it clearly for the first time. Short. Dark. Balanced for quick thrusts rather than slashing.

Something cold settled in her stomach.

She blocked another strike. The impact sent fresh agony through her shoulder, and she felt the stitches tear. Warm blood started spreading down her arm. She was slowing down. The exhaustion was catching up with her, the accumulated damage of three days of survival dragging at her limbs like chains.

The daggers were the only thing keeping her alive. Their superior balance, their perfect weight distribution, the careful craftsmanship that made every parry fractionally easier, every strike fractionally faster. Like the difference between rusted iron and masterwork steel. Right now that margin was the only thing between her and a corpse.

He could have killed her then. She saw the opening he had, the angle that would have put his blade through her throat. He didn't take it.

Why didn't he take it?

She attacked instead. Stopped thinking and let her body do what it had been trained to do. Fast. Brutal. The techniques she'd perfected in the years since a man with grey eyes had disappeared from a room above a butcher's shop. If she was going to die, she was going to die moving forward.

He met her strike for strike. Matched her speed even as hers started to flag. Countered her angles with precision that felt almost contemptuous. But something was wrong with his rhythm now. Something hesitant. He was pulling strikes that should have landed. Giving her openings he shouldn't have given.

She didn't understand. She didn't try to understand. Her brain had stopped working properly somewhere around the second minute of the fight. All that was left was muscle memory and survival instinct and a bone-deep rage that refused to let her fall.

"You're telegraphing," he said.

The words hit her like a fist to the chest.

"Watch the shoulders."

The words were wrong. They belonged to a different street, a different year, a man who'd left. Her guard slipped. Just for a heartbeat. Just long enough for his blade to open a line across her side, blood welling up hot and immediate through her shirt.

She knew that voice.

No. She didn't. She couldn't. It had been fifteen years and voices changed and people changed and this was just a Guild killer who happened to know the same lessons she'd learned from someone who'd left without saying goodbye.

But her hands were shaking now. And not from exhaustion.

She attacked again. Wild this time. Sloppy. The kind of fighting she'd trained herself never to do because it got you killed. But she needed him to stop talking. Needed him to stop sounding like someone she'd buried in an empty room above a butcher's shop fifteen years ago.

He blocked. Countered. Could have killed her and didn't. Again. And again. And again.

Why wasn't he killing her?

Her next thrust was pure desperation. No technique, no precision, just a blade aimed at center mass and a prayer to gods she didn't believe in. He sidestepped, caught her wrist, twisted.

The pain was blinding. One dagger clattered to the cobblestones. He twisted harder and the other followed, dark metal ringing against stone. He had her. His blade at her throat. His grip on her wrist like iron. Like a trap that had decided to bite.

She knew that grip.

Gods, she knew that grip.

For one frozen heartbeat, they stood there. His blade against her skin. Her blood dripping onto the stones between them. The market silent around them, holding its breath.

He hesitated.

She didn't.

Her free hand found the knife in her boot, the one she kept for moments exactly like this. She drove it up under his ribs in one savage motion. The same angle she'd used on the man in the alley when she was nine. The same thrust, angled up, finding the soft space between bone and muscle. She felt the wet give of flesh, the catch of something vital, the shudder that ran through his body as the knife found its home.

He made a sound. Not a scream. More like a cough, surprised and wet.

His blade fell away from her throat. His grip on her wrist loosened. But he didn't let go entirely. His fingers closed around her arm, weak now, the strength bleeding out of him with everything else.

"Shadow," he said.

The world stopped.

She knew that name. No one called her that. No one had called her that in fifteen years. Not since a man with grey eyes had walked into the shadows and never come back.

He dropped to his knees. The knife was still in him, her hand still wrapped around the hilt. She could feel his heartbeat through the blade, slowing, stuttering, fading.

His other hand came up. Trembling. Reached for his mask. Pulled it down.

The moonlight caught his face.

Grey eyes. Slate grey. Knife-blade grey. The skin was more weathered and the stubble flecked with gray, but it was a face she knew better than her own. Despite the fifteen years written into the lines of his brow, he was still the man she had waited for on the butcher's stairs until the hope had finally run dry. "No," she said.

The word came out broken. Meaningless. A denial of something that was already true.

Rook looked up at her. Blood on his lips. Blood on his chin. Blood spreading across his dark clothes, black on black in the moonlight. His eyes found hers and held them, and for one terrible moment she was nine years old again, standing in a room above a butcher's shop, breathing in the smell of leather and woodsmoke and wanting it to stay.

"No," she said again. "No, no, no . . ."

Her legs gave out.

She hit the cobblestones hard, knees cracking against stone, and she didn't feel it. Couldn't feel anything except the knife in her hand and the heartbeat fading through the blade and the grey eyes looking at her like they'd been waiting fifteen years to see her again.

All of it came flooding back. The hand on her shoulder. The warmth she'd wanted him to put back. The laugh that cracked his weathered face into something almost human. "Watch the shoulders, little shadow." The grip that taught her how to hold a knife without looking like she was going to drop it. The way he'd caught her when she stumbled, his face inches from hers, something passing between them that she'd never been able to name.

The empty room that smelled wrong. Too clean. Too still. The smell fading with every breath she took, like she was killing it by wanting it too much. Six days of checking the stairs and hating herself for it. Her feet had always been traitors when it came to him.

The rule she'd carved into her bones: if someone can leave you, they will.

She'd killed him.

She'd killed him with the technique he taught her so she'd never be helpless again.

"I didn't . . ."

The words wouldn't come. Nothing would come. Her throat had closed up and her eyes were burning but she couldn't cry, couldn't scream, couldn't do anything but kneel there with her knife in his chest and watch him die.

"I know." His voice was wet. Fading. Each word cost him something he couldn't afford to spend. "That was . . . the point."

He reached for her. His hand found her face. The touch was featherlight, trembling, nothing like the iron grip that had caught her wrist in this same market fifteen years ago. Just an old man bleeding out in the dark, touching the face of the girl he'd taught to survive.

"I'm sorry," he said. "I'm sorry I left. I'm sorry I came back."

Her hand found his. Pressed it against her cheek. The same cheek his blade had nearly opened when the fight started. She couldn't speak. Couldn't think. Couldn't do anything but hold onto him while the last of his life poured out onto the cobblestones.

"You were . . . the only good thing," he said. "The only thing I ever did . . . that wasn't . . ."

He didn't finish. His eyes went distant. His hand went slack.

And then there was nothing left of him but a body and a blade and the girl who'd put them together.

***

The sound that came out of her wasn't human.

She didn't know what to call it. Something raw and animal that tore its way out of her chest and echoed off the empty stalls and disappeared into the night like it had never existed.

She didn't let go of his hand.

She knelt there in the dark with her knife in his chest and her fingers wrapped around his, and she felt everything she'd locked away for fifteen years come pouring out like blood from a wound that had never healed. The cupboard. Her parents burning. The man in the alley when she was nine. Weston dying in the dirt. Daven begging. And now this. Now this.

She'd told herself she'd never let anyone close enough to leave her again.

She'd been right.

Something cracked open inside her. The emptiness she'd been carrying since the cupboard, the numbness that had kept her functional, the cold space where feelings used to live. It fractured. Like something that had been holding together by sheer force of will had finally run out of will. She could feel it breaking apart, all the walls and armor and dark humor that had kept her functional for fifteen years just . . . shattering.

She bent forward until her forehead touched his chest. Until she could smell the blood and the sweat and underneath it, faint, almost gone, the ghost of leather and woodsmoke and something sharp like metal.

"You bastard," she whispered. "You absolute bastard."

She didn't know how long she stayed like that. Minutes. Hours. The moon moved across the sky and the shadows shifted and the blood went cold and sticky on her hands and still she didn't move.

When she finally lifted her head, her eyes were dry. She hadn't cried. She couldn't remember the last time she'd cried. Maybe the cupboard. Maybe before that. The tears had dried up somewhere along the way, and they weren't coming back now.

But something else had broken loose. Something that had been holding her together. The sarcasm wouldn't come. The dark humor that had always been her armor, her blade, her way of keeping people from seeing the wound underneath. She reached for it and found nothing. Just empty space where the defense should have been.

He'd taught her that too. The jokes. The deflection. The sharp tongue that kept the world at arm's length.

She looked at his face. The grey eyes were open, staring at nothing. She should close them. That was what you did for the dead. A small dignity. A final kindness.

Her hand moved before she could stop it. Gentle. Trembling. She brushed her fingers over his eyelids, closed them, let her palm rest against his cheek for one long moment.

“You left,” she said. Her voice was hollow. Empty. Nothing like herself. “You left and you never said why and I waited for you like an idiot and you were here the whole time. In the Guild. Working for them. Killing for them. And they sent you to kill me and you came. You came.”

She swallowed.

“Why didn’t you run?” was what she wanted to ask. The answer didn’t matter. He’d come. He’d come, and he’d let her kill him because he couldn’t bring himself to kill her first.

The short blade was still in his hand. Dark. Perfectly balanced. Built for quick thrusts rather than slashing. She’d wondered, once, what had happened to that knife. He’d taken it when he left. Kept it all these years. Through everything. Through whatever the Guild had made him do. He’d kept the knife he’d used to teach her.

She pried it from his fingers. Her hand slipped once on the blood before she got a good grip. She held it up in the moonlight. The weight was exactly how she remembered. The balance was exactly how she remembered. Everything about it was exactly how she remembered, except now it was covered in his blood and hers and the memory of what it used to mean.

She tucked it into her belt. She didn’t know why. She just couldn’t leave it there.

She finally pulled her blade from his chest. The sound it made was wet. Final. She cleaned it on his shirt because that was what you did, wiped the boot knife that had killed him, and slid it back into place.

Her daggers were still on the cobblestones where they’d fallen. She retrieved them. The dark metal was cold now, slick with blood. She didn’t clean them. Let them carry his blood for a while longer.

She should leave. She knew that. Someone would come eventually. The Guild would want confirmation. The Watchers made rounds even in the dead of night. Staying was stupid, dangerous, the kind of mistake that got you killed.

She stood there anyway.

Looking down at him. At the body that used to be the first person who'd ever seen her as something worth teaching. The first person who'd made her feel like she might survive this city. The first person she'd ever wanted to stay.

She'd been nine years old, standing in his room, breathing in the smell of him, and some traitorous part of her had wanted him to put his hand back.

She was twenty-four years old, standing over his body, covered in his blood, and some traitorous part of her still wanted that.

Her feet had always been traitors when it came to him.

"I'm sorry too," she said.

Then she walked away.

The Merchant Quarter stayed empty. The shadows stayed deep. And somewhere in the distance, a torch guttered and died, leaving nothing but darkness where the light had been.

She didn't go back to the safehouse. She couldn't. Mirael would be there, and Mirael would see her face, and Mirael would ask what happened, and she couldn't. She couldn't say the words. Couldn't make it real by speaking it out loud.

She walked until her legs gave out. Found an alley. Slid down the wall until she was sitting in the dirt with her back against cold stone and her hands still covered in blood that had started to dry and crack.

The city breathed around her. Distant sounds. Distant lights. The endless pulse of Garnath that never stopped, not even in the dead of night, not even when someone's world had just ended in a market square that meant nothing to anyone but her.

She sat there until the sky started to lighten.

She didn't sleep. She didn't move. She just existed, if you could call it that. Breathing because her body wouldn't stop. Bleeding because she hadn't bothered to bandage the wounds. Waiting for something, though she didn't know what.

When the first light of dawn touched the rooftops, she finally stood.

Her body moved like it belonged to someone else. Some other Selene who hadn't just killed the first person who'd ever made her feel like she was worth something. She walked through streets that were starting to wake up, past vendors setting up stalls, past early risers heading to work, past all the normal people living their normal lives who had no idea what had happened in the market square a few hours ago.

She needed something. She didn't know what. Something that wasn't sleep or food or the safehouse with its walls closing in.

She needed to remember why she was still alive. What she was fighting for. What made any of this worth the price she kept paying.

She needed Kira.

CHAPTER 30: Kira's Name Day

Selene found Kira in the corner of Mother Gessa's cellar, knees pulled to her chest, watching the other children eat.

Waiting. The way strays wait at the edge of a meal until they're sure no one will chase them off.

"Come on," Selene said.

Kira looked up. Those eyes. Crystal blue, too old for her face. The same color Selene saw in mirrors and tried not to think about.

"Where?"

"Out."

Kira unfolded without another question. She crossed the cellar floor in quick, silent steps and slipped her hand into Selene's. Small fingers. Cold. Thin enough that Selene could feel the bones beneath the skin, the fragile architecture of a child who had never eaten enough.

Mother Gessa looked up from the bread she was slicing. Her eyebrows rose, but she said nothing. Just nodded once, a small smile tucking into the corners of her mouth, and went back to her work.

Outside, the morning was gray but dry. The kind of overcast that couldn't decide if it wanted to rain. Garnath smelled like salt and smoke and the fish guts rotting in yesterday's buckets. Kira walked close to Selene's hip, matching her stride, eyes moving across the street the way street children's eyes always moved. Watching. Counting. Noting exits.

"Where are we going?"

"The docks."

"Why?"

"Because it's your Name Day."

Kira's steps faltered. She looked up at Selene with something that might have been confusion, or wonder, or both tangled together.

"How do you know about that?"

"Gessa told me."

Silence. Kira's hand tightened in Selene's, her thin fingers pressing harder.

"She remembers," Kira said quietly. Like the idea surprised her.

"She remembers all her lambs."

They walked. Through the market where vendors were still setting up, crates thudding onto tables, voices arguing over placement. Through the tangle of streets that led from Southside toward the water. Kira was quiet, but Selene could feel her thinking. Could feel the questions building up behind those too-old eyes.

"I didn't have a name before," Kira said finally. "Before Gessa."

Selene looked down at her. "What did people call you?"

"Girl. Sometimes nothing. Sometimes things I don't want to remember."

The words were flat. Matter-of-fact. The way children described horrors when they'd lived with them long enough that horror became ordinary.

"Two years ago," Kira continued, "Gessa found me behind her shop. I was eating from her garbage pile. She brought me inside and gave me bread and asked my name. I didn't have one. So she said she'd give me one. She said everyone deserves a name."

"What did she call you?"

"Kira. She said it meant 'light.' She said I had light in my eyes even though I wouldn't look at her." A pause. "I still don't know if that's true. About the light. But I like the name."

"It's a good name."

"She told me that day would be my Name Day. The day I became Kira instead of just 'girl.'" Her voice got quieter. "No one ever remembered before. Besides Gessa. And now you."

Not a birthday. Street children didn't have those. But it was the day she'd gotten a name, and that was close enough. Six becoming seven, counted from the day someone bothered to notice she existed.

Selene didn't know what to say to that. So she said nothing. Just kept walking, Kira's hand in hers, heading toward the water.

***

They passed the warehouses where dock workers moved crates and shouted numbers at each other, past the cargo cranes and the ships being loaded, until the chaos faded and the seawall curved out toward the quieter stretch.

Selene's feet knew this path. Her body remembered it before her mind caught up, and by the time she realized where she was leading them, it was too late to turn back.

The gap in the seawall. The stone steps leading down. The flat rocks just above the waterline where fishing boats bobbed in the distance.

She stopped. Her chest tightened.

She hadn't been here in seventeen years. Not since before. Not since Papa.

The smell hit her first. Salt and fish and wet stone, the same smell that used to cling to Papa's clothes when he came home. The sound came next: water slapping against rock, the distant cry of gulls, the creak of boat hulls. Sounds that used to mean safety. That used to mean Papa would be home soon with stories about ships from far-off places.

Her vision blurred at the edges. Just for a second. Just long enough that she had to blink hard and focus on the texture of the stone beneath her boots.

"Selene?"

Kira's voice. Small. Concerned.

Selene looked down. Kira was watching her face with those too-perceptive eyes, seeing something Selene hadn't meant to show.

"I'm fine."

"Your hand got tight."

Selene realized she was squeezing Kira's fingers. She loosened her grip, but didn't let go.

"Sorry."

"It's okay." Kira looked at the water, then back at Selene. "This place makes you sad."

Selene looked at her. Seven years old and already reading people like text on a page.

"It used to make me happy," Selene said. "A long time ago."

Kira nodded slowly. Like she understood. Like she already knew that happy places could become sad places, that memory could poison the ground it walked on.

"We can go somewhere else," she offered.

Selene looked at the rocks. At the water. At the place where she used to sit with Papa and listen to him name the boats.

"No," she said. "We're here now."

She stepped through the gap in the wall and started down the stone steps. After a moment, Kira followed.

***

The flat rock was the same. Smaller than Selene remembered, the way childhood places always shrank when you came back to them as an adult. But the same rock. The same angle. The same view of the harbor mouth where the fishing boats came and went.

She used to fit in Papa's lap here. He'd wrap his arms around her and point at the ships and make up stories about where they'd been. Some of them were probably true. Most of them probably weren't. She'd never know now.

Kira sat beside her, legs dangling over the edge, feet not quite reaching the water below. Her eyes were huge, taking in the harbor, the boats, the endless gray-green expanse of water.

"It's so big," she said.

"The harbor?"

"Everything." Her voice was hushed. Reverent. "I've never seen this much sky before. The buildings always cut it up."

Selene looked up. She was right. Out here on the rocks, past the seawall, the sky opened up in a way it never did in the cramped streets of Garnath. Just gray clouds and pale light stretching all the way to the horizon.

"I've never been to the edge of things," Kira said. "It feels like the world goes on forever."

"It does. Further than you can imagine."

"Have you seen it? The rest of the world?"

"No. I've never left Garnath."

Kira considered this. "Do you want to?"

The question caught Selene off guard. No one had asked her that before. She'd never asked herself.

"I don't know," she admitted. "I don't think about things like that."

"Why not?"

"Because wanting things you can't have is a waste of energy."

Kira turned that over in her head, the way she turned everything over, examining it from angles before she responded.

"Maybe," she said finally. "Or maybe wanting things is how you figure out what to do next."

Selene looked at her. Seven years old. Three years of having a name. Already sharp enough to cut through defenses Selene had spent seventeen years building.

"Where'd you learn that?" Selene asked.

"I didn't learn it. I just thought it." Kira's eyes went back to the water. "Gessa says children think things adults forget how to think. She says that's why she listens to us."

Selene didn't have an answer for that. So she sat with it instead, watching the boats move across the harbor, feeling the cold of the rock through her trousers and the warmth of Kira's small body beside her.

***

Time passed. Selene lost track of how much. The sun moved behind the clouds, invisible but present, and the light shifted from morning gray to midday pale.

Kira asked questions. Endless questions. The kind children asked when they finally felt safe enough to be curious.

"What are those boats catching?"

"Silverbacks, probably. Maybe mackerel if the school's running."

"How do they know where to find them?"

"Experience. Luck. Reading the water."

"Can you read water?"

"No. My father could."

The words slipped out. Selene heard them leave her mouth and felt her jaw tighten. She hadn't meant to say that. Hadn't meant to open that door.

Kira was quiet. Waiting. Present.

"He worked here," Selene said. The words came slowly, dragged up from somewhere deep. "Not on the boats. On the docks. Loading and unloading. Keeping track of what went where."

"Was he good at it?"

"He never got fired. So probably."

"Did he like it?"

"He never complained."

"That's not the same as liking it."

Selene's mouth twitched. "No. It isn't."

A gull cried overhead. The water lapped against the rocks below. Somewhere in the harbor, a man shouted something Selene couldn't make out.

"He used to bring me here," she said. "After work sometimes. When there was time. He'd sit right here on this rock and tell me about the ships. Which ones came from far away. What they were carrying. He made up stories about the captains. I think most of them were lies, but good lies. The kind you want to believe."

Kira listened. Her body had gone still the way it did when she was paying attention with everything she had.

"What happened to him?"

The question was gentle. The way Kira asked about boats and fish and everything else.

Selene should lie. Should say he got sick, or went away, or any of the easy answers that ended conversations. She'd told that kind of lie a hundred times to a hundred different people. It was easy. Automatic.

She opened her mouth to tell it again.

"Bad men came to our house," she said instead. "When I was seven."

Her voice didn't sound like hers. It sounded like someone else talking, someone far away, using her mouth to say words she'd never said out loud before.

Kira's eyes widened, but she didn't speak. Didn't move. Just waited.

"I hid. My mother put me in a cupboard and told me not to come out. No matter what I heard." Selene's hands were shaking. She pressed them flat against the cold rock to hide it. "My father didn't hide. He stayed. They asked him where I was. He wouldn't tell them."

Her throat closed. She had to force the next words through.

"They killed him for it. For not telling them where I was."

The harbor blurred. Selene blinked hard, forcing her vision to clear. She would not cry. She hadn't cried since she was seven years old, sitting in a gap between buildings with smoke in her hair and nothing inside her chest. She wasn't going to start now.

"My mother too," she said. The words were barely a whisper. "They killed her too. And then they burned our house. And I stayed in the cupboard like she told me to, until the smoke got too thick to breathe."

Silence. The water moved. The gulls cried. The world kept going the way it always did, indifferent to the small tragedies unfolding inside it.

Kira moved closer. Her small hand found Selene's arm and rested there. Light. Barely any weight at all.

"I'm sorry," she said.

Two words. Simple. The kind of thing people said when they didn't know what else to say.

But Kira meant it. Selene could hear it in her voice, feel it in the warmth of her small hand. She wasn't performing sympathy. She wasn't filling silence with noise. She was just sorry, the way one survivor was sorry for another.

Selene's throat ached. Her eyes burned. She didn't trust herself to speak, so she just nodded.

They sat like that for a while. The water moved. The clouds shifted. Eventually Selene's hands stopped shaking.

"I was five when Gessa found me," Kira said quietly. "You were seven when you lost them. We both got found by the street first." Selene looked at her. Black hair tangled from sleep. Thin face. Eyes that had seen too much.

"Yeah," she said. "Same as me."

***

"I'm hungry."

Selene blinked. She'd been watching the light change on the water, not thinking about anything, which was rare enough to feel strange. Like she'd set down a weight she usually carried without noticing and her body didn't know what to do without it.

"Yeah?"

"My stomach is making sounds."

"That happens when you're hungry."

Kira looked at her with something that might have been exasperation. On anyone else, anyway. On Kira it was just a slight narrowing of the eyes, the ghost of an expression.

"I know that."

"Then let's fix it."

They climbed back up the stone steps. Selene's legs had gone stiff from sitting, and she stretched them as they walked, working the cold out of her joints. The city noise was louder now, the midday traffic in full swing.

The food stalls along the outer dock were crowded. Workers grabbing meals between shifts, sailors spending coin before shipping out, the usual chaos of people who needed to eat fast and get back to work. Selene guided Kira through the crowd with a hand on her shoulder, steering her around elbows and cart wheels.

She found the stall she wanted. Old woman with a brazier, frying something in a pan that smelled like onions and pork fat. Simple food. The kind Papa used to bring home wrapped in paper, still hot, grease soaking through.

"Two," Selene said, holding up fingers.

The woman looked at Kira, then at Selene. Her eyes moved between them, noting the matching black hair, the similar blue eyes. Whatever calculation happened behind her expression came out in her favor.

"Pretty daughter," the woman said, wrapping two portions in brown paper.

Selene opened her mouth to correct her. Stopped. Let it go.

"Thank you," she said instead, and paid.

They found a spot against a warehouse wall, out of the flow of foot traffic, and sat with their backs to the rough wood. Kira unwrapped her portion carefully, like the paper itself was worth saving. Street habit. Everything might be useful later.

The food was meat and onions in fried dough. Hot. Greasy. Exactly what it was supposed to be.

Kira took a bite and her eyes closed. A small sound escaped her throat, something between satisfaction and surprise.

"Good?" Selene asked.

"Mmm."

They ate. Kira ate slowly, savoring each bite, making it last the way children did when they weren't sure when the next meal was coming. Selene watched her from the corner of her eye.

Sauce gathered at the corner of Kira's mouth. A smear of grease on her chin, just below her lip.

Selene reached over and wiped it away with her thumb. The gesture was automatic. Thoughtless. The same motion Mama used to make across the dinner table, a thousand years ago.

Her hand froze halfway back to her lap.

She stared at her thumb. At the grease glistening there. At her own hand, which had done something soft without permission, something maternal, something that had come up from the grave of her childhood and moved through her before she could stop it.

Her chest tightened. Her breath came shorter.

"Selene?"

She looked up. Kira was watching her with those too-knowing eyes, holding her food in both hands, perfectly still.

"You're doing it again," Kira said quietly.

"Doing what?"

"The thing where you get far away. Where your face goes empty."

Selene forced herself to breathe. Forced her hand to drop to her knee. Forced her expression into something that might pass for normal.

"I'm fine."

"You don't have to be fine," Kira said. "Not with me."

The words landed somewhere soft. Somewhere Selene had stopped protecting because she'd forgotten it existed.

"Eat your food," Selene said. Her voice was rougher than she meant it to be. "Before it gets cold."

Kira looked at her for a moment longer. Then she went back to eating, her eyes still on Selene's face, watching her the way she watched everything.

***

"Can we play a game?"

They were walking back toward the quiet stretch, full and warm and moving slower than before. The sun had broken through the clouds, weak but present, throwing pale light across the water. The afternoon was sliding toward evening.

"What kind of game?"

"I don't know." Kira's brow furrowed. "I don't know many games."

"What do the other kids play at Gessa's?"

"Running games. Chasing. I don't like those."

"Too loud?"

"Too many people. Too much touching."

Selene understood that. She thought for a moment.

"I know a game. My . . ." She stopped. Started again. "Someone taught me, when I was your age."

Papa. On this exact stretch of seawall. The memory was there suddenly, vivid and sharp: his big hands guiding her smaller ones, showing her the flick of the wrist, laughing when her first ten stones sank straight down.

She found a handful of small stones on the ground. Flat ones. Good for skipping.

"You throw them at the water," she said. "Try to make them bounce. Like this."

She flicked her wrist. The stone skipped once, twice, three times before sinking.

Kira's eyes went wide. "How did you do that?"

"Practice. Here." She pressed a stone into Kira's palm. "Flat side down. Flick your wrist, don't throw."

Kira tried. The stone hit the water and sank immediately.

"Again," Selene said. "Lower angle."

She tried again. Sank again. Her jaw tightened, that stubborn look that Selene recognized from her own mirror.

"Again."

The third throw sank. The fourth skipped once before going under.

Kira gasped. A small, sharp sound of surprise. She spun to look at Selene with eyes that were suddenly startlingly bright.

"I did it!"

"You did."

"Did you see?"

"I saw."

Kira grabbed another stone. Tried again. Sank. Tried again. One skip. Tried again. Two skips.

And then she laughed.

The sound hit Selene somewhere deep. Somewhere she'd stopped guarding because she'd forgotten it was there. A child's laugh. Unselfconscious. Pure. The kind of sound that came from someone who had, for just a moment, forgotten to be afraid.

Kira threw another stone. It skipped three times, and she spun around with her arms out, a motion that was half celebration and half sheer disbelief that she could do this thing, that her body could make something beautiful happen.

Selene felt something move in her chest. Something rusty and unfamiliar, pushing up from somewhere deep.

She tried to swallow it down. Failed.

The laugh came out of her before she could stop it.

It sounded wrong. Rough. Like a door that hadn't been opened in years, hinges screaming against the rust. It hurt, almost, the way unused muscles hurt when you finally moved them. Foreign in her own throat, in her own mouth, like she'd forgotten how to make the sound and her body was relearning it in real time.

Kira stopped spinning. Stared at her.

"You laughed," she said. Hushed. Like she'd witnessed something rare.

"No, I didn't."

"Yes, you did. I heard it."

"Must have been a seagull."

"Seagulls don't laugh like that."

"How do you know? You've never been to the docks before."

Kira's mouth twitched. Just a little. Just at the corners.

"You're smiling too," she said.

Selene touched her own face. Her cheek muscles were doing something they hadn't done in years. It felt strange. Wrong. Like wearing someone else's expression.

"Must be the wind," she said.

"There's no wind."

"Then it must be the company."

Kira looked at her for a long moment. Then she smiled too. A real smile. The kind that reached her eyes, that softened her whole face, that made her look like what she was: a seven-year-old child who had, for just one afternoon, gotten to be a child.

Selene's chest ached. A different kind of ache than she was used to. The full kind.

She didn't know what to do with it. So she just picked up another stone and skipped it across the water, and Kira grabbed one too, and for a while they just threw rocks at the harbor while the sun painted the clouds orange and gold and the city breathed in the distance.

***

The light was dying. Orange and gold bleeding into purple at the horizon, the sun disappearing behind the rooftops of Garnath. The afternoon had bled away without Selene noticing.

They sat on the rocks again. Closer to the edge now. Kira's head was tilted back, watching the colors shift across the sky.

"We should go back," Selene said.

"I know."

Neither of them moved.

The water was turning dark, catching the last of the light in ripples that looked like scattered coins. Somewhere in the harbor, a ship's bell rang. The evening shift changing over.

"Thank you," Kira said. Quiet. Not looking at Selene. Looking at the water, at the sky, at the light fading from the world.

"For what?"

"For today."

"It was just food and rocks."

Kira shook her head slowly. Her hair caught the last of the light, dark strands turning almost copper at the edges.

"It wasn't just that." She was quiet for a moment. "No one's ever taken me anywhere before. Just to take me. Just because."

Selene didn't know what to say to that.

"At Gessa's, people come and go," Kira continued. "They bring food sometimes. Or blankets. Or they take children away to other places. But no one ever just . . . takes you out. To show you things. To sit with you."

Her voice was steady, but there was something underneath it. Something fragile.

"You showed me the water," she said. "And the boats. And how to make rocks dance. And you told me about your papa. You didn't have to tell me that."

"No," Selene agreed. "I didn't."

"Why did you?"

The question hung in the salt air. Selene turned it over, looking for an answer that made sense.

"I don't know," she admitted. "I've never told anyone that before."

Kira nodded. Like she understood. Like she knew what it meant to carry secrets that had never seen daylight.

She leaned over and rested her head against Selene's arm. The way children did when they trusted someone completely, when they'd decided this person was safe, this person wouldn't hurt them, this person would stay.

Selene didn't move away.

The warmth of Kira's head against her bicep. The weight of it, so small, so fragile. The absolute trust in that gesture, a child putting herself in Selene's hands without hesitation.

This was what she'd wanted. Even if she hadn't known it until now. To give Kira one good day. One day where she didn't have to count exits or watch for threats or wonder where her next meal was coming from. One day where she could just be seven years old and throw stones at water and eat hot food and laugh at nothing.

The day Selene never got.

She put her hand on Kira's head. Her palm against the messy black hair, feeling the warmth of the small skull beneath, the impossible fragility of it. The gesture her mother used to make. A lifetime ago. In a house that didn't exist anymore.

She let it rest there. Longer than she meant to. Feeling something crack inside her chest, something that had been frozen so long she'd forgotten it could thaw.

Then she pulled her hand back.

"Come on," she said. Her voice was thick. She cleared her throat. "Mirael will wonder where we went."

Mirael. Who had finally met Kira two weeks ago. Who had sat in Gessa's kitchen and watched Selene be soft with someone and hadn't said a word about it after. That had felt like forgiveness. Or the beginning of it.

Kira stood. Brushed off her clothes with the automatic movements of someone who was used to being dirty and had stopped caring. She looked up at Selene with those too-old eyes in that too-young face.

"Can we come back?"

"Maybe."

"To this spot? Where your papa took you?"

Selene looked at the water. At the rocks. At the place where her childhood had ended and where, today, something else had started. She didn't have a word for what that something was. Wasn't sure she wanted one.

"I don't make promises," she said.

Kira nodded. She'd already learned that lesson, probably. About promises and how they could break.

"Okay," she said. "Maybe is okay."

They climbed the steps back to the seawall.

The city was louder now, the evening traffic picking up, people heading home or heading out depending on how their lives worked. Lanterns being lit in windows. The smell of cooking food drifting from doorways. Garnath settling into its evening rhythms.

Selene walked. Kira walked beside her, matching her stride, her small hand finding Selene's again like it belonged there.

They didn't talk.

Selene's head was full of things she didn't have words for. The smell of salt and fish and wet stone. The sound of Kira laughing. The feeling of her own laughter coming out of her throat for the first time in seventeen years. The weight of Kira's head against her arm. The warmth of that small skull under her palm.

She'd given Kira one good day.

And somewhere in the giving, she'd found something she thought she'd lost forever. The knowledge that she could still feel something other than the emptiness. That the walls she'd built weren't as solid as she'd thought.

They were never stone. Just old wounds. And old wounds could crack open in both directions.

The sun finished setting behind them. The sky deepened from purple to black. Stars started appearing, faint points of light that the city glow almost drowned out.

Kira's hand was warm in hers. Small. Trusting.

Selene held it tighter.

The city swallowed them back into its noise and its crowds and its endless hungry motion. Just another evening in Garnath. Just two people walking home.

Except it wasn't. And they both knew it.

CHAPTER 31: Still Here

Viena found her at the Broken Wheel.

Selene was sitting in the back corner, nursing a drink she hadn't touched, watching the door out of habit. The tavern was half-empty in the late afternoon lull, the regulars not yet arrived, the daytime drinkers already gone.

Viena crossed the room without hurrying. She moved the way she always moved. Deliberate. Unhurried. Like a woman who had learned that rushing made you look weak.

She sat down across from Selene without asking permission.

"You're hard to find these days."

"That's the idea."

Viena signaled the barkeep. Waited until a drink arrived. Took a sip that was more ritual than thirst.

Selene waited. Viena didn't make social calls.

"Looks like the Paladins have more problems than looking for you." Viena set her cup down. Her voice was the same as always. Flat. Professional. The voice of someone who traded in information and never let it touch her. "They're dealing with corruption in their own ranks."

Selene didn't move. Didn't react. Just watched Viena's face and waited for whatever was coming next.

"The man who killed your Paladin friend. He's been taken into custody."

Your Paladin friend. Like Weston was a category, not a person. Like he was a transaction Selene had made and lost.

"Custody."

"Silverhold. Internal investigation. The official language is 'corruption and conduct unbecoming,' but you know how that goes. Could mean anything. Could mean nothing."

Selene's hands stayed flat on the table. Her face stayed empty. Inside, something shifted. A door closing. A drawer sliding shut.

"Do they know why?"

"Why what?"

"Why he did it. Who ordered it. What Weston saw that made him worth killing."

Viena shrugged. The gesture was small, economical. "If they know, they're not sharing. The investigation is internal. Which means it'll take months, produce a report no one reads, and end with someone getting reassigned to a post in the ass-end of nowhere."

That was how it always worked. The system protecting itself. The truth buried under procedure and official language and the slow grinding wheels of institutions that existed to perpetuate themselves.

Weston had believed in that system. Had worn its uniform, carried its sword, died with its name on his lips.

And this was what it gave him. Custody. Investigation. Conduct unbecoming.

"Is he talking?" Selene asked. "The one who did it."

"I don't know. Probably not. Men like that know the rules. Keep quiet, take the reassignment, wait for it to blow over. Talk, and you become the problem instead of the solution."

Selene nodded. The motion felt distant, like her body was doing it without consulting her.

"I thought you'd want to know." Viena was watching her. Reading her the way she read everyone. Looking for the angle, the leverage, the thing she could use later. "You two were . . . close. Or close enough."

Close enough. That was one way to put it.

Weston had stood in front of her in an alley and told her she deserved better. Had looked at her with those earnest eyes and believed, really believed, that the world could be fair if people just tried hard enough. Had died on a stone floor because he'd done the right thing and the system he served had decided that was inconvenient.

"Now I know." Selene's voice came out flat. Controlled. The voice she used when she didn't want anyone to see what was underneath.

Viena waited. A beat. Two. Giving her space to say something else, ask something else, do something other than sit there with that empty expression.

Nothing came.

"That's it?" Viena raised an eyebrow. "No questions? No demands? No charging off to Silverhold to put a knife in the man who killed your friend?"

"Would it help?"

"No."

"Then that's it."

Viena studied her for a long moment. Something moved behind her eyes. Not sympathy. Viena didn't do sympathy. But something adjacent to it. Recognition, maybe. The understanding of one survivor looking at another.

"You've changed." It wasn't a compliment or an insult. Just an observation.

"Everyone changes."

"Not like this." Viena stood. Straightened her coat. "A year ago, you would have been halfway to Silverhold by now. Consequences be damned."

Selene looked up at her. "A year ago, I still thought answers meant something."

Viena didn't have a response for that. She left a coin on the table for her drink and walked out without looking back.

The door closed behind her. The tavern settled back into its quiet hum. Somewhere in the kitchen, someone dropped a pot. A dog barked in the street outside. Life resumed, indifferent.

Selene sat with her untouched drink and let the silence fill the space Viena had left.

Weston was dead. His killer was in custody. There would be an investigation, a report, a quiet resolution that resolved nothing. The man who'd ordered it, whoever that was, would never be named. The reason Weston died would stay buried under official language and institutional protection.

She could chase it. Could go to Silverhold, find the man, put a knife in his throat the way she'd done to Daven. Could demand answers, force confessions, tear the truth out of someone's dying mouth.

And what would that give her? Another half-sentence. Another smile. Another dead end dressed up as closure.

She'd tried that. It hadn't worked.

Weston believed in institutions. Believed that the system could be good if good people worked within it. Believed that truth and justice were things you could find if you just looked hard enough.

Selene didn't believe that anymore. Maybe she never had.

She left the drink on the table. Put a coin beside it. Walked out into the fading afternoon light.

The city didn't notice. The city never noticed.

***

The room at the Veiled Lantern smelled like old wood and cheap perfume.

Selene closed the door behind her and leaned against it. The stairs had felt longer than usual. Her legs ached from walking, from sitting on cold rocks all afternoon with Kira, from the simple exhaustion of being awake for too many days in a row. Even her jaw was sore, like she'd been clenching it against words that came out anyway.

Now there was something else underneath the tired. Something heavier. The weight of Viena's words settling into the place where she kept all the things she couldn't do anything about.

Mirael looked up from the narrow bed by the wall. She had a candle burning on the crate beside her, and something in her hands that might have been mending. Her fingers went still when she saw Selene's face.

"You're back."

"I'm back."

The room was small. Two beds, a crate, a window that let in the sound of rain starting outside. The kind of temporary refuge they'd learned to find over fourteen years of running and hiding and waiting for things to get worse.

Mirael set down her mending. She didn't ask where Selene had been. Didn't ask about Kira. She'd learned years ago which questions Selene would answer and which ones would hit a wall.

"You look tired."

"I am tired."

"More than usual."

Selene pushed off from the door. Crossed to her bed, the one closest to the door, and sat on the edge. The mattress was thin, stuffed with something that had given up its shape years ago. She started unlacing her boots.

Rain tapped against the window. Soft. Steady. The kind of rain that could fall all night without anyone noticing.

"Kira's at Gessa's," Selene said. "She's safe."

"I know. I checked."

Selene looked up. Mirael was watching her with that expression she got sometimes. The one that was too careful, too attentive, like she was reading words that Selene hadn't written yet.

"You checked."

"I always check."

Fourteen years. That was how long Mirael had been doing this. Covering the gaps Selene left open, catching the details Selene forgot, being the eyes in the back of Selene's head that she never asked for and couldn't survive without.

Selene pulled off her boots. Set them by the bed where she could reach them fast. Old habit. The kind that didn't go away even when the danger was somewhere else.

"I saw Viena." The words came out before she decided to say them. "On the way back."

Mirael's hands went still in her lap.

"And?"

"The man who killed Weston. He's in custody. Silverhold. Internal investigation."

Silence. The kind that waited for more.

"That's all?"

"That's all there is. That's all there's ever going to be."

Mirael was quiet for a moment. Processing. Reading the spaces between Selene's words the way she always did.

"You're not going after him."

It wasn't a question.

"No."

"Good."

That was it. No lecture about justice. No arguments about what Weston would have wanted. Just good, and the understanding that some things weren't worth chasing.

Selene let out a breath she didn't know she'd been holding.

"I took her to the docks," she said. Changing the subject. Moving forward. "The quiet part. Past the warehouses."

Something shifted in Mirael's face. A different kind of stillness.

"The place your father used to take you."

Selene didn't ask how she knew that. Mirael knew everything. Fourteen years of watching, listening, remembering. She probably knew Selene better than Selene knew herself.

"Yeah."

The rain picked up. Harder now. Drumming against the roof, running down the window in crooked lines. Somewhere below, muffled laughter drifted up from the common room, the sounds of the Lantern doing what it always did.

"How was it?"

Selene stared at her boots. At the scuffed leather, the worn soles, the laces she'd have to replace soon.

"She laughed," she said. "I taught her to skip stones. She laughed."

Something shifted in Mirael's face. Selene saw it from the corner of her eye. That softening that happened when Mirael let her guard down, when she forgot to keep her expression neutral.

"And you?"

"What about me?"

"Did you laugh?"

The question sat between them. Selene should lie. Should shrug it off, change the subject, put the wall back up where it belonged.

"Yeah," she said. "I did."

Mirael had to clear her throat before she spoke. "Good. That's good."

Selene pulled off her outer shirt, leaving the thin undershirt beneath. The room was cold, but she'd slept in worse. She swung her legs onto the bed and lay back, staring at the ceiling. Water stains spread across the plaster in patterns that looked like continents on a map she'd never seen.

The tired went deeper than muscle now. The kind of tired that came from carrying something heavy for so long that you forgot you were carrying it until you finally set it down.

She'd told Kira about her father. She'd never told anyone that before. All that time with Mirael, and she'd never said those words out loud.

And now Weston. Another thing she was carrying. Another weight she couldn't put down, couldn't do anything about, couldn't fix or avenge or resolve. Just another half-truth to file away with all the others.

The bed creaked. Footsteps, soft on the wooden floor. The mattress dipped beside her.

Selene didn't open her eyes.

Mirael lay down next to her. Close enough that Selene could feel the warmth of her through the thin fabric. Close enough that their shoulders almost touched.

She didn't ask permission. She never did anymore. Somewhere over the years, this had become something they did. Mirael slipping into Selene's bed on the bad nights, the cold nights, the nights when the walls felt too thin and the world felt too large. Selene never invited her. Never held her. Never asked her to stay.

Never kicked her out either.

"You can sleep," Mirael said. Her voice was barely above a whisper. "I'll watch."

"You don't need to watch."

"I know."

Selene opened her eyes. Turned her head on the flat pillow. Mirael was lying on her side, facing her, close enough that Selene could see the flecks of gold in her brown eyes.

All that time. All those years, this woman following her, fighting beside her, bleeding for her. All those years of Mirael slipping into her bed and Selene pretending not to notice. All that time of something neither of them named because naming it would make it real, and real things could break.

"I told her about my parents," Selene said. "About what happened."

Mirael's breath caught. A small hitch. Barely audible over the rain.

"You've never told anyone that."

"I know."

"Why her?"

Selene looked at the ceiling again. At the water stains. At the shadows moving across the plaster.

"I don't know," she admitted. "She asked. And I just . . . said it."

Mirael was quiet. Processing. Selene could feel her thinking, feel the questions she wasn't asking, feel the weight of all those years of patience pressing against the silence.

"I'm glad," Mirael said finally. "That you could tell someone."

There was something underneath the words. Something that ached. But Mirael didn't let it surface, and Selene didn't dig for it.

The rain drummed on. Steady. Patient. The kind of sound that could fill a silence without breaking it.

Selene's eyes were heavy. Her body was sinking into the thin mattress, her muscles loosening one by one, the tension she carried like armor starting to come apart.

"Sleep," Mirael said again. Softer this time. "I'm here."

Selene should say something. Should thank her, or push her away, or do something other than just lie here letting Mirael watch her fall apart at the seams.

She closed her eyes instead.

Mirael's hand found hers on the blanket. Light. Barely any pressure. A question and an offer wrapped into one gesture.

Selene didn't pull away.

She let herself feel it. The warmth of Mirael's fingers. The sound of rain on the roof. The smell of old wood and cheap perfume and something underneath that was just Mirael. Soap and ink and that lavender she put in her clothes to keep the smell of Garnath at bay.

For the first time in weeks, the weight lifted. Not all of it. Not Weston. Not her father. Not the half-words and half-truths that would follow her forever. But enough. Enough to breathe. Enough to rest.

For the first time in weeks, she wasn't counting exits or listening for footsteps or running through contingencies in her head. She was just tired. Bone tired. Soul tired. The kind of tired that only came when you were safe enough to feel it.

And Mirael was here. Mirael was always here.

Selene let go.

***

The rain continued through the night. Steady and cold, the way Garnath rain always was in this season. It drummed on rooftops and ran through gutters and puddled in the streets below, ordinary and endless.

The candle burned down to a stub and guttered out. Darkness filled the room, broken only by the faint gray light from the window.

Mirael stayed awake for a while, watching Selene's face in the dimness. Watching the lines smooth out, the tension fade, the mask slip away into something softer. Something younger. Something that looked almost like the girl Selene might have been, once, before the cupboard and the smoke and the emptiness that moved in to fill the space.

She didn't move her hand. Didn't pull Selene closer, though she wanted to. Didn't whisper the things she'd carried for fourteen years and never said out loud.

She just watched. And eventually, she slept too.

The rain fell. The city breathed. The night passed the way nights always passed in Garnath, one hour bleeding into the next, unremarkable and ordinary.

Somewhere in Silverhold, a man sat in a cell and waited for an investigation that would bury more than it found.

Somewhere in the Lowers, a girl named Kira slept in Mother Gessa's cellar, dreaming of stones skipping across gray water.

And in a room at the Veiled Lantern, two women held hands in the darkness and let the world turn without them.

EPILOGUE

The archive smelled like dust and old paper.

Serith closed the door behind him and turned the lock. The room was small, windowless, lit by a single oil lamp on the desk. Shelves lined three walls, stuffed with ledgers and correspondence and the accumulated secrets of two decades. His private collection. The things that didn't exist in any official record.

He crossed to the desk and sat. The chair was hard, uncomfortable by design. He didn't come here to relax.

The journal lay where he'd left it that morning. Plain leather cover, water-stained at one corner, the spine cracked from years of use. Unremarkable. The kind of thing a person might carry everywhere without anyone noticing.

Daven had delivered it himself. Walked into this very room, set it on the desk, and left without a word. Professional to the end.

He was dead now. The woman had cut his throat in a warehouse before he could finish whatever he'd been trying to say. Seventeen years of reliable service, ended by a loose end that should have been tied off when she was seven.

Serith opened the journal to the first page.

The handwriting was neat. Educated. The kind of penmanship that came from early training, from a household that valued appearances. It matched what his sources had told him about the woman called Mirael. Good family, bad circumstances, years on the streets that should have ground the refinement out of her but somehow hadn't.

He began to read.

***

I'm starting this journal because I need somewhere to put the things I can't say. Selene would laugh if she knew. She doesn't believe in writing things down. "Paper can be stolen," she says. "Memories can't."

She's wrong about that. Memories can be beaten out of you. Starved out. Burned out. I know. I've lost so many already.

But I need this. I need somewhere to be honest, even if it's just with myself.

So here it is. The truth I'll never speak out loud:

I love her. I have loved her since the first night, when she pulled those boys off me in the alley behind the tanner's shop and didn't ask for anything in return. Fourteen years ago. I was seventeen and starving and so tired of being afraid, and she looked at me with those cold blue eyes and said "Can you walk?" She didn't ask if I was hurt or what had happened. Just those three words. And when I said yes, she turned and started moving, and I followed her, and I've been following her ever since.

She doesn't know. Or she does and pretends not to. I can't tell anymore.

***

Serith turned the page. Drew a thin line in the margin. Wrote: *attachment—fourteen years. Exploitable.*

***

She came back with blood on her hands again tonight. Wouldn't tell me whose. I cleaned the wounds on her knuckles and didn't ask questions. That's what we do now. I clean, she bleeds, neither of us talks about it.

I know what she is. What she does. I've known since the beginning. The first time I saw her kill a man, I should have run. Any sane person would have run.

I stayed. I watched her wipe the blade on his shirt and check his pockets for coin, and I thought: this is the safest I've ever been in my life.

What does that make me?

***

I've memorized her scars. All of them. The one on her left shoulder from the fishmonger's son who thought she'd be easy. The thin line across her ribs from the job in the Merchant Quarter that went wrong. The old burn on her forearm that she won't explain, that I think is from before. From the fire. From when she was seven and the world ended.

She doesn't know I've mapped them. She doesn't know I trace them with my eyes when she's changing, when she thinks I'm not looking. She doesn't know I've imagined touching them a thousand times. Running my fingers along each one. Learning the texture of everything she's survived.

I would never. She doesn't want that from me. She's made that clear without ever saying a word.

But I imagine it anyway. In the dark. When she's sleeping three feet away and I can hear her breathing and I want so badly to cross that distance that my whole body aches with it.

***

Serith underlined a phrase. Wrote in the margin: *physical locations of scars—identifying marks.*

***

She fucked someone again last night.

I heard them through the wall. The sounds she makes for strangers. The gasps and the moans and the way her breathing changes when she's close. I know those sounds better than I know my own voice. I've heard them a hundred times. Two hundred. Through every thin wall in every cheap room we've ever shared.

It was a man this time. Deep voice. Rough. He kept saying her name wrong, calling her "Sel" like they were familiar, like he knew her. He doesn't know her. Nobody knows her. Not even me, and I've spent fourteen years trying.

I lay in my bed and listened to her fuck him, and I didn't cry. I used to cry. The first year, I cried every time. Now I just lie there and wait for it to end. Count the sounds. Track her breathing. Wait for the moment when she comes and I feel something crack inside my chest that never quite heals.

She always comes back to our room after. Always. Smelling like sweat and stranger and that musk that clings to skin after sex. She never says anything. Just cleans herself at the basin and climbs into her bed and falls asleep like nothing happened.

I watch her sleep on those nights. Watch the mask slip away. Watch her face go soft and young and almost peaceful.

And I think: I would let you destroy me. I would let you break me into pieces and I would thank you for it. Because at least then you'd be touching me.

I will never say that out loud. I will never write it again after tonight.

But it's true. God help me, it's true.

***

Serith paused on that entry. Read it twice. Then moved on without annotation. Personal weakness. Operationally irrelevant.

***

There's a child now. Kira.

Selene found her the way she found me. Stray. Starving. Street trash that nobody wanted. Seven years old with eyes that have already seen too much.

I should love her. She's just a child. She's done nothing wrong.

I hate her.

No. That's not true. I don't hate her. I hate what she represents. I hate the way Selene looks at her. The softness that comes into those cold blue eyes when Kira is nearby. The way her hand hovers near the girl's shoulder like she wants to touch but can't remember how.

Fourteen years I've waited for that softness. Fourteen years of bleeding for her, fighting for her, lying awake listening to her fuck strangers and pretending it doesn't carve pieces out of my chest. Fourteen years of being the one who stays, the one who's always there, the one who would die for her without hesitation.

And a seven-year-old gets what I never could. In weeks. In days. Without trying.

I watch them together and I can't breathe. Selene brings her food. Checks on her at Mother Gessa's. Walks slower when Kira is beside her, matching the child's pace. Little things. Things she's never done for me.

It's the age. I know it's the age. Seven. The same age Selene was when whatever happened to her happened. She sees something in that girl. Herself, maybe. The child she used to be.

I understand it. I do.

But understanding doesn't stop the jealousy from eating me alive.

I'm not jealous of a child. I'm not. I'm not that small, that petty, that broken.

But I am.

God forgive me, I am.

***

Serith drew a line under *Kira*. Wrote: *child—seven years old. Leverage. Locate. Monitor.*

He turned more pages. Skimmed entries about safe houses, about routes through the city, about contacts Mirael had cultivated over the years. Useful intelligence. He marked the names, the locations. Cross-reference with existing files. Fill in the gaps.

Near the end, the handwriting changed. Shakier. Written in haste.

***

They found the daggers. I don't know how. I don't know what it means.

Selene won't tell me where they came from. Won't tell me why everyone suddenly wants us dead. She just said we need to move. Tonight. Pack light. Leave everything we can't carry.

I'm scared. I haven't been this scared since before her. Since the streets, since the cold, since I was alone and waiting to die.

Something is wrong. More wrong than usual. I can see it in the way she checks the windows, the way her hand keeps drifting to the knife at her hip. She knows something she isn't telling me.

She always knows things she isn't telling me. That's how we work. She carries the weight so I don't have to.

But this time feels different. This time feels like the weight might crush us both.

If something happens to her, I don't know what I'll do. I don't know who I am without her anymore.

That should terrify me. It doesn't. It just feels true.

I should stop writing. I should pack. I should be ready to run when she says run.

But I needed to put this somewhere first. Just in case. In case we don't make it. In case this is the last time I have a chance to write anything down.

I love you, Selene. I have always loved you. I will love you until it kills me, and probably after.

You'll never read this. No one will ever read this.

That's the only reason I can write it at all.

***

The entry ended there. The rest of the pages were blank.

Serith closed the journal.

She'd written that the night of the fire. Hours before Daven's team moved in. Hours before the smoke and the flames and the desperate scramble out a back window.

She thought the journal had burned at the fountain with the thief. She didn't know the real journal had been handed off before the fire was lit. Didn't know Daven had been waiting for it. He sat in the lamplight for a long moment, the silence of the archive pressing in around him.

The woman Selene. The loose end that should have been tied off seventeen years ago, when her parents burned. The daughter who wasn't supposed to exist. The daggers that should have stayed buried.

And now this. A journal full of devotion and weakness and tactical intelligence, written by someone who loved her more than her own life.

He opened to the inside cover. Wrote in small, precise letters:

Primary Asset: MIREAL Approach: Isolation from SELENE. Incremental. Exploit attachment, jealousy, fear of abandonment. Secondary Asset: KIRA Approach: Threat to child forces SELENE exposure. Use as leverage against both women. Timeline: Before network rebuilds. Before the girl becomes useful. Note: MIREAL believes journal destroyed in fire. Maintain that assumption.

He set down his pen. Closed the journal. Held it in his hands for a moment, feeling the weight of it. All those words. All that desperation and longing poured onto paper by a woman who thought she was alone with her secrets.

He had read private journals before. Hundreds of them, over the years. Diaries of merchants and nobles and spies, full of their petty grievances and hidden shames. Information was information. Secrets were currency.

But this one.

This one he would keep close.

He extinguished the lamp. Sat in the darkness for a while longer, thinking.

Then he stood, tucked the journal inside his coat, and walked out.

The archive swallowed his footsteps. The door closed behind him.

In the hallway, a servant waited with a message. Serith took it, read it by the light of a wall sconce, and nodded once.

"Tell them I'll be there within the hour," he said. "And send word to our contacts in the Merchant Quarter. I want eyes on Mother Gessa's establishment by morning."

The servant bowed and disappeared.

Serith walked on. The journal pressed against his chest like a second heartbeat.

Behind him, the archive sat empty. The lamp stayed dark. The silence settled back in like dust.

For Kira...

GLOSSARY

CHARACTERS

Selene Araveth Protagonist. A skilled contractor operating in Garnath. Orphaned at age seven when her parents were murdered in a house fire. Trained by the Guild. Carries a pair of relic daggers and a wooden star pendant that belonged to her mother. Age twenty-four during the main events of the story.

Mirael Selene's partner and closest companion. An information broker and former thief who has traveled with Selene for fourteen years. Maintains contacts throughout Garnath's underworld. Operates out of the Veiled Lantern.

Kira A young street orphan with crystal-blue eyes. One of Mother Gessa's "lambs." Selene sees echoes of her own childhood in Kira and becomes protective of her.

Rook A veteran Guild contractor in his late thirties. Though his hair is beginning to silver at the temples, he remains in his physical prime; rugged, methodical, and exceptionally patient. Known as one of the Guild's most efficient "cleaners," he possesses a tactical mind that prioritizes discipline over raw instinct. He was sent to Garnath on high-stakes Guild business, where he became the unintended mentor to a young Selene.

Weston A Paladin stationed in Garnath. Unlike most of his order, he genuinely believes in justice and protecting the innocent. His idealism puts him at odds with the institutional corruption around him.

Daven A contractor connected to old money interests. Known for his forgettable face and unsettling smile. Referred to as "the knife" in contrast to the Guild's institutional threat ("the hammer").

Mother Gessa An elderly woman who runs an unofficial orphanage in Southside. Provides food, shelter, and protection for street children she calls her "lambs." Tells stories of the old gods to the children in her care.

Viena An information broker who operates in Garnath's gray markets. Professional, detached, and well-connected. Trades in secrets and intelligence.

Serith A name connected to Dragoncrown and old money. Mentioned in connection with contracts and political influence.

PLACES

Garnath A coastal city where the story takes place. Divided between wealthy districts like the Merchant Quarter and impoverished areas like the Lowers and Southside. Known for its salt air, fish markets, and institutional corruption.

The Lowers The poorest district of Garnath. Narrow streets, overcrowded tenements, and limited Paladin presence. Home to many of the city's desperate and forgotten.

Southside A working-class area of Garnath near Tallow Market. Location of Mother Gessa's cellar.

The Merchant Quarter A wealthier district of Garnath with cleaner streets and better-maintained buildings. Home to merchants, minor nobility, and old money families.

The Veiled Lantern A brothel in Garnath where Selene and Mirael maintain a room. Offers discretion and asks few questions of its long-term residents.

The Broken Wheel A tavern in the Lowers. Neutral ground for certain kinds of business. Has a back room for private conversations.

Tallow Market A market area in Southside. Vendors sell candles, rendered fat, and other goods. Quieter after dark.

Silverhold The Paladin headquarters and prison facility. Where internal investigations are conducted and prisoners of significance are held.

The Docks Garnath's harbor district. Includes working wharves, warehouses, and quieter stretches of seawall away from the main traffic.

Bridgewater Street Location of the Paladin outpost where Weston is stationed. A former courthouse repurposed for law enforcement.

ORGANIZATIONS

The Guild An organized network of contractors (assassins) operating throughout the region. Hierarchical structure with established rules and protocols. Issues contracts, enforces standards, and eliminates those who become liabilities. Known for patience and inevitability rather than speed.

The Paladins An official law enforcement and military order. Ostensibly dedicated to justice and protection but riddled with corruption. Different outposts vary in their adherence to ideals versus institutional self-interest.

Dragoncrown An old money family or organization connected to political and economic power. Their influence extends through hired intermediaries rather than direct action.

TERMS

Contractor A professional killer for hire. May operate independently or through the Guild. Distinguished from common murderers by skill, discretion, and adherence to professional standards.

Contract A paid agreement to eliminate a target. Guild contracts carry institutional weight and expectations. Breaking or failing a contract has severe consequences.

The Knife and the Hammer Informal terms distinguishing between types of threats. "The knife" refers to personal, targeted violence (like Daven). "The hammer" refers to institutional, inevitable force (like a Guild contract).

Lamb/Lambs Mother Gessa's term for the street children under her protection.

Name Day A birthday. The day a person's name was given to them.

Mark A target for observation, theft, or elimination.

Ground Terrain chosen for an engagement. "Chosen ground" refers to a location selected in advance to provide tactical advantage.

OBJECTS

The Daggers A pair of relic blades Selene carries. Exceptionally well-crafted with perfect balance and unnaturally sharp edges. The steel seems to shed blood rather than hold it.

The Wooden Star A pendant Selene wears. Given to her by her mother the night her parents died. A keepsake and the last physical connection to her family.

MYTHOLOGY

Vaeryn A figure from old stories. In Mother Gessa's tellings, Vaeryn is associated with watching over lost children and collecting the names of those forgotten by everyone else. Whether Vaeryn is a god, a spirit, or simply a story varies by teller.

ABOUT THE AUTHOR

Adger R. Matthews II started drawing before he started fighting, and started fighting before most people start high school. Art school in his late teens. Military at seventeen. Two combat deployments to Iraq. Then years behind the wheel as an owner-operator long-haul truck driver, crossing the country with stories building in his head that wouldn't stay quiet.

He now serves as a DoD civilian logistics officer stationed in Thessaloniki, Greece, where he writes, records, and runs Soul Forged Studios between the margins of his day job. The UNWRITTEN universe, his sapphic grimdark dark fantasy series, began as a single character who refused to stop surviving. It has since grown into novels, full-length rock albums, a tabletop roleplaying game built for veteran mental health, and a creative ecosystem that refuses to stay in one lane.

His characters carry scars they didn't earn cleanly. His stories are about broken people who keep moving forward anyway. *Selene: Origins* is his third published work in the UNWRITTEN saga.

www.soulforgedstudio.com

adger@soulforgedstudio.com

"Every epic world begins with a single unwritten truth."

ABOUT SOUL FORGED STUDIOS

Soul Forged Studios LLC is an independent creative studio built around a single universe and a simple conviction: stories should do more than entertain.

The studio publishes the UNWRITTEN novel series, produces original music under the band name UNWRITTEN, and develops SOULFORGED, a tabletop roleplaying game designed for emotional processing through collaborative storytelling. Its digital tools division builds AI-assisted resources for independent authors, starting with First Light Beta Reader.

Everything Soul Forged Studios creates lives inside the same world. The novels tell the story. The music lets you hear it. The game lets you live it.

SOUL FORGED STUDIOS *Forging Stories. Shaping Worlds.*

THE STORY CONTINUES

UNWRITTEN: The Awakening *the Soul Forged Saga, Book One*
A thousand years after the world was rewritten, a street thief carries something that should not exist. Across collapsing kingdoms, a Paladin feels the same pulse stir within her own soul.
Some truths are too dangerous to survive history. Some loves are too powerful to stay dead.
Available now in hardback, paperback and eBook.
www.soulforgedstudio.com

www.ingramcontent.com/pod-product-compliance
Lightning Source LLC
LaVergne TN
LVHW100502110826
845146LV00002B/491

* 9 7 9 8 9 9 3 2 5 0 4 2 7 *